THE LOVE INTEREST

CALE DIETRICH

THE
LOVE
INTEREST

FEIWEL AND FRIENDS
NEW YORK

A FEIWEL AND FRIENDS BOOK
An imprint of Macmillan Publishing Group, LLC

THE LOVE INTEREST. Copyright © 2017 by Cale Dietrich. All rights reserved.
Printed in the United States of America. For information, address Feiwel and Friends,
175 Fifth Avenue, New York, N.Y. 10010.

ISBN   9781250107138

Book design by Anna Booth

Feiwel and Friends logo designed by Filomena Tuosto

TO KIA

PART ONE

LOVE INTEREST

CHAPTER
ONE

ALL FOUR WALLS OF MY CELL ARE MIRRORS.

The light on the ceiling flashes red and pinpricks of crimson bounce around the room. *Red, huh?* That's a bit sudden, seeing as the last examination was only a couple of weeks ago. I grin at the light, and my smile is reflected by the endless versions of myself that surround me. The light flashes again.

I drop into a push-up position. The concrete floor is so cold my hands go numb then start to burn. Up, down. Up, down. A strand of mousy-brown hair falls over my eyes. That color will be the first thing they change about me.

If I'm chosen, that is.

If I'm good enough, that is.

On flash nine I jump to my feet. Gritting my teeth, I grab my shirt and pull it up and over my head. The voice of the LIC's events coordinator rings through my mind: *When you're examined, be proud to display the bodies you've worked so hard to create. You're all incredibly beautiful young men, and you should relish the chance to show everyone how handsome you are.*

I scrunch the shirt in my hands for a second—just a second—crushing it beneath my grip. Adrenaline pumps through my torso and my arms, making them feel electric. I toss the shirt into the corner of the room, then lower my eyes and force myself to do what they want me to do every morning: look at the boy/man/whatever I've become.

The countless hours I've spent working out have obviously had an impact. Still, I'm far from perfect. I mean, I have abs, which took *forever* to show, and I'm proud of my arms. But my skin is stormtrooper white, I have a mole on my left hip I'm really self-conscious about, and my chest is getting hairy. When did that happen? I touch my now-hairy chest. Oh great, another thing to stress about. I wish I could tell myself that it's nothing, that they'll fix whatever flaws I have if I'm chosen, but I can't. Another boy was once dismissed because they said his nose was unpleasant. If an oddly shaped nose is enough to get rejected, I'm sure my pale, weirdly hairy body isn't far behind.

I don't linger on my face. It's not hideous or anything, it's just kind of boring. Plus, it's destined to be changed. I close my eyes and try to get rid of the depressing thought. To make it through, I need to be positive.

I've worked frigging hard on my body, though. I open my eyes, then flex my biceps and smile. I've definitely bulked up since the last examination, and I hope I'm not too big to be a Nice. All the *super*fun and superrigorous personality testing they make us do here has shown that Nice is the disposition for me. But they've made a mistake. Me, a Nice? Yeah, right. Sure, I try to be friendly and I don't like hurting people's feelings, but that doesn't mean I'm a Disney prince.

The light flashes again. I pull my trousers down, leaving me dressed only in sky-blue trunks. As I throw the pants away, my door hisses and slides open. I wince and raise a hand, my forearm protecting my eyes from the burning whiteness of the hallway.

I walk outside and stop in front of my door. The others are already standing in front of their cells. The floor of this hallway is white concrete, but the walls and ceiling are long, smooth mirrors.

Dozens of guys are visible, all dressed in the same trunks as I am. Most are busy staring at themselves, fixing their hair, practicing their smiles, or flexing their biceps, but a few are looking from side to side, sizing up the competition. *Those are the threats.*

We don't talk.

We know better than that.

"Turn," booms a tinny voice.

With a shuffling sound, we turn to the left and stare down the hallway. In front of me is a guy so ridiculously buff I instantly lose all pride I have in my body and seriously wonder why I even try. His back is muscles on muscles on muscles. How does he even work those muscles out? Extremely complicated yoga?

It turns out the back belongs to a not-so-complicated guy named Robert. He says that name was given to him by his birth parents, but that's a huge lie. We aren't the result of loving families: we were taken, probably as infants, from families that couldn't care for us. Some people think our parents were tricked into giving us up, believing we were going to a family that wanted us. Others think they sold us to the LIC. I lean toward the former because the thought is comforting, and to me, that's more important than the truth.

Unlike Robert, all I have is a number: 412.

Robert's a Bad for sure. It's evident in the confidence-killing meatiness of his back and in the uneven tribal tattoo that covers his right shoulder. Even the people in charge here must think he's 100 percent Bad, as someone borderline like me would never get permission to destroy his so-called wholesome image as he's done. He catches me looking and his top lip curls into a snarl.

"You may now proceed to the main hall."

My feet plod on the icy concrete as we walk down the hall. Moving slowly, we pass through a set of frosted-glass doors into a large rectangular room. There are no windows, so the only light comes from the long fluorescent tubes that run along the roof. The light is just a touch too bright; the dial turned a fraction too far.

At the front of the room is a huge screen. Beside it is the events coordinator, a slim man wearing a tailored black shirt tucked into dark-gray slacks. Usually he's the pinnacle of male grooming, but today his short hair is messy, spiking up in uneven tufts, and his pants are slightly creased.

"Hey, guys," he says. "I know you weren't expecting an examination today, and I'm *super* sorry about making you do this, but it's kind of an emergency. A particularly important young woman has shown signs that she's ready to select a partner, so two of you have to be sent in right away. We're looking for a boy-next-door Nice and a mysterious, tortured-soul Bad."

Aren't they always?

"Five Nices and five Bads from this floor have been identified as a potential match, so, obviously, they'll be examined. And guys, I know this test is late notice, but I'm your pal, so you can trust me when I say that if your number is on the screen, it's there for a reason. It means our complex compatibility algorithm has concluded that she will fall for you if you spend time with her. How cool is that? Now, let's see who made it to the next round."

The screen flashes and the numbers appear. I scan the list, my heart racing. Come on . . .

Yes!

My number is there, in the very middle. Thank you, complex compatibility algorithm! I take back all the times I called you rigged. It's been over a year since my number last appeared, and in that time I've totally committed myself to being the perfect Nice. Now I'll find out if that's enough to succeed, or if I'm destined to die before I'm even given a chance to fight for my life.

"Nices go through the door to the left, Bads to the right. If you're not sure what your disposition is, that's fine, the color of your number will tell you. Nices are blue, Bads are red."

My number is blue, confirming my suspicions: they think I'm a Nice. I quickly glance at the other chosen guys. I ignore the Bads, because they never pick two Love Interests from the same floor, so these Bads will never be anything to me. The Nices all have light hair and boyish faces. *She has a type.* Three of them are about my age, but the one directly in front of me is much younger, probably eleven or twelve. He has no chance of passing this examination, but is going to be forced through it anyway.

I clench my hands into fists. He shouldn't be here. I can't say anything now, because if I do we'll both be punished, but if I fail the examination I'm going to take him aside and make sure he knows I care about him. The boy shuffles toward the doorway. I wait for a second, because Nices don't lead, then I join the line. The glass panes separate, revealing a square room. We enter.

In the doorway I tense. At the back of the room, standing still, is a Stalker. I've seen one in person only a few times, but fleeting encounters have been enough to give me nightmares.

It's a tall robot, standing at around eight feet, with a hulking, all-black body. That's not the worst part, though; that honor goes to its head, which looks like a mannequin's: no eyes, no nostrils, lips pursed. Right now, the body is totally black, which means it's currently dormant. My heartbeat steadies. It can't move unless its lights are on, so this one isn't here to hurt anyone. It's here to keep us in line, and to remind us what will come after us if we disobey.

The door at the back of the room opens, and a short, round man in a striped navy button-down and black slacks enters. *They'd kill me if I looked like that.* A stethoscope hangs over his shoulders.

He hooks the stethoscope into his ears, then walks up to the first boy, who is flexing his biceps. The doctor ignores the showboating and presses the metal end of the stethoscope against the boy's chest. After a few moments, the doctor switches the stethoscope for a tape measure and measures the boy's torso. I was the last to enter this room, so I'm at the end of the line. Now I feel like that was a mistake. What if they find the perfect Love Interest before they get to me?

As I wait my turn, I stand with my back straight and my fists clenched. After what feels like forever, the doctor beckons the boy in front of me forward. The kid takes a tentative step toward the doctor, then raises his hands. He's so small. The doctor narrows his eyes, and the boy lets out a little sob that breaks my heart.

"Runt," says the doctor. "Get out of here. Next."

The kid scurries away. I step forward, taking his place, and the doctor presses the end of the stethoscope onto my chest. The metal is freezing, but I keep my face expressionless. Still, I can't control my heartbeat, so he must know I'm feeling *something*, even if he doesn't know what it is. He'll probably put it down to nerves, and that's partially true, but if I've done my job right he'll never suspect that I'm feeling frustration or maybe even anger at the way they're treating the kid. A Nice would never feel such unsavory things.

He pulls the stethoscope away. "Arms up."

I raise my arms over my head. He leans in close and wraps the tape measure around my chest and pulls it tight, pinching my skin. I grit my teeth. He smells like cinnamon candy and body odor.

He takes a step back. "Flex."

I tilt my arms back, arch my spine, and flex my biceps as hard as I possibly can.

As he wraps the tape around my right bicep I notice there's a blue line drawn on the measure. It must be to make sure I'm not too big. Bads can be as buff as they want, the bigger the better, actually. For a Nice, the aim of the game is lean. I need to look friendly and cute, but when I take my shirt off I need to be ripped. Just in an approachable way that doesn't look like I work out much. Like these muscles happened accidentally, the result of playing outside with a golden Labrador or good genes or something like that.

My bicep falls within the acceptable bracket, so he moves across and checks my left.

"Good job," he says as he drops the tape measure. My mouth falls open an inch before I catch it. I've never been complimented by a doctor. Not even once. "Now tense." He places his palm on my stomach and presses. I feel my own firmness against his skin. He pulls his hand away and nods at the hair that covers my chest. "That'll need to be fixed. Nices can't be hairy. But other than that, your body is in excellent condition. Great work."

I want to jump up and down, or pump my fist, or do something to show how freaking fantastic his words have made me feel, but I remain still.

He turns to the guard. "This one and that one—" He tilts his head toward the boy at the front of the line. In the corner of my vision, I see him turn and look at me, sizing me up. I keep my attention focused on the guards, as if not looking at him will wipe him from existence. "—can advance. The others aren't ready."

I crack and turn to face my competition. He's got hazel eyes, and his nose and shoulders are covered in freckles. He looks like an average nerdy-in-a-hot-way Nice.

For my sake I hope that's all he is.

"You first," I say with a gesture toward the door.

When he thinks they aren't watching, he narrows his eyes at me. "How kind of you."

I blink, startled. I didn't even think that he might be offended by the offer. Obviously he thinks I was being a smartass or something, but I really wasn't, it was just instinct.

"Sorry," I say. "I didn't mean to . . ."

The door opens. He sneers one last time, then steps through.

Suddenly the room is eerily quiet. So this is it. My interrogation, also known as my best shot at getting out of here this year. I exhale. I know I'm as prepared as it's possible to be, but I can't shake the feeling that my best efforts aren't enough, and that I'm doomed to spend my whole life here. The thought makes me shiver.

After an eternity, the door slides open. I gulp, then step forward. The door whooshes closed behind me.

The room is plain, the walls smooth and featureless. Sitting at a stainless steel table is a trim man with rigidly perfect posture and solid gray hair. Despite his hair color, his eyes are bright and his face is mostly wrinkle-free, so pinning his exact age is difficult. I'd guess late thirties or early forties.

He gestures toward the seat. "Congratulations on making it this far. My name is Rodger Craike, and I'm the manager of the Love Interest Compound. You will call me Mr. Craike or sir, nothing else."

He picks up a tablet and starts scrolling. I sit and peer at the screen. *Huh.* It's filled with reports from my monthly integration exams. Because the LIC is so isolated, we have to take classes to keep up with pop culture, and each month we're quizzed to make sure we're keeping up to date. It's usually about big movies, popular TV shows, and hit songs, which we are required to know by heart in case of karaoke or sing-alongs. For Bads and select Nices, sports are included, but I don't have to learn about that because they decided I'm more of a nerdy-boy-next-door type. Thank goodness. Anyway, we do all this so we can "integrate seamlessly" with the real world when the time comes. Their words, not mine. I know my test scores are good, but he's frowning at them like I failed every single one. *Why?*

"I should thank you, sir," I say, trying to draw his attention away from whatever is wrong with my scores. He keeps reading. "For giving me the gym equipment and the food. I wouldn't look this way without you."

"We provide the equipment, you do the work." His eyes flick down over my body. "And you've done an exceptional job. You'd be surprised how many Nices ruin their bodies by making themselves too big. But you understand what it means to be Nice, don't you?"

I shrug my shoulders. "I hope so."

He tilts his head back and laughs. Recovering, he leans forward. "Maybe, after all this time, we've found a genuinely nice guy."

Or someone smart enough to know how to play the system.

"Enough pleasantries. As the manager of the LIC, it's my job to make sure every Love Interest is the right man or woman for the job. So I'm going to ask you a few questions to see how well you've applied yourself to your time here. Are you ready to begin?"

I nod.

"What disposition are you?" he asks.

"Nice."

"Why do you think that?"

"All the tests told me that's what I am."

"You think they made a mistake?"

Yes.

"No, it's not that," I say. "It just feels weird to call myself Nice; it seems boastful. I'm not perfect by any means, but I think I'm a nice person. Plus, I'm so obviously not Bad. I'm good at making people laugh, not manipulating or intimidating them."

"Some people would say making someone laugh *is* manipulating them."

"Some people," I say, "would say if laughter is a manipulation it's the best one there is. It makes people feel good. Who cares how that end is achieved?"

He looks down and starts typing something on his tablet. The room fills with the sound of his fingertips hitting the screen. I breathe in through my nostrils, then exhale slowly.

Finally, he lowers the tablet and rests it on the table. "A lot of Nices have told me they'd give their life to save their rival if they could. Would you be willing to do that?"

I look down at my hands. The true answer to this question is the reason I know I'm not a genuine Nice: I'm not ready to die, and I'm not willing to give up my life for anyone else. I've always known that if I made it out of the LIC I'd fight as hard as I could to make sure I got the girl and survived. It's what I hate about myself the most.

I meet his stare. "I would be willing to do that. Sacrifice myself, I mean. I'd do it in a heartbeat."

He grins. "You know what I think? I think you're a great actor. I know you're lying, yet I find myself believing you. It's truly a rare gift."

I tense, and it spreads through my entire body, with cold dread creeping down from my cheeks to dwell in the cords of my shoulders. *He knows.*

"Oh, don't look so scared; it's a good thing. You're going to be a spy, after all, so being able to act is one of the most valuable skills you could have. And you clearly are a natural liar. But I'm not interested in an actor who needs to memorize lines; you need to be able to improvise. So answer these questions with the first thought that enters your mind. If you pause, you'll fail. Now, why do you think your Chosen should pick you over your rival?"

"I don't. I just hope she does."

In his eyes, I see him ticking the boxes.

Modest? Check.

Humble? Check.

"Elaborate on that," he says.

"I want her to pick whoever will make her the happiest. And if she's a better fit with him, I'll gladly accept my fate."

A total pushover? Check plus.

I imagine myself standing naked in a massive steel room: the incinerator. Feeling the cold dry air on my skin, the metal beneath my feet. The split second of agony before the roaring orange flames turn me into ash. *Stop thinking about that. Focus!*

"There must be some good things about you," he says. "Tell me about them."

"I'm a good listener. And I can be funny sometimes, I guess."

"If you caught your Chosen kissing your rival, what would you do?"

I lower my eyes and bring on the tears. When I feel them behind my eyelids I look up at him, my entire body radiating hurt. I stare at him for a moment, drop my mouth open a fraction, then turn my head away.

"I'd look at her like that. Then I'd walk away. Next time I saw her she'd probably apologize if I were still in the running, so I'd tell her she doesn't ever have to explain herself to me, and that I only responded in that manner because I love her so damn much. I'd tell her I'm glad it hurts because it proves how much I care."

"Would you fight for her?"

"If I had to, yes."

"When will you first try to kiss her?"

"I won't. I'll wait until she kisses me. But I'll kiss her on the cheek after our first date."

"What would you do if she texted you in the middle of the night and said she was lonely?"

"I'd drop everything and run to her as fast as possible. I'll be there for her whenever she needs me. No matter what."

"Now, I have one last question, and in many ways, it's the most important one, so think for a second before answering. If you get it wrong, you'll be dismissed."

I wipe my sweaty palms on my legs. This is it. One last question.

"I'm ready," I say.

"Do you think you will fall in love with her?"

I smile, because I know the answer, and that means I'm finally getting out of the LIC. There's no way I can get it wrong, because the answer to this question has been drilled into me every single day I've been here.

"It doesn't matter," I say. "She's the hero of this story, so how I feel is irrelevant."

He leans back on his chair and grins.

"Correct."

CHAPTER
TWO

CRAIKE LEFT AFTER THAT, LEAVING ME ALONE in the room to stew. He never told me explicitly that I made it, so I have no idea if I passed or if I have to go back to my cell to wait until another girl is ready. On one hand, he seemed pleased with my answers, but he also saw right through some of my lies. Does he know how fake I am? He definitely won't send me out if he knows. My interview replays in my mind, with each repeat narrowing in on my more cringeworthy lines. *I had one shot and I screwed it up.*

With a whoosh, the door slides open and a tall girl with straight blond hair enters. She's dressed in an oversized blue flannel shirt, torn black jeans, and white sneakers. In her hands is a white iPhone, which must be showing something fascinating as she's staring at it intently. Under one arm is a pile of neatly folded clothes. Men's clothes.

She places the pile on the table. "Get dressed."

"Thanks." I stand and grab the shirt. It's a white dress shirt and the material is soft and silky. I put it on. It fits tight against my body, hugging my shoulders and tapering in at my waist.

"It's not just for you. It's hard to work when I'm distracted by . . ." She gestures toward me with one hand as her voice trails off. I'm not sure if she's talking about my abs or my crotch.

"Thank you?" I say as I button up the second button. "It's nice to know I can be a distraction." I pull the pants, gray slacks, up over my hips and fasten the silver clasp. Then I sit down. "Maybe it means I have a shot after all."

She finally looks up from her phone. "Here's hoping. Now that's done, I'd like to do this."

She raises her hand, offering me a high five.

I slap her hand, and she beams.

"Congrats, man!" she says. "You made it through! That's a big deal. Oh, and I should introduce myself. I'm Kaylee, your coach."

"My *what*?"

"Your coach. I'm here to give you love advice, if you need it, that is—and trust me, you probably do. I'm your own personal relationship counselor. And, luckily for you, I'm the best at what I do."

"And that is?"

"Making important young women fall in love with fakes like you. I'll be with you the entire time, telling you what to say, giving instructions on how to act, that sort of thing. When they transform you, a device like this"—she taps on the table, which creates a hologram of a silver ball about the size of a pea—"will be injected behind your ear. It lets us keep track of you, plus, it'll allow us to communicate. And don't worry, this isn't the

Suicide Squad, it's not a bomb to stop you if you go AWOL. We have Stalkers for that. This little beauty is mainly so I can make sure you don't say the wrong thing. During a lot of the important conversations you'll have with your Chosen, I tell you what to say. On those days, you're just my pretty puppet. Sound good?"

I cross my arms over my chest. Already the silky material feels cold.

"It sounds perfect."

"Great! And it's not like I'm in your head all the time, you will get to have *some* time alone with her. I'm only there for the big moments—first dates, first kisses, that sort of thing. The quiet moments are yours. Also, I'm the person you can talk to if you want a set piece. You know, a dangerous event or something that dramatically flings her into your arms. I've seen a Chosen totally change her mind about a guy because of a well-timed set piece. Now, don't you want to see who you've been assigned to?"

A.K.A. the girl who decides if I live or die.

"I sure do!"

"Great! Isn't this exciting? You're about to see the girl you could spend the rest of your life with."

Well, in that case, I *really* hope she's beautiful. Why is she showing me this? It's not like it changes anything.

She swipes her hand to the right, and the tiny silver device zooms away and is replaced by a blue-tinted hologram of a girl. She's looking up at something in the distance. Her face is nondescript, pretty in a way that doesn't stand out, aside from the cute little freckles on her nose. Her brown hair is tied back into a ponytail.

She's not a supermodel or anything, and for that I'm grateful. She looks like a nice, normal girl.

A girl who would choose a Nice boy.

"Her name is Juliet. She's been marked as important ever since she was five years old, when she aced her Mensa test. We've monitored her ever since. When she was seven, she started inventing, producing things that people with graduate degrees would struggle with. Her brain, it . . . it operates in a way that's so far ahead of everyone else. The world's top universities have been trying for years to get her to enroll with them, but she's rejected them all because she wants to have a normal high school experience. She's one of a tiny handful of people in the entire world who we believe have a higher than ninety-seven percent chance of reaching the top of their chosen field. Her inventions will shape the lives of every single person on earth one day. Or, at least, that's what the head honchos here think."

I tilt my head to the side and look at the hologram of Juliet again. "Why are you sending us in now?"

"She's only just started being interested in boys, as proved by a series of, well, blunt Google searches. We expect her to make her choice before she leaves for college."

I keep eyeing the shimmering hologram of Juliet. Of the person I must make fall in love with me.

"If you know so much about her, why are you assigning her two guys?" I ask. "Wouldn't it be easier to create the perfect guy for her? Like a scientist or something?"

Kaylee's smile falters. "I want you to promise me something, okay? Don't talk like that in front of Mr. Craike. He straight up doesn't like people who ask questions, and trust me, if he doesn't like you you're screwed. But it's a legitimate question, so I'll answer it. Sending in two guys is much more effective than sending a guy on his own. One of the reasons is that it forces her to make her choice sooner; being in demand has that consequence. The second reason is that they tried sending in Solos and, well, it didn't work that well. They made one perfect guy for each girl, like a science whiz for Juliet, and you know what happened?"

"No idea."

"The Chosen ignored the Love Interest and fell for some random person in her class. This baffled the scientists, but it made perfect sense to me. I never fall for anyone predictable; it surprises me every single time. Seriously, I fall for the *worst* guys. So having two guys in the running as opposed to one makes sense because it increases our odds. Now, do you have any more questions? After the surgery our conversations will be monitored, so I won't be able to be as honest with you as I can be right now."

I pause for a second, thinking it over. This isn't an opportunity I can afford to waste.

"Do you think she'll pick me?"

Kaylee shrugs. "It's possible. For you to win this you need to present yourself as a man she can depend on. Her life is going to get pretty wild, and she knows it. Someone nice, secure, and stable will be a good thing for her. She's probably looking for someone who she can come home to after a big day who'll remind her of simpler times. Someone who'll cook her dinner and care for her children. But there's a problem."

My heart thunders.

"Juliet is, let's put it simply, not your typical Chosen. She likes to shake things up. It's part of the reason my bosses are so interested in her. Any sane person in her position would pick a Nice, but Juliet is daring. The innovative mind that makes her worth monitoring is what makes her so unpredictable. She might not even care about things that appeal to most people, or the pressures of society. Don't let her appearance or her dreams fool you—making Juliet choose you is going to be tough."

"That depends on my rival. Do you know who he is?"

She nods.

"You'll meet him pretty soon. He's good, man. Like, real good. When I met him he turned on the charm so hard I nearly fell apart on the spot. He's much more charming than you. You should be careful. He's a killer, that one."

"Maybe I'm saving the charm for the real deal."

She rolls her eyes. "Let's hope so. Well, I'm out of time, so I have to go. This will be the last time I see you while you look like this! And don't worry too much about the procedure. You're lucky—I think they're only going to make superficial changes, so it shouldn't hurt that much." She taps the spot behind her ear. "Talk soon!"

She skips out of the room, leaving me, once again, alone. I sit for a few minutes, my fingers drumming on the table, my legs bouncing up and down, my posture reverting to its natural hunch.

Whoosh.

I look up. Standing in the doorway is a boy. He's a Bad, that's obvious, but he's unlike any Bad that I've ever seen. He's slim, maybe even skinnier than me, but his biceps fill the black leather jacket he's wearing. The collar of his gray T-shirt dips low, showing a small stretch of smooth skin. Unlike most Bads, who seem to favor military-style buzz cuts, his hair is long and stylishly messy. It screams, *I'm the lead guitarist in a punk band you're not cool enough to know about*. It's jet black, though. Of course it is.

A grid of red light appears in the middle of the room, separating us. The air hums with static.

He steps forward and raises his hand so his fingertips hover an inch away from the light. "It must be to stop me from killing you."

"Or me from killing *you*."

"You wouldn't do that, would you? You're my rival, which means you're a Nice guy, and Nice guys don't kill people. It's a pleasure to meet you."

THIS BOY WILL KILL YOU.

The door whooshes closed behind him.

He scratches the back of his neck with one hand. "I guess they wanted us to meet before it all starts."

"I guess so."

"And, well, before they change us. Apparently all this"—he waves a hand in front of his face—"is about to get seriously shifted."

"I don't know what you want me to say to that."

"You could say you're sorry? You know, offer me some of that classic Nice guy sympathy?"

I shake my head. "Yeah, that's not really my style."

He leans back, inspecting me. "For a Nice, you're not very nice, are you?"

I smile. "Nope!"

He laughs. "I'm not that Bad either. But hey, what can you do? Maybe we could ask them to swap our dispositions?"

"Um, I'm going to go ahead and respectfully pass. The only

reason you'd want to switch this late in the game is because you know she's going to pick the Nice."

His face falls, and my smile falters, then fades. All I can think about now is him standing alone in the middle of the incinerator.

I breathe in deep, then exhale. I can't think of him like that. I've always known whoever I went up against must die, so I can't start feeling bad about it now. Not when the guilt could distract me from my goal. "Listen, man, I want to say I'm sorry. I wish it didn't have to be like this. I don't want you to die."

That's a lie.

He's staring at me with one eyebrow slightly raised, but the corner of his mouth keeps twitching up, so very close to a smile. "Maybe you are Nice after all. Maybe I should be worried."

He grabs the chair and swings it around so the high back faces me. The legs screech against the concrete. Then he sits down, with his chest pressed against the chair's backrest and his hands propping up his chin, which is covered in a few days' worth of black scruff. A large patch on his right cheek is totally hairless.

He looks me in the eye. His eyes are a rich, earthy brown, so startlingly normal that they'll probably be changed. Brown is too boring for a Bad. I hope I'm wrong, because he's incredibly handsome already. Any improvements would just increase the chances of her falling for him at first sight.

"I realized something," he says. "This is the last moment we have to be ourselves. As soon as they call us, we'll stop being us and we'll start being Love Interests, with our whole identities changed to fit what she wants. So I want to take this moment, the last moment of being me, and avoid all that competitive bullshit and spend a second saying what I truly think. And seeing as you're here, I want to have, like, an actual conversation with you. My—no, our—last one. So what do you say? Would you like to talk, properly talk, with me?"

I'm a bit weirded out by his friendliness, but I definitely don't want to hurt his feelings, so I just nod.

"Great. So, what makes you tick? Like, seriously. Not the answer you'll give Juliet. What do you really feel? About yourself, about this place? About anything."

He can use this against you.

"You first."

He nods. "Fine. If I had a choice of anything to do with the rest of my life, I'd want to be a paramedic. I like the idea of the adrenaline, but also that I'd be able to help people. I'm really bummed that it's too Nice a profession for a Bad. I like comic book movies but I can't be bothered to read the books themselves. I spend an embarrassing amount of time thinking about my parents. Actually, the amount of time I spend thinking about them isn't embarrassing, but what I think is. I've convinced myself that I was stolen from them and that they're out there right now, desperately hunting for me. I know it's optimistic bullshit, but no matter how hard I try I can't shake that image of them. Lastly, the thing that scares me the most about this whole thing is that for me to survive, you have to be destroyed. Like, best-case scenario for you if you lose is mind-wiping, and even that's unlikely—so I'd probably be sending you to your death. The fact that I want you to go through that so I don't have to terrifies me, man. So . . . what about you?"

The rational side of me is telling me to keep my mouth shut, to use the information he gave me to derail his efforts to make

Juliet fall for him. It's also possible everything he said was a lie, a way to get a head start before the game has truly begun. I shouldn't trust him. Yet this other, louder part of me is looking at the guy in front of me and seeing something other than competition. Someone who knows how I feel. Someone who's been through everything I've been through. Someone I don't have to lie to because we both know what we are.

I look down at the table. "Most people think I'm a kind person, a genuine Nice, but I know I'm not."

"Why is that?"

"I . . . I know the cost of my survival and I still really want to live. So I guess all you need to know about me is that I'm capable of hurting you to ensure I win. I'm dangerous, I know I am." I catch his stare and hold it. "You should be afraid of me."

"If you're not a nice person, why are you a Nice?"

"They think I'm Nice, and I'm not in a position to correct them. Do you think they'd let you switch if you wanted to become a Nice? They have plans and expectations for all of us, and I want to survive, so I've learned to act like I am the boy they want me to be. So far it's worked out pretty well."

The light on the ceiling flashes.

He points at it. "Well, that's us. I guess this is it for now. So say good-bye to this face, Nice guy, and I'll see you out there, I suppose. And don't feel bad about trying to win. I think that's the only way we'll make it through this with our sanity intact. Let's give it our all and let her decide. That way she kills one of us, and neither of us has to feel guilty. Because I wouldn't be able to cope if I had played any part in killing you, even if you wouldn't feel bad about killing me. So do we have a deal? We'll both give it everything we have? No regrets, no backing down, and no guilt when she makes her choice."

I wish my brain worked like that, like I could just say no regrets or guilt and then not feel it. But I know myself, and I know the guilt will crush me if I win and he dies. Still, he wants to pretend it's that simple, that our emotions can be contained by a spoken contract, and I'm willing to entertain him. Plus, if I'm being totally honest with myself, I want to keep pretending for as long as possible that I don't care at all that he could die because of me.

So I accept his offer, and it feels like the contest has truly begun.

CHAPTER
THREE

I'M NAKED ON A STEEL SLAB. I'M NOTHING MORE than a chunk of beef. Meat to be sliced and chopped and turned into something usable. All offcuts will be discarded.

My arms and legs are bound to the table, encircled by freezing stainless steel bands. The bands pinch at my wrists and ankles, pulling at the strands of hair they trapped when they snapped shut. Above me are two circles of white light. A man wearing a surgeon's mask advances toward me holding a black marker. He places the tip of the pen right on my hairline, then scrapes it across my skin, all the way down to the middle of my eyebrows. I close my eyes slowly and lick my dry lips.

He tilts his head to the side, inspecting my face. He reaches forward and grabs my bangs. "We'll change his hair. And his eyes. Get the needle."

I strain my eyes to keep watching him. *Like looking at him is going to stop him.*

A nurse swings a boxlike metal contraption around so that it hangs above my face. It's attached to a long metal arm that connects to a white machine that stands beside the table. I stare right into the pointy ends of two shiny silver needles. I exhale and try, unsuccessfully, to make my body stop shaking.

"How blue do you want?" asks the nurse.

The doctor peers into my right eye. Even though he's wearing a surgeon's mask, I can smell his breath, which reeks like the bottom of a garbage bin. He moves across and looks at my other eye.

"As blue as the ocean. I want her to think of water when she looks him in the eye."

"What about his jaw?"

He moves his gloved hand up and grabs my chin. He yanks my head to the side, and his cold fingers run along my jawbone. His grip tightens and he slowly turns my head in the other direction, so that I'm looking at the wall with the door. It's white and has no door handle, like every door in the LIC. His fingers jab in harder, like he's trying to separate my jawbone from my skin.

The grip fades, and my head lulls back into position.

"It needs to be stronger." He jabs the pen into the tip of my chin. "We'll need to cleft this a little bit."

"And his body?"

"I can hear you, you know," I say. "And can I suggest something? I always wanted my ears to be level. They're a bit lopsided, as you can probably tell. So maybe you could, you know, fix that?"

"Be quiet," snaps the doctor. "Speak again and I'll do everything without painkillers."

I close my mouth, instantly regretting my decision to speak.

What was I thinking? Nices don't challenge authority. Ever. I'm nervous, so I hope he'll let it slide, but I have to be better. Mistakes like that in the real world will get me killed.

He huffs, then places his hand on my chest and pinches some of the hair that's growing there.

"This," he says as he makes a fist, gripping a few small strands. His hand lifts up, and my chest rises up with him until my bonds stop me. He keeps pulling until the hair rips out. I drop back down, squirming in agony. "Needs to go." He jabs me in the gut. My body bends forward, but the bonds catch me and snap me back into place. "Other than that, he's in fine physical condition. His muscles are of adequate definition to create arousal."

"What about his . . ." The nurse looks down at my crotch.

No no no.

"Are you a child? Are you talking about his penis?"

She nods.

"Well," he says. "It's not very impressive as it is, is it?"

My flight instinct kicks in, and suddenly all I can think about is getting out of this fucking room. Ignoring the pain in my wrists, I pull as hard as I can, trying to free my hands. All I end up doing is flailing. What can I do? I can't just lie here and let them do this to me. I start to buck and kick, hoping desperately that a miracle will happen and something will break and I'll be free.

The doctor places his gloved hand on my chest and presses down hard, stilling me. My rabbitlike heartbeat thuds against his palm.

He leans in close. "That's what you get for snark. Now, team, are you ready to begin?"

"Yes sir," they answer in unison.

"Good. Then let's start with his eyes."

The doctor grabs the big white machine with both hands and pushes it into position above my right eye. Then, with his smile obvious in the pinch of his mask and the twinkle in his eyes, he places a mask over my nose and mouth.

Blackness swirls.

I splay my palms.

Kick my feet.

Finally, the black takes over.

I SIT UP, SCREAMING. BUT THERE'S NO PAIN. I raise my hands to my face and marvel at the freedom of my wrists. The room I'm in is like my old room, but the walls are plaster, not mirrors, and the bed is soft. A bunch of clothes are in a messy pile on the floor. I must've kicked them off mid-nightmare.

I lift up the fluffy blanket. I'm totally naked, and everything down *there* looks exactly the same as it used to. My manhood is still *my* manhood. I smile, then bite my lip. My chest looks funny. Every single hair is gone, leaving me feeling cold and slightly tingly. I run my hand along my chest. It feels slippery. My skin is also a few fractions darker than before, now a nice, even farm-boy tan, and the mole that used to sit on my hip is gone.

I slide out of bed and pull on a pair of blue boxers, then a pair of chinos. As I'm deciding between navy and green shirts, the door opens.

It's Kaylee. She's dressed in a red-and-black flannel shirt and tight white pants.

"Hi," she says, pulling a white earbud from her ear. She

covers her eyes until I pull a shirt, the green one, over my head. As I tug it down she drops her hand and takes a step forward. "Wow. Dude, you should look at yourself. They haven't changed much, but seriously, what they did makes you look so much cooler. You're stunning!" She looks behind her, checking to see if the coast is clear, then reaches into her pocket.

"We aren't supposed to show you mirrors so soon after your operation, but this isn't a mirror so it should be fine. Man, I love technicalities."

She passes me a white iPhone. I stare at the dark reflection that appears on the screen.

The boy looking back at me isn't me. His hair is golden blond, his eyes are vivid blue, and his nose is perfectly straight. Also, his chin is noticeably more pronounced. In fact, the first thing someone might notice would be his strong jaw. He's an idealized version of myself, what I wished for whenever I felt ugly or unlovable. It's myself through the lens of someone who loves me.

I practice my smile. Oh God. It's now crooked—nice touch. I peer closer, turning my head to the side, paying particular attention to my cheeks. No freaking way. They're faint, and only visible when I'm smiling, but this fact is unavoidable: they gave me dimples.

"Are you impressed?" asks Kaylee.

I pass the phone back to her. "Yeah, I look great. They did an exceptional job."

I mustn't have put enough effort into my tone, as she crosses her arms. "You're still recovering, so I'm going to let that one slide. Oh, and you've officially been given a name. It's Caden, C-A-D-E-N. Get used to responding when people call you that."

A name.

I have a freaking name.

Caden.

I think it over and over in my mind until it starts to sound odd.

My name is Caden.

"First things first. I've already set up your home and selected your outfits, so that's all taken care of. I'm still working on your scripts, but I've printed out the first few and have them ready for you. All that's left is one last meeting with Mr. Craike. Then we'll take a plane to your new place. Isn't this exciting? You're finally getting out of here, Caden." She claps her hands together, which makes her bracelets chime, then she pouts. "Aw, I'm kinda jealous. Now, do you have any last questions before you go? You can ask me anything—just remember that whatever you say from now on will be monitored."

"There *is* one thing that's always bugged me," I say. "I'd like to know why the LIC is so focused on pairing us in high school. Like, wouldn't it be better to send us in when we're a bit older? No one finds the love of their life while they're a teenager."

"You haven't read any YA novels recently, have you?"

I shake my head. "I prefer sci-fi. Why? What does that have to do with anything?"

She looks up at the camera that's attached to the ceiling and shrugs.

I want to ask her why she's acting so weird, but the door opens and Craike appears so I clamp my mouth shut. The shoes he's wearing are so polished they shine, reflecting the harsh white light.

"Kaylee," he says, offering a wide smile. "What a pleasure it is to see you."

"The pleasure is mine, sir. But don't scare my boy too much, okay? I need him in fighting condition. He's going to meet Juliet later on today."

"I won't," Craike says. "I promise."

He winks at me and I tense, because if his tone didn't give away that he was lying, the wink definitely did. Which means whatever he's about to show me could be absolutely horrific.

CHAPTER
FOUR

KAYLEE WAVES AT ME, THEN WALKS OUT OF THE room. When the door closes behind her, Mr. Craike steps forward and touches the table. Blue light erupts from the surface.

"Caden," he says, his tone flat. "You look much better."

"Thank you, sir."

He taps the screen and a grainy hologram appears. The video is dark and kind of blurry, and the brightness ratio is skewed. Night vision, I presume. He presses *pause*, then walks around the desk to stand behind me. His hands slide upward, then clamp down on my shoulders. His icy cologne fills my nostrils. I want to shrug him off, to get his awful, cold hands off me, but I keep my shoulders slack.

He pushes me forward and I stumble closer to the projection. My eyes focus, and I realize I'm looking at a quiet alley.

"The thing about actors, Caden, is that they can never be trusted. So let me be very clear—I don't trust you. I was once a seventeen-year-old boy, and I can recall the fire you have in your chest, the drive that pushes you to defy authority. So know that those feelings aren't even remotely original, and that fighting against me, no, against *us*, is a losing battle."

He taps the screen and the hologram unfreezes. A man, handsome, with a slender body and glasses, runs down the alleyway. He reaches a door and slaps his hand against it once, twice, three times before he gives up, turns around, and raises his hands above his head. I guess he's a Nice, because he's wearing a bulky knitted sweater and he just gives off that kind of vibe.

"Don't worry," whispers Craike. "His rival was chosen. He was going to be killed anyway. We decided his passing could serve, well, demonstrative purposes. We were kind to him in that way. His death has saved many lives."

"Please," cries the man. "Let me try again with another girl. I'm so much better now; I know I'll win if you give me the chance. Please. Please!"

A hulking, all-black figure walks past the camera and advances toward him. The guy's expression turns terrified—he's realized that he's been trapped by a Stalker. The man screams, then the figure moves impossibly fast—a dark blur—and grabs him by the throat. The Nice's eyes go wide, then wider still, so they're bulging from their sockets.

I need to watch this, even though I know how it's going to end. It's awful, and it's going to haunt me for the rest of my life, but I can't look away. And that's not just because Craike is here and I can't disobey him. I need to watch so that I know, precisely, what will happen to me if I'm not convincing enough as a Nice. *This is why*, I think. This is why I've worked so hard, to make sure that what is happening to this Nice will never happen to me.

I blink and keep watching.

The Stalker's hand grips tighter. The skin of the man's neck flows out and covers the hand. The Nice coughs and gags, choking. His body is still fighting for life, even though he must know he's done for. Blood spurts as the fingers sink right through the skin. The Nice's eyes roll back into his skull. The monster's fingers and thumb touch, crushing the spine. And that's it: the Nice's body crumples and lands on the ground in front of the sleek black feet. His head remains in place, gushing blood, supported only by the cold metal hand.

"Turn around, Caden."

I spin and stare right into a muscular black chest. It's smooth and nearly featureless, missing both nipples and a belly button, like a child's doll. Little rivers of pulsing white light ripple through the skin, shimmering almost like starlight. My blood chills, and I tilt my head up. A still, black metal head is glaring at me. I gaze into the flat panes where the eyes should be and it seems that *something* is looking at me.

"Now," says Craike.

The Stalker's hand shoots out and grabs me by the neck. The fingers are freezing cold. My face starts to burn. I kick my feet and dig my fingernails into the smooth metal, but its grip holds firm.

Craike grins. His bottom teeth are yellow and crowded, all the little teeth at odd angles mashed up against one another. "This is a Stalker. It's the most advanced robot ever created, the perfect killing machine. If you ever stray from the script or try to run, we will send him after you. And he will rip you apart."

The flat black panes glare at me.

"Enough," says Craike.

The Stalker releases me and takes a step backward. Little

pulses of light run from the tips of its fingers all the way to the middle of its chest, where a cluster of light glows.

"We are not releasing you. We are sending you out for a purpose, and you will always be ours. Even if you win the contest you'll work for us, giving us all the information about your Chosen that we require. Is that very clear?"

How could he be clearer? He might as well have told me the rest of my life will be awful no matter what. Death by incineration is a thing of nightmares, but life for a successful Love Interest isn't exactly a happily ever after. After winning, the Love Interest needs to be a perfect partner to prevent his Chosen from ever moving on.

Also, he must betray a person who loves him every single day. I force the thought down, trying to keep it from showing in my eyes.

"Crystal."

"All right. Now, sit. There is one last thing we must discuss now that I know I can trust you."

Rubbing my burning neck, I sit down. The hologram fades away.

Craike sits too. "I want you to tell me what you think the LIC trains Love Interests for. I'm sure a smart boy like you has some theories. Answer truthfully or you'll be punished."

My first instinct is to ignore his threat and lie anyway, to make him think I haven't thought about this as much as I have. But he's already shown that he has an excellent bullshit detector, so I have to tell the truth.

"I think this is all about surveillance," I say. "Only super-important people are assigned Love Interests, right? I think you want our Chosen to fall for one of us so that she'll tell us all her secrets. And then we'll tell those secrets to you."

He smiles, but his eyes remain cold. "You know more than most. Do you have any questions about our motives? Most do, and we have nothing to hide here. An informed Love Interest is an effective Love Interest."

I'm shocked, but I don't let it show. I've spent a huge portion of my life trying to figure out what the LIC is training me for. I've known for a long time that they're teaching me to be some sort of spy—that's obvious from some of the classes they make us take—but I've never known *why*. I sort of figured I'd always be kept in the dark about most of the ins and outs of their operations. That's just the way they are.

"The only thing I don't understand," I say, "is why the LIC values secrets so highly. I mean, you've gone to all this effort"—I gesture to the Stalker—"to create this place and train Love Interests, just to spy?"

Craike places his hands on the table. "Let me put it this way: how much do you think people are willing to pay for a piece of information that could end a presidency or destroy a rival company?"

"A lot?"

"A lot is correct. Love Interests acquire information for us, and then we sell that knowledge for more money than most people earn their entire lives. You were incorrect, though, in assuming we deal in secrets, because we don't. We didn't train you to tell us *gossip*." He spits the word out like it's dirty. "We deal in information. The right piece of information can be truly devastating if it's precisely aimed. You'll be surprised by how willing people are to hand over information that could ruin them to the people they love. The LIC has been profiting from people's affection for centuries."

"Centuries?" I ask. I'd guessed because the LIC is so high-tech that it was a fairly new organization.

He nods. "Yes, the LIC has existed for hundreds of years, and we have Compounds in eleven countries. Almost everyone you think of as important or influential had, or has, a Love Interest beside them, hiding in plain sight."

He touches the screen. The hologram appears again. He swipes, and a black-and-white photograph appears. It's of an old president whose name I can't remember. He's standing on the steps of the White House, waving at a group of people. Beside him is his wife. She's waving at the crowd with one hand. I'm sure most people wouldn't notice anything abnormal about her, but now that I know what she is, there's something about her frozen smile that's horrific. She isn't there to support the man she loves on a monumental day in his life.

She's a spy.

The photo vanishes and is replaced by a wall of images. Each one is similar to the one of the president; someone important, from athletes to movie stars, is standing in the limelight. But they aren't the ones I focus on. I'm focusing on their partners, the monsters hidden in plain sight.

"I hope," says Craike, "the knowledge that you are now a member of the world's most covert and most powerful spy organization inspires you to make the right decisions when you enter the real world. You're going to do good work out there, Caden, I can tell. I don't mean just for us, but for the world: you'll help us keep everyone safe from the tiny few who have real, terrifying power. If she picks you, that is." He taps the screen once, and the hologram disappears. "Now, come on, it's time to go."

Leaving the Stalker in the room, we make our way into a long hallway lined with empty cells. We walk through a set of double doors to a small courtyard. The grass is plastic and neon green. There's one palm tree and a small fountain filled with white-and-orange koi fish. Four huge decorative mirror shards, each easily double my height, have been stabbed into the grass.

In the shade of the tree, a bunch of rejected guys are standing, chatting. Their disappointment shows in the sag of their shoulders. We're sort of friends—well, as close to friends as we can be given that one day we could become mortal enemies.

Still, their faces bring up some of the best memories I have: watching movies in the rec room with 105, lifting weights with 304, and goofing off in behavioral psych classes with 63.

I've lived with most of these guys since I was eleven, which is when I was moved from my foster home to the LIC. I might not be friends with all of them but they're the closest thing to family I have. I spot 413 in the group. We aren't friends but he came to the LIC the same week I did, so we'll always have that binding us, even if I do find him kind of annoying.

In his defense, he *did* introduce me to Nicki Minaj, and he'll always get points for that. Sure, he only showed me the "Anaconda" video because, well, Nicki and those dancers. But the song stuck in my head, and afterward I listened to it on repeat until I'd memorized each of the verses. Now she's my favorite musician by a huge margin.

413 waves at me. Should I say goodbye to him? What do I say

to someone I'm probably never going to see again? I can't say what I want to say, which is: thanks for introducing me to Nicki, but I still think you're a tool.

"If you'd like," says Craike, "you can say goodbye to them."

"Thank you, sir."

I walk away from Craike and approach 413. He offers his hand.

"You made it?" he asks.

I nod as I shake his hand. This is . . . odd. He's usually such a bro, and as such, I didn't think he was capable of just a handshake. Usually he likes elaborate greetings with knuckle bumping and back tapping. Now, though, shaking his hand, he seems softer, and I'm worried that I've judged him too harshly.

"Yep, I did," I say. "Looks like I'm getting out of here."

He must hate me for leaving while he's still stuck here. He must think I'm rubbing his face in it.

He pulls me into a hug. "Go crush it out there, man. And who knows, maybe in a couple years we'll both be out and I can have you over for dinner or something. You know, like normal people."

"Yeah, definitely."

I force the statistical improbability of that happening out of my mind, then return to Craike.

"They hate you," he says.

I nod. "They're just scared. They're almost eighteen so they know they have limited time, because everyone knows the adult Compound is more selective than ours. No one wants to stay at the LIC forever." He narrows his eyes, which makes me blush. "I mean, no one wants to grow old without being assigned."

We both know this doesn't happen. Either you're chosen

while you're desirable or you vanish, either to be incinerated or, in rare cases, mind-wiped and repurposed into some other role, like a parent or older brother or something. Being repurposed is far from ideal, though, as they say it strips you of all personality, leaving you a shell of the person you used to be. We both know that winning is the only way to live a life somewhat worth living.

"The fact that I was chosen," I continue, "means they have one less shot at being assigned while they're still young adults. Some of them already have their transfer forms. It makes sense that they're afraid."

"Fear is useless. If they want to get out they need to work hard. It's the only way through."

Easy for you to say.

At the end of another long, mirrored hallway is an elevator. Craike presses a plastic card onto the wall to the left of it. A square panel illuminates, showing a photo of Craike above the words ACCESS GRANTED. The sound of machines whirring fills the air.

He turns to me. "Did you enjoy your time at the LIC, Caden? Sometimes I can't wait to get away from a place, only to leave and discover I was happier than I thought."

I look down the pristine reflective hallway. Will I miss this place? *No freaking way.* But he's staring at me, so I smile and say: "Sure, I mean, I'm sad about leaving my friends, but I'm excited to finally live the life I was born to live. To become the real me, you know?"

The doors slide apart. We walk inside. He taps his card onto a screen beside the buttons, then presses the button marked 1. The elevator rises.

"Caden, the only person a liar can't fool is a better liar. And boy, I can see right through you."

I turn away, my cheeks reddening.

He keeps looking at me. "So let's hope Juliet isn't a very good liar."

"Yes, let's."

The door opens, revealing a massive hangar. Sitting in the middle of the room is a gleaming white jet. Two workers in gray overalls are pulling at chains at the back of the room, slowly opening the door to reveal a long gravel runway.

And the sky.

It stretches on and on and on. It's bloody endless.

"We can't be disturbed as we transport Love Interests," says Craike. "And a private jet is the most efficient manner of discreet transport."

In front of the steps that lead to the door of the jet is Kaylee. She sees me and starts jumping up and down, waving ecstatically.

Hey, Caden!

Her voice rings through my mind, clear as day. Startled, I take a step back. She laughs, then taps the spot behind her ear.

Don't freak out in front of Craike, all right? It's bad form.

Can you hear me?

Of course I can. This is good, we need to practice talking telepathically. And no, I can't always read your mind. Only little bursts. Now, I'm going to hug you.

She sprints toward me and grabs me in a hug. My arms go slack as she squeezes, but my obvious awkwardness only makes her grip me tighter. "It's time. Come on, man, smile! You're finally getting out of here. You're going to a small country town in Virginia called Mapleton. It's got all these little bookstores and coffee places and ugh, it's so cute. You'll love it there."

Craike's warning rings in my ears. *You'll always be ours.*

"I'm sure I will!"

"You *have* to see the inside of the plane. It's decked out to the absolute max. I'm talking leather seats, wide-screen TVs, the newest gaming consoles, and, best of all, a full bar." She flings her arm around my shoulders. "Maybe a drink or two will settle those nerves before you meet Juliet? God knows alcohol was probably invented to help hapless Romeos like you. So come on, let's go!"

I climb up the steps, bouncing up and down, trying to make myself appear almost as giddily excited as Kaylee. I figure it's what a Nice would do. At the very top, I turn and look back. Craike is staring at me with his arms tight across his chest. His eyes are cold and his mouth is set in a sneer. "Don't forget what I said, Caden."

Step out of line and you will die.

"I never will."

Then I walk through the doorway into the plane.

CHAPTER
FIVE

KAYLEE WASN'T KIDDING, THE INSIDE OF THE plane is stunning. The carpet is the color of cream, and there are only four seats: massive, soft leather things that recline fully. At the back of the plane is a small bar, and behind it is a glass shelf stocked with every type of alcohol imaginable. Alcohol wasn't allowed at the LIC, but I've seen enough TV to know it's supposed to be delicious. My mouth waters.

Two of the seats are occupied. A prim-and-proper-looking girl with her red hair pulled back in a tight bun sits in one. She catches me looking and her eyebrows furrow, making her square glasses slip down her pointy nose.

In the other is my rival.

But it's not him anymore.

His eyes are now a shining, emerald green. His face has been restructured so now his jawline is stronger and his nose is slightly bigger and dead straight. His cheekbones are high points beneath his eyes and his teeth have been bleached so that they're impossibly white. Even the little hairless patch on his cheek is gone, and now the bristle on his cheeks looks almost like a full-on beard. I thought he was handsome before, but now he's in a whole new league. Like, before he was the lead guitarist of a punk band I'm not cool enough to know about, but now he's the dreamy lead singer of a mainstream pop-punk band who is going to ride the line between cute and sexy all the way to the bank. It's just . . . his eyes are so vibrant, and his hair is so perfectly messy. I can't look away.

"Judy," Kaylee says with a stern nod to the prim girl.

Judy moves her head lazily upward and blinks slowly. "Kaylee. It's so nice to see you. How was the funeral of your last boy? I heard the flowers were beautiful."

He and I keep looking at each other.

"I need a drink," I say, and I head toward the bar. I pass him, and as soon as I do I sense movement; he's slid out of his chair to follow me.

I grab the fanciest bottle of scotch I can find, a squarish bottle with a blue label, and start pouring it into a small square glass. The amber liquid sloshes against the bottom of the cup.

My rival is behind me. "So," he says. His hands are in his pockets and his shoulders are slightly hunched. "I was given a name. They want me to go by Dylan, but you can call me Dyl, if you'd like. I prefer it. It feels more like my choice, not theirs, you know?"

I turn away from him and spin the lid back onto the bottle. My grip on it tightens, forming a tight seal. Of the two of us, he's better-looking. By a wide margin. After everything I've done to turn myself into the perfect Nice, he could win because of his pretty eyes and stupidly cute smile. It's bullshit.

He could star in a CW show, for crying out loud! He's a scruffy Abercrombie model! He's . . .

He's looking at me.

"Dude," says Dyl. "What's the deal?"

I place the bottle down and turn to face him. The glass of the bottle clatters against the granite of the bar.

"You've changed. A lot."

His mouth drops open slightly. "Is it bad?"

I shake my head. "No. But you don't look like a real person anymore. I mean, seriously, who the fuck has bright-green eyes?"

He laughs. "I do, apparently. Now pass me a scotch, Nice guy. I've always wanted to try it."

I pause. Should I do this? The LIC wouldn't want me to. I peer past him and see that both Kaylee and Judy are distracted by their phones, so I pour a drink and pass it to him. They want me to hate him, and if I can do something that goes against their wishes but doesn't get me in trouble, I'm absolutely going to do it.

He's staring at me, grinning like he noticed that I hesitated but poured him the drink anyway. *Damn it.* He raises his drink to his lips and winces. "This doesn't smell how I'd imagined."

I smell my own, which stinks like burning acid. I thought it'd be sweet and woody.

"Well," he says. "It's too late to back out now. Cheers!"

Our glasses clink together, then, at the same time, we take big gulps. The liquid sets my mouth on fire. Coughing, I slam the glass back down onto the bar. Through watery eyes I see Dyl. He's doubled over, spluttering his lungs out. He looks ridiculous.

I laugh. Like, genuinely laugh.

I can't remember the last time I laughed like this.

He starts to laugh too, and somehow, that makes everything better.

I recover and take a deep breath. My mouth and my windpipe are numb and sort of cold. It feels funny yet kind of nice. *Is this what being drunk feels like?* Dyl straightens up, beaming, his smile showing off those goddamn perfect teeth.

He wipes his eyes. "I owe you, man. Imagine that, Juliet and me at a party, me a Bad, and then I can't even handle a sip of scotch. I'd be a joke!"

My smile fades as I remember why I'm on this plane. Why I exist. The only thing I should laugh at is one of Juliet's jokes. Without her around, I don't matter, so feeling anything when I'm not near her is a waste of energy. Also: I helped Dyl, which is something I can't afford to do. He's right, if he'd spluttered like that in front of Juliet it would've cracked apart his tough-guy persona. Giving him that drink was a mistake. All I can do now is hope that it wasn't a big, life-ruining mistake.

Caden, what are you doing? says Kaylee's voice in my mind. *I told you, that boy is dangerous. He's not your friend. I repeat, he is not your friend. Come back to your seat right now!*

I slide past him and make my way back down the aisle. When I reach my seat I sit down and clasp the buckle of the seat belt over my waist.

From the other side of the plane, Kaylee glowers at me. A strand of golden hair has fallen out of place, and now it dangles in front of her eyes, which are brimming with rage. The intensity of her stare shocks me, and I look down at my seat belt.

Don't be an idiot, Caden. I want to win, to show Judy I'm better than her. Don't let him destroy you before we've even begun.

So that's all she cares about? Great. I turn in my seat so my back is to Kaylee. The plane is moving, and now I'm out of the LIC. I guess it's a big deal, but I'm still recovering from Kaylee's scolding and my own self-loathing, so I don't really feel anything.

I squint and look out the window. All I can see is a long stretch of brown earth and then the sky. The sunlight is golden, and I imagine the smell of it, clean and free of chemicals. I'm as free as I'll ever be now. Holy shit! The feeling, bright and hot, overwhelms my shame. I'm finally a part of the real world. Maybe I can't do *anything* I want, but it's definitely better than before.

I remember Dyl spluttering after he sipped the scotch, and smile. *Don't forget what you are.* The only reason I'm on this trip is to reach Juliet. Even though it feels like it, it's not a big deal. Right now I'm nothing, a blank page waiting to be filled. I shouldn't feel anything until I meet Juliet. But man, that was funny. *He's* funny.

All I have to do to survive is make sure that boy dies.

My smile fades.

CHAPTER
SIX

THE PLANE TOUCHES DOWN IN A SMALL, PRIVATE runway in the middle of a farm. The flight passed pretty quickly as, thankfully, there was a TV screen that dropped down from the ceiling. The only options were eighties movies, so I watched *The Breakfast Club* and then the first third of *The Princess Bride*. But for the most part I spent my time staring out the window. The countryside we were flying over was so big and so flat it fascinated me.

"Are you coming, Caden?" asks Kaylee.

I unbuckle my seat belt and force the Nice into my voice. "Yep."

When the door opens, Kaylee reaches across the bar and swipes three cans of Coke, tucking them into her handbag. Then we disembark.

Outside it's flat and barren and the air smells like burnt sugar. Past the fields of swishing grass and the green mountains is the impossibly blue sky. At the top of the stairs, I pause with my hands on the cold metal railing, marveling at the world in front of me.

Everything is vibrant and colorful. The sun is rising, peeking out against the mountains, but the air on my skin feels dreamily warm.

"Yeah, yeah," says Kaylee. She's already off the steps and is standing in front of a shiny white limousine. "The world is beautiful. Big whoop. Now come on, I want to show you your house. I spent a lot of time working on it, so you need to appreciate it!"

I walk down the steps. On the other side of the plane, Dyl is disembarking. He raises one hand and waves.

I don't wave back.

Rather, I clamber into the limo after Kaylee. Inside is a row of black leather seats. Kaylee is sitting with her back pressed up against the door. Tinny classical music pumps from a speaker on the ceiling. The windows are tinted so dark I can't see outside.

The limo starts up and pulls off the side of the road onto the highway. Kaylee cracks open a can of Coke, filling the limo with the scent of sugar.

"Can I . . ." I start, then I shut my mouth. Soda, even diet soda, is a banned substance at the LIC, and asking for it now feels way out of line. It's only Kaylee, and she's so laid back it's easy to forget who she works for, but that's a mistake I can't afford to make. Kaylee is my boss, and I'm not free, so I need to tread carefully around her.

She smiles. "Oh my God, have you ever had a Coke before?"

"Not since I hit puberty."

She reaches into her bag and pulls out a can. Then she offers it to me.

"It's up to you, Caden. You can drink it if you want to, but remember, you're going to have to take your shirt off in front of

Juliet at some point, and your body is perfect right now. Do you want to risk losing your physique over one tasty beverage?"

I push down all the thoughts telling me to grab the drink and finish it in one go, and shake my head. "No, you're right. I've worked too hard to ruin it now."

She beams and puts the Coke back into her bag. "Good choice. So, just to keep you in the loop about what's happening, right now we're going to go to your home, the place you'll live while you're competing. Oh, and you'll meet your parents. They aren't your real parents, but I don't think you're dumb enough to think that. Seriously, some Love Interests get so excited, like I'm taking them to their birth parents. It's totally pathetic. By the way, do you remember your birth parents? I read that some people have memories of their infancy."

I look down at my hands. My only memories are of foster parents who only pretended to love me because it was necessary for development, then mirrored walls, red-clad guards, and a promise of a better life if I became a good enough liar.

"Well," she says. "I guess you don't want to talk about that. That's fine. Anyway, you'll meet the people we've chosen to be your parents. I didn't have any control over the mom, but I did pick the dad. Not that that means much, as all the good ones were already taken. So he's, er, a bit rough. I'd stay away from him as much as possible if I were you." She glances down at her watch. "Okay, it's five-thirty now, which means you've only got a little bit of time to get ready before school starts. And have a guess who is going to be there. . . ."

"Jennifer Lawrence? No freaking way!"

She rolls her eyes. "No, unfortunately for you, she's already been paired. For real, though, Juliet is going to be there. So, on the drive over, I want you to read this."

She reaches into her shiny gold handbag and pulls out a few sheets of paper that are clamped together by a black clip. I glance at the first page. It's like a movie script, only my name is in big block letters above some of the dialogue. The page is titled "First Meeting."

She leans in closer. "This is your script. Obviously, I can't predict exactly what Juliet is going to say, but I've studied her for a while and I can make a pretty informed guess. Just make sure you keep the idea of each line and tailor it to what she says. Hit all the right beats and you'll be fine. Craike told me you showed him in your interview how great an actor you are. Now is the time to use those skills. You'll need them."

I flick through the pages, quickly counting ten. Each one is full to the margins with script. There's only one page for our first meeting, but there are others for things like first date and first kiss.

"So it's all fake?"

"There's no such thing as fake. As much as it sucks to admit sometimes, everything that exists actually exists and everything that happens actually happens. Do I look fake to you? Does the paper you're holding not feel solid? This is real. It's just unusual. Think of it like a great romance. People in those never come together in the way they expect. All this stuff with the LIC and me and everything could be the setup for your kick-ass love story."

Yeah, because manipulative liars make great partners.

She gasps. *Oh crap, she heard me.*

"Sorry," I say. "I just thought I'd get to talk to her with my own words."

"There's plenty of time for that. But, trust me, a good first impression can often be the difference between winning and losing. Speaking of, when you're out there, I want you to always keep your eyes on the prize. The contest will be called when it becomes clear that she's chosen one of you as her partner. Basically, as soon as she declares her love for one of you in a big, meaningful way, it's over, and the rejected Love Interest will be removed. Sorry, I got off topic. What was I talking about?"

"First impressions."

"Ah, yes. You need to make sure in the first second she sees you that you present yourself as a viable romantic option. Screw it up and you'll be constantly fighting an uphill battle to make her view you as someone she could love. Now, you need to get your backstory right."

"My backstory?"

She rolls her eyes and lets out a long sigh. "Yes, Caden, your backstory. You can't tell her you're from the LIC, can you? When Juliet was a child, shortly after she aced her Mensa test, a plant was placed in her school. Wait, you know what a plant is, right?"

I shake my head. I have a pretty good idea what a plant is, but I'd like to hear what Kaylee has to say about them.

"They're nothing special," she continues. "They're just kids who are particularly good at acting. We send them out for a while, and then they come back to the LIC. When they grow up, they become Love Interests, just like you. Anyway, this plant and Juliet became best friends, but then his nice, gentle father died in a boating accident and they had to move away. It was so tragic. You are that boy, returned to her after all these years. And don't worry, the plant was homeschooled, so the only people you need to keep continuity with are Juliet and her parents. Anyway, today, at school, you get to surprise her by showing up out of nowhere." She taps the script on my lap. "Which leads to this scene."

"So this plant's name, it was Caden, right?"

"Yeah, it was."

Not even my name is really mine.

I turn and look out the window, trying as hard as I can to get rid of that thought before it inflicts even more damage. *All I am is a Love Interest. Without that, I'm not even worth a name.* "What happened to the other Caden?"

"Oh, it's kind of funny—you've actually already met him! He was the Nice you went up against in the final round. To be honest, I'm glad Craike picked you—that guy was *so* smug. But that doesn't even matter. You're the real Caden now, so stop talking and start reading. I need your performance to be perfect. And, well, you need it to be perfect as well, obviously. Have you seen what they did to Dylan? He's the hottest thing I've ever seen. I'm telling you, a guy would have to be very nice to make me forget about him."

Her words linger. *You're the real Caden now.* She's kind of right, and it fills me with something like confidence. Unlike my time at the LIC, where what they wanted from me was kind of vague, I now know exactly what I need to do to survive. I need to become Caden, a sweet, funny Nice guy, and I need to make Juliet fall for me.

It's what I have to do.

———————

THE LIMO PULLS TO A STOP IN FRONT OF A white house. It's made of wood and is probably best described as quaint, but that's putting it charitably. It has two roofs—a peaked one that covers the porch and a second, higher one. The plain wooden front door leads to a small, sun-bleached porch enclosed by a white railing. A lot of the paint has chipped away, revealing the dark wood beneath. The front yard is filled with weeds, and the plastic garbage bin that sits on the curb is overflowing.

Kaylee stands in front of the house beaming, proudly presenting it with a flourish of her hands. "Whaddaya think?"

I cross my arms. It looks like a gust of wind could blow it over. Or crack it apart. I want to tell her how shit it is, but I know I can't.

"It's, well, a fixer-upper. But that's cool! It's a nice break from living in a spaceship. It feels more real, you know?"

She blinks slowly. "Don't play Nice with me, Caden. I've been inside your head and I know you're not the boy you pretend to be. You have no idea how much effort it takes to make a house look this awful, and I want credit for all my work. I did it because it'll make you seem endearing to Juliet. Your parents are already in there. Well, the woman is pretending to be your biological mom and the man is your stepdad. Don't mess that up, because Juliet will obviously remember the accident that killed your dad and it'd be almost impossible to recover from a slipup that big. Oh, another thing: don't try getting close to them, they're pretty messed up. Remember, they're people who were deemed unfit to be Love Interests, so they had their, um, minds refreshed. Unfortunately, we haven't perfected the process, and they're always a little . . . Well, you'll see. And, on top of all that, they never got the chance to meet their soul mates, so it makes sense that they're pretty broken."

Soul mates? Is she serious? A Love Interest would never think that their Chosen is their soul mate. We may be perfect for her, or at least we can act like we are, but the relationship is always skewed in her favor. A Chosen is never tested to see if a Love Interest will fall for him or her. It's always the other way around.

"Are you even listening, Caden?" she says, pulling me from my thoughts. "This is important. Now they pose as the parents of new hopefuls like you. But they're grieving, remember that. They lost the only person they'll ever love. Because of that, some of them can be downright nasty. Obviously not around your Chosen, but when it's just you, it'd be wise to keep your wits about you. I can't stress that enough."

"Hearing you loud and clear."

"Good. Then let's go."

We clamber out of the limo into the warm sunlight. I take in a deep breath through my nostrils. A pair of chirping sparrows fly past the house and over a yellow pickup truck.

I touch the sun-warmed metal of the truck. Kaylee reaches into her pocket and produces a key ring. She tosses it to me and I catch it with one hand.

No freaking way.

"Is this mine?"

My enthusiasm is reflected in her grin. "It sure is! Are you a good driver?"

"I'm the worst! But who cares?"

"Well, start practicing. Girls like boys who can drive."

I stare at the truck. *This is mine.* "Thanks so much, Kaylee. Really."

I actually mean it.

Kaylee leans against the hood of the limo. "You're such a boy sometimes. Well, Caden, this is it for now. I'll be in contact, though." She pulls me into a hug. After patting my back once, she moves away, but keeps hanging on to my biceps. "Good luck today. I'm rooting for you, and not just so I can show Judy who's the best coach. Remember that I'm on your side whenever things get tough, all right?"

"Sure."

She rubs my right bicep with one hand, then lets go. "Oh, and one last thing. We'll be able to communicate via your implant most of the time, but if I don't answer, you can contact me on this number." She reaches into her bag, pulls out a white business card, then hands it to me. Her number is etched into it in shiny silver ink. I move it from side to side, marveling at the shine. "But only contact me in a real emergency, okay? I have a life, remember."

"Noted."

She nods once, then walks back to the limo. As the door slams, I spin around and make my way up to the house. I reach the door and rap my knuckles on it. *Okay, Caden, guard up, Nice face on.*

The door swings open, revealing a woman in her late thirties. She's very good-looking, with an angular face and remarkably pale-blue eyes. She's easy to look at in a model-like, appreciate-from-afar kind of way, but she's not someone who actually turns me on. She's too stern-looking and, quite frankly, too old for that.

"You must be Caden," she says, her voice flat.

"That's me!"

"Well, welcome to this old shithole." I look past her and inspect the place. It's obviously past its prime. The TV that sits in front of a faded maroon couch is square and bulky, an antique, really. The kitchen is cramped and cluttered with plates covered in crusted-on food.

"Why couldn't you have been a Bad?" she asks. "They always get mansions. And now, because of you, I'm stuck in this dump."

I look past her, taking the place in. "I'm sorry that you don't like it here, but it's not so bad, is it? I think it's kind of charming."

She narrows her eyes and fans her fingers through her knotty hair. "So that's how this is going to be?" She lets out a weary sigh. "Fine. Your room is up the stairs and down the hall. Don't make any noise, I'm watching *Judge Judy*."

She walks back to the couch and slumps down.

I step over a pile of rank-smelling clothes into a small room with a tight staircase. I climb it. At the top is a long hallway with three doors: two bedrooms and one bathroom. My guess is that my room is the one opposite the bathroom at the far end of the hall. The prospect of it being *my* room makes me smile. This is my house. It's not much, but it's mine. Just to be sure, I gently push open the door of the room closest to the staircase and peer inside. It's trashed, the floor covered in dirty, crumpled clothes, moldy pizza boxes, and other garbage.

In the middle of the mess, on the bed, is a great bear of a man. He obviously used to be Bad: even asleep, his face is set into a snarl. He's shirtless, and his chest is huge, taking up a massive portion of the double bed. He moans, and I quickly but quietly close the door. If a man like that saw me staring at him while he was asleep, it wouldn't end well for me.

I reach my room and pause. This is it. The moment I've dreamed about forever. No matter what it looks like, this room has to be better than my cell.

I swing the door open. It's surprisingly plain. A simple metal bed frame with a single mattress covered in a navy sheet is jammed into the far corner of the room. A white desk is pressed against the opposite wall, and a wooden chest of drawers is tucked into the corner. The walls are bare but, thankfully, plaster, not mirrors. There's one mirror in the room, a freestanding antique in the far corner, but I can spin that around if I want. And then I'll finally be able to sleep without having to look at myself!

I walk to the window and push it open. Outside is a small stretch of brown-tiled roof, then there's the porch, the front yard, and the road. Beyond that is an overgrown paddock surrounded by a barbwire fence. A black cow raises its head and looks in my direction, its jaw bobbing up and down as it chews.

This is my view! Every morning when I wake up, this is what I'll see. Because this is my room! It's basic, sure, but it's clearly not a cell. It's a normal person's bedroom, and it's all mine. I can put posters on the walls! They'd probably have to be approved or something, but I can't think of any reason why Kaylee would say no to that request.

I turn back and look at the desk. Beside the computer is a stack of beaten paperbacks, obviously taken from the LIC's library. I actually miss going there. It wasn't a full library or anything, as the collection was strictly regulated, featuring the bare minimum required to let us pass as regular teenagers. Still, there was a lot of good stuff there if you knew how to look for it. The sci-fi and fantasy section was particularly good, probably because our learning about Narnia or whatever was much safer for them than our learning about the real world.

I smile as I pick up the first book, a copy of *The Martian* I've read at least five times. I go through the pile and find a lot of the books I found refuge in when things got bad at the LIC: *Ready Player One*, *Neuromancer*, and *Dune*. These books helped me get through some pretty terrible stuff, and it's only now that I'm out that I've realized how attached to them I am. They're all a part of me, and these copies, the exact ones I read at the LIC, are the copies I want on my shelf for the rest of my life.

Caden, can you hear me?

Sure can. And Kaylee, thanks for the books. They're . . . They mean a lot to me.

I know! You told me you like sci-fi, and I keep track of these things.

Still, I think you should take them back. I'm out now, so I don't need them as much as the guys who are still there. Yeah, you should definitely take them back.

Nonsense, Caden. If you care that much, I'll make sure there are new copies for the library. But those books are yours now. Anyway, what do you think of the place?

I glance around my room. *I freaking love it.*

That's great! Now, your school uniform is in the closet. Shower, shave, and get yourself ready. Have you memorized the script?

Not yet, but I'm working on it.

Good. Now get ready. Make yourself pretty for your girl!

I open the closet, revealing a chest of drawers and silver coat hangers. Hanging from them are five short-sleeved white shirts with a navy logo in the middle. Then there's an assortment of button-downs, some plain and therefore wearable, but there's a lot of plaid. Oh my God, so much plaid. Next are two suit jackets, one black, one navy. Finally, there's a black cotton T-shirt with a familiar green label on the chest.

Starbucks? What's that doing here?

Oh yeah, I forgot to tell you, I got you a job. How good are you at making coffee?

Um, I'm probably the worst coffee maker in history. I've never tried! I didn't even think to learn, but obviously I should've. I . . .

Don't stress, Caden. It doesn't matter that much. I got your "mom" to act like a concerned parent who wants to give you a reason to get out of the house after school. The manager there's a good guy, so he's given you a few trial shifts. Most important, Juliet goes there every single day after school, so you'll get a lot of extra time with her. Also, it'll make you seem responsible, which is a big thing for Nices. Your first shift is tonight. But aside from that, what do you think of the rest of the clothes? I tried to pick things I thought you'd like.

I run my hands through the clothes. Not one item is sky blue. I'm not sure how she knows me well enough to guess what kind of clothes I like to wear, or why she thinks I'm plaid's biggest fan, but I'm grateful Kaylee took the time to say something nice. If she likes me, maybe she'll put more effort into keeping me alive.

They're great. Thanks so much.

No worries. Now get dressed like a big boy; I'm sure you can figure out the school uniform. I'm out!

I pull a short-sleeved dress shirt from its hanger, and then grab a white undershirt and a pair of long gray slacks. I take a pair of undies, gray Calvin Kleins with a white waistband, from the pile and make my way out into the hall.

In the hallway, Dad scratches his bloated, hairy stomach. *Gross.*

"Know your place," he says. "And we won't have a problem."

He pushes past me, bringing with him the sharp stale scent of body odor. He walks into the bathroom and kicks the door closed behind him. A certifiable army of insults to hurl at him swarms my mind, but I force them down. He's big and probably violent, but I'm strong, I know I am. I can handle him. Not that it would ever get to that point, because I can't ever challenge him.

A Nice would silently go back to his room and wait. So that's what I do.

Once I'm in my room, I place the bundled-up pile of clothes on the end of the bed and turn on the computer. It's a laptop, sleek and gray and awesome. It boots up. I open Google and stare at the search box. It looks like I could search for anything, but I know my searches will be monitored. I have to make sure I never search for anything that could get me in trouble.

I open the desk drawer and find that it's filled with gadgets. I pick up a phone, a Samsung, and tuck it into my pocket. Underneath a bundle of cords is an iPod in a blue case. It must be there so I can listen to the music that Juliet likes, but I'll probably be able to load some of my own music—including, of course, Nicki Minaj's entire discography—onto it. It's been a while since I've had a headphones-in listening session in my room, so I should have one soon. Plus, like always, applying her words to my life will let me steal a little bit of her behemoth self-confidence, and confidence is what I need if I'm going to win this thing.

The toilet flushes and the bathroom door swings open. Dad walks out, still scratching his gut. It's covered in little white flakes of God knows what. I scoop my clothes up and walk in after him.

The stench hits, so thick I can taste it. My eyes water and I cough and gag.

Harsh male laughter sounds down the hall. There's a pause, and a woman's follows suit, a high-pitched cackle.

I slam the door closed. Worried the stench will infect my clothes, I reopen the door and throw them into my room. Then I undress and step into the shower. A limp stream of lukewarm water trickles over my body. I squirt a splash of body wash onto my hand and rub it into my chest, creating a foamy white lather. Lifting my arms, I rub it into my armpits. I squint, marveling at the hairlessness of my underarms. Apparently, a Nice is not allowed any body hair at all.

The smell of the neon-blue gel, slightly like fruit punch but mainly like chemicals, fills my nostrils, covering the stench of shit. I tilt my head back and let the water run through my hair and down over my face. It feels pleasant, warm, and slightly refreshing.

As the foam runs down my body the smell comes back with a force. I grin. This is his attempt at intimidating me? It's almost funny. I stifle a giggle as I turn off the taps, shutting the water off. I rub the towel through my hair so it spikes down over my forehead, then drag the towel across my chest, mopping up as much water as I can. Then I wrap it around my waist and step out of the bathroom.

In the hallway is Dad, dressed in my uniform. It's obviously too small for him, as the shirt is strained to capacity. One of the buttons, the one beside his belly button, has burst, and the fly of the gray slacks is unzipped. He's standing there pouting, with his wrists as limp as possible and his butt sticking out. Oh wow, Kaylee *really* wasn't kidding about the slim-pickings thing.

"Look at me," he says, his voice high-pitched. "I'm Caden. Aren't I a pretty boy? Look at me waddle!" He shakes his bum and flails his limp wrists around. "I work out all the time, and I . . ."

I grip the towel around my waist. I *have* to ignore him. He wants me to break character, to reveal my real self, and that's not something I can ever do. If I let my anger show, he wins, so I keep my eyes down and enter my room. I close the door and discover, thankfully, that it has a lock. I slide the latch across then drop the towel. My face is burning so hot the feeling has flowed down my neck to my chest, which feels like it's on fire.

I run a hand through my dripping hair and take in a deep breath through my nostrils. I'm pacing in a small circle on the carpet. I did the right thing. It feels awful to let him get away with it, but it was the right call. I have to recognize that, because it's the only way to deal with stuff like this.

My heartbeat slows to its normal tempo. I finish drying myself, then grab a pair of briefs, bright red this time, and step into them. Once I'm dressed I glance at my phone to check the time. Crap, I should've been out the door two minutes ago! I pull on a pair of socks, then black dress shoes. There. Done.

I take a step toward the door, then double back and grab my script from the desk. I'll have to read it on the bus.

My fake dad's in the kitchen now, still in my uniform, sipping from a bottle of beer. He takes a sip and eyes me. "I wear it so much better, don't you think, Patty?"

"Shut up!" she screeches back, and she grabs the remote and

points it at the TV. The green volume bar slides up. "Can't you see I'm busy?"

"Well, I'm off," I say with a cheery wave. I'm acting Nice because I have to, but a childish part of me wants to spite this guy. What should I call him? I was hoping to call them Mom and Dad, to get some sense of normality, but that's obviously not in the cards now. Maybe I could call him D? That's perfect because it does technically stand for *Dad*, but it also has a second meaning, one only I'll know. "See you later, D."

D sneers at me. "I look forward to that *so* much."

I wince, then slide past him, pressing my back against the wall to avoid his girth. He's not fat, exactly, just solid, and he smells like the beer he's drinking: salty and acidic.

The school bus is outside the house, waiting for me almost expectantly. I jog down the steps and run up to the bus door. The driver is a short black woman with straight hair. She smiles, and I feel the tension leave my shoulders. Not everyone out here is horrible.

"First day?" she asks.

"Yep."

She pulls a lever and the door hisses closed behind me.

"Sit near the front. Some of the kids at the back can be pretty savage to you blazer types."

"Thanks."

I find a spare seat near the front of the bus. I swing into it as the bus pulls onto the road.

I'm on my way, Juliet.

CHAPTER
SEVEN

MAPLETON ACADEMY IS A SLEEK, MODERN PRIVATE
school surrounded by a black fence. The windows gleam in the
sunlight. It's so picturesque it could be a set. But it's not. I repeat
it like a mantra. *It's not a set.* This school is real. Everything
that's happening is real, because I'm finally in the real world.
Dyl and I are the only things here controlled by the LIC.

I step off the bus and take a moment to appreciate the beauty
of the school. The buildings are obviously new, and all the walls
are smooth and freshly painted. There's no grime, cracks, or creeping weeds. Flower beds filled with rosebushes and other colorful
flowers I have no hope of identifying are scattered around the
place.

Caden?

Yeah?

It's Kaylee, obviously. How are you feeling?

I'm still a little freaked out about you being in my mind.

*Get over that real quick. You need to be in position in twenty
seconds. Do you see the steps that lead into the school?*

In front of me, past the open gate, is a set of concrete steps that lead into a cream-colored building. Between me and the steps is a speckled concrete pathway filled with students bustling around, chatting or playing handball.

Sure do.

Run! Juliet is making her way down the hall. You need to be outside waiting for her. Go!

I sprint toward the steps, ducking and diving between the herd of students. They all glare at me as I pass. Once I reach the steps I skid to a stop. There are three steps, then a set of navy double doors.

Put your arms out in front of you!

What?

Do it!

I move my arms forward.

The door swings outward and Juliet steps out. She looks like her hologram: beautiful in a simple, unboastful way. She steps forward, and her ankle twists on the first step. She falls. I take a step toward her and she smashes into my chest. Hair flies into my face, making my eyes water and my nose itch. I blink the tears away and lower her to her feet.

Her hands remain on my chest, with her fingertips curling slightly above my shoulders. She looks down. Her books are in a pile around our feet. She bends down, but I move faster, scooping them up. I pass them to her, and our eyes meet. *Time to win this thing.* My eyes widen slightly, as if with a flicker of recognition.

"Juliet?"

She moves a strand of hair away from her eyes, tucking it behind her ear. She's peering at me with her head tilted to the side and her eyes narrowed. She's kind of short, and her head just reaches my chest. Strangely, it makes me like her more. "Do I know you?" She doesn't sound unfriendly, just curious.

"I guess not," I say, looking down at the top of her head. "We used to be friends. But it's been a while, and I sort of knew you'd forget me." I extend a hand and offer my best smile. "I'm Caden."

She takes a step away from me. Her eyes are twitching, looking over my face, studying every minute detail. *Come on, Juliet, put it together. If you don't, I'm screwed.* Slowly, recognition dawns on her and her mouth drops open, the edges of her lips curling into a smile.

"Shut up! Caden? Caden Walker?"

"The one and only."

She squeals and flings herself at me. Her arms wrap around my neck. She smells like floral perfume. I hug her back, pressing her against my chest. She's soft and warm, and touching her feels nice. Not in a I-want-to-rip-her-clothes-off way, but in a friendly way, like I'm genuinely happy to see her and she's genuinely happy to see me.

We pull apart. "So, you remember me?"

She playfully pushes my arm.

"You were my best friend, Caden; I'd never forget you. I just . . ."

"Didn't expect me to be here? Well, I worked my ass off to get a scholarship to afford it. But I did it, and here I am."

"Oh my God, I didn't mean that! I just meant that I, um, I didn't expect you to look like . . ."

Scratch the back of your neck. Make sure your shirt pulls up. Show her your stomach.

I raise a hand and scratch the back of my neck. For a second, and only a second, her eyes flick down and gaze at the sliver of skin that is showing, then she glances at the floor. She looked! But did she like what she saw? Are my abs good enough to impress her?

I tuck my hands into my pockets and fidget, giving her my best Nice-guy puppy-dog eyes. "Like what? I'm not disappointing you, am I?"

She laughs. "Come on, man. You know you're gorgeous. You used to be this sweet little boy, and now you're freaking buff!"

"Well, I won't be for much longer," I say. "I had to help out on Grandpa's farm over the summer. Spending days riding horses and lifting hay bales had this side effect. I'll be back to my normal scrawny, pasty-white self in no time."

"Don't apologize, you look great. Different, but great. Now, what's your first class?"

"Trig."

Her face falls. "Oh. I'm in AP calculus. And I really have to go. But I'll see you at lunch, right?"

"Absolutely."

"Great. Come on, I'll show you to class. You've got Mr. Corhedge, and he's a grumpy little troll. You definitely don't want to be late on your first day or he'll make you pay for it for the rest of the year."

Together, we walk through the double doors and enter a long hallway. Wasn't she going somewhere? I should ask her where she was—

STOP! It's Kaylee. *Don't be a freaking idiot! If she remembers where she was going she'll leave and you'll lose some time with her.*

I press my lips together. Inside, students are bustling around, grabbing books from lockers or heading toward classrooms. A girl with a huge tumble of curly hair and a thin Asian guy are holding hands in front of the boys' bathroom. They're staring into each other's eyes, and they seem so focused on each other that I bet I could scream at them and they wouldn't even notice. Will I ever have that with Juliet? Will I ever be able to look at her without thinking about the fact that we only met because I'm a Love Interest?

"Do you have your locker yet?" she asks as she stops in front of one and opens it. Inside all the books are sorted alphabetically. A black-and-white picture of a man and a woman, presumably her parents, is stuck on the back of the door. "If you don't, you'll need to go to the principal's office before class. Have you done that yet?"

I'm out of script!

Improvise, man! Use words!

"Is something wrong, Caden?"

"No, I'm fine. It's all a little overwhelming, that's all. And no, I haven't, I only just got here."

She looks down at her watch. "I know the feeling. Head down the hall and take the first right. The door at the end of that hallway is his office. Sign in and head to class."

"Will do."

She bites her bottom lip. "See you around, Caden. I can't wait to properly catch up."

"Neither can I."

She grins, then spins and makes her way down the hall. As she walks, the people around her glance at her. A surge of protectiveness flares in my chest. Is this love? Is this what it feels like?

After being signed in by the principal—a short, balding man with an overly firm handshake—I'm assigned a locker. When I find it, I see it's right next to Juliet's. Of course it is.

The next time I run into her is during lunch. She's sitting at the far end of the courtyard in the shade of the school's chapel. She's sitting with her back against the stone wall, next to a thin black girl who could easily be a model.

I walk up to Juliet. "Hey."

Juliet smiles. Damn, she's pretty. I got lucky. Who knows, maybe in time I could actually fall for her.

"Hi, Caden."

"Well, hello," says the could-be-model girl. "Where have you been hiding my whole life?"

"Natalie!" says Juliet. "He's not a piece of meat."

Oh yes I am.

"Not hiding," I say, fidgeting. "Just on the other side of the country. I'm Caden, it's a pleasure to meet you."

She ignores me and turns to Juliet. "He's not *the* Caden, is he?"

Juliet looks me in the eye. She squints in the brilliant sunlight. I can feel the warmth on the back of my neck. "The one and only."

"Now I know why you wouldn't shut up about him." Natalie turns to me. "Wait, is he blushing? That's so adorable I think I'm going to die on the spot!"

Juliet pushes herself up off the wall. "Come on, Caden. Let's catch up."

We stop in the corner of the playground and sit down on a long silver bench in the sunlight. She turns to face me.

"Caden, I need you to fill me in. What happened after you left? You never responded to my messages and . . ." Her voice trails off. "Sorry. I wanted to be friendly. But man, that was so unlike you. Whenever I'd check my in-box I'd hope that there would be a message from you, saying hi. That's all I wanted. What I got was four years of radio silence and a bunch of shitty feelings. And then you show up at school with no warning? What's the deal with that?"

I scratch the inside of my palm. "Mom said I was never coming back. She told me it was best to forget about you, so that's what I tried to do. I know it doesn't excuse my behavior, and I'm sorry I didn't reply, but I didn't handle being away from you that well."

"So you shut me out? Why is that better?"

I fan a hand through my hair. I imagine Craike staring at me, judging my performance. "I can't explain it, but I was a kid, and writing to you reminded me of how much I wished I was sitting next to you. I tried to make other friends, but that didn't work; I never clicked with anyone as much as I clicked with you. I resented them for that. And I knew if we kept messaging the pain would get worse. So I was a coward and I stopped. I'm sorry, Juliet, and if I could go back, know that I would message you every single day."

She looks down at her black dress shoes, and her hair falls over her face. Her hands, which are dotted with freckles, are shaking. Why is that happening? What am I doing wrong?

I slide an inch toward her. "But I'm here now, Juliet, and if there's anything I can do to make it up to you, I'll do it."

"Anything?"

"Anything."

She smiles a sheepish smile. "Well, there *is* one thing. Later on in the term." She rolls her eyes and chuckles. "No, it's stupid. Forget I said anything."

"I said I'd do anything, Juliet. I meant it."

Two little bursts of pink light up her cheeks.

"Well, for my art project, I need to do a, um, portrait. And I need a subject. And, well, there aren't a lot of guys willing to pose for me, because it has to be, um, you know."

I gulp a hard swallow and raise both eyebrows. "How naked are we talking?"

She tilts her head back and laughs. "Oh God . . . only shirtless. I can look up pictures online for the rest of you and . . ." She laughs again. "I know I sound kinda weird right now, but I promise I'm not. I'm like, 'Hi Caden, I haven't seen you in ages, now come into my house and strip for me.' Sorry. Forget I said anything."

I shake my head. "I said anything, so I'll do it. It just means I need to stay away from the cafeteria." I pat my stomach. "I need to make sure I keep this figure. And I was looking forward to letting myself go. But it would be my pleasure to do this for you, Juliet."

"Thanks, Caden. Really."

The bell rings. She skips back to her friends, leaving me alone on the bench. I watch her go. So that's the only girl I can ever be with. She's pretty, and she seems nice. It could be so much worse. I guess I got lucky.

How'd I do?

Kaylee's laughter sounds in my mind.

She invited you to her house to get naked. You've got this in the bag.

It's what I suspected, but hearing it confirmed makes me grin. I look back at Juliet. She's back with Natalie, who is leaning toward her, trying to get her attention. From across the courtyard Juliet raises a hand and waves at me. I smile and wave back.

Dyl's a dead man.

CHAPTER
EIGHT

I'M ON MY WAY TO THE STARBUCKS DOWN THE street from the school when a drop of rain hits the back of my neck. I frown and look up. The day has turned south, and the air is thick and muggy, the sky filled with gray clouds. Rain splatters against the road. I tuck my hands into my pockets and shuffle-jog the rest of the way, treading carefully to make sure I don't fall on the slippery ground.

I reach the store and swing the door open. As part of my "cultural education" at the LIC I was shown pictures of Starbucks, but I've never actually been inside one. This store matches the ones I was shown in the classes, with wooden walls, a shiny counter, and a chalkboard displaying the menu. It smells like syrup, coffee beans, and whipped cream, and I breathe it all in. Now I know why they're so popular. The very air of this place is delicious.

Only two tables are occupied, one by an elderly couple who are both sipping cappuccinos, the other by a stern-looking guy in a sharp suit who is sipping from a to-go cup while he checks his phone.

A buff black guy, maybe early thirties, in a too-tight black shirt and green apron makes his way around the counter. His smile is wide and his eyes light up with it, making me feel like he's genuinely pleased to see me even though we've never met. Looks like I'm not the only one here who can act.

"Are you Caden?"

I nod. "Yep."

"Good, good. I'm Levi, the manager here. Your mom told me a lot about you and I'm happy to have you on the team." He claps his hands together. "So, did you bring your uniform?"

I raise my backpack slightly.

"Great. There's a bathroom down the hall. Go get changed and wash your hands, then come out here. Remember, when you're in uniform you represent the company, so smile all the time. And never say anything rude to a customer, even if they're being rude to you. If you do those two things, you'll do fine. Get going! The after-school rush is going to get here any minute."

I enter the bathroom and step into a stall. After getting changed I check my reflection in the long horizontal mirror. The shirt is too small, and the sleeves press tight against my biceps, which I'm sure was intentional. I push my bangs down, then leave the bathroom holding my bag in my hands.

"There he is!" says Levi. "You look good, man. Black is your color. Come with me, I'll show you around."

No new customers have entered the store while I was getting changed, though one more staff member has appeared, a girl with messy mousy-brown hair and terrible posture. She's by the coffee machine, slowly cleaning a silver strainer with a blue cloth. There's a hole in her nose where a ring obviously should go, but she must've removed it for work. Her name tag tells me her name is Iris.

Levi leads me into a cramped storeroom. The shelves are stocked with sacks of coffee beans, rows of mugs, and bottles of syrup. Oh goodness, this room smells even better than the rest of the store. I breathe in deep then let out a happy sigh. Levi reaches around a sack of coffee and retrieves a folded green apron that's wrapped in plastic.

"You'd be a medium, right?" he says, and I nod. He passes it to me. The plastic crinkles.

"Good. I have a lot of them but they never get used. Most of the people who work here are girls or the types of guys who barely eat or exercise. It'll be nice to have another actual man around here. Now put that on and I'll show you how to use the cash register. Don't stress, it's easy. If Iris can do it, I'm sure you can. Oh, and you can leave your backpack in here if you're ready to start."

Time passes pretty quickly. Fat drops of rain are splattering against the windows, drenching the green umbrellas outside. It's been pretty quiet, so Levi's been showing me the ropes. My initial judgment of him is quickly disproven, as he's obviously a genuinely nice guy. He patiently showed me how to use the register and explained the basics of the coffee machine. He also made me this month's special, a butterscotch latte, so I could suggest it to customers. It's sweet and a tiny bit bitter, which is exactly how I like my coffee, so I don't have to lie when I say I like it.

I'm sipping the latte when the door opens. It's Juliet. She's wearing an oversized gray hoodie, tight black yoga pants, and UGG boots. The rain has dampened her hair, making it darker and super curly. It hangs casually over her shoulders. The cold has made her nose red and her cheeks pink. I wish this weren't our first day, because if this were happening after a flirty relationship had been established, I could hug her to warm her up. I'd press her against my chest, and she'd smell the cologne Kaylee picked out for me, one that apparently includes a note or two that Juliet loves. Right now, though, I need to keep my distance, because hugging her would be mega-creepy, especially if she figures out that I'm only doing it so that she can smell me.

"Caden?" she says, stepping forward. "What are you doing here?"

Her eyes cross from me to Levi.

"Wait, you know Juliet?" asks Levi. I nod and he turns to her. "Do you want the regular?"

"Yeah, thanks, Levi," she says. Levi taps the screen in front of me, then moves across to the coffee machine and starts frothing some milk.

Juliet is still looking at me. "So you work here?"

"Have to pay the bills somehow."

"I still can't get over this," she says as she reaches into the pocket of her hoodie and pulls out a green leather wallet. "I haven't seen you for so long and now you're . . . here."

She taps her credit card against the card reader. It's accepted.

"It's weird for me too," I say. "But it's a good weird."

"Totally!"

The receipt is printing so slowly. I scratch my elbow; Juliet pretends to be fascinated by a bag of chocolate-covered coffee beans. Where's Kaylee? Why isn't she giving me a line?

"One tall peppermint mocha," says Levi, placing a steaming cup on the counter. Juliet picks it up, brings it to her lips, and lets out a contented sigh.

"Thanks, Levi. And thanks too, Caden. I promise I'll be more normal later. It's just seeing you still kind of freaks me out. I mean, you were MIA for so long and now you work at my favorite place on the freaking planet! It'll take some time to convince myself you aren't going to leave again. I'm sorry I'm not more normal."

"Take all the time you need, Juliet. I'm not going anywhere." She's smiling as she walks away.

I SLUMP DOWN ONTO MY BED, THE EVENTS OF the day replaying in my mind. I raise my hands behind my head and nestle down, getting comfortable. Well, I can't get too comfortable, because I'm still wearing my muddy Chucks and I don't want to wreck my sheets. But undoing tight laces now would be *way* too much effort. I compromise by grabbing a towel from the floor and shoving it under my feet. Once that's done, I lie back down.

Where was I? Ah yes. Juliet.

Her round face. Her hair, so soft and so dark. Her perfume, like flowers, which smelled so incredible when mixed with the rain at Starbucks. The splattering of freckles on her nose and cheeks. Her quick laughter and the warmth of her smile.

Is it possible she will ever like me? Why would she? Isn't it obvious to her that I'm a massive liar? Then again, she did ask me to come to her place and get naked. She wouldn't ask that of me if I didn't do at least something right.

I smile a wide grin. She's the perfect girl. In time, I could fall for her, and maybe that wouldn't be so bad. I know being a Love Interest means I'll always have to keep some things from her, but wouldn't it be nicer if I loved her? It would make my job easier, and make this situation feel more normal. I think of her, and the possibility of developing genuine feelings for her, until I fall asleep.

A knock sounds on my window, the one that looks out over the roof. I sit up and instinctively pull my blanket over my crotch. I check my phone; it's 3:00 a.m. Yawning, I spin around.

Perched outside my window is Dyl. He's dressed in a plain white shirt under a leather jacket, skinny jeans, and brown boots. He's crouched down so the entirety of him is visible, framed by the window. I grab a shirt from where I threw it when I went to bed. As I tug it down I slide out of bed, painfully aware of the fact that my lower half is covered only by thin blue boxers.

I slide the window up and stare at him. "What are you doing?"

He reaches into his bag and pulls out a bottle of beer. He offers it to me. "I tried this, and man, you need to check it out. It's the most delicious thing ever. Get some clothes on and get out here!"

I eye him warily. "How do you know where I live?"

He laughs. "Oh man, I'm sorry, I didn't even think about that. I asked Judy and she told me your address. I told her it was so I could keep my eye on you, but really it's because I was bored and I wanted to hang out."

I scoop up a pair of chinos from the floor and step into them. I need to play this carefully. Dyl is here, for some reason, and that reason can't be because he wants to spend time with me, *especially* if Judy is involved. I can't think for a moment he's here to be my friend. If Dyl is here, it means he's playing the game.

Only he's underestimated me. He thinks he can play me and I won't notice.

Oh man, I'm going to mop the floor with him.

I clamber out of the window. He's already sitting on the edge of the roof, his legs dangling. I sit down beside him, leaving a gap of about half a yard. Still, it feels too close for comfort.

He offers me the beer, and I take it. It's cold, and the paper label is soaking wet, so it slides underneath my fingers. How many calories does it have? Probably a lot. I turn the bottle around and check the label.

He narrows his eyes. "Seriously? Come on, man, one freaking beer isn't going to turn you into Homer Simpson. Live a little!"

I glance at him. His eyes are bright, filled with joy and enthusiasm, like he's actually excited about me trying beer. He's acting. He must be. And he's good. Maybe I do need alcohol. I take a big swig. It tastes how my new stepdad smells: bitter and nasty. Wincing, I force a swallow and smile. "Yeah, this is super delicious."

He turns to me. "You hate it, don't you?"

"I didn't say that."

"Come on, man. I thought we weren't going to lie to each other. We're the only people we can tell the truth to, remember? You don't have to lie to me about small stuff, or anything at all, really. If you don't like something, you can tell me. I promise I can handle it."

"Fine, I don't like it. It's bitter and tastes sort of like watered-down piss."

"There we go, the real Caden shows himself. Also, are you an expert on the taste of watered-down piss?"

"No, of course not. Why would you say that?"

He laughs. "I was being sarcastic, Caden. I guess they didn't teach you that at Nice school."

"I was being aggressive, Dyl. I thought for sure they would've taught you that."

I take another sip of the beer. This time, now that my taste buds know what they're in for, it's not that bad. It tastes sort of crisp, like an apple, and the dryness is pleasant.

"Actually," I say, "this is pretty nice. Thanks."

"You're welcome."

We sit there for a few moments in the silver moonlight, our legs dangling in thin air. Every time he moves, the leather of his jacket makes a rustling sound. The warm wind has buffeted his hair, and now a few long, straight strands have fallen out of place from behind his ears to the front of his face, in front of his impossibly green eyes. His surgeons did an exceptional job with him. It's hard to take my eyes off his face, and it's causing a weird tightness in my throat, making it difficult to breathe.

He drums his fingers on his thighs. "So you met Juliet today. How was it? Was it everything they told us it would be? Was it the best moment of your *whole* life?"

The sarcasm is strong in this one.

"Getting out of the LIC was the best moment of my life," I say.

He tilts his beer toward me. "Amen to that." I clink the neck of my bottle against his.

"But it was nice. She seems like a cool girl. What did you do today? You weren't at school."

"I was planning my big entrance. It's going to be epic. You could be standing naked right in front of her and she wouldn't even notice."

His eyes go wide.

"Uh-oh," I say with a grin. Maybe it's the alcohol, or the fact that he looks so mortified, but I find his mistake kind of funny. "You screwed up, Dyl. I never told you she asked me to model for her."

He nods. "Yep, that was a pretty major fuckup. I'm not cut out for this whole lying thing, in case that wasn't screamingly obvious." He takes a swig of his beer. "The beer is definitely not helping."

"It doesn't matter," I say. "Because she definitely would notice me if I was naked in front of her. I'm kind of spectacular."

"Well, look at you, you smug bastard. Fine, I'll tell you the truth, I'm pretty excited about meeting her. What do you think of her? Do you like her?"

"What do you mean?"

"Didn't you listen at all at the LIC? Who someone likes isn't always easy to explain. There are some factors for attraction, like symmetry of faces and muscle definition, but most of the time the reason someone likes someone is a big fat mystery. Just because you've been assigned to her doesn't mean you automatically like her. Love is more complicated than that."

I grip my bottle tight. "I get that, but you asked me if I liked her like it matters. But it doesn't. Our Chosen has to fall for us but we don't have to fall for them. How we feel will never matter."

"Well, that's a load of crap."

I blink, startled. No one talks like that, especially not a Love

Interest. I almost expect a Stalker to appear out of the darkness and rip Dyl apart. I shiver and hug my arms to my chest.

He glances at me. "Have you seriously not thought about whether you might like her? Don't you want to fall in love?"

"It's nice if we happen to fall for our Chosen, but it's not like it changes anything."

Our eyes meet, and he doesn't look away.

For the first time, I start to wonder if love is, in fact, necessary.

CHAPTER
NINE

IT'S A FREE PERIOD, SO I SHOULD BE STUDYING, but I'm not. I'm staring at the door. At any moment, Dyl will make his move to pull Juliet away from me. She's sitting to my left with her head down, staring at a textbook. Everyone around her is chatting, yet she's actually reading. My lips curl up into a small smile. *Any moment now.* The smile fades. My entire body is shaking and my knees are bouncing up and down. I grip my thighs, bunching up the silky material of my slacks.

What's he going to do?

Juliet starts writing something in her notebook. With her head turned to one side, her hair falls on the other side of her face in a straight brown line. She looks pretty, sure, but looking at her doesn't stir anything in me. It's an observation, cold and clinical. Why isn't *anything* stirring in me? What's wrong with me?

She looks up at me. "What's going on?" she whispers. "You look freaked."

I muster up a grin and glance down at my history textbook.

On it is a photo of some old white guy who is apparently super important. According to the book he fought for people's rights. Just not mine, apparently. I place my hand over the caption and try as hard as I can to recall his name.

I push the book away. "I'm realizing how much I'm screwed. I have no idea who half these people are."

"I know it seems scary, but it's not so bad if you break it apart and tackle each area on its own. I actually kind of love it. If you want, you could come over after school and I could bring you up to speed? I told Mom and Dad you showed up at school yesterday, and they'd love to have you over for dinner. That's only if you want to, obviously, and I know you're really smart because you're on a scholarship and I didn't mean to imply that—"

"Juliet," I say with a grin. "I'm really flattered, and I could use the help. But you don't have to if you don't want to. I'm sure you're swamped with your own stuff."

"I want to. Seriously, it would be my pleasure. And besides, I wasn't asking. Mom is expecting you to come over tonight. So, can you make it?"

"No, I can't. My calendar is absolutely full."

Her face falls. "Oh. Right. Cool. Maybe another time."

I laugh. "Juliet, I'm joking! I wouldn't care if Beyoncé herself wanted to hang with me. I wouldn't miss dinner with you and your family for anything."

"Now I know you're lying. Anyone would pick Beyoncé over a boring dinner with me and my family."

"I wouldn't."

She smiles.

You're lucky we made you hot, Caden. If she wasn't attracted to you she would've barfed.

Get lost, Kaylee!

Ugh, fine.

She's looking down at her feet. "So, dinner at my place tonight. At seven?"

"Absolutely."

"Good. Because Dad's already organized everything. He's making roast chicken. Wait, you're not vegetarian or vegan or anything like that now, are you? It's cool if you are, obviously. Maybe I should've talked to you before we planned everything."

"It sounds perfect."

"Great."

"Great."

At lunch, I sit between Juliet and the could-be model from yesterday, Natalie. I take a bite of my plain cheese sandwich. My parents hadn't wrapped the cheese properly, so now it's hard, cracked, and the color of mustard. But it was the only thing in the fridge, aside from a huge selection of beers. When I saw them I wondered what Dyl would think, and that made me smile. *Together, we can try them all.* Juliet turns to me. "You still look nervous, Caden. Is there a problem?"

I shake my head. "Nope. Everything's cool."

"You don't need to lie to me. We're old friends, remember?"

All I do is lie to you.

I imagine telling her the truth. Sitting her down and telling her what I am, who I work for, and the real reason I look the way I do.

How would she deal with the revelation that I'm not the sweet, kind guy she thinks I am? Her face, warped by rage and sadness, fills my mind. Nothing could be worse than Juliet looking at me like that.

Then I think of the Stalker, sleek and black and impossibly strong, holding a detached head in its hands.

My head.

My eyes are closed, but my mouth is open. My tongue is sticking out, pink and flaccid. The skin of my cheeks is pale.

A torrent of blood gushes from the jagged stump of my neck. It falls onto my limp, crumpled body. The blood has drenched my clothes, making my white shirt cling to my muscles, showing the definition of my pecs and my abs.

That's why I lie. It isn't my choice. It's what I have to do.

"You're my best friend," I say. "I'd never lie to you. I'm tired. That's all."

"Good. Because you'd tell me if something was bothering you, right? Even if it's the smallest thing, you could tell me, like when we were kids."

"Right."

THE DAY PASSES AND DYL STILL HASN'T SHOWN up. After the final bell, Juliet stops me before I get on the bus.

"So tonight, at seven. Ignore what I said about studying—it was an excuse to get you to come over. But this is me, being brave and saying that I want you to come over. After you've already said yes. Anyway, do you have a car?"

"I do."

"Well, do you want to drive or should I swing by your place and pick you up?"

"The thing is, I only got my license a few weeks ago and I'm not confident driving on my own yet. I know that sounds pathetic but . . . I'll catch the bus. It'll be fine."

"No way, Caden. I just had an idea. Why don't I meet you at your place and then we can walk together? It can't be far. Plus, this way, I can show you how much the town has changed while you've been gone! It'll be great, it's so pretty at night. So are you in?"

"Sounds perfect."

"Great, see you tonight."

I STARE AT MY CLOSET.

What should I wear?

Kaylee huffs. *Didn't you get my e-mail? You need to check those. Wear slacks, the black shoes that aren't school shoes, and the white long-sleeved shirt with the white buttons. You know, the nice one. Leave the top two buttons unbuttoned, show her a little bit of man-cleavage. Is your chest still hairless?*

I peek down my shirt. The skin there is smooth.

Sure is.

Good. Then maybe undo the third button accidentally or something.

You think she'll like me if she thinks I can't dress myself?

I think she'll think you're hot, and honey, that never hurts. But fair point.

I get dressed in the outfit she told me to wear. I undo only the top button.

Make your hair neater. Actually, I've changed my mind about the buttons, do them all up. You're about to meet her parents, so you need to look extra presentable. Still sexy, though, like a hot business-man. Also, no pressure, but you need to make sure they like you, otherwise this whole thing is over. Juliet isn't going to side with a Nice who her parents don't like.

I grab a comb and run it through my hair, parting it to one side, ensuring it's pressed down over my scalp.

Is there a script for this?

Nope, there are too many variables to predict the conversation. I e-mailed you a few conversation starters, but for the most part, you're alone. Anyway, are you ready to go?

I glance at my phone. It's 6:05.

We're meeting at 6:30, Kaylee.

So? You're a Nice, you need to show up early. Now get that fine body of yours out there and wait like a proper gentleman!

I ruffle the shirt to show off my chest. *My man-cleavage.* I snort as I step into the hallway. I stop, and then turn around and grab my iPod, figuring that if I'm going to wait, I may as well listen to music. Plus, the right songs will be like a last-minute pep rally for myself. I tuck the iPod into my pocket and leave my room.

In the living room, M and D are sitting in front of the TV watching the news. The sight of M makes me wonder about female Love Interests. We were kept separately, obviously, so I don't know much about them. My guess is that they're pretty similar to male Love Interests, only they were trained to attract men, not women.

D turns in his seat. "Where are you going?"

"Juliet invited me over."

"Use a condom." He scratches his chin, which is covered in prickly regrowth. A river of dried pasta sauce runs from the corner of his mouth to his jaw. "Or don't. Knock her up for all I care. That'll probably force her to pick you. And that's all you want, isn't it?"

M doesn't even look up from the TV.

I stop in front of the door and wave. "Bye."

They ignore me.

Outside, I tuck my hands into my pockets, protecting them from the slight chill in the air, and jog through the front yard. She's not here yet, obviously, so I sit down and lean my back against the streetlight outside my house. The metal is cold and the grass is damp. I pull out my iPod and put my still-slightly-tangled headphones in. I go straight to pop Nicki, because while I like her other stuff, I need something upbeat and energetic right now. The song I choose is "Va Va Voom," because the beat is so fast and it's so good and it always makes me feel unstoppable. It's a hit of sugar, a sip of soda. It's sweet, delicious musical candy.

The chorus hits and I lean my head back. So this is it, my first maybe-date with my Chosen. My whole life has been leading to this moment. All my training, everything I've gone through, it's all been to turn me into a guy who can sweep Juliet off her feet. I . . .

Hang on.

Across the road, about five feet away, are three sleek black vans. I've never seen them here before. I stand up and glare at them. Something shiny catches the streetlight, drawing my eye. I tilt my head and peer through the gap between the vans. *Oh no.*

Behind them is a motorbike.

This is it. This is Dyl's big entrance.

SHIT!

I take my headphones out, then jog across the road to the vans, imagining Dyl and Judy huddling inside one of them, waiting for the perfect moment to strike.

"I see you," I hiss through gritted teeth. "Get lost!"

The vans remain still. In the distance I can see Juliet walking down the street. She has headphones in and is looking down at the ground, so, thankfully, she hasn't noticed me yet.

I sprint back across the road to my position. But I don't take my eyes off the vans, and my clammy hands are balled into fists. *This is it!*

Juliet reaches me and waves. Her face is pale and her hair is slightly frizzy. She's dressed in a knee-length jacket, tight pants, and brown boots. A royal-blue scarf is wrapped around her neck, and a brown handbag is slung over her shoulder. I'm not a robot or anything; I can tell that she looks überpretty. Yet my heartbeat remains steady, and nothing even remotely primal pumps through my blood. *Why?*

She stops in front of me. A vanilla-like scent fills the air. "You're early."

I shrug. "What can I say, I was excited. And I was thinking that maybe I could drive. It's dark, and it could be unsafe."

"Dude, it's barely even dark and I walk by myself around here all the time. We'll be fine. Come on, it's not far, and it's

exercise! Plus, I frigging love the way the town looks at night."
She looks past me at my house. "Is that your place? It's . . ."

Did she just say *frigging*? My favorite fake swearword? *Be still, my beating heart.*

"It looks like shit," I say. "I know."

She shakes her head. "I was going to say it's quaint. I like it."

"So are you ready to go?"

Don't boss her around, Caden. She's in charge, remember.

Luckily, she nods. "I am. Let's go."

The streets are quiet and empty, so we walk in the middle of the road. Her shoes click against it. Our path is lined by parked cars. The moon and the stars are out in force, and the houses give off a golden glow. She was right, the town is beautiful at night. I *frigging* love it.

Every now and then I peer over my shoulder, checking on the parked cars.

"I'm really glad you've come back, Caden."

"What makes you say that?"

"Just this walk, I guess? It's not a big deal or anything, but before you came back I'd accepted the fact that you weren't a part of my life anymore. I didn't like it, but I'd accepted it. So this . . . um, it's hard to explain, but it feels like a bonus? Like the movie of our relationship ended, and now I'm in this weird little future-bubble that includes you. And I like it. I'm so happy that I get to have small moments with you again."

"I like being back too. I finally feel real again."

"What do you mean?"

"I always wanted to come back. Always. Everything that

happened between saying goodbye to you and now doesn't feel like it really happened. Like the boy who did those things wasn't me."

"Do you ever think about the last time we saw each other? It's sort of immortalized in my things-I-think-about-before-bed bank."

I nod. "I think about it all the time."

You're digging yourself into a hole.

She places her hand in her pocket, then pulls it out and scratches her arm. "What do you remember about it? Like, what's the image you think of when you think of it?"

"Uh . . ."

Up ahead, a black van screeches around the corner and starts speeding toward us. Juliet grabs my wrist and pulls me forward. Together, we leap from the road onto the grass.

"What the hell?" Her face is scrunched up. "What a dick!"

The van reaches us and slams on the brakes. Torrents of gray smoke billow from under the van and the smell of burning rubber tickles my nose. The door swings open, and three rough-looking guys clamber out. Their faces are narrowed in identical sneers, and their hands are tight fists.

One of the guys steps toward us. He's bald, and his compact body is dressed in a leather jacket. He cracks his knuckles. "Well, hello. That's a lovely bag you have there, miss. It's worth a lot, am I right?"

Juliet grips her bag tighter. I step in front of her and shield her with one arm.

The man laughs. "Oh, and *you're* going to stop me?"

This is Dyl's big entrance, Caden! Derail it!

He steps forward and takes a wild grab at Juliet. She jumps out of the way. If I do nothing, Dyl wins. I clench my hands into fists. This is the one time breaking character is a viable option, because I need to make sure I don't play along with Dyl's plan. He'll expect me to play Nice, and I can't do what he expects me to do. Then again, Juliet is in danger, and a Nice would turn to violence to protect her. It's the only time a Nice ever would. From the corner of my eye I see a single beam of light, a motorbike, coming toward us. Dyl, on his way to "save" us.

Screw that noise.

I step forward and punch the guy right in the face.

His nose cracks as a bolt of pain shoots from my knuckles to my wrist. He staggers backward, pinching his nose, which is pumping blood. Pure pain sings under my skin. I wave my hand through the air, biting my lip to stop the scream that's turning my chest to meaty shreds.

The guy I punched is glaring at me. "Kill him," he barks.

Shit!

The two others leap toward me. I bring my hands up to protect my head. Hits come from everywhere and I fall, hard, to the ground. A steel-toed boot digs into my stomach, sinking in so deep his toe touches my spine. I roll onto my back. A boot stomps down on my chest. I grab his foot and try to trip him, to bring him to my level so I can punch him somewhere soft, but another kick hits my ribs and my arms go slack. *That's it, my ribs are broken.* I curl into a ball. Juliet flings herself at one of them, getting in a strong punch. She's clinging to his back, hitting him in the face, scratching at his cheeks. He throws her away with one hand. She tumbles and falls.

Right into Dyl's chest.

Dyl shoves her away and pushes up his sleeves. He punches the guy kicking me, and it's a perfect punch. It hits the guy in the jaw and then his fist carries on downward. The goon spins and falls. The other guy charges, but Dyl recovers and sends a quick jab into his throat. The man coughs and splutters, then stumbles backward and falls to the ground.

Dyl straightens up, his chest heaving. In and out, in and out. He raises his hand, sweeping a few strands of dark hair back into place. Someone must've pulled on his collar in the chaos of the attack, because now a jagged line is cut into his shirt, revealing his collarbone and a small, but definitely noteworthy, stretch of skin. He doesn't seem to have noticed it, but I can't look away. Was it on purpose? Did Judy do it to show off his body? I stare at the exposed part of his chest and my mouth goes dry.

Dyl turns and steps over me to reach Juliet, who is sitting on the grass. He looks like a freaking badass superhero. And he saved me. I was hurting and he stopped it. All I want to do is thank him, but Juliet is right there, so I can only watch.

He offers Juliet his hand.

And she takes it.

"Thank you," she says. "Who are you?"

"Doesn't matter. Are you all right?"

She bobs her head up and down.

"Good. It was stupid of you to be out here alone. Don't do it again."

He walks away, ignoring her flabbergasted expression, and grabs his bike, lifting it up from where he ditched it. He swings his leg over it and sits down.

"Wait," she says. "Don't talk to me like that. And I wasn't alone, obviously. Caden is right there! So are you blind as well as rude?"

Dyl looks down at me and sneers. "Close enough. Do you go to Mapleton?"

Close enough? What the . . . ? I breathe in through my nostrils. It's not him, not really. This is the Bad version of Dyl. He doesn't mean what he says. He's acting. My heartbeat slows.

"I do." There's a definite edge to her voice.

Good, I think. He didn't get away with insulting me. I'm glad, because if she hadn't said anything I might've, and that would be way out of character.

"Great," he says, his voice rich and deep. "I start there tomorrow. Maybe you could buy me lunch or something. You owe me for saving you."

"I don't owe you anything."

"Keep telling yourself that, sweetheart." He spins his shiny black helmet in his hands.

Juliet scowls as Dyl puts the helmet on. He revs the throttle and then, without another word, rides off into the night. Juliet stands in his exhaust fumes, her hair a mess, her chest heaving.

I push myself up off the road and make my way over to her, pinching my nose to stop the bleeding.

"Oh my gosh, Caden." She rushes toward me and places her hand on my face. "Are you okay? Wait, I'll call an ambulance."

"There's no need, Juliet, I'm totally fine."

I need to get control of this, because spending tonight in the hospital is the furthest thing from romantic. Plus, I need to show her that I'm dependable and safe. I need to show her that if she makes plans I'll be there for them.

"It doesn't hurt that bad. And, honestly, hospitals freak me out. I'll heal better away from there, trust me."

"You sure?"

"Absolutely. I'll call one for them, though, just to make sure they're okay."

They got what they deserved, but I figure a Nice would care about them no matter what. The guy I punched lets out a moan that almost makes me feel bad for him. The key word being *almost*: I'm pretty sure he's the reason my left kidney is currently stabbing my other organs. I pretend to dial 911, then tell the "operator" what happened and our location. If I thought they actually needed help, I'd call the real line, but my guess is that they're just pretending to be injured. Even if I called the real number they'd clear out of here before the ambulance arrived.

Once the "call" is over, I make my way over to Juliet. "The ambulance is on the way. We don't have to hang around, though."

"Really? Won't they have questions?"

"They said it's fine, they'll call me if they need more info. We can leave."

That's a lie, but luckily she buys it, and we head toward her place.

Once we reach her house, Juliet opens the door. A woman, presumably her mother, is in the foyer. She's dressed in a dark-green wool turtleneck.

Her name is Daphne, call her that. She'll be surprised you remember. Also, shake her hand. She likes professional greetings.

"Daphne," I say as I offer my hand. "It's a pleasure to see you again."

She shakes my hand, then turns to Juliet, her eyes narrowing. *Did I do something wrong?*

"Don't stress," says Juliet. "We're fine."

Daphne spins and glares at me.

I raise my hands in surrender. "I'm fine. Honest."

"You don't look fine, Caden! You're going to bleed all over my carpet! Juliet, I need answers. Right now. What happened to you?"

"Fine, Mom, on the way over some guys tried to take my bag. Caden and a bystander stopped them. It's not a big deal, even Caden thinks so."

"It most certainly is a big deal!" She pulls a phone from her pocket. "I need to call the police. Do you remember what they looked like?"

"Mom, please listen to me, they ended up a lot worse than we did. If we call the police Caden could get in trouble. And all he was doing was protecting me, so I don't want that. Plus, if Dad finds out about this he'll never let me go out. Like, ever. So can we please drop this? Trust me, it's what I want, and it's what Caden wants as well."

Daphne's features soften. "Are you sure, Juliet?"

"I am."

"Then it's settled." She places her hands on her hips and glares at me. "Jesus, Caden, you haven't changed at all. Come with me, I'll get you cleaned up for dinner. Richard!" she hollers. "Bring a shirt down from your closet."

What does she mean I haven't changed at all? Was the first Caden a troublemaker? Shouldn't Kaylee have told me?

Richard pops his head out from the kitchen. He has Juliet's round face, kind eyes, and brown hair that's buzzed super short. "What?"

"You heard me! Now go. Caden, follow me. Juliet, set the table."

I follow her down a long hallway. We walk to a small white-tiled bathroom. A shiver runs down my spine at the sight of the bathroom, so clean, so similar to the LIC. I pause at the door-way, my toes wiggling into the comforting softness of the hall carpet, the air in my lungs feeling cold and clammy. I recall my mirrored cell, the classes that felt like torture, and the constant feeling of dread that accompanied every single day at that accursed place.

Daphne is standing in front of a gold-framed mirror, riffling through a first aid kit. She looks up and narrows her eyes. She does it the exact same way Juliet does: an expression that is clearly supposed to look stern, but actually looks cute. "What are you doing? Get in here."

I shrug my shoulders. I'm free now, and I'm never going back there, so there's no need to panic.

I walk into the bathroom and stop in front of her. She steps closer and peers at the cut on my temple.

"It's just a scratch. He was probably wearing a ring. Does your head hurt?"

Obviously.

"It's not that bad," I say.

She turns on the tap. "That's a good sign. Now wash the blood off and then put this"—she hands me a Band-Aid—"on the wound. You'll be fine. And be quick about it! I'm starving." Richard passes her a shirt and then she passes it to me. I start to grab it.

Her grip on the shirt tightens. "Just so you know, Juliet's life has been so peaceful since you left. You show up and one day later this happens. I'm starting to think you're a drama magnet, Caden."

She releases the shirt and rushes out of the bathroom, closing the door behind her. I take my shirt off and take a second to check my body for injuries. There's a fist-sized bruise on my lower back, but other than that I'm fine. I probably should tell someone about the bruise, but that could mean Juliet sending me home and I can't risk that.

Carefully, I put on the new shirt, which is a navy dress shirt with black buttons. It feels soft and silky against my skin. I splash hot water onto my face and rub until my cheeks turn red.

My face still looks alien, too perfect to be me. Even though I'm tired and stressed, my skin looks tan and clean. The skin under my eyes matches the rest perfectly: there's no darkness. Even with the injuries, including a small cut that slashes through my right eyebrow, I look good.

I splash one last handful of water onto my stupid perfect face and walk out of the bathroom.

In the dining room, Juliet and her mom are seated, chatting. I walk in and the conversation nose-dives. Juliet dips her head slightly and smiles, but one hand reaches out and fiddles with her fork. Her mother raises one hand and places her thumb under her chin, inspecting me like I'm a piece of art. Which I guess I am. All I'm missing is the doctor's signature on my ass.

Richard enters with a tray containing a golden roasted chicken, crispy potatoes, and carrots dripping with oil. The smell of it makes my mouth water.

"Caden," he says as he places the tray in the middle of the table. After pulling off his oven mitts, he walks over to me. "Look at you!" He squeezes my shoulder. "I hardly recognize you! You've lost a lot of weight. Now sit, and let's see if we can put some of those pounds back on."

"Sounds like a plan!"

I take a seat opposite Juliet.

"So what happened to you?" he asks as he slices into the chicken. "Why were you bleeding onto my carpet?"

"Just some thugs."

"*Just some thugs*?"

"Yep."

Juliet leans forward. "It wasn't a big deal, Dad."

"It *is* a big deal! You think I'm going to let you go out at night alone now that I know . . . thugs are roaming the streets!"

Juliet rolls her eyes. "Dad, we have company. Can you not be overprotective for two seconds? And look at this." She shows him her fist. The knuckles have been scraped raw. "I punched one of the guys. I'm not defenseless."

He puts his knife and fork down and turns to me. "No offense, Caden, but this is a conversation I need to have with my daughter right now. Juliet, if the streets aren't safe, you aren't going to go out alone. It's that simple."

"Richard," says Daphne. "It's fine. Trust me."

Juliet thumps her fist down on the table. "Why am *I* being punished when they attacked me?"

"You aren't being punished, you're being kept safe."

Juliet scrunches up the napkin she was holding. "Dad, drop it. Let's have dinner."

"Fine."

"Fine."

Daphne turns to me. "See," she says. She's smiling fondly. "Even though you've been gone for so long, some things haven't changed. These two are still fighting the same old fights. It's kind of comforting, isn't it?"

I chuckle. "Yeah, it is."

Juliet lets out a little burst of laughter, and the mood of the entire room lifts. Her dad passes me a helping of chicken, two potatoes, and half a carrot. I pour a splattering of gravy out of a jug with a cow on it over everything and serve myself a huge scoop of cauliflower casserole. Then, to finish everything off, I grab a roll and bite into it. It's soft and fluffy and the best thing I've ever tasted. Obviously, bread wasn't allowed at the LIC. We practically lived on steamed chicken breasts and green veggies.

Whoa, Caden, watch those carbs.

Do you expect me to not eat? That'll look weird.

Fine. Just be careful with your portions.

Juliet's plate matches mine, and she's eating with such ferocity I feel it's okay to ignore Kaylee and do the same. I cut off a big slice of chicken and stuff it into my mouth. It's so freaking delicious I'd smile if my mouth weren't so full.

"My God, look at the two of them," says her dad. "It's like they're never fed. I promise we do feed her, Caden."

Juliet and I glance at each other, grin, and dive right back in.

After dinner, I'm leaning back on the chair with my hands on my stomach. Kaylee is yammering on about something, but I'm so full and dreamily content that I don't listen.

Juliet's hands are resting on her extended stomach. She actually does look slightly pregnant.

"Dad, I have something to tell you." She snorts.

I extend my own stomach. "Well, Juliet, I have something to tell *you.*"

We burst out laughing. Both her parents roll their eyes in exactly the same way.

"I'll go get dessert," says Daphne. "Although let it be said that I don't think giving either of you sugar is a good idea if you find *that* joke hilarious." But she's smiling a soft smile, so I know she doesn't mean it.

Juliet keeps looking at me, and every time I catch her looking, she turns her head away and pretends she wasn't watching.

Sorry, Dyl.

Your play didn't work. You hit me.

But you're the one on the ground.

CHAPTER
TEN

AFTER DINNER, JULIET INVITES ME FOR A TOUR around her house. Obviously I accept, so I'm following her as we walk on the sandstone edge of her pool. There was no script, so I've had to improvise. Kaylee's in my ear in case I get stumped by a particularly tough question, but for the most part, I'm on my own. I decide I should pretend to be an excited guy who is stunned by her affluence. So far, I think I've pulled it off.

I dip my hand into the water.

Invite her for a swim. It would be great for her to see your body.

It's too soon, Kaylee. Trust me.

Juliet's house is a freaking mansion. Like, it's way too big for the three people who live here. There's a gym almost as large as the private ones at the LIC, a tennis court, a guesthouse bigger than my house, and even a sauna. Every time I see something new I gawk at it and Juliet blushes.

She stops walking and faces me. "I know it's a lot. But it's not like it's inherited money. Both Mom and Dad have worked hard to have all this."

She's explained that four times now. Her mom is a famous cookbook author, and her dad is a lawyer. Growing up, she spent a lot of time with her grandparents. But now that she can look after herself, her relationship with her parents has improved. Well, that's the story she tells, but there's something in the way she delivers it that makes me doubt her.

"Do you get along with your parents?" I ask.

"I guess. They pretty much let me do whatever I want. Dad's controlling sometimes, but what father isn't, right?"

"Right."

She gasps. "Oh, Caden, I'm so sorry to talk about dads after what happened to you. That's the height of selfishness, complaining about a controlling father to someone who lost his. I'm so sorry."

Oh crap. I totally forgot that she thinks my dad is dead! I blink rapidly to fill my eyes with tears. "It's okay, Juliet, it happened a long time ago. I miss him, and I always will, but you don't need to treat the subject with kid gloves. I had a dad I loved, and then he died. It sucks, but it happened."

She frowns. "Is your stepdad nice?"

I shake my head. "He's horrible. He took most of Dad's money and blew it on bad investments, so now we have pretty much nothing. It's all right, though; I don't let it get me down."

"It's a miracle you turned out to be as kind as you are, Caden. I'm just realizing this was a bad idea; it's like I'm boasting about having all this stuff when it really doesn't matter. You must think I'm the most entitled snob ever."

"Juliet, I think you're amazing, and all this stuff is mind-bogglingly cool. This was fun. Truly."

She eyes me warily. Then she spins and starts walking away, her feet balancing on the very edge of the stone. The moonlight reflects in the aquamarine water, casting a weird blue light over everything.

Stare at her until she notices.

Why? That's so creepy.

She'll like it, trust me.

I look up and stare at Juliet. It takes her a few seconds, then her eyes meet mine and she blushes.

"Why are you looking at me like that?"

I shrug my shoulders. "I can't help it."

"I—I," she stammers. "I have no idea how to respond to that, so I'm going to ignore it. Anyway, Caden, I can't believe I almost forgot to show you my absolute favorite thing. Do you want to see my lab?"

"Your *what*?"

"My lab . . . it's short for *laboratory*."

"I know, it's just, um, I didn't expect you to have one. That's so cool! Of course I want to see it."

We walk away from the pool onto a long stretch of grass. At the other side is a gray shed. She unbolts the door and opens it, then flicks on the light, revealing a huge cluttered workspace. There are three long metal benches evenly spaced above a smooth concrete floor. Each one of them is overflowing with metal contraptions, circuit boards, and pieces of smashed-up computers. It truly does look like the workspace of a mad scientist.

"I spend most of my time here," she says. "If I ever need to get away from everything and create, this is where I come. I love making stuff, if you can't tell. What do you think?"

Beside her is a rack of test tubes. Each one is filled with glowing blue liquid. I'm genuinely impressed. "This is the coolest place I've ever seen!" I say. "It's like a museum. Can I touch stuff?"

"If you're gentle, sure."

I pick up a weird, shiny glovelike thing. It's shaped like a hand, with the fingers connecting to a black Velcro strap that would fit around my wrist. Each of the fingers is a thin wire. At the very end of each wire is a silver pad.

"What's this?"

She rushes toward me and plucks it out of my arms like it could sting. Gently, she places it back down on the bench.

"That's one of the very few things in this whole room that could actually kill you. I call them Bolt Gloves."

The name reminds me of static gel, an ointment they have at the LIC. A Love Interest puts it on his hands or torso before coming into contact with his Chosen, so that when they touch, the Chosen gets a faint electric shock. Thankfully, Kaylee decided I don't need to use it. Wearing it is incredibly painful, as it shocks the Love Interest constantly before it's washed off. I nearly cried the first time I had to put it on my chest.

"Now you officially have my attention," I say.

"I'm trying to come up with a more effective device for personal defense. The idea is that you wear the glove, and to activate it all you have to do is press down on whoever is attacking you. Then, *zap!* It sends electricity through them, eliminating the threat. They work for the most part, but the amount of electricity they produce would still be fatal to all but the sturdiest people. So they don't really work at all, because I don't want to create anything that kills people. I'm aiming instead for seriously maimed. Like, imagine if I'd been wearing it tonight? I could've stopped the fight before it started."

I point to the test tubes filled with glowing blue liquid.

"What's that?"

"Oh, that's not finished yet, but it's supposed to be an alternative to sunscreen. My idea is that you apply this gel once a month and then you have complete protection from UV. Goodbye, sunburn. It doesn't work yet, but I'm sure I'll figure it out eventually."

"That's incredible, Juliet. This whole place is. When did you become such a genius?"

"I guess we both changed while we were apart. I got smart and you got hot."

Her cheeks go red, then she points to the door. "But that's enough for now, huh?"

But I'm barely listening.

Because my Chosen called me hot.

It's still early, says Kaylee's voice in my mind. *But that sounded a lot like checkmate.*

I'M IN BED, WATCHING THE CLOCK SLOWLY TICK by. It's midnight.

After I got home, I cleaned my room, mainly because I was still processing my time with Juliet and it felt good to be doing something with my hands. Also, I was trying to figure out what to say to Dyl if he asked about it. Do I tell him she called me hot? At the moment I'm leaning toward not telling him, because even though we're competing I don't want to hurt him unnecessarily. I may not be Nice, but that doesn't make me mean.

Now the floor is clear of clothes, my desk is dish-free, and everything has been wiped down. The room smells like the lemony cleaning chemicals I used, fresh and sharp. I've even left two bottles of beer that I swiped from the fridge on my desk. In case, well, Dyl decides to show up.

A knock sounds on my window. *Yes!* I slide out of bed, pull on a shirt and a pair of sweatpants, then walk over and open it. Dyl is there, in the darkness, grinning at me. He looks so different now that he isn't *Dylan*, the heroic badass. He's smiling and his eyes are wide and friendly, not narrowed like they were when I last saw him. I like this version of him so much more. He's wearing a black shirt and dark jeans.

"You're wearing black," I say. "*What* a surprise."

"Are you all right?" asks Dyl. He's peering at my face. What's that look in his eyes? Is it sympathy? I raise my hand and touch the bruise on my right cheek. Aside from that, there's the cut on my eyebrow, but the pain feels like a headache; annoying, but not crippling. I'd actually forgotten about it.

"I'm fine," I say as I step outside, passing him a beer as I make my way out. "It's totally fine."

"Good. I was worried. I told them not to attack you, but apparently you attacked them? What's with that? They were supposed to try to mug Juliet, but when I got there it was a full-on brawl. I had to improvise."

I bow my head slightly, nodding. "I figured out it was your big entrance. It made sense to try to derail it. Sorry."

He laughs. "Don't be sorry, I'm not mad at you. I just can't believe you punched him in the face." He grabs my hand and lifts it up. Just grabs it, like it's no big deal, like it's okay. He peers at scrape wounds on my knuckles. "That's pretty badass, Caden." I realize he's literally holding my hand. I flinch away and rest my hand on my jittery thigh.

He looks at his own knuckles, which are bloodless. "I didn't actually hit them. It was all rehearsed. And you wouldn't believe how much Judy shouted at the guy who hit you. He was supposed to make you look weak compared to me, but he ended up wounding you, and everyone knows . . ."

"Wounded guys are hot," I say, finishing his sentence. This lesson was drilled into us at the LIC, so it makes sense that Judy would be mad. In his anger, Dyl gave me an advantage and turned his big entrance into a positive for me. If I were his coach, I'd be livid.

"His name is Tom," he continues. "He's actually a pretty great guy. He seemed upset that he had to hit you. I'm sorry too, Caden. I really am."

"What? Why? This is a fight, remember. A contest."

"It is. But I don't want to win this by hurting you. I just don't."

"You say that now, but when it comes down to it we'll be scratching each other's eyes out. It's human nature."

"Human nature sucks sometimes."

He didn't disagree.

He lies down. His black shirt pulls up a little, showing a sliver of his stomach. He has abs. I shouldn't be surprised—all Love Interests have them—yet I find I'm kind of shocked by his body. What would Juliet think if she saw us side by side with our shirts off? Whose body would she prefer? I have a feeling it'd be his. *I prefer his.*

He clears his throat. "Man, you need to lie down and see the sky from this angle. It's so cool."

I lie down beside him. Our faces are separated by only three tiles, but we aren't looking at each other. We're looking up at the sky. It's navy, pinpricked by tiny dots of silver light.

"It's beautiful," he says. "Did you ever dream of doing just this while you were at the LIC?" I shake my head, and he continues. "I did. All I wanted was to spend hours looking up at the stars. I seriously thought about it almost every night.

"We could do that now—if you want to, obviously, it's not a big thing. But we literally could look at it for hours. We don't have to, though, if you have other things to do or something."

He tilts his head slightly and looks at me. His stare is a little too intense, so I look down and focus on his neck and his perfect stubble. After the bristle of his chin, there's a long stretch of smooth skin that arcs down until it reaches the collar of his shirt.

I steel myself, then look up and meet his stare. "I'm in if you are."

Because it's the truth.

I've never been more *in* in my life.

CHAPTER
ELEVEN

"HERE'S OUR HERO!"

Natalie grins as I approach the table. She's sitting alone, but she's holding her head high and her posture is perfect, so she looks perfectly comfortable in her solitude. I don't have this ability. Whenever I sat alone at the LIC, I was sure that everyone was judging me. The fact that she can sit by herself and not give a crap what anyone thinks makes me respect the living daylights out of her.

I sit down beside her. On the table, a ham sandwich rests on a sheet of plastic wrap beside a metallic pink water bottle. Natalie is Juliet's best friend, and as Kaylee has repeatedly told me, it's vitally important that she give me the seal of approval. Luckily, Juliet chose well, as Natalie is kind and good-natured. Spending time with her is fun, so I'd do it even if my life didn't depend on it.

"Getting beaten up is heroic now?" I say. "Wait, I'll get Spider-Man on the phone; he probably needs to know this."

She chuckles. The more I see of Natalie, the more I notice how beautiful she is. Her face is—I can't believe I'm saying this—heart-shaped, and her skin is flawless. What's most attractive about her, though, is her constant smile, and her funny/kind/warm personality, which is seriously top tier.

"So where's Juliet?" asks Natalie. "This is the first time I've seen you apart in, like, forever."

"Bathroom."

She smiles knowingly, and scoops a piece of sliced carrot into a low-calorie avocado dip. "Seriously, funny guy, what's the deal with you and her?" She bites down, and the carrot crunches loudly.

"What do you mean? We're friends."

She rolls her eyes. "Please, you can tell me the truth. You two are *so* obvious. I mean, you guys got mugged yesterday, and yet today both of you are all smiles. It's weird."

"Did she say anything about me?"

"Nope. But Juliet isn't the type to talk about what she feels. Here she comes now."

I turn my head and see Juliet walking across the courtyard. She raises one hand and waves, then points to the water fountain. She walks to it and joins the small line that's formed in front of it.

Natalie gives me her best death stare. "I don't need to tell you that if you hurt her I'll end you, do I? I'm a black belt, just so you know. I could crush your neck with one punch if I wanted to."

"That's oddly specific."

"Because it's specifically what I'll do to you if you hurt her. I'll crush your neck."

A guy stops in front of our table. He's got black hair that

tumbles over his forehead in pressed-down curls. His face is long, making his eyes look slightly dopey. "Natalie? Who's this?"

He sits down beside Natalie and instantly places his hand on her thigh. He's got a huge, bulky body, easily double the size of hers. Even sitting, I have to tilt my head up a bit to meet his brown eyes.

"Trevor," says Natalie, "this is Caden. Caden, this is Trevor. He's my boyfriend."

She slides across on the seat to get closer to him, her slim body nestling against his gigantic torso. His hand moves up her thigh. Do they even know I'm here? They're a note of bad music away from a porno. "I was saying I think Caden and Juliet are a thing."

"About time," says Trevor. "I thought Jules was going to end up an old spinster at the rate she was going."

Natalie slaps his arm. "Trev, you're embarrassing him. And besides, Caden was telling me that they're just friends. And I *totally* believe him."

Juliet reaches the table and sits down beside me. I mouth the word "hi," and she smiles and tucks a strand of hair behind her ear. She does that a lot. I wonder what she's thinking about when she does it.

"What're you talking about?" she asks.

"Spinsters," I say.

"That's oddly specific."

Natalie smirks. She tilts her head a fraction to look past me, and the smirk fades. Juliet is also looking in the same direction. Her eyebrows narrow.

I spin around and get a good look.

It's Dyl.

He's wearing the school uniform, but it's at least one size too big, as the white shirt hangs off his lanky frame and the gray slacks rest low on his hips. The top button is undone, and his hair is a dark, spiky mess. His cheeks are still covered in rough stubble, even though the school dress code prohibits facial hair. Actually, he probably avoided shaving *because* it's against the dress code. Either way, it suits him.

He strides across the courtyard like he owns the place, with his head up high and his arms level with his shoulders. He finds an empty seat in the shade of a tree and sits down, then he reaches into his backpack and pulls out a small book with a pale-blue cover. He opens it to a bookmarked page and starts reading.

Trevor glares at him. "Is that poetry? Who the fuck reads poetry?"

I stifle a laugh. Then I notice Juliet. She's leaning slightly forward, her chin resting on her fist. Her eyelids are drooping slightly. "Lots of people do. Hundreds of poetry books are published every year. *Someone* must read them."

"I'm telling you," says Trevor. "There are only three types of people who read poetry for fun. First, English teachers or majors. Second, people who want to be poets themselves. Third, people who want to seem impressive. Seeing as that guy is obviously not in category one or two, I declare him three. Caden knows what I'm talking about."

Do I ever.

Natalie nudges him again. "Just because you're shallower than a Michael Bay movie . . ."

"Have any of you heard what happened to him?" asks Juliet.

"Everyone in the bathroom was talking about it. If that happened to me, I'd probably read poetry too."

Dyl turns a page of his book.

I turn back to Juliet. "What happened to him?"

"It's awful, Caden. His house burned down, and his parents were, well, they didn't make it out. So his rich aunt adopted him, which is why he moved here. He lives in a big mansion on the coast, the one fenced off from everything. I think it's really brave of him to be at school so soon after it happened. So maybe we should be nice to him."

So *that's* his backstory. Classic, painful, and effective at generating massive amounts of sympathy. No one would get through that without being tortured, and even though I know it's all a lie, I can't look at Dyl the same way. He's acting like he's hurt, and him hurting hurts me. *Good job, Judy.*

"Let's stop talking about it," says Natalie. "It's making me feel bad. And I didn't get to finish boasting to Caden about my stunning boyfriend." She rubs Trevor's chest. "He's going to the Olympics. Everyone in the know says so. It's been expected of him ever since he was a kid."

He raises his hand. It's almost the size of a dinner plate. "I've got big hands. And even bigger feet."

My eyes flit to the side to get a glimpse of Juliet. She's still staring at Dyl. My heart starts to thunder.

Get the attention away from him!

"The Olympics?" I say, a little too loudly. "That's interesting."

Natalie grins and grabs Trevor's hand. "Yeah, Trevor's a swimmer, and he's one of the best in the country. Freestyle's his specialty, which means he's the fastest of the fast. He's totally going to the Olympics. Actually, the school's swimming carnival is coming up. It doesn't count for anything, that's *so* beneath him, but he's still going to swim."

"Aw, babe," he says, and he plants a firm kiss on her cheek. "I love it when you get all proud. But yeah, I mean, the carnival isn't much, seeing as I've already qualified for nationals. Oh, and hey, just so you know, nationals are in DC this year, so you're totally welcome to come and watch if you'd like. I'd like to get a little cheer squad going. Anyway, enough about me. Do you swim, Caden?"

"I prefer running. There's less chance of drowning. Also, fewer old guys in Speedos."

He chortles. "That's very true. But you should get used to it, because like Nat said, the carnival is coming up. You can watch if you like—it's all these girls do—but it's more fun to be in it."

Thank you, Trevor. A swimming carnival means one thing: an excuse to take my shirt off in front of Juliet.

Caden! This is—

So perfect, right?

Yep, it's amazing. Make sure you say yes, but don't seem over-eager or anything.

"Yeah, um, that sounds great. It's worth a shot, right?"

"Exactly! I like your attitude, man!"

Juliet moves for the first time since Dyl appeared. She tugs at the front of her shirt. "I wonder what he's reading. He looks really into it."

I stare at him. His head is bowed, and the book is open on his lap. His face is still, almost serene. I imagine a bomb going off behind him and him not even flinching. He turns a page. What's he reading? What combination of words could be so damn entertaining? I want to walk over to him and straight-up ask. I imagine him looking up from his book and smiling at me.

Maybe I'll see him tonight. Maybe I can ask him then.

That makes me smile.

CHAPTER
TWELVE

I CAN'T SLEEP. I'M ON MY BED WITH MY BLANKET pulled up over my body, leaving my head and my bare shoulders exposed. My ceiling is white, and a massive crack runs from one end to the other. To pass the time, my eyes follow the seam as it twists and spirals across the plaster. Dad's loud, honking snores vibrate through the entire house.

The noise is annoying, but that's not what's keeping me up. There are two possible explanations for my current insomnia: the first is that I'm in the middle of a fight for my life and that's stressing me out. It makes sense. I can't help but think that there must be more I can do to make Juliet like me. Every interaction with her is burned into my memory, each moment taken apart and scrutinized. Was I Nice enough? Did I charm her? Did she look at me and see a man she could spend the rest of her life with? Also, does she even want to meet her life partner right now? Or ever?

The other explanation is a little more confusing: Dyl. Even though I'm stressed about the contest, every now and then I think about him, or, more specifically, the prospect of him visiting me tonight, and I grin. I can't help it. The nights he visited were two of the best nights of my life. Talking to him, I don't feel so conflicted. He knows what I am, and I know what he is. We both know we're on guard, and we both know we're lying about things, so I don't feel like I'm taking advantage of him. With me, he knows what he's getting, yet he keeps coming back for more.

I hear a grunt, and I spin around and close my eyes. The roof groans and I hear a body slide up onto the tiles.

Footsteps thud across the shingles.

The window rattles.

I close my eyes tighter and curl into a small ball. But a grin has cracked my face. I know he can only see the back of my head, so smiling doesn't matter. He'll think I'm still asleep. He's outside right now, waiting for me. I know what he'll look like, and that's making a weird giddy feeling swirl in my stomach.

The knock sounds again, louder this time.

I sit up and my eyes catch his for a second. His mouth is hanging open, a sign he's still breathless from the climb up. I scratch the side of my head as I climb out of bed. This time I don't bother getting dressed before I walk over to the window.

"Hey," I say as I unlatch it. "You're getting predictable." I pull on my pants. Wait, he's not looking at me. His eyes are on the window frame, and he's digging his fingers into the wood, chipping off the brown varnish. Is it because I'm shirtless? Why doesn't he want to look at me without my shirt on? I zip up my fly. "That's not very Bad of you." I pull a navy sweater over my head. Before he came over, I tried on a bunch of different sweaters, trying to find the right one. This one fits perfectly, pressing kind of tight against my body, showing a hint of my pecs and biceps.

He rolls his eyes. I climb out through the window and sit on my spot on the edge of the roof.

He sits down beside me. His long, thin hands are clasped together. "I'm sick of being Bad. It's bullshit, man. This whole thing. Did you see me today, at school?"

"Of course I did. Everyone noticed. More important, Juliet definitely did. I was meaning to ask you, what were you reading? You seemed really into it."

His face falls. "Seriously, you fell for it too? It was stupid and boring and I hated it. It was all acting, and I feel so fake. Even when I was reading that boring-ass book like it was book eight of Harry Potter, all I could think about was how I couldn't wait to come here tonight. It's the one time I feel like myself. Do you know what Judy wants me to do?" I shake my head. "She wants me to start being mean to Juliet."

"What?"

"Yep, tomorrow in gym class I need to be aggressive toward her. You know she's taking self-defense as an elective, right? Well, tomorrow I'm supposed to hurt her a little bit."

He's telling me too much. A part of me wants to tell him to shut up, to stop handing me his life. I know I can't do that. He's exposed his soft underbelly, so I have to get in as many hits as I can. It's who I'm supposed to be.

"That's horrible!" I say. "And, quite frankly, stupid. Why does Judy think that will make Juliet like you?"

"Apparently it'll make me seem like a tortured soul who is lashing out, because I can't handle all the epic, sexy pain within me. And apparently *that* will make Juliet think she can fix me, to help me deal, and that will make her fall for me. I dunno, a lot of it doesn't make sense to me, but wouldn't it take a lot more than a crush to get over the death of my parents?"

"Whatever, Batman."

He tilts his head back and laughs. "At least I'm not going to give her diabetes. And fair warning, as part of my tortured-soul thing I have to start being mean to you. Apparently that will make me seem strong and make you seem weak. Because strong nowadays means being a total dick. I just want you to know that I don't mean what I say to you out there, it's just acting. I think you're an awesome guy. I probably didn't write it anyway; Judy scripts pretty much all my conversations because she's scared I'm going to screw it up."

"What?"

"She thinks I'm too soft to be a good Bad and that you're taking the lead because of it. She says I have to make you look pathetic, otherwise I'll lose and, well, you know what'll happen. What's Kaylee's strategy for you?"

"She doesn't have one. I think she thinks I'm doing well."

"Has she told you when you're going to kiss her?"

"Not yet. Do you know when you're going to?"

"Yeah, it's at the costume party at the end of the semester."

"What costume party?" I ask.

"Yeah, there's going to be one, I'm sure you'll hear about it soon. Judy wanted our love story to have a big moment, so she sent a donation to the school board in order to fund it. Anyway, I'm going to be dressed as a devil. My costume is the most ridiculous thing I've ever seen. It's a red domino mask and horns, and then I'm shirtless, with a pair of these pointed bat wings attached to my back, and then red leather pants. I'm going to look like a total fool. Plus, I have to do so many crunches to look good in it that my abs hurt all the time. Like, even right now, they ache." He pats his stomach. "Right here."

"And you're going to kiss her?"

He scratches the back of his hand. "Yeah, I am."

That sort of hangs in the air for a while.

"Are you looking forward to it?"

He fidgets. "I guess. I mean, the only practice I've had is during kissing classes, so I'm worried about screwing it up. Kissing has to be more than a physical skill, right? Because I know about lip pressure and when to use tongue and all that, but what about the connection? What if I screw that up? I just don't think a perfect kiss is something that can be taught."

"I feel the same. I wish there was a way to get better at it."

My heart is pounding. Can he hear it?

God, I hope he can't hear it.

"I've got an idea," he says, and he leans forward, fixing his eyes on the dark horizon. He's all jittery, like an excited puppy. "Come with me."

I remain in my spot. "Where are we going?"

"Have you ever been for a drive? And I'm not talking about in the limo on the way here. I'm talking an actual drive, with the wind in your hair, the whole sky above you, and the world in front of you. It's the most amazing thing in the world, and I'd like to show it to you."

"Of course not." I roll my eyes at my own bluntness. "I mean, no, I haven't."

"Would you like to?"

I nod. "But first, I need to know something."

"I'll tell you anything. What's up?"

I exhale, yet it doesn't release the cramped, cold feeling in my chest. I have to warn him about me. Otherwise this will all be over in a few weeks and he'll be dead. The other option is that he's playing me, and if that's the case, I need him to know I'm not falling for his act.

"Why did you tell me your whole plan?"

He doesn't flinch, not even for a second.

"Huh," he says as his eyes widen. "I guess I did. Put that on the list of stupid things I've done."

"Don't lie. If you were that stupid you never would've made it through the tests at the LIC."

"You think I'm playing you?"

"I'm not an idiot, so yes, I think you're playing me. I know what our relationship is. Hell, it's pretty much all I can think about sometimes. And then nights like this come along and my guard goes down and I start having a good time until you do something suspicious like tell me your whole plan and then I feel like an idiot. Because we're rivals, Dyl. We aren't supposed to get along. And if you think I'm not going to use everything you just told me against you, then, well, I think you underestimated me. Trust me, I'm not a threat you can dismiss."

He closes his mouth and turns to the left. When he looks back, his eyes are slightly glassy. "You're one of the very few people on earth I can be honest with. I know that's not something you can give me in return, and that's fine, it's who you are, but I'm not built to lie. It turns me into a man I hate. So, trust me, I know I could be handing you the gun that shoots me. I really do. But I can't keep lying to everyone all the time. You . . . you're a vent. Telling you the truth keeps me sane."

"Please don't call me a vent."

He looks down and chews his bottom lip.

"I prefer controlled burn," I say.

"Done. Now that that's out of the way, CB, do you want to go for a drive with me? I promise I'm not playing you and I promise you won't regret it."

I nod. "Lead the way."

Together, we leap down from the roof and cross the damp grass to his car. It's a black convertible. It's not sleek like most modern ones: it's big and boxy, and it looks a little bit like a monster.

"I want one," I say.

He opens the passenger door for me. I step inside and sit down. I can feel the cold, smooth leather even through my sweater. It smells dry and earthy and perfect.

"I'd let you drive," he says as he gets situated in the driver's seat, "but Judy would have an absolute fit. She thinks this car is like the ultimate way to make Juliet fall in love with me. Like, she'd take one look at it and instantly throw herself at me. If I crashed it they wouldn't need a Stalker. Judy would rip me apart all on her own."

I lean back in my seat. There's no headrest, so my head sits against the top of the seat. I curl my body slightly so that my cheek rests against the leather.

"I don't want to talk about that. Just drive."

And drive he does. The world around me turns into a blur of

darkness, broken only by the glowing golden orbs of the street-lights. We drive over a bridge, high above a vast stretch of navy water. I turn my head and look at him.

He's staring forward, his face set once again in a determined look, the same one he used when he was reading from the book of poetry. Both his hands are gripping the steering wheel tight. Without moving his head, he moves his hand down to grab the stick shift, and his foot kicks forward, changing gears. The engine makes a soft roar and the car surges forward.

The sight of him makes me smile.

My eyes widen, and I sit up straighter.

Crap. Ohhhhhhh crap.

I like him.

The realization crystallizes in my mind, making every encounter I've had with him make so much more sense than it previously did. Or maybe it's not so much a like, but I definitely feel *something* for him. Something more than most guys feel toward other guys.

I imagine him laughing on the plane, then I picture myself looking at him and recall how the sight of him laughing made me laugh harder. Nope, there's no need to lie to myself. I like him. *Crap!* I like him. *Good job, brain, you can't have him, so you decide you want him. Typical.*

The scary thing is that I've felt something like this before, back at the LIC. It was for Toby, a Nice a year older than me who had floppy brown bangs and a deep voice that didn't match his skinny body at all. He took me under his wing when I first arrived, and he even insisted on calling me Sam, because his philosophy was that everyone should have a proper name. I didn't know it was a crush at the time; I was pretty sure I was straight.

I just thought I really, really wanted him to like me, because he was cool, popular, and knew more about *Star Wars* than anyone else. I should've known what I felt was actually something, as the mere thought of him was enough to make me grin, and I did go hard when I saw him take his shirt off before an examination.

I cried when he left, and then the feelings faded until I pretty much forgot about them. I just thought it was a weird thing that happened once and would never happen again. Yet, here we are, starting round two.

Wait, what about Juliet? I like her, sure; she's a lovely girl. Smart, funny, and pretty. I thought I could fall for her. Now those thoughts feel like wishful thinking from a naive boy. With guys, it's different. It's always been different, I just didn't realize how different until now. I've always liked how they look, and I've always felt drawn toward boys with bright eyes or cute smiles or jaws lined with stubble. With girls, it always felt very conscious, like I was pushing my thoughts in a direction they didn't want to go. And now I know why it felt like that.

I exhale, but my heart is still beating really hard. This is a thing that happens to people. It's not unprecedented. It's, like, a legitimate thing. And that thing that happens to people? It's clearly happening to me. Because, all of a sudden, all I can think about is what it would be like to hold his hand.

I push the thought away. I can never pursue anything with Dyl, or any guy for that matter, so this has to be kept down. This . . . crush or whatever it is can't go anywhere, because Dyl isn't like me. The odds of that are so, so slim.

But in the corner of my vision, I see him turn his head and look at me, just how I looked at him.

PART
TWO

ANTAGONIST

CHAPTER
THIRTEEN

"CADEN!" SCREAMS M. I SIT UP AND YAWN, SCRATCHING
the matted hair on the side of my head. At the LIC they shaved us
every three weeks, keeping it short. I was due for a shearing the
week I left, so this is the longest it's ever been. How long have I
been out now? A couple weeks? I check my calendar: it's been
nineteen days. "Someone's at the door for you."

"Wait, why am I waiting for you?" says Kaylee from down the
hall. "You work for me, remember?"

Quick footsteps sound. *Crap.* I slide out of bed and pull on a
white shirt. My room is a mess, so I scoop up the clothes on the
floor and throw them into my closet. The desk is still cluttered
and my bed is unmade, but there just isn't enough time to do anything about that. I straighten up as my door swings open.

Kaylee stands in the doorway panting. She's wearing a sky-
blue dress and heels. "Caden, we need to talk."

I swallow hard. Memories of my regular nighttime activities—
Dyl and I, in his car, driving through the city—replay in my mind.
Each night we go somewhere different. It's rapidly become the

part of the day I look forward to most. That must be why she's here, to scream at me for spending so much time with him. Or maybe she tuned in to my nonplatonic thoughts about him. I meet her stare. "We do?"

"Of course we do! The costume party is coming up, and we need to choose your costume." She sits down at the computer. "Now, the theme is good versus evil. So, obviously, you'll be dressing up as someone good. Do you have any ideas?"

Whew.

"Jesus? He's one of the good ones, right?"

She rolls her eyes. "Now is not the time to try to be funny, Caden! This party is a huge moment in the school's social calendar. Plus, Juliet will be in a costume. And you know what that means?"

"Truthfully, I don't have a clue."

"She'll be more open to things! That's why costume parties exist. You mustn't forget, most people are always forced to be themselves, which totally sucks, by the way. By wearing a costume, Juliet gets a chance to do what you and other Love Interests are so fortunate to do every single day and become someone else. And when you're someone else, it's easier to be brave and act on what you really want. So, at this party, I think Juliet will make her first move. I bet she will kiss one of you. If you show up as Cletus the Slack-jawed Yokel, the chances of you being the one she kisses go *way* down."

"Oh man, that was my dream costume! I even had a perfect bit of straw picked out."

"Very funny. Now, how much skin do you want to show?"

Her fingers tap on the keys, and a black box pops up on the

monitor. It's a program I don't recognize. On the screen is a blond 3-D character in white briefs standing on a gray box. Beside him is a table filled with clothes. It looks sort of like Create A Sim, only someone has gone to an extreme amount of effort to make sure this avatar looks super buff. Like, comic-book level of absurd, unreachable muscle definition.

I frown. "Is that supposed to be me?"

"Yes. Now, you can go as a sexy angel. It's a classic. How are your abs?" She reaches across, grabs the hem of my shirt, and lifts it up. I flex, making my stomach muscles shudder. Is my body all I am to her? Haven't I shown that my strength, as a person *and* a Love Interest, comes from my mind, not my body? If Juliet is falling for me, surely it isn't because I have abs. They probably help, sure, but there's more to me than that, right?

"Still good," she says. "But not as good as they used to be. Do more crunches."

The insult stings, but I push through it. "Do you think Juliet would want me to be naked? That's what Dyl is doing. I should go as something modest but funny. I know her, and that's what she'll like."

"Like what?"

"You're the one who works for an all-knowing spy organization. You tell me!"

She bounces up and down on her seat. "Caden! I've got it! Juliet's favorite character is Spider-Man. She's, like, borderline obsessed with him. I'll order you a costume. There, you won't have to be naked, but it'll still be sexy. How's your butt?" She pushes me around and stares at my backside. I bow my head slightly, feeling like a hunk of beef.

"It's good. One of her favorite things about Spider-Man is his butt in tights. Seriously, the amount of times she's Googled 'Spidey-butt' is sort of embarrassing. But that ass of yours will be like a wet dream of hers."

Gross.

"Great."

She slides off the chair and stands up. "You should be grateful I care this much, Caden."

"Because I have *so* much to be grateful for in this life I'm living?"

She crosses her arms. "What's going on with you? You never used to talk to me like that."

I could tell her so many things. I could tell her that, sometimes, I'd rather say what I think than some scripted Nice guy answer. That spending time with Dyl has shown me how satisfying it is to be myself, or that being Nice is becoming more difficult.

The flare of defiance quickly dies, leaving a gigantic expanse of freezing-cold fear in my chest. A Love Interest is who I am, and it's all I'll ever be. Questioning that, or letting people like Kaylee know that I'm questioning it, will result in my death. I'm sure I'll fondly recall my snarky comments while they march me to the incinerator. I rub my eyes. "Sorry, I'm just tired."

She's clearly not fooled. "Careful now, Caden. You're doing well, but this contest isn't over yet. Anyway, you actually do have a lot to be grateful for. At least you're not a Solo."

"Why is that?"

"They have to have the traits of both a Nice *and* a Bad. You think you have to act? You should see the hoops those poor guys have to jump through. Also, they have to be obsessed with their Chosens, like to the point where they don't do anything other than obsess over them. At least this way you get some semblance of a life outside of your relationship with Juliet. Like your time with Dylan."

My eyes widen and a queasy feeling builds in my gut.

"Oh, don't look so scared, I get that you've become friends, and that's fine. It'll only become a problem if it interferes with your relationship with Juliet. Speaking of Juliet, is it working? Is she falling for you?"

"Um, I think so?"

"Well, are you falling for her? How does she make *you* feel?"

"She . . . she makes me the happiest man on earth."

Kaylee raises an eyebrow. "I hope you're more convincing with her. Now, it's time for you to get ready for school. I'm going to get the costume and I'll leave it under your bed. It'll be ready for the party on Friday. Isn't this so exciting?"

———————

A HUGE BANNER THAT SAYS MAPLETON ACADEMY COSTUME EXTRAVAGANZA is tacked on the wall. Beneath the words, a male devil and a female angel are posing and smiling. Beside them are the words GOOD VS. EVIL written in silver and red glitter respectively. Beneath that, Batman is punching the Joker and Harry Potter is casting a spell on Voldemort. It looks like a banner made by a five-year-old using newspaper clippings and a hot-glue gun.

Juliet and I are standing in the middle of the hallway, inspecting the poster. Around us, students rush past. It's sports day, so everyone is dressed in blue polo shirts and gym shorts. It's also freakishly hot, like to the point where my shirt keeps sticking to my back.

I turn to her. "I wonder what makes it an extravaganza."

Natalie and Trevor are behind us. His arm is slung over her shoulder, and they're making googly eyes at each other. Their obliviousness to the rest of the world has become a sort of joke between Juliet and me. Whenever we get a spare second, we pull stupid faces at them and wait until they respond. It usually takes a while.

"Don't doubt this party's extravagance, Caden. It's going to be off the freaking chain! I'm talking streamers, I'm talking fruit punch, I'm even talking balloons of differing colors!"

I laugh, but it's short lived. I'm lying to her. She's hilarious and kind, so it's easy to pretend we're real friends. Then I remember who I am and all that comes crashing down. I'm not, nor will I ever be, her friend.

All I'll ever be is the scumbag who manipulated her into falling in love with him.

She frowns. "What's up with you? That sounded fake and you look tired."

I can't let anything show, but I feel like screaming. That's two people today who've seen right through my act. I'm slipping, and I need to up my game if I want to survive. From now on, I'm going to be Nice all the time and I'm never going to let the real me show. Any thoughts or feelings that don't fit the role need to be eliminated.

I rub my cheeks. "I can't get anything past you, can I? You're right, I didn't sleep well for some reason."

"Oh good, I thought you were sick or something. Because in case Trevor let you forget, the swimming carnival is tonight, and it would be fun to have someone of my own to cheer on for once."

Be daring, Caden. Ask her if it's a date.

Blood rushes to my cheeks. "Oh cool, yeah, sweet." My voice is a pitch higher than it usually is, and it sounds frail. I don't need to act nervous because I *am* nervous. If I ask her out too early and she rejects me it'll be tough to make her like me in the way I need her to. "Sounds good."

"Did someone say my name?" asks Trevor. "I swear I heard someone say my name."

Juliet reaches her locker and opens it. "I was telling Caden about the carnival today." She pauses. Sitting in the middle of her locker, in front of the perfectly organized books, is a single red rose.

"Caden," says Natalie, slapping my arm. "You're a sweetheart!"

"It wasn't me," I say.

"Oh."

I press my fist against my locker. Dyl never told me about the rose. And unless Juliet has another suitor, one who hasn't shown his or her face yet, he put the rose there. Yet he didn't tell me about it. I can't blame him, because I never tell him anything about what I plan on doing with Juliet, but still, this is noteworthy. He normally tells me everything.

Juliet shelves the book she was holding and closes the door. *Good,* I think. She left the rose in the locker, which must mean she doesn't care about it. Or maybe she's saving it for later? I wish I could just ask her how she feels about it, but that would draw more attention to the romantic thing Dyl did. I need to act like it isn't a big deal, even though all I can think about now is that stupid red flower.

"We were talking about the swimming carnival," I say. "You know, the one that I'm going to win this afternoon?"

Trevor chuckles. "Man, if you beat me, my dream would be dead, but I would *still* feel sorry for you. I have no idea what kind of punishment Natalie would dish out to whoever beats me, but I know it would be brutal."

We move away from the locker and turn the corner, and then we walk through the double doors into the gym. It's a big, open room, with white walls and timber floors covered in blue mats. Plastered on the walls are posters of sweaty, half-naked men and women with body builders' physiques surrounded by phrases like YOU CAN DO IT and LIVE YOUR DREAM.

In a messy circle in the middle of the room is the rest of our class, as well as a dark-haired man in a white martial arts uniform that looks tough and uncomfortable. The fabric doesn't fit together properly, revealing some of his pale and hairy chest.

Behind him is Dyl. He's stretching his arms, his face set in his Bad sneer. He raises his arms above his head and stretches, showing a sliver of the V-shaped muscles of his stomach. As always, his hair is messy and there are dark circles under his eyes, but they somehow make him look good. *Tortured*, as he would say.

The instructor claps his hands together. The sound booms around the room, making me flinch.

"First up, we're going to do some sparring. Break into pairs and face each other on the mats. And no going with anyone you're dating—this is Self-defense, not Hand-holding One-oh-one. Now go!"

Dyl breaks away from his spot and strides toward us. I freeze. He reaches us and I realize he's here for Juliet, not me. My cheeks redden. He's not himself right now. In this moment, he's not my friend. He's a Bad, and I need to be a Nice. It's the way things are.

"You're with me," he says, looking her in the eye.

"I am not."

"You are. You need to learn how to defend yourself and I can teach you. Now come on."

"I can defend myself!"

"That's why I had to beat those guys up for you? Come on."

I step between them. "I'll go with you, Juliet."

Dyl's hand presses on my chest, above my heart. I can feel my heartbeat thudding against his palm. He pushes hard, and I stumble backward.

"You've done enough, mate," he says. "You can't even protect yourself, let alone her. Juliet, if you want to learn to defend yourself, come with me. This is your last chance."

She tucks a strand of hair behind her ear.

And she walks to him.

Natalie rushes up to me. She's smiling, but my entire body is shaking with rage and sadness and God knows what else. *He won.*

"No need to look so glum, Caden. I won't go *that* hard on you."

"Sorry, it's just . . ." I turn my head and look at Dyl and Juliet. They're touching. *Fuck fuck fuck they're touching.* "That is happening."

Natalie squeals and jumps up and down. "Oh my gosh, are you *jealous*? You are, aren't you? That's the sweetest thing I've ever seen. I knew you liked her! I knew it! Now stop being so obvious and fight me."

I raise my hands to the sides of my head as Natalie walks into position. She moves slowly, taking big, sweeping steps. Her legs snap together and she grins.

"Ready?" she asks.

"Sure am."

She ducks down and spins. Her shin hits the back of my calves. My legs fly out and suddenly I'm looking up at the ceiling. *Whack!* My back hits the mat first, then the back of my head follows, rattling my brain. I stare up at the high ceiling as my lungs splutter for air. A dull ache forms at the spot where my head first hit. Natalie walks over and offers her hand. I grab it and she pulls me to my feet.

She's grinning. "You're weaker than you look."

Through watery eyes I look at Dyl. He's holding Juliet close to his body. Really close. The entire length of his body is pressed against her. His hands are wrapped around her wrists, moving her through the motions of a punch. Her face is set in concentration, exactly like his. His eyes flick up for a heartbeat, find mine, and his lips curl upward.

Then he turns his attention back to Juliet.

FOURTEEN

SELF-DEFENSE WAS THE ONLY CLASS I HAD WITH Juliet today, so I spent every other class planning our next encounter. I didn't see Dyl either, and that made everything worse. It took every little piece of self-control within me to stop myself from sprinting out of the classroom to track them down. What if they were alone? What if they were still looking at each other like they were before? There are so many possibilities and they all suck elephant balls.

The lunch bell rings, signaling the end of the school day, because the entire afternoon block is devoted to the swimming carnival. I leave the classroom, shove my books back into my locker, then head out into the courtyard. At our spot are Juliet, Natalie, and Trevor. They're leaning in a row against the chapel. Everything looks normal. I reach them and wave.

"Hi," I say.

Juliet lifts herself up off the stone wall. "Hey, Caden, sorry about not going with you in Self-defense. That Dyl guy can be pretty persistent, huh? He's asked me to go with him, like, every class."

"He sure can."

Trevor steps toward me. "Have you got your trunks, Caden?"

My face falls. "Wait, that's today?"

His eyes go wide. "You can't be serious, man! I've told you, like, every single day for the past two weeks!"

I laugh, and turn around and show him my backpack. "I'm messing with you, Trev. Of course I do."

He lets out a sigh. "Good. Can we head to the pool now? I want to get there early to be as prepared as possible."

"Sounds like a plan."

We set off down the quiet street. The school is on the very edge of town, at the top of a hill, which means we have to walk downhill to reach the Mapleton Aquatic Center. It's a Wednesday afternoon, so the town is pretty quiet. Most of the parking spaces are empty, and the shops are occupied only by lonely shop assistants. Trevor and Natalie walk in front of us, his arm around her shoulder. She's holding a black gym bag.

I turn to Juliet. "So did Dyl teach you anything? He was kind of right, it would be good for me to learn how to defend myself."

"Yeah, he did. He told me to aim for the eyes or the throat. He said punches are mainly for show, and that a quick jab to someone's eye can end a fight in a second. He's really smart."

"Can you two be quiet?" asks Natalie. She's rubbing Trevor's forearm. "Trevor needs total silence in order to get into the right headspace."

Huh? Kaylee wrote me an entire conversation to have with Juliet on the way to the pool, and now I have to give up on it? I breathe in. *Think about it rationally, Caden. What would a Nice do?* The answer comes to me quickly. A Nice would listen to his Chosen's best friend and keep his mouth shut.

So I shoot her a smile and shut my mouth, and the rest of the walk passes in silence. Eventually, we reach the pool. It's surrounded by two rows of sun-damaged bleachers, the silver metal dulled by years of neglect. Just past the entrance is a small bathroom. People dressed in school uniforms of differing colors are swarming around the place.

Inside, the air is thick and muggy and reeks of chlorine. Trevor takes in a deep breath that fills his enormous chest, making it look even bigger. His skin is a few shades paler than it normally is.

Natalie rubs his biceps. "You'll be fine, babe. Remember, this is just a practice run for nationals. That's the one that matters. Just focus on getting a good time."

He jumps up and down and shakes his arms. "Yeah, but Dad said that everyone is getting faster, and the cutoff for Olympic trials is going to be at least half a second quicker than last time. If I can't get low twenty-threes now, when there's no pressure, then I'm totally boned at nationals."

"Don't stress," says Juliet. "Trev, you've got this." Her eyes land on me. "Good luck to you too, Caden."

"Right," says Trevor. "Thanks, guys. Caden, you're with me."

He takes the bag from Natalie and plants a quick kiss on her cheek. Then he turns and walks down a long hallway.

I follow after him. "So what's the plan?"

"We'll get changed, then we have to go back out and wait until our turn is called. Oh man, I'm so nervous."

"You know they're right, though, don't you? I'm sure you'll do fine."

He chuckles. "Yeah, man, I hope so. But if I want to make the Olympics one day, which I do, I need to get a good time today. I know this race doesn't mean much, but getting twenty-four or something now would be a nightmare, and it'd be almost impossible to bounce back from that. So I guess it's normal to be a little nervous."

Up ahead is a brick bathroom. Inside, there are three rows of benches. Two shirtless guys are in the corner of the room, chatting. Trevor dumps his bag on the closest bench, then he grabs the bottom of his shirt and pulls it over his head. I gape for a second before turning away. He's maybe even bigger than Robert, the Bad from the LIC. He's not as shredded as Robert is, but still, Trev looks stronger. I guess it's because his muscles actually have a purpose; they're not for show like a Love Interest's are. I chance another look. His skin is paler than I thought it'd be for someone who swims all the time, and a few dark moles cover his skin, one beneath his left nipple, another beside his belly button. They're imperfections, obviously, but they're also endearing. His body is unique in a way that mine will never be.

I shake my head and the thought dislodges.

I make my way to a bathroom stall and switch into my board shorts, which are blue and come down to just above my knees. I keep my shirt on, because if I'm going to strip, I need to do it in front of Juliet.

I walk out. Trevor is now wearing thin gray pants but is still shirtless. He looks down at my trunks and frowns. "Are you serious, man? You're wearing board shorts?"

"What's wrong with them? I got them especially for this."

"Don't you know how much they slow you down?"

I fidget. "I didn't until now."

He dismissively waves his hand. "It's cool. Sorry, I forget sometimes what I care about doesn't matter that much to other people. Let's go see the others."

It takes an hour for us to be called. I spend the time in the bleachers next to Juliet, watching the races, occasionally scanning the crowd for Dyl. Trevor sits on the row in front of us with his huge body bent forward. Natalie massages his shoulders, occasionally rubbing his back and telling him, "You've got this, babe."

A speaker crackles. "Seventeen-to-eighteen boys for the fifty freestyle."

"This is us," says Trevor, and he stands up.

I rise and take a step after him. I should take my shirt off now, but to do so would be kind of weird because Trev is already shirtless, and I can't make it seem like I'm stripping in front of Juliet deliberately.

Trevor presses a knuckle to his forehead. "God, Caden, this is like baby steps. Do you plan on swimming in your shirt?"

I shake my head.

"Then it can't come to the pool. Come on, shirt off, hurry up."

Thank you! I grab the collar of my shirt and grip it tight for a second, like I'm nervous about taking it off. Then I pull it over my head in one swift movement. I keep my eyes down as I scrunch it up and stuff it into my backpack, using the movement as an excuse to flex a bit. I chance a glance at the girls as I'm zipping up my bag. They're both staring, no, gaping at me. Natalie's mouth is open and her eyes are wide. Juliet is chewing her bottom lip.

"Fuck, man," says Trevor. "And you say you don't lift? Fucking liar."

I cross my arms, covering my chest. A Bad would smirk, maybe even put on a show. But I need to be awkward and uncomfortable, like I'm as shocked by my body as they are. "I . . . um, it's not that impressive, is it?"

"You're gorgeous," says Natalie. "Own it, man!"

I blush on cue, then scratch the back of my neck, tensing my muscles as I move. If I've pulled it off, I'll look nervous but still mega sexy. It's a fine line, but it's one of the textbook Nice moves and I've practiced it countless times. I think I've got it down, but I can't bring myself to look at Juliet to see if it's had the desired impact.

"Let's go, Tyson Beckford," says Trevor. "You've given the girls enough of a show."

We turn and walk away. As we step down off the bleachers I turn and look at Juliet. She's whispering something to Natalie, which could mean anything. She could be talking about, I don't know, how cute/buff/handsome I am, or about how she now thinks I'm a huge douche with no class for stripping in front of her. Trevor steps closer to me.

"You can wear your shirt to the pool," he says. His eyes have lit up with maniacal glee. "But you should've seen Juliet's face. You're going to be in her dreams tonight and you're welcome for that, man."

I scratch my forearm. "I'm that obvious, huh? Do you think she knows I like her?"

We reach the sign-in area, which is just a row of plastic chairs basking in the sun guarded by a man holding a clipboard. He writes our names, then lets us pass.

Most of the spots in our row are already taken, occupied by guys in various stages of undress. I check them out, then realize what I'm doing is out of character, so I turn to Trevor. He's also looking at the other guys, but it's pretty clear he's just sizing them up as threats rather than, well, appreciating them in the way that I do.

He notices me staring and points to two free seats. We make our way to them and sit down. My eyes snap open as the bare skin of my lower back starts to sizzle. I leap forward and rub the middle of my back with one hand, then lean forward so my back doesn't touch the backrest. Still, I can feel the heat of the seat through the thin material of my shorts.

"To answer your question, Juliet is the smartest person I know," says Trevor, who is seemingly oblivious to the hellfire he's sitting on. "If I figured it out, she probably has as well."

But you haven't got it figured out. You're so wrong it hurts.

Dyl appears out of the bathroom and starts walking toward us. He's wearing a black T-shirt and track pants, and his hair is swept back behind his ears. He reaches the sign-in area and quickly signs in. Then he walks up to our row and picks the seat right next to mine. I sit up straighter and breathe out. *Come on, man, don't blush. That's embarrassing.* But he's about to take his shirt off, I know he is, and I'm also shirtless, which is making the whole thing feel dangerously sexy. Like he could grab me at any moment and kiss me and I'd finally find out what it's like to touch another guy's naked chest. My stupid body betrays me, and I go kinda hard and my cheeks grow warm. *Fan-freaking-tastic.*

Dyl glances at me, then, silently, he pulls his shirt up and over his head.

His torso is even better than I thought it'd be. It's not textbook Bad, because he's not like a body builder, but I like what he has way more. He's slim, but he's got serious muscle definition, ticking off the classic hot-boy trio of pecs, abs, and abdominal V. And that's not even mentioning his biceps. God, his biceps are a joke. Most of his torso is smooth, but a small amount of dark hair covers his chest. I didn't think I was a chest-hair type of guy, but judging by the erratic things my heart is doing at the moment, I totally am. With a smirk, Dyl takes his track pants off, and I go even harder, because imagine if we were alone in a bedroom and he did that?

He drops the track pants and starts rolling his right shoulder. Now he's wearing black trunks, and they're sort of tight and they make him look so freaking good. They're pulled down just enough to show the green waistband of his underwear, which Judy must've told him to do; it draws attention to his abs and to his underwear itself.

This is a major problem, because I'm fully hard now and I'm going to have to stand up soon. *Crap!* I lick my dry lips and try to think of anything other than Dyl's bare chest, but it's like he's giving off this weird warmth, and I can feel this strange, sexy-as-hell energy in the space between us.

Farts. Old people falling over. Puppies. Old people having sex.

A horn blares and Trevor stands up. *Shit!* Old people doing nasty stuff to each other is doing the trick, and I've calmed down enough that I'm pretty sure my crotch won't draw any attention. I take in a deep breath then stand up with Trevor, keeping my eyes as far away from Dyl as I can, just in case the mere sight of him is enough to cause a boner aftershock. Still, his chest lingers in my memory. I focus on the speckled concrete and try as hard as I can to dislodge the image.

The sun warms my bare shoulders, making my skin feel golden. Copying Trevor, I step onto the block and look out at the long stretch of still blue water that's waiting for me. I roll my shoulders and chance a look at Dyl.

He's staring right at me. He winks.

The horn blares, and I'm struck with a second of confusion. Dyl leaps forward, his arms pointed in front of him.

Go, Caden, go!

I leap forward and smash into the pool, my chest slapping the water so hard it instantly starts to sting. I kick my legs and straighten up, but everyone else is already half a body length in front of me.

He winked he winked he winked.

Why would he do that?

His face is stuck in my mind, the confident tilt of his stubbly chin, his long, dark eyelashes, his scarily knowing smile. Did he notice that I was larger than normal? *Ignore him.* It's what I have to do. I kick my legs harder and pull my open palms through the water. I fall into a rhythm and pick up speed. Now I'm close to the others. The blue-tiled wall is up ahead. I give one last kick and move my hands forward.

I touch the wall. Breathless, I stand up and take in a few gulps of air before checking the scoreboard. I came in fifth! I officially didn't lose!

"Not bad for a newbie," calls Trevor. He's smiling a huge smile.

"Did you do it?" I ask.

"I'm not sure, but I think so! It felt really fast."

We high-five. Trevor pushes himself up and out of the pool. I figure if I attempt to copy him I'll slip and look like an awkward fool, so I make my way over to the ladder. When I reach the top, I notice that Natalie and Juliet are standing on the edge of the grass, holding towels. Natalie shrieks and runs into Trevor's arms. She slaps into his body and he picks her up.

"Twenty-three ten!" she calls. "I told you you'd do it!"

"Holy shitballs!"

"You did it, babe! If you can do that again at nationals, then you'll definitely make the team."

I reach Juliet. She offers me a white towel.

"Thanks," I say, grabbing it and rubbing my hair.

Someone touches my arm for a second, then shoves me. I totter a few steps to the right, and Dyl takes my place in front of Juliet. I'm sort of expecting her to be looking at him with outrage for pushing me. But she's not, and I can hardly blame her. A dripping-wet punk rock Adonis is bare-chested right in front of her. His hair spikes over his forehead, and it makes his eyes look even greener, almost like they're emerald.

Dyl places his hands on his hips. "Are you going to congratulate me?"

"For what?" asks Juliet. "Coming in second?"

"Silver is still a medal, so yes, I deserve praise. Especially when I'm competing against a titan over there. Are you going to congratulate me or not?"

"Decidedly not."

"Have it your way."

He turns and walks away. But I'm watching her, and her eyes dip for a second, tracing down his back, settling on the two dimples above his ass, then darting to the bleachers. Then I realize I'm staring at him, so I turn away.

Oh crap, I think. She just had her chance to look at us both shirtless.

And she chose him.

AFTER THE SWIMMING CARNIVAL, I HAVE A SHIFT at Starbucks. It's pretty much the same as every other shift, with me taking orders while Iris makes coffees and Levi chirps cheerily along. Even though it's a nice day, the store is still pretty quiet, and I can tell that both depresses and confuses Levi. He told me his boss blames him for the store's underperformance, and if it continues this way he'll be fired. So he spends most of his time staring at the door, as if wanting it bad enough will make people rush into his store.

I join him, and spend most of my shift staring anxiously at the door, waiting for Juliet.

She doesn't show.

FIFTEEN

IT'S THE NIGHT BEFORE THE PARTY, AND I CAN'T
sleep. My costume is under my bed, still in the box it arrived
in. I haven't tried it on, because the prospect of not looking
good in it freaked me out so much I postponed trying it on, and
kept postponing, and now it's the day before the party and I don't
even know if my freaking costume fits. I'm a moron. *Such* a
moron.

A knock sounds.

I grab my pillow and put it over my head. It's probably just
the wind or something rattling the window, like it always is. I'd
prefer not to deal with the disappointment I get when I realize
that, once again, the roof is empty. It's been a week since Dyl last
visited, and there's no reason for him to ever come back. It's for
the best. The contest is heating up, and that part of my life is over.
It hurts, but deep down I know it's for the best. I can't help but
be myself when I'm around him, and that's dangerous.

The knock sounds again.

"Dude, get up!"

Grinning, I roll over and look out the window. Dyl's there, dressed in a black button-down. He raises his hand and jingles his keys.

I sit up. Do I want to go with him? I shouldn't. I should close my eyes and wait until he leaves. It's what a smart Nice would do. But I really want to go. Like, more than I've ever wanted anything. Maybe even more than I want to win the contest. I never thought I'd want anything more, but I thought these visits had stopped for good and now I've got the chance to do it again. It might be a dumb decision, but I need to see where this night will take me. I'll always regret it if I don't.

I get dressed, then make my way over to the window.

"It's been a while," I say as I duck through the window onto the roof. I try to keep my voice flat, but my enthusiasm breaks through, lighting it up. "I was starting to think you were bored with me."

"No way, man. I've just been busy plotting nefarious plots. Secret nefarious plots, so don't try to get me to tell you about them. Judy would rip my balls off. But I'm sorry about vanishing on you like that. I actually missed our drives together, even if I was too stressed to organize one."

I jump down and land on the ground with an *oomph*. Dyl lands beside me. As he straightens up I cross the front yard and clamber into the passenger seat. Once inside, I lean back and watch him make his way around to the driver's seat.

"I have a question," he asks as he sits down. "Are you hairless everywhere? At the carnival you looked like a waxing salon ad." He slams the door shut and turns on the engine. "It must've hurt."

"No more than having your eye color changed."

"But doesn't it grow back?"

"I think they removed the follicles, so no, it doesn't. Juliet likes it, and that's the important thing."

"That's a shame. You'd look good with chest hair."

He's staring at me, and I look away to keep my attention away from his lips, which are curved into a smirk.

"Are we going somewhere?" I ask. My mouth is dry, so it comes out kind of raspy. "Or are we driving for the heck of it?"

He chuckles as we pull into the street. "*Heck*? Jesus, Caden, I think you're becoming Nicer every time we speak. What happened to the boy I should be afraid of?"

"You think my manners make me less scary?"

"I never thought you were scary." But he's grinning, so it sounds more like a compliment than an insult. "Not even once."

I lean my head back and look up at the stars.

He winked at me. At the pool, he winked at me, and I can't stop thinking about it. I want to ask him why he did it, but he's not bringing it up and I'm never going to. Not now, not ever. That would be like admitting that that second mattered to me, and for some reason the thought of him knowing that makes me feel all shaky.

"And to answer your first question," he says, "I'm here for two reasons. The first is beside you."

I look down at the seat beside me. On it, sliding around, is an iPod. It's attached to the car by a black cable.

"Press Play."

I roll my eyes. "It's not the Smiths or Sufjan Stevens, is it?"

He laughs. "No way, man, they're Nice bands. If I was being

a Bad right now, we'd listen to Black Sabbath. Or Metallica. So just shut up and press Play."

I tap the screen. It displays a black-and-white photo, the cover art for a song called "Midnight Show" by the Killers. The song starts with synths, then the guitars kick in.

"I found the only way to make driving better. It's angsty rock music. Judy loaded it all onto my computer for Love Interest reasons, but it turns out I genuinely love some of it. I bet you'll like it too, so I'll shut up now and let you listen."

I keep looking up at the stars as they zoom by, becoming lines of silver against the navy sky. The song is beautiful, a slightly aggressive voice singing catchy poetry backed by electric guitars. The singer sounds as frustrated as I feel sometimes.

The song ends and I open my eyes.

Dyl glances at me. "Did you like it?"

I loved it, but I can't help but think that it's not as good as Nicki Minaj. Nothing is. There are lots of reasons why I can't ever say that to him, so I stay silent.

"I'll take that as a yes. Do you have a favorite band, Caden?"

I desperately search my brain for a band he'll think is cool.

"Oh no," says Dyl. "You're good, but I can always tell when you know an answer but change it. Your forehead goes all crinkly for a second. Tell me the truth, man. I won't judge."

"Fine," I say. "Nicki Minaj is my favorite. She's not a band, but she's my favorite musician, and I figure that's what you were asking. I know she wears silly costumes and stuff sometimes, but she's a fantastic wordsmith, maybe the best one ever, and listening to her makes me feel like I can do anything."

Here it comes, he's going to judge me because she's too girly, or because she's a rapper, or because . . .

"Huh," he says. "Good choice. I love her 'Monster' verse. Do you know that one? The one with Kanye?"

"I do!" I say. "It's a great song. One of my favorites, actually."

"Well, we'll have to go for another drive and listen to it. You might think she's the best wordsmith ever, but my vote for that award would go to Brandon Flowers. So do you want to finish his album? I bet you'll like it."

I nod, and we listen to the entire album. During the closing notes of the final song, Dyl pulls the car off the road. Up ahead is a dark, creepy forest and a small wooden shed.

I cross my arms. "Are you serious? You brought me to a murder shed?"

"It's not a murder shed, Nice guy, it's a cool shed in the middle of nowhere that I found when I was driving and I thought it was awesome. And, like every awesome thing I find, I wanted to show it to you. Because we are both living with limited time, and life should be lived while we have the chance." He tosses me something. It's a silver flashlight. He's holding one exactly like it. He flicks it on, and a long beam of golden light erupts from the end. "We're exploring."

I turn back and look at the shed. "There's either a murderer or a dead body in that thing."

He grins. "Possibly both."

I grip the flashlight tight as we leave the safety of the car and head toward the shed. As we walk, my thoughts drift to Kaylee. Surely she would've said something by now if she was listening in? She's usually only connected when she knows a big conversation with Juliet is coming up, but then again she has popped in randomly a few times, so I probably should check.

Hey, Kaylee, are you there?

Nothing.

"What are you doing?" asks Dyl. "You spaced for a second."

"I was just checking if Kaylee is listening."

"And?"

"We're alone. If we aren't, she's not saying anything."

"Oh, cool."

The ground is soft and squishy, and every step sends a small wave of grayish mud up the edges of my Chucks. In front of the shed is a small overgrown veggie garden and a chopping block. Embedded deep in the block is a rusty ax.

Dyl steps up the first step. The wood creaks under his weight. He freezes, his entire body tense. The only sound is the rustle of the wind through the trees and the occasional high-pitched chirp of crickets. He places his palm flat on the dark wood and pushes. The door swings open, letting out a low screech. The light of the moon illuminates only a small stretch of the shack, and I can see half of a wooden dining table.

Dyl enters first, his body hunched, ready to spring back should the expected ax murderer leap forth. But the shed is still, and his body relaxes, his posture reverting back to its usual confident semi-slouch. His hand fumbles around on the doorframe and then he grins, his white teeth glowing in the shadowy murk.

He flicks his finger upward and orange light floods the shed.

"Quick, get in before anyone sees you."

I step inside and he swings the door closed behind me. Inside, it's a small square room, with a dining table, two chairs, and an empty kitchen counter with a dirty sink loaded with dishes. A moth-eaten mattress and a balled-up blanket are pressed against one corner. The counter is moldy, and the taps are covered in flaky brown rust.

Dyl flicks the lights off.

"What are you doing?" I ask.

He grins. "It's sexier this way."

I step toward the door and yank it open. His eyebrows furrow and he blocks my path with one hand.

"Get out of my way," I say.

"What?"

"I said get out of my way."

His arm remains on the door. "Dude, calm down. I meant it was sexier in the way, like, scary is sexy. That sort of thing. What did you think I was saying?"

I let go of the door handle and face him. For the first time, I realize I'm taller than him, and I stare right at the tip of his nose, just under his neatly trimmed eyebrows. "I don't know why you brought me here, that's what. And why you treat me the way you do. Because, Dyl, you're treating me like I'm an idiot and I'm just not. I know the game we're playing. I do. And you act like we aren't competitors and you show me cool things but when does it stop? And why did you even start it? Why did you bring me here? And why did you say you wanted to make it *sexier* for us alone in a small room?"

He's staring at the floor.

I step toward him. "Why did you bring me here, huh? You're such a big fan of the truth, so why don't you tell me? What are you afraid of?"

He looks to his left. "I brought you here to kiss you."

"Are you joking?"

He sucks on his bottom lip and faces me. He looks like he's in pain.

"It's not like that, it's . . ." He runs a hand through his hair and spins away. Once he completes his little circle he steps toward me. "I'm going to kiss Juliet tomorrow. And I need practice. I thought you'd understand because you need practice too. I brought you here because no one in town will see us and it seemed like a good idea. I thought we could kiss each other like teenage girls do in sitcoms to prepare for the real thing. I'm sorry if that's weird."

I clench my hands and keep looking him in the eye. *Prepare for the real thing?* Oh God, he doesn't even know how much of a real thing this is for me. The enormous reality of this is why kissing him isn't an option at all. I want to do it, sure, but I never can. It'd be like willingly putting myself at the top of a very slippery slope, with massive spikes covered in razor wire at the bottom.

"Why would I want you to be good at kissing her?" I say, more to myself than to him. If I say rational words, maybe I can force myself to act rationally. "Did you even think for a second that you not being good at kissing Juliet would be a good thing for me? We're competitors, Dyl. Above everything." I gesture at the space between us. "Above all of this, that's our relationship. Man, I shouldn't have to say these things to you. I really shouldn't. But you and I, we're not anything close to friends."

"You're my only friend."

"Don't lie. Not now. What makes you think I'd want to help you do this, Dyl? Do I look suicidal to you?"

He grabs my shoulders. I shake them off, so he tucks his hands into his pockets.

"I was dumb, okay, and I was lying. I brought you here to kiss you because I want to kiss you, all right? I want to kiss you because I want to kiss someone, just once, because *I* want to do it. And as soon as one of us starts dating Juliet it'll be cheating and I know neither of us will do that. But we're not hers yet. We're free men. And I, well, I feel something when I'm around you. I don't understand it and I don't want to, but there's something about you that creates this urge within me. Like, whenever I'm around you I can't help but focus on your mouth, and I find myself imagining what your lips would feel like against mine. So I want to kiss you, all right? It's embarrassing and weird, but I want to kiss you."

I stare at him. *He's just like me*, I think. He wants to kiss me as much as I want to kiss him. His back is bent slightly, and his thin body is shaking. He's looking at me with wide eyes, like whatever I decide to do next is going to be the most important thing that has ever happened on earth.

Then again, it could be a trick. It could be. It probably is.

"I know this is a trick," I say. "But I don't care. I want what you want too. One real kiss. So let's do it."

"Thank God."

I step forward and force him backward so that his back is against the wall. Surprise is in his eyes, so I grin, then lean forward and press my lips to his. His stubble is prickly but his lips are soft, oh eff are they soft. He pauses, and I step even closer so that our foreheads and chests touch. We're both gulping down air. Damn, his skin is warm even through the shirt. His hands move up and fumble with the hem of my shirt. *What's he doing?* I feel his hands slide under my shirt, where they move across my stomach to my hips. Every part of me that he's touching feels unbelievably amazing. Like, who knew palm-to-hip contact would be this frigging hot? But it totally is.

"Sorry," he says, and his hands slide out from under my shirt. "I got a bit carried away."

"I'm not complaining, man."

"So I can keep going?"

I look into his eyes and nod vigorously.

He grins. "Sweet."

He leans forward and kisses me again, stronger this time, forcing me back a step. He's no longer leaning against the wall, but now his entire body is pressed against mine. His hands go under my shirt again, higher than they did before, up to my ribs. I raise my hands and he pulls my shirt over my head. I get only a second to breathe before he's kissing me again.

I should stop. No, I need to stop.

I ignore my thoughts and start unbuttoning his shirt, revealing his chest. Once all the buttons are undone he grins, which melts me, then he shrugs the shirt off his shoulders and throws it away.

I look at him for a second, and he just looks at me.

"Sweet," he says again, then he grabs me by the back of my neck and brings my lips to his.

It feels freaking incredible. He tastes sugary, and he smells like cologne, and his body keeps brushing against mine, which makes me want more of him. More contact. More of everything, really.

Oh my God. This is Dyl! My Dyl. And I'm kissing him!

He starts kissing my neck and I chuckle.

He pulls his head back and his eyebrows pinch together. "Am I doing something wrong?"

"No, it's just, you definitely don't need practice."

"Neither do you."

"So should we stop?"

"Do you want to?"

I shake my head.

"So why should we?"

There are a million reasons to stop.

I ignore them all and kiss him.

SIXTEEN

REGRET. OH, BLOODY REGRET, I'VE SEEN YOU on TV but never had the chance to feel you in real life. And man, you freaking suck. I roll over in bed, rubbing my eyes as I move. They feel dry, like my eyelids are abrasive. But the post-hookup regret most people on those shows feel is after a character had sex with either a friend or an unattractive stranger. This was just kissing. We literally kept our pants on, yet my head feels like it's collapsing in on itself. What if Kaylee saw us doing what we were doing? What would the punishment be?

The image of the Stalker holding my head flashes in my mind. Only this time, there are two blood-drenched bodies on the ground, one in white, one in black. Its free hand rises, revealing another head: Dyl's. The Stalker presses the two heads together so that the lips touch.

I slide out of bed and realize I'm fully clothed. After what happened in the shed, taking my clothes off felt dirty. So I climbed into bed with all my clothes on and, after hours of replaying the events that took place, I fell asleep.

I grab my towel from where it's all balled up on the floor. It's still damp. I fling it across my shoulder and head out into the hall. D is walking toward the bathroom wearing only red silk boxers. A faded blue towel hangs around his neck.

"Don't even think about it," he growls.

I duck into the bathroom and slam the door shut. He smashes into it and the whole room shakes. I press the button on the door handle and it locks with a click. Was that the right thing to do? A Nice wouldn't do that. I breathe in through my nostrils. One of the things I liked most about kissing Dyl was the recklessness of it, the feeling of ignoring common sense and following my gut, giving a big middle finger to the consequences. But the night is over, and I'm a Nice, so I need to act like it. I'm going to shower as fast as possible, and then I'm going to apologize until D forgives me. It's what I have to do.

With that in mind, I undress and step into the limescale-covered shower. As I close the door he shouts a shockingly profane string of insults at me. It's so awful it's almost comical, and even though it's incredibly nasty, he does deserve credit for somehow managing to be sexist, racist, *and* homophobic within the space of ten seconds. *I'm going as fast as I can!* I turn the tap as far as it goes, which does nothing to heat the water up. I brace myself and step into the cold water. I wash my chest, then duck my head into the spray, wetting my hair.

I shut off the taps and stand, shivering, in the shower. He's still screaming. I grab my towel, dry my body as well as I can, then put my old boxers on. I'll change them when I'm back in my room, but I know he's going to make a scene, and I'd rather not deal with him totally naked. I wrap the towel around my waist. I can do this. I've worked so hard to become the perfect Nice, and all he wants is for me to break character. If I show him how mad he makes me, he wins.

I open the door and step outside.

His face is blood red. "You arrogant little shit!" he says. "I was on my way to the bathroom and you went in first!"

"I'm sorry, sir, I didn't—"

His hands shoot out and shove me in the chest. I take a step backward and grip the towel around my waist really hard.

"Who do you think is in control around here, huh?" he asks. "You act like you're big and important, but you're nothing. No one expects you to win, so I'm the one who matters, because I'm the one who will still be alive in a month. Trust me, I'm counting the days until they march your entitled, flamboyant ass to the incinerator."

He steps into the bathroom.

I feel myself lift away from the train tracks. This is going to be a wreck. It's unavoidable. A voice tells me to stop, to keep being Nice, but it's quiet and soft. It knows I'm already gone.

"I am."

He steps back out into the hallway. His body is bent forward and his breath stinks like beer. "What did you say?"

"You asked me who I think is in control around here. I know who is. It's me."

He snarls and leaps forward. Both his hands smack into my chest, the force making my ribs vibrate. I take two quick steps back before my feet can't keep up and they fall out from under me. I land hard on my ass. His foot comes down and presses on my sternum, giving me an excellent view of his gnarled toenails. Tufts of straggly black hair protrude from the base of each of his toes. He wiggles his foot, pressing me down into the carpet.

"I'm stronger than you! I'm in control, you little maggot!"

"You're not!" I spit. "I'm the Love Interest. I'm the one who matters! You're a washed-up failure who is jealous of me because this is as good as your life is ever going to get!" I shove his foot off me. Small clods of dirt remain on my chest. "Touch me again and I'll make sure they incinerate *you*. Got it?" I breathe in and sit up. "In my story my real dad is dead; you're my stepparent. You can be replaced. Got it, *Dad*?"

He stares at me. "Got it," he mumbles, his face reddening. He turns and walks into the bathroom. He closes the door softly.

After getting dressed I start to cool down, and the stupidity of what I did starts to sink in. I sit on my bed and rest my head on my hands. What's wrong with me? I just broke character, something I swore I'd never do. But I did it. I start shaking and my eyes fill with tears. What if something like that happens when I'm around Juliet? How fast, and how violently, I stopped being Nice haunts me.

Still, I have to go, so I stand up. I close my eyes and take in a deep breath, settling myself, then I head down the stairs. M is in the living room, lying on the couch, her head propped up by red pillows. *The Doctors* is on. I open the front door and see that the bus has stopped at the house two doors down from mine.

Shit! I forgot my costume!

I chance one last look at the bus, then sprint back through the house to my bedroom. I guess I could drive if I miss the bus, but I don't really want to, because driving still freaks me out. Inside my room, I pick up the dirty clothes that I'd previously kicked under my bed and throw them away. Then I pick up a gray box and tear it open. Inside is my Spider-Man costume.

I grab it and shove it into my bag. Then I run down to the bus. The bus driver, whose name always escapes me, gives me a friendly smile, which settles my heart rate a little bit. It's not enough to calm me down, though, as the memory of my epic fuckup lingers.

At school, Juliet, Natalie, and Trevor are standing near Juliet's locker.

"Hey, Caden," says Juliet with a small smile. "Do you have your costume for the party?"

I open my locker. "It's not a party, it's an extravaganza, re-member? And yeah, I do."

She snorts and pushes away from the locker. "Yeah, you're right. It should be a lot of fun. But hey, can I talk to you for a second?"

Uh-oh.

I nod, and we walk to a quiet spot at the edge of the lockers. She leans against the wall. Normally the prospect of having one-on-one time with her would make me smile. Right now, as a side effect of my recent activities, which have been distinctly not Nice, my hands start trembling. I tuck them into my pockets.

"So, Caden," she says. "You know how, when you first got here, I needed someone to model for me?"

I nod slowly. Kaylee scripted a scene about me modeling for Juliet, so I know which direction to steer the conversation. "Yeah. Are we ready to start? I've been doing a lot of chin-ups and have been avoiding the free drinks at work to make sure all this"— I gesture toward my chest—"is ready."

"No, it's . . . Don't take this the wrong way, but I asked Dyl to pose instead. I'm good friends with you now, so staring at you pretty much naked for hours would be weird for me, and I think he would help me do well on the assignment. That's all this is about, getting a good grade. Is that cool?"

I frown and my shoulders slump. In the script, she said yes, and I model for her. Kaylee even wrote a few witty one-liners for me to say while I was posing. Now I've lost all that time with her. I can't help but think that kissing Dyl, or my outburst this morning, is what caused this.

"Juliet, I totally understand. I'll do whatever makes you happy."

School passes slowly because all I can think about is the fact that Juliet chose Dyl over me. Point blank, she picked him. I think about pretending to be sick so I can leave early, but that's what the Caden who got me into this mess would do. For me to claw my way back into this contest, I need to fully recommit to being a Nice. My true thoughts and feelings are the enemy, so I need to bury them.

After lunch, I head down the hallway to English. Dyl is walking toward me, staring at his stupid poetry book. I glare at him. He's going to strip in front of Juliet. I picture the way he'll slowly pull his shirt up and over his body. The way he'll grin as he balls it up and throws it away. How the ridges of muscle along his ribs will ripple as he flexes.

I think about grabbing him by the shirt and shoving him up against a locker. I'd press my forearm into his neck, just above his collarbone. I imagine his eyes, wide and startled, and the way his mouth would drop open for a second before he'd smirk and call me Nice guy.

He never forgot about the contest. Not even for a second. All day I've been distracted and he's been making moves to pull Juliet away from me. I want to scream at him, to ask him how he could kiss me and then keep playing like nothing has changed. Instead, I clench my fists and walk past him.

After the final bell, Juliet is waiting for me outside my classroom. She's leaning against the wall, glancing at everyone as they stream out of the room.

"Hi," I say as I approach her. "It's nice to see you."

She bites her lip and detaches from the wall. We make our way down the hall toward the exit. "Caden, you know you can tell me what you actually feel, right?"

I gulp. "What makes you think I don't?"

"Just the way you've been acting today. Like, it seems like you're upset about me doing the art assignment with Dyl, but you don't want to let it show. It's fine if you're mad at me or whatever, but please don't pretend to feel something you don't. It's what my dad does and I can't stand it. Promise that you'll never do that to me?"

"I promise," I say. "Well, from now on, anyway. In case it isn't screamingly obvious, I'm not cut out for this whole lying thing. You can see right through me. So yeah, I'm a little bit upset that you're doing the assignment with Dyl because I was looking forward to spending time with you. That's it. I'll get over it."

"Thanks for being honest, Caden. But I want you to know the reason I'm doing the assignment with Dyl is that I like you so much, not the opposite."

"For realsies?"

"Yep, for realsies. To do the assignment you'd have to be half naked. It'd be weird with you because, you know, you'd be shirtless."

"I wouldn't mind."

Too bold, Caden. Get awkward, fast!

My smile drops. "About the me-being-shirtless thing, I mean. Sorry, I was trying to sound sexy and I epically screwed it up. Pretend I didn't say anything."

She laughs. "It's okay, Caden. I like the idea of seeing you without a shirt on. It's . . . it's why I asked in the first place. But, well, our relationship is different now. It's stronger than attraction, or at least I think it is. So I don't want to screw it up by throwing a whole lot of lust into it, especially when you're naked and I'm not. So let's drop it, okay? Speaking of dropping it, Trevor and Natalie are coming over to my place before the party starts to get ready. Do you want to join us?"

"*Dropping it*? What is this, a Pitbull song?"

"Move past the bad segue, Caden."

"I do as you command, Juliet. But wouldn't I be intruding?"

She shakes her head. "Dude, they both love you. And I . . . I like you a lot, so it'd be awesome if you came. No one is being sympathetic by inviting you over. We like spending time with you because you're funny and cool, so it's for our benefit as much as yours. Plus, we may even have a couple drinks before. Mom is cool about alcohol as long as we don't get drunk, so she got us a bottle of wine. It's going to be really fun, and I want you to come. So are you in?"

Am I in? I'm as in as it is possible for me to be. I thought for a second that I'd ruined everything, but maybe the few times the real me emerged he didn't do as much damage as I thought. I still need to be very careful about how much I let my personality come through, but it's not as grim as I previously imagined. I'm not out of the running yet.

"Lead the way," I say.

CHAPTER
SEVENTEEN

JULIET'S HOUSE IS ONLY A COUPLE HUNDRED yards away from the school, so the four of us are walking there, following the paved pathway beside the road. As we pass under the school gates I recall the e-mail Kaylee sent me last night. She thought it'd be a good idea to take advantage of my friendship with Juliet in order to damage her relationship with Dyl. Kaylee said that Juliet would listen to me as long as I didn't come across as a "possessive fedora-wearing asshole." Those were her words, obviously, but I agree with the sentiment.

I turn to Juliet. "So how much of Dyl have you been seeing?"

"Not much. Why do you ask?"

"He seems to like you a lot. It's kind of creepy."

"Liking me is creepy?"

Oh boy. Wrong tack.

"No, of course not—I mean, you barely know him and he seems kind of obsessed. Liking you isn't creepy at all. It's the most obvious thing in the world."

"Barf. But I get what you're saying. He's intense. I think that's just how he is."

I could tell her so many things about him. But my feelings toward him are too strong, and I know if I say anything else it'll come across as self-serving and bossy. I may as well start whining about how nice guys never get the girl, so I shut my mouth.

We walk around a large lake. In the middle of the water is a fountain that looks like a leaping goldfish vomiting water from its mouth. The lake itself looks sludgy and slightly green, partly covered with rotting leaves. The path we're walking on is cream-colored concrete that's filled with cracks. Juliet's shoes make a satisfying clicking sound with every step.

"Do you like anyone, Caden?" asks Juliet. "You've been here awhile, so have you spotted anyone you could see yourself dating?"

She's giving me her best doe eyes and her arms are swaying, her fingers curling inward, making a semi-fist. This is a test. She's mining for information about my feelings. This is a good sign. It means she cares.

I shoot her a sly grin. "Maybe one."

"You aren't going to tell me who it is, are you?"

"I might," I say. "I just want to make sure she likes me back first."

She skips ahead to catch up with Natalie and Trevor. When she reaches them she stops and looks back at me. "Caden, she's probably waiting for you to do the same thing." She shrugs. "Just saying."

She turns around and falls into step with Natalie and Trevor.

I tuck my hands into my pockets and start whistling. Juliet just told me what she wants: she's interested, but wants me to make the first move. I think about what the LIC taught me about that. One of the best Nice strategies is a big romantic first date. It's settled. Tonight, at the party, I'm going to ask her out.

At her house, her mom opens the door. She's dressed in a sleek black pantsuit but her blondish hair is ruffled, like she's been running her fingers through it a lot.

"Caden," she says as I step into the doorway. "No injuries this time?"

"None at all."

"Great. Now, I've known you for a long time so I don't feel bad asking for help. Richard's in the kitchen preparing some snacks for you guys. Can you go and help him? Juliet, set the table."

Juliet puts her hands on her hips. "Mom, I told you this is a casual thing."

"Nonsense. We don't do casual." She points at Natalie and Trevor. "You two can go watch TV if you'd like. Caden, Juliet, snap to it."

Natalie and Trevor stare into each other's eyes.

"I could get used to this," says Natalie.

"So could I, babe. Why do you think I want to go to the Olympics so bad? Win one medal and it's, like, rock star treatment for the rest of your life!"

"Well, you'd better win! A girl could get very used to this lifestyle." She playfully punches his chest. "And I'm rather fond of you. I'd hate to ditch you for the guy in the next lane. But I will do it. If he beats you, that is."

I head into the kitchen. Richard is wearing an apron and carefully slicing a slab of smoked salmon. Little pieces of pink gel cling to the edge of the blade.

He places the knife down on the white stone counter top. "It's great to see you again, Caden. But shouldn't you be fraternizing with the other youth?"

"Daphne told me to come and help you."

He wipes his hands on a green dish towel. "Of course she did. That's not a problem, is it?"

"Not at all! What do you need?"

He points to an empty white bowl. Beside it is a bag of sea salt–flavored chips.

"Can you open that and take it out to the table? There are some dips in the fridge; can you take those as well?" I nod. "Thanks, Caden, you're a lifesaver."

I squeeze the bag and open the chips, unleashing a salty smell. My mouth starts to water as I dump the chips into a bowl. Then I open the fridge and retrieve two clear plastic containers. One is filled with brownish dip and the other is green, presumably avocado. Both look delicious, and both are obviously off-limits for me.

"They're homemade," says Richard as he washes an apple in the sink. "Daphne's own recipe. Trust me, once you've tried them, you'll make your own from scratch too. It's *so* much better than that store-bought garbage."

"I bet it is!"

Carrying them, I walk out into the living room.

It's a wide room, with two brown leather couches placed in front of a huge wide-screen TV. On the wall to the left of the TV is a massive mahogany bookshelf. One side is devoted to thick legal textbooks, and the other is filled with brightly covered cookbooks. In front of the books are various knick-knacks, like a small golden cannon and a framed photo of a baby in a white gown. It's like a mural devoted to her family. A piece of minimalist art is on the other wall.

On the couch, Natalie is sitting on top of Trevor, kissing him. Her hair has fallen over both of their faces. I blush as I walk past them and place the food down on the coffee table. The only other thing on the table is a big hardcover book filled with photos of the ocean. I flip it open, trying to ignore the sucking and slurping coming from the couch. A harsh laugh sounds.

"I take it you're not a fan of PDAs, Caden?"

"Is anyone?" I crack open the container of avocado dip. It smells heavenly and makes my stomach rumble. *No way.* I need to think of my abs.

Trevor tilts his head and looks at me. "Dude, I have a question for you."

"Shoot."

"Have you ever kissed anyone?"

"Trevor," says Natalie, her tone harsh. "Don't be mean."

"I'm not being mean. But come on, look at him, he's blushing at the sight of us. He's the most innocent thing I've ever seen."

What should I say, Kaylee?

No response.

I shrug my shoulders. "It's fine. Um, yeah, I have. Kissed someone, I mean. I'm not as innocent as I look."

Isn't that the truth.

"I don't believe that for a second. Who have you kissed?"

Dyl. I kissed Dyl, and it was possibly the best moment of my life.

"Does it matter?"

"It does, man. I want to be your friend and I know none of your romantic history. So fill me in! Who was she? What did she look like?"

His use of the word "she" makes me flinch. He said it so confidently, like I would only ever want to kiss girls. I know that's not the case, and that wanting to kiss another boy is perfectly normal, but he doesn't seem to know that. What am I supposed to do, contradict him and make this a big thing? I could never do that because I'm a Love Interest, but the fact that he didn't even give me the option to be gay makes me want to throw something at him.

"I'd like to know too, Caden," says Natalie, her tone soft, like I'm pathetic even though *they're* the ones who started this conversation. They brought it up, and now they get to judge me because my answer is unsatisfactory to them? Why is that fair? "If you want to tell us, that is. It's cool if you don't. Have you ever been in a relationship?"

"I'd rather not talk about it." I step backward out of the room. "Sorry."

I return to the kitchen. Richard is reaching up to the cupboard above the stovetop. His body is fully stretched out, but he can't seem to reach the saucepan he's trying to grab.

"Here," I say. I walk over and quickly grab the saucepan. Then I pass it to him.

"Thanks, Caden. Daphne wasn't really thinking when she designed this place. She figured since she does the most cooking it wouldn't matter that I can't reach the pots!"

I chuckle. "Do you need any more help?"

"If it's not too much trouble, there's one last thing. Can you chop up this celery for me?"

A gigantic piece of celery is sitting on a wooden chopping board. I walk toward it and pick up the silver knife. I cut off the head, then slice the body into thin slivers.

Hey, Caden, it's Kaylee. Sorry I was slow, I had a date, but I'm here now.

"You and Juliet seem to be getting along," Richard goes on. The celery crunches beneath the knife. "Is there anything you want to ask me? I'm here now."

"We aren't dating, if that's what you're asking. We're just good friends."

He blinks. "Wow, I wasn't expecting you to be so blunt."

"Keeping secrets isn't my thing."

"That's a rare quality. And if you respect me enough to be honest I will return the favor. I think you're a good young man, Caden, I really do. And I think you would be kind to Juliet. But you must understand, it's my job to make sure she becomes the woman she was born to be. She's destined for greatness, you must know that, and, well, all boys your age hurt girls eventually. You just do. So I want you to think hard about what your relationship with Juliet is, because—"

"Dad?" Juliet is standing in the doorway, glaring at him. "What are you doing?"

"I was talking to Caden about—"

"I can't believe you! Caden and I aren't even dating and you're already freaking him out!"

"But you will be soon enough. I see the way you look at each other. I'm not as smart as you but I'm not an idiot, Juliet."

"You can be sometimes, Dad. Seriously, I don't know what you want from me. You want me to get married, yet you don't want me going anywhere near boys or, God forbid, having sex! It's like you want me to be alone but are also judging me for not having a serious boyfriend!"

He puts the pot he was holding down on the counter. "You've got so much potential, Juliet. I don't want you throwing it all away for the first hot boy you see." He turns to me. "Not that I think you're hot, Caden. I'm using lingo to try to relate to her. I read it in a book."

"Dad, seriously, *please* stop talking."

"I'm just trying to protect you, Juliet. That's all. You'll probably thank—"

"Caden," interrupts Juliet. "Come with me. I'm done. So done."

I follow her out of the kitchen into a small hallway. The walls are lined with framed photos from holidays she and her family have been on. In the one closest to her, Juliet is standing in front of the Colosseum with her arm flung around her mom's shoulders.

Right now, she's leaning against the wall, her head pressed limply against the plaster. I lean on the wall opposite from her. Our legs are inches apart.

She rolls her eyes. "I'm sorry about him. He's dramatic. We both are, in a way. It's embarrassing—you probably think I'm a brat. A spoiled, rich brat."

"He was being pretty weird. I'm on your side, Juliet. Not his. Not now, not ever. And you're not a brat."

"You're too nice to me sometimes," she says, but her voice is soft. She looks up at me. "It makes me feel like I can get away with anything."

"It's because you can. You could hate *Star Wars* and I'd still forgive you. I can't think of one situation where I wouldn't take your side."

"Now that's not true. You don't like me spending time with Dyl. I can see it in your eyes. It's like you're jealous."

She picked that up? Crap, that means I need to be more careful. I'm lucky because being jealous of Dyl fits the persona I've created, so it's not going to make her doubt my character. But it's dangerously close to my real feelings. And if I've learned anything, it's that my real feelings only hurt me.

"I'm not jealous of him. I'm intimidated, I think. He's a scary dude. Do you remember when he beat up those guys? I don't like the idea of you spending time with someone that violent."

"He's not scary, he's different. He's unlike anyone I've ever met. I'm usually pretty great at reading people, but with him I come up with nothing. I mean, he beat up those guys, sure, but do you remember that book of poetry he was reading? I asked him about it, and he let me borrow his copy. It's really tattered, and a few of the lines are highlighted. Thugs don't read poetry, Caden. Plus, he only beat up those guys to save *us*, remember? He told me he hates hurting people, but he's willing to do it when it's necessary."

"That's bull. You missed it, but I saw him when he was fighting. He was grinning like a loon. He was loving it."

"Oh. That's a bit weird."

Critical hit!

"Anyway," she says. "You aren't jealous of him, exactly. I think you're jealous we're spending time together."

If I'm going to ask her out tonight, I need to start being bold. "I *am* jealous of that. And I'm not ashamed of feeling that way."

"Oh." She smiles. "I wasn't expecting you to be so blunt. But this is a party, and I don't want to talk about Dyl right now. Come on, it's time to get into our costumes!"

I get dressed in a simple guest bedroom. It's a cream-colored room with a single bed and one tall stand-alone mirror pressed into the corner. With the skintight spandex on, but with the mask off, I make my way over to the mirror. I ruffle my hair, making it look messy, and practice my quizzical expression. I look pretty good. Not as good as Dyl probably will, but the costume makes my muscles look bigger than they actually are, and the blue of the suit makes my eyes pop.

Kaylee, mask on or off?

Off for now. Put it on when you get to the party. It'll put some distance between the boy she knows and the seriously hot man you are now. She'll check out your pecs and then be like, damn . . . Wait, that's Caden?

I swing open the door. Outside, walking right past, is Juliet. She's wearing a royal-blue dress with frilly white lace on the chest. I do a double take. Is that really her? Now that she's wearing a white wig and blue contacts, she somehow looks more grown up. Her eyes move down from my face to my chest. I breathe in and tense, making my pecs and abs go rigid. Her stare stops at my belly button. I wish I had a link with her like I have with Kaylee. I'd give anything to hear what she thinks when she looks at me.

"Spider-Man," she says. "Oh my God, I love it!" She steps

forward and pinches the material on my chest. She also pinches some skin and I wince. I bend over, placing my hand on my stinging flesh. It hurts, sure, but I play it up because wounded guys are hot. "Oh, sorry, wow, this thing is skintight, huh? It's so good, so detailed. Where did you get it?"

I chew my bottom lip. Because I have no freaking clue where Kaylee got this costume. "Online."

"Yeah, but where online?"

Kaylee?

Just say Amazon.

"Amazon. But enough about me. You're Alice, right? From Wonderland. Is she good or evil?"

Pretend she has an eyelash on her cheek.

But she doesn't.

That's why I said to pretend.

I lean forward and gently pluck an imaginary hair from her cheek.

"Eyelash," I say, and I blow on my fingers, releasing the non-existent eyelash.

She's blushing and looking at the floor, so I guess Kaylee's play was a success. "Thanks, Caden. What was I talking about? Oh, right, if Alice is good or evil. I think she's clearly a hero, but she's not very good, seeing as she's sort of bonkers. Although I was sort of hoping to avoid a night of people asking me that question."

Call her pretty.

"No, it was just me being dumb. She's obviously good. And you look great, Juliet. The wig and the contacts, they make you look . . . different."

"That's the point of a costume, Caden."

"You know what I mean."

Her smile drops. "I do. Or at least I think I do. You're a lot easier to read than Dyl is, but you're still a bit of a mystery to me, Caden Walker. Now let's go see what horrendous couples costume Nat and Trev have come up with. We may need a bucket. For, you know, when we barf."

In the living room, Trev and Natalie are holding hands. He's wearing an orange-and-blue basketball jersey under a brown leather jacket. Natalie is wearing a white V-neck and blue jeans. A plastic tube is hooked into her nostrils.

"No," says Juliet.

"Okay?" asks Natalie.

"Okay," answers Trevor.

Juliet and I glance at each other.

"Barf," we say at the same time.

"You don't like it?" says Natalie. "Seriously?"

Juliet grabs her by the forearms. "Don't be silly, I love it. It's sickeningly cute. But how do Hazel and Gus fit the theme?"

"People don't have to save the world to be good," says Trevor. "John Green gets that, and I do too. All you have to be is honest and kind, and then you're good."

His words ring in my mind. Because, by his criteria, I'm a bad person.

CHAPTER
EIGHTEEN

THE PARTY IS IN THE SCHOOL'S GYM, WHICH IS a fact they've tried to cover up with streamers, posters, and flashing neon lights. But the reality of the location is obvious in both the squeaky sound the floor makes every single time someone takes a step, and in the smell, like stale sweat, that hangs over everything. *Why not just have fun?* I ask myself. One night. One good time. It's the perfect chance to ignore everything ahead and just go wild.

I wish I could be that guy. I really do. But this party is a big event, and I need to be on my game, making myself as Nice as possible. One mistake could be the end of me, so I have to be perfect.

Juliet is beside me, swaying along to the music. Her pink, glossy lips are pressed together. I could kiss her tonight. It would be a good thing if I did, because if Kaylee's right, which she usually is, one of us will kiss her tonight. And it should be me. It's not that I want to kiss her, because I don't; it's just strategy. But the idea of Dyl kissing her makes me clench my hands into fists. I'll kiss her just to stop *that* from ever happening.

A pop song starts to play and Natalie grabs Trevor by the arms and pulls him into the crowd. Juliet's eyes focus in on someone. I follow the direction of her gaze and see a figure at the back of the gym leaning against the wall, his figure cast in darkness by the shadow of the bleachers.

Dyl.

Game on, Bad boy.

He peels himself off the wall and cuts a path through the crowd toward us. He's dressed exactly how he said he would be, only he was wrong when he said he'd look foolish. So wrong. He looks freaking incredible. He's shirtless, and his crunches have obviously paid off, as his stomach is taut and defined, and each little bump of muscle is clearly pronounced. Over his shoulders are two brown leather straps, and attached to them is a pair of crimson bat's wings. Horns of the same color protrude from the top of his head.

He smiles.

Next to him, I feel like a child. I'm a kid dressed up like a superhero. And he's a full-grown man. It radiates from him, in the tilt of his chin, the uneven manner in which he walks, in his borderline obnoxious I-fuck-people-and-I'll-fuck-you smile.

"Hey," he says.

"You're missing some of your costume," says Juliet. But her throat keeps bobbing up and down. *She likes him.*

"No one seems to be complaining," he says with a wave of his hand. He nods at a group of girls at the front of the crowd. They break out in a fit of giggles and flock closer together, their arms and chests touching as they whisper to one another. Their eyes keep flitting in Dyl's direction. I want to tell them to back off, because they aren't a part of this story and they never will be. "It's my duty," he continues. "People who look like me owe it to everyone to show off our bodies." He flexes his biceps. The girls squeal. Who are they? Were they hired by the LIC?

I turn back. He's still flexing. Holy frigging frig, his biceps are huge. My mouth goes dry.

"Well, I'm not impressed," says Juliet.

"Don't lie, Juliet. It's unattractive." He steps closer to her. "You want to touch me, don't you? To run your fingers along my body, to feel my lips on yours. It's okay, Juliet. I want you to feel me too. I want you to do whatever you want to me." He steps away. "Just ask, Juliet, and I'll do it, no exceptions. All you have to do is ask, and I'm yours."

I blink my watery eyes and gulp down a swallow. Dyl winks at Juliet, then heads toward the group of girls. Juliet watches him as he walks past. Her eyes trace down his spine; then she smacks her lips.

"Do you want a drink?" I ask.

She looks up from the floor and brushes a strand of hair away from her face. "Umm, yeah. That would be lovely, Caden. Thanks."

I duck away from her and head toward the main table. It's covered in a red plastic sheet and is loaded with snack foods. Stupid Dyl. His offer was hot, sure, and it would take a strong person to turn down that offer from someone as attractive as him, but Juliet is a strong person. She'll say no. At least, I hope she will.

A thin boy with square glasses and blond hair sees me as I approach and smiles at me. He's wearing a purple vest and tie over a white dress shirt, and he's holding a microphone in his hands. His shirt sleeves have been rolled up, revealing a sleeve of tattoos on his forearms.

"Hi," he says as I grab two plastic cups.

I grip the cups, making the thin plastic crinkle. "Hey . . . Sorry, do I know you?"

I scoop the ladle into the punch bowl, filling the metal spoon with purple liquid and a couple of floating blueberries. It smells like melted sugar.

"Not yet," he says. "But that's the whole point of things like this, isn't it? To get to know people?"

"I guess."

"And I've seen you around school and you seem like—"

I peer closer. Wait, is he blushing? He is: his cheeks are burning red even through the darkness. He chews his chapped bottom lip and looks me in the eye. "—someone I would like to spend some time with, if you, um, catch my drift."

"I've gotta go," I say, looking down at my two cups, which are now full. "See ya around, maybe?"

He grins. "Yeah, totally!"

I spin away and walk toward Juliet. *What was that about?*

She's bobbing her head along to the beat, and the pink light reflects in her glassy eyes. I hand her a cup. She grabs it and takes a sip. "Who was that?"

"Huh?"

"That guy who was talking to you. It looked like he was asking you out."

My eyebrows furrow. "Did he?"

"Well, what did he say to you?"

"He thought I seemed cool and he wanted to spend some time with me . . . if I 'caught his drift.' Huh, he *was* asking me out, wasn't he? Wow, I didn't even notice."

She scoffs. "Boys can be so thick sometimes. Yes, Caden, he was asking you out. Are you going to say yes?"

I freeze. "No."

"Why not?" she asks. "Caden, it's not a big deal if you're gay. You know that, right?"

"This isn't Tumblr, Juliet, straight men do exist here. I like girls."

She laughs, and the tense moment passes. *Whew.*

"Sorry," she says. "I know it's a horrendous cliché, but you're so well put together, and so handsome, and it's not like it would matter to me if you were, but I'll admit I was curious about your sexuality. Because sometimes I can't tell if you're flirting with me or if we're just really good friends."

Ask her out now.

What?

Right now. Tell her it would matter to you because then it means you wouldn't like her. Which you do.

"We *are* good friends," I say. "But that doesn't mean I wasn't flirting with you."

I don't think my heart has ever beat so fast. If I screw this up, I'm a dead man. Also, Kaylee was listening in. Now she knows what I honestly think, and that's absolutely terrifying. It could become an issue for me down the road, but I can't stress about it now. I need to focus on Juliet.

"Oh," she says.

"I like you, Juliet. I always have. But I'm not a boy anymore, I'm a man, and I like you in a way that I didn't before. And I would love to go out with you sometime."

"I'm going to stop you there," she says.

Everything slows down and all I can think about is the LIC, with its shiny mirrors, neon-white lights, and skintight, sky-blue clothes. I failed. I failed so I'm going back. I was too forward too soon and I screwed everything up. I—

"Yes," she continues. I finally look up at her, just in time to see her smile. "I would absolutely love to go out with you! So there's no need to stress. Pick something for us to do and ask me properly then, because I'm guessing this was an impulse and you should make a plan. Also, I don't want to think that you asked me out to prove you aren't gay. We're too special for that, and if we end up together for a long time I don't want this to be the story of how you first asked me out. Oh God, I'm going to leave now before you think I have this big plan for our future, like a notebook filled with Mrs. Walker doodles or something. Which I don't! Truly. Ugh, I'm shutting up now. I'm going to go and find Nat and Trev. So bye."

She dashes away.

Did I do well, Kaylee? She said yes. That's good, right?

I don't know. It's too early to tell, but she seemed a little bit uncertain. The date you take her on is going to have to be an absolute killer.

I walk into the crowd. The beat coming from the massive speakers makes my entire body vibrate. I slide between two girls and suddenly I'm surrounded by bodies. Facial features are only detectable when the neon lights flash. I roll my shoulders and crack my neck, then I start to dance. The music is good, and eventually I start to drift away, focusing only on my movements and the beat. I run my fingers through my hair, messing it up, and lose myself to the music.

CADEN!

What?

Juliet! Go to her now!

I shove my way through the crowd. People scowl at me as I pass.

She's at the back of the gym. With Dyl. Alone. Run!

I finally break out of the mosh and stop beside the food table. I can see her. No, I can see *them*. At the back of the gym, a muscled, naked back is writhing against her. The wings bob up and down as he sucks like a vampire at the spot of skin beneath her ear. She's pressed against the wall. He pulls his mouth away from her glowing white skin and runs his hand through her hair. And then he leans forward and whispers something.

STOP THEM, CADEN!

Their lips touch. She closes her eyes and slides her tongue into his mouth. My blood turns to slushy ice water. Around me the sound and movement of the party continue in slow motion, but all I can see is the two people in the shadow of the bleachers.

Kissing.

Tears fill my eyes.

"Caden?"

I blink rapidly and turn. Natalie and Trevor are walking toward me.

"Oh man," says Trev. "That totally sucks. I'm so sorry, dude."

Natalie reaches to grab my hand. I flinch away. "Are you okay, Caden?"

"Peachy, Natalie. I just . . . I'm going to go."

To get to the exit I have to pass Dyl and Juliet. But all I can think about is the door, so I break away from Natalie and Trevor and head toward the closed double doors. There's a long, empty stretch between me and the exit. Every step feels like it takes an eternity.

I wipe my eyes as I reach the door.

"Caden?"

It's Juliet.

I look at her. She's staring at me from over his bare shoulder. He's not even looking at me; he's still kissing her neck. Why isn't he looking at me? Surely he's thinking about how this would make me feel. All I can see is the rippling movement of his back muscles as he moves his hands up to her face, and the dark strands of his hair. He pulls away from her neck, giving me a glimpse of his face. His mouth is hanging open and his eyelids are drooping slightly.

I wipe my eyes with the back of my hand and swing the door open. Outside is a long corridor. It's empty, and most of the streamers that used to hang from the ceiling have fallen and now lie on the floor. Everything is still.

And the Academy Award goes to Caden Walker! Man, you looked so hurt!

I splutter as the tears turn into a full-on sob.

I am hurt! He was kissing her! I'm dead, Kaylee.

Oh.

I burst through the doors into the crisp night air. Through watery eyes I look up and notice the moon is nearly full, casting a silver glow over the parking lot. Suddenly woozy, I make my way back to the building. There, I press my back against the brick wall and try to take in a deep breath, but all I get is a shuddery gasp.

They picked each other over me.

So I'm going to die.

CHAPTER
NINETEEN

I'M LYING ON MY BED ON TOP OF MY BLANKETS with my hands resting on my stomach, thinking about the two most important kisses of my life. First, the night I kissed Dyl. Second, Dyl kissing Juliet. No matter what I try to do I can't get the images out of my head. My legs are crossed, so my left ankle sits atop my right. Cool fall air is blowing through my open window.

My iPod is resting on my chest. I'm listening to *Hot Fuss*, the album Dyl and I listened to in the car. The songs are all sort of romantic, but they aren't love songs; they're too angry and tinged with sadness for that. Still, I can't help but think that Dyl deliberately picked this album for us to listen to. Did he hear these songs and think of me? Or did he just like it?

One of the songs, called "Andy, You're a Star," is pretty clearly about a crush that the lead singer has on another guy. That song, that inclusion, is the one I can't shake from my mind, and it's the song I've listened to more than any other. Surely Dyl would know the meaning of it. I mean, we kissed, and he seemed to really like it, so there's a pretty decent chance he's a little bit gay or bi. A straight guy couldn't kiss me the way that he did.

Caden, are you awake?

I sit up and pull my earbuds from my ears. How long was Kaylee listening in? Or, more important, what does she now know about me? I should stop spending all my time thinking about Dyl, but it's not like I can control it. If I could get rid of the thoughts, I would. So she probably now knows what I think about him, but I'm not going to be the one who starts *that* conversation. If she wants to talk about it, then I'd have to do it, but for now she seems to be content pretending my feelings don't exist, and that's fine with me.

Yeah, I am.

Good. It's not over yet. Get dressed.

Why? It's done. She kissed him. I'm dead.

Stop being melodramatic—she's not even with him anymore. You can go and talk to her. Oh, and don't wear a jacket. I've made you a set piece. I rigged the top of the lookout, so wait for my instructions and then do everything I say. If you do that, she'll forget about Dyl. Trust me.

I almost laugh. Since when is trusting someone that easy? I turn and glance out my window. Strong wind is pummeling the trees, and the air smells like rain.

I stand up. Dyl isn't giving up. He's still playing this awful game. Even after we kissed, he still wants me to die. After everything he's said to me, every moment we've shared, he hasn't changed his mind. Am I going to let him kill me? No fucking way. If I lose, it'll be because of Juliet. Dyl will *never* outplay me.

I pull on a gray shirt and a pair of skinny chinos. Then socks and my black Chucks. The mud from the walk to the shed is still dried onto the soles. I bang them together to dislodge as much of the muck as possible, then I creep through the house and walk outside. I stop on the sidewalk overlooking the paddock. The cows are on the ground, their heads curled inward. Only one is still upright.

What now, Kaylee? I'll do whatever you need.

Walk all the way down the street. Then up the hill, to the lookout.

I walk on the sidewalk, past the place where we were mugged, until I reach the hill. I climb over the closed gate, ignoring the CLOSED AFTER 6 P.M. sign. A paved pathway cuts through the forest, going straight up the hill. The forest itself is still, just a lot of leafless trees, fallen logs covered in fuzzy green moss, and mountains of brown and yellow mulch. The path up is steep, and my legs start to burn.

When I reach the top, I'm above the town. It stretches out in front of me, glittering golden against the navy sky. A small raised box is embedded in the top of the cliff face: a lookout.

Juliet is leaning against the railing, looking out at the town. She's leaning forward, with her arms bent and her head in her hands.

Tell her you're here. Don't scare her.

"Juliet?"

She spins and looks at me. Her cheeks are glistening, and the tip of her nose is red. She's still wearing her Alice dress, but her feet are bare. I turn away from her and notice her high heels are on the bench. One is upright, the other has fallen onto its side.

"Caden?"

I nod and step up onto the metal platform. The metal mesh dips a little under my weight.

She turns toward me, but her hand remains on the railing. "What are you doing here?"

"I come here when I need to think," I say. "What are you doing?"

She looks back out over the town. I walk over to her and follow her gaze. The town looks much bigger than I thought it was, filled with so many houses. I spot the school. So many things happen there, yet from here, it looks like nothing, just a tiny speck of light. I turn to face Juliet. She's holding her head high, and the wind is making her hair flutter.

"I'm a mess," she says. Her voice is an octave lower than usual. The slightly zany spark that usually lights up her tone is missing. "I told you I'd go out with you and then I kissed Dyl. Who does that? I think he just surprised me. I mean, he's always flirty when he models for me, but I didn't think anything was going to come of it. But tonight he was extra flirty, then he led me to the spot by the bleachers and he kissed me and I kissed him back. Seriously, what's wrong with me? I should've said no."

"Nothing's wrong with you, Juliet."

"But you looked so hurt! I don't want to make anyone feel like that. Especially not you."

I look down, shaking my head. "Don't ever be sorry for making me feel what I feel. That was one sad moment, sure, but you've made me feel so happy countless times. Even if you break my heart it would be worth it. You're special, Juliet, and I know you're going to have boys falling for you your entire life. Don't ever let them make up your mind."

"You're too kind to me," she says. "You know, I was doing fine until you showed up. And then Dyl appeared and everything got so complicated."

You have no idea.

"Do you like him?" I ask. "Dyl, I mean."

"I'm not sure."

"Do you like me?"

"I love you, Caden. I'm just not sure if it's in the way you want me to."

I grip the railing tight. "I want you to feel how you want to feel, Juliet." I drum my fingers against the metal. "So, was he a good kisser? We're friends, remember! I want to talk to you about this stuff."

"It was actually my first kiss, so I don't have anything to compare it to. But yep, it was hugely agreeable. He even tasted good, Caden."

I snort. "What, pray tell, did he taste like?"

"I don't even know—like boy, I guess?"

Caden, I've made you a dinner reservation at a fancy restaurant. Ask her out.

"Oh, Juliet, I decided where we should go on our date. I booked us a table at . . ."

Mario's on the waterfront. Seven-thirty, tomorrow.

I repeat what Kaylee told me.

Juliet smiles super wide. "You still want to go out with me?"

"Of course."

"Oh my God! I thought I'd screwed everything up. I freaking love that place! Seriously, they have this pesto chicken pasta that's pretty much my favorite meal ever." Her eyes narrow. "How did you know?"

"I didn't, I guess I just got lucky. So that's a yes? You'll go out with me?"

"Yes, it's a yes. And Caden, I'm sorry about kissing Dyl. I don't know what I was thinking. I get so swept up in him that I don't feel like myself when I'm around him, you know?"

I know, Juliet. Oh boy, do I know.

"Let's go," she says. "It's freezing up here."

I jump down off the railing. She follows behind me.

She screams. I spin around in time to see her smash into the ground. She's on her back, holding her thigh. Her knee is red and bloody.

Take off your shirt and give it to her.

On the ground, Juliet is whimpering.

You did this to her, Kaylee. My voice sounds angry.

I did. Show her you'll make her feel better when she hurts herself. You'll thank me for this later, Caden.

I pull my shirt off and crouch in front of her.

"Caden, what are you doing? It's freezing."

I look into her eyes, and scrunch my shirt up so it's like a cloth. "I need to stop the bleeding."

She nods, giving me permission, and I press the shirt to her bloody knee. She winces and lets out a hiss. I tie the shirt around her wound, and then place my arm under her knees.

"Grab my neck," I say. "I need to get you out of here."

She loops her arms around my neck. I bend my knees and rise. She's actually quite light.

"I don't know what happened," she says quietly as I begin our descent. "I was fine and then it was like the ground shifted. It was weird, Caden." She leans her head against my bare shoulder. "I'm so lucky you were here."

They did this. They hurt her.

Kiss the top of her head and tell her everything will be okay.

I ignore the voice in my head.

A HARD KNOCK SOUNDS ON MY WINDOW. I SLIDE out of bed and open it. Dyl lingers there, staring at me. It's been a few hours since I last thought about him, as my anger at Kaylee has been brewing within me, consuming all other thoughts. I've punched my pillow so many times it's now limp and lumpy.

"We need to talk," I say as I open the window. "They went too far today. They . . ."

I look at his face.

His eyes are puffy and red. His bottom lip is wobbling. "Caden."

My anger melts away. "Dyl, what's wrong?"

He sniffs and wipes his nose on his jacket sleeve. "Can I come in?"

I look around at my bedroom and realize that no one I care about has ever been in it. I'm suddenly conscious of the smell, which is like me before I go to bed: sweat mixed with my deodorant, and it's tinged with the slightly sour smell of unwashed clothes. What will he think about that? Will he think I'm dirty?

"Yeah, man," I say. "Sure."

He clambers inside. As soon as he's in I pull the window shut. That makes the room seem even smaller, and the air feels warm and cramped, reminding me of the cabin where we kissed. I shove that memory away and push the window open again.

He looks around. "So this is your room."

"It sure is."

He wipes his eyes with his sleeve. "Judy spent the last hour screaming at me. Apparently my kiss wasn't good enough, and Juliet agreed to go out with you. She thinks it's over." He sits down on my bed, which makes the mattress screech. "So I'm officially dead."

I recall how I felt after I saw them kissing, and realize he's probably feeling the same mix of anger, sadness, and self-loathing.

"It's not over yet," I say. "I'm not winning—you've still got just as good a shot as I do." I'm not sure if that's the truth, but it's what he'll want to hear, and I'm willing to lie to make him feel better.

"Don't, Caden. Please, I don't want you to lie to me tonight."

"I'm not lying. It's just a date, Dyl. And she said she enjoyed kissing you. Besides, I know what it's like to kiss you. Trust me, she won't forget about it in a hurry. So it isn't over. You need to keep fighting."

"Why should I? I won't be able to live with myself if I let my only friend die, and the only other option is her choosing you and then I'm dead anyway. I can't win and . . ."

"We've got time, Dyl. This world is our playground until she makes her choice. We can do whatever we want until then. It's not done. Don't give up. I . . . I won't be able to handle it if you give up. You need to hold on."

He gulps. "I'm not sure if I can, Caden."

Silence fills the room.

I sit down beside him. "If you need anything," I say, "just ask."

He crosses his arms. "Well, there is *something* I want. Can I sleep here?"

"What?"

"Not on your bed, just on the floor. I don't want to go back to my house. I hate it there, it's so big and my fake aunt is so terrible. All I want to do is sleep here tonight. Please, Caden. I promise I won't bother you."

Is this fake? My gut tells me it's real. What could he possibly hope to achieve by coming here like this? Being fragile and helpless is never a good strategy. That leaves only one option, one I desperately want to be true: he wants to spend time with me. I walk to my closet, open it, and pull out a pillow and a blanket.

"You can stay," I say. "As long as you don't try anything."

He hugs the blanket and pillow. "Thanks." He places the pillow on the floor. "For a lot of things."

I jump up onto my bed and nestle down. "You're welcome, I guess."

He lies down on the floor. I realize that we're both staring up at the same ceiling, the same one I've stared at countless times.

"I have a question for you," I say, turning my head to the side to look at him. "Why do you like me?"

He faces me. "What?"

"Like, why do you even like spending time with me? You're always coming to my window, but I don't understand why. I just . . . I'm not a Nice, not really anyway, so I don't see why you like spending time with me."

He sits up and crosses his legs. "Are you serious?"

I bob my head up and down.

"God, Caden, you're one of the nicest people I've ever met. It's why I like you so much. Seriously, you're my best friend. Not that that's saying much—I didn't have any real friends at the LIC—but I think that makes what we have even more important to me. Let me be clear on this: you're my first real friend *because* you're nicer to me than everyone else is. So what on earth makes you think you're not a Nice?"

"I told you before, I want to win this game, even though I know what'll happen to you if I win. I can't be a Nice if I think like that. I just can't be."

"Caden, what will happen to me if you win is not your fault. Nor is wanting to win. That's human nature. So you, my good friend, are officially a Nice. End of story. All right?"

"I guess."

He lies back down. "Anyway, we should get to bed; it's getting late. This is weird, but do you mind if I take my shirt off? I can't sleep with it on."

I gulp. "Oh yeah, that's fine."

"Sweet. Night, Caden."

"Night."

He takes his shirt off, then rolls over and, after a couple minutes, falls asleep. I stare at the wall with my body turned away from him.

Caden?

Yeah?

I've seen this happen before. He thinks you'll back away from Juliet out of kindness to him. And then, as soon as you do that, he'll pounce. You need to cut him loose.

I wish I could be that guy. I wish I could be ruthless and sever all connections with him. I wish I could let him die and then continue with my life like nothing had changed.

But that's not who I am.

CHAPTER
TWENTY

I'M STANDING IN FRONT OF MY MIRROR DRESSED in a white shirt and black slacks. The belt around my waist is unclasped, so the ends poke out above my crotch, and the top three buttons of the shirt are undone, showing my smooth chest.

I raise my hands to do up a button and realize they're shaking. I fumble with the button a few times, but my fingers feel puffy and useless.

Awww, look at you, all nervous before your big date. It's sweet. Juliet will like it.

And that's what's making me nervous.

Caden, don't feel guilty now. I'm sure he wouldn't if he were in your position. End it quickly and then let it be done.

I take in a deep breath, which slows the shaking in my hands, then I bring them up and button the last few buttons. I pop my collar and wrap a black tie around it. Once it's done up properly, tied in a perfect full Windsor, I look at myself one last time. I look like a perfect Nice, with flawlessly styled blond hair, dreamy ocean-blue eyes, and a heroic jawline. Even though I've looked like this for a while now, I can't help but be taken aback by how picture perfect I look. The disconnect between the textbook Nice boy staring back at me and the messed-up guy I really am is staggering.

I grab the jacket that's resting on the end of my bed and put it on. The suit is tailored perfectly, making my shoulders look broad and my waist look trim. I fiddle with the knot of the tie, moving it up so it sits right against my Adam's apple. It feels like I'm being choked.

A bouquet of tulips is on the kitchen counter. They're her favorite. Make sure you don't forget them. And Caden, I decided to let you take control of this date. I'll be listening, obviously, and will be there if you have any questions, but you've shown you can handle it on your own. So I'm going to make some popcorn and just watch you do your thing. I'm actually looking forward to it.

Thanks, Kaylee.

Don't sweat it, man. Go crush it out there.

I brush a few wispy golden strands of hair up and away from my forehead. So I'm on my own for this date. This means if I screw it up it's my fault. Also, if it goes well and Juliet starts to fall for me, I'm the one responsible for what happens afterward.

Can I do something that could kill Dyl? I'm not sure I can anymore. Not without destroying all the parts of me I like. I miss the old me. He would've breezed through this date and celebrated as Dyl was marched away by a Stalker. Stupid feelings, making me all soft.

I push the tie up farther. I'll go on the date. It's what Dyl would do if he were in my situation, so he'll understand. That said, I won't aggressively go for her heart, I'll just act the same way I always do around her. The date will still be a win for me, but not so drastic a win that she forgets about Dyl entirely. That's the best I can do for him.

I leave the room. In the kitchen, M is staring at a vase filled with pink flowers.

"They're lovely," she says, looking at the flowers, not at me. She runs her fingers along one of the petals, gently brushing it. "So they're obviously not for my benefit."

I pause in the doorway to the kitchen. "No, they aren't. But I can probably get you some if you want."

She laughs a soft laugh, and pulls a single flower from the bunch and presses it to her nose.

"That's a very nice offer," she says as she makes her way back to the TV. "But that's not what I want."

She's staring at the TV now, so I know she won't respond. I scoop up the bouquet; a thin stream of water drops from the green stems. Once the stream turns to a trickle, I pull them out of the vase and walk toward the door.

"Good luck," says M. "Don't end up like me."

I stop in the middle of the doorway and look at her. But I can't think of anything to say to that, so I duck outside and walk to the truck. I swing the door open and gently lay the flowers on the passenger seat.

––––––––––––

THE DRIVE ACROSS TOWN IS UNEVENTFUL. Once I reach Juliet's house, I park and walk up to the door. I knock on it once. I pull my fist back to knock again and the door swings open.

Richard is standing in the doorway, dressed in a navy suit over a pressed sky-blue button-down and a black skinny tie. His hair has been combed and his posture is more upright than it usually is, like wearing fancy clothes has increased his confidence.

He smiles warmly. His teeth are slightly yellowed in the way a lot of men's his age are, probably from drinking too much coffee. "Caden," he says, stepping aside to let me in. As I pass him he claps me on the shoulder. "Where did you get that suit? It's stunning!"

"Honestly, I can't remember. Are you going somewhere?"

Daphne steps down from the staircase. She's wearing a gold dress and is clutching a white leather purse with a gold clasp. Her makeup is impeccable and her nails are covered in shiny red nail polish.

"Caden," she says, grabbing me by the biceps and placing a dry kiss on my cheek. "You look so handsome. I'm sorry, but we have to run. We've got our own reservations at George's. I think Juliet's in the shed."

She walks past me and then, together, they leave. I watch as they cross the yard to their car, a silver Mercedes convertible, and Richard opens the door for her. Hoisting up the hem of her dress, she steps inside. The sight makes me smile.

I realize I'm being weird, so I turn and walk through the empty house to the shed, rubbing my cheek with my sleeve as I walk. Inside, I can hear metal scraping against metal. It smells like burning rubber and acidic smoke. I pound my knuckles on the metal door, which makes a dull thud, but the sound of the machines continues.

I open the door.

"Hello?"

Juliet is behind a bench, partially hidden by a variety of scientific contraptions I have no hope of identifying. She's got on a plain gray T-shirt and she's wearing plastic goggles that make her eyes look absolutely massive. Her hands are stained with grease. She lowers the small drill she was holding and the sounds stop, making the entire shed eerily silent.

"Goggles," she says, pointing a finger. She's holding a bunch of black wires, peering intently at the exposed ends. I turn in the direction she pointed and find a shelf filled with goggles. I grab a pair, put them on, then walk over to her and offer the flowers.

"I got these for you," I say. "It seems dumb now, I should've gotten you something you actually like, but . . ."

"They're beautiful, Caden. But you're early," she says. "Too eager, huh? Too excited to try the pesto chicken?"

I shake my head. "Nope, I'm on time." I show her my phone, which is displaying the time. Her face drops.

"You're joking, right? You moved it forward or something."

"What's that old saying? About flying time?"

She drops the wires. I notice it's the Bolt Gloves. Only now they're darker, almost black, and the base mechanism is bigger.

I gesture toward them. "Bolt Gloves, right?"

She nods and pulls off her goggles. "Ever since the attack I've been perfecting them. But shit, that doesn't matter right now. Caden, come with me, I need to . . ." She looks at her grease-covered hands. ". . . shower and, oh God, I'm so sorry, I can't believe I lost track of time."

I laugh. "Juliet, it's fine. Take your time."

I want to ask her about her leg, to see if she's okay, but she was already pretty weirded out by the fact that she fell and I don't want to draw attention to the set piece. It's odd, I genuinely want to do something nice, but my ties to the LIC are preventing me from doing so. Instead, I take off my goggles and put them back on the shelf. Then we walk to the house.

As we step inside she says, "I bet you've never had this problem, huh? Never dated a girl as unorganized as me."

Sorry, Caden, I know I said I would let you do this but I can't help myself. Make sure you tell her you haven't dated anyone. It'll make her feel special. Okay, I'm shutting up now.

We walk inside and stop beside her bedroom door.

I scratch the back of my neck. "Um, this is kind of weird to admit, but this is my first date. I guess I just never met anyone I liked enough. Until now."

"Huh," she says as she steps into her bedroom. She grabs a white bra and a pair of underwear from her chest of drawers. I blush and stare at the floor. She passes me, and she smells like burning hair. "I'll be, like, five minutes. You can wait in the living room if you'd like. Okay, I'm going to stop talking now because I've made us late enough as it is."

She ducks into the bathroom. I lean against the wall, the back of my head resting against the cold plaster, my shoes sinking into the carpet. I'm about to go on a date with my Chosen. It's strange, because I must've thought about this moment almost every night before I fell asleep while I was at the LIC. Back then, I imagined it would be straightforward: I'd play my role, she'd fall for me, and that would be it. I never imagined that I would feel bad for my Chosen, or that I would be this worried about what will happen to my rival if I win.

It's my first date, so I should be nervous and excited, but right now all I feel is sorry for her. She's in there, getting ready for a date with a boy who she thinks likes her. What she gets is me, liar extraordinaire. And, if things go my way, she'll spend the rest of her life with me. She'll never get a real date or a real partner. She deserves one, but I have to take that from her if I want to live.

When she steps out, she's put on makeup, so her skin glows. Her eyelashes have been extended using some sort of bottled trickery, and it looks fantastic. She's wearing a navy dress dotted with specks of silver and different-colored circles. No, not circles. Planets. The specks of silver are stars.

She's wearing a space dress.

It's the best piece of clothing I've ever seen. It's cute and kind of funny, and it makes me ache more than ever for the future I'm taking from her.

"Ready to go?" she asks.

I keep staring at her.

"Caden, what's going on?"

I look down at her feet. She's wearing black high heels with thin straps that wrap around her ankles. I meet her eyes.

"You look beautiful, Juliet."

I mean it.

She blushes. "Thanks. And you look nice as well, Caden. Very suave. Should we go?"

I nod, and we walk through the house to the carport, where a gold Mazda is waiting for us. She opens the door and we climb in. The passenger seat is pushed right to the front of the car, leaving no leg room. I pull on a small lever beneath the seat and it slides backward.

She turns on the engine. "Dad bought this for the family so I would learn to drive a manual," she says. "Only he didn't ask if I wanted to learn a manual, which I don't. So I'm sorry if the ride is a bit bumpy."

I'm sorry about interrupting again, Caden, but you should definitely ask her about her family. It'll—

Kaylee, do you seriously think I don't know that? I've got this.

Fine! I'll stop.

"How are you and your dad getting along?"

She rolls her eyes as we pull out of the carport. "There's always friction. Anytime one of us speaks we annoy the other. I know it drives us both up the wall but we can't stop it."

"You're too similar, I guess."

"Ouch. But you're probably right. What about your parents? Do you get along with them?"

I think of M, and the deep indent she's left on the couch. And D, the great bear of a man who always reeks of alcohol. Then I think of the big blank space that is my real parents.

"I dunno. They kind of do their own thing. I'm just sort of there."

"I find that hard to believe—they've got you, the poster child of manners and charm, and they don't care?"

"Not really."

"Well, screw that. And screw them. I think you're great."

She flicks on the turn signal and pulls to the curb in front of a bustling restaurant. Out the front is a small balcony. Lights have been wrapped around the railing, and they glow in the fading sunlight. Inside, people sit at the tables eating large plates of Italian food. Waiters dressed in black duck and dive between the tables, carrying plates of food or removing dirty dishes. I breathe in through my nostrils. It smells like parmesan cheese, tomatoes, and garlic.

We get out of the car and walk to the front of the restaurant, where a girl with shiny brown hair pulled back into a tight ponytail smiles at us. She's dressed in a black dress shirt and a loose skirt.

"Hello," she says. Her accent is distinct yet unfamiliar, clearly from some European country. Maybe Sweden? She's staring at me expectantly. "Do you have a reservation?"

"Yeah, we do. Under Walker."

She checks a black folder. Her eyes scan the page for a second, then they light up. "Ah yes, Mr. and Mrs. Walker, what a pleasure, may I take you to your table?"

"We aren't married," says Juliet. "We're seventeen."

"Oh. My apologies. You seem to be very fond of each other; it radiates from you. It's a beautiful thing. Let me take you to your table."

We're led through the restaurant to a wooden balcony. We pass through rows of occupied tables to one that's positioned in the very corner.

The waitress places two clipboards down in front of us. "You're lucky," she says as she pulls a lighter from her pocket and lights a circular candle in the middle of the table. "This is the best table in the restaurant. It's usually booked for months, but there was a cancellation this afternoon. I was told to give it to the cutest couple I saw. I chose the two of you." She smiles, then walks away.

We sit down. I realize that we're up fairly high, overlooking the river. The lights from the restaurant are reflected as golden spheres in the black water. The table closest to us is occupied by a family of four. The youngest, a girl with curly yellow hair, is using her hands to reorganize the spaghetti on her plate into some sort of artwork. Her small face is smeared with tomato, and she's grinning, which makes me smile.

I pick up the clipboard. Attached to the front of it in fancy golden paper is the menu.

"Get the chicken," says Juliet. She's staring at the menu, and her hair has fallen over her face in the way it always does when she looks down. "Trust me, you won't regret it." She laughs a slow laugh. "God, look at me bossing you around, Caden. Choose what you want, ignore me; I'm obviously a control freak."

I place the menu down in front of me and rest my hands on top of it. The flame of the candle between us flickers. It smells like vanilla.

"The chicken sounds lovely."

She mimics my movement and meets my eyes. Her long, thin hands rest on the paper. She's obviously scrubbed her hands, but still, a faint trace of black grime is apparent on the top of them. Her nails are chipped and jagged.

She flips the menu over and looks at the back. "So we've decided? Ugh, now we have to wait ten minutes until she comes back so we can order."

"Yeah, I wish there was a button or something I could press that would tell her we're ready. Because, like, most of the time I don't care about browsing the menu, I know what I want."

"I know, right? But it feels sort of rude to not look at it, so a lot of the time I pretend to read it in case they're watching. I imagine some poor chef looking out from the kitchen who has spent hours devising the perfect dish only for people to ignore it because they know what they want and never question that or try something new. It must be heartbreaking."

I look over at the kitchen. A big man in a chef's uniform is barking orders at a boy dressed in black. The boy's shoulders are hunched, and his eyes are semiclosed, almost like he's wincing. It's like, *Please-don't-talk-to-me-and-let-me-do-my-job*. The chef barks one last thing, and then the waiter sprints out of the kitchen carrying two steaming plates of pasta.

I look back at the chef. My heart does not break for him.

"So how is Starbucks going?"

"It's all right. It's part of my routine now, I barely even notice it. I feel bad, though, because Levi is such a nice guy, but the store is always pretty quiet. He thinks he's going to get fired. It's the only Starbucks on the planet that isn't always crowded."

"That's a shame. The coffee is great there, everyone knows it, but it's a small town and there aren't many people here who want to spend five dollars on coffee no matter how nice it is. We're instant-coffee types here, if you hadn't realized."

"That's kind of sweet, actually."

"Sweet in the boy kind of way or in the girl kind of way? Like, is it awesome or is it cute?"

"Both."

She laughs, tilting her head back. The waitress returns.

"Ready to order?" she asks, placing a water carafe and two glasses on the table.

"Pesto chicken fettuccini," I say.

"Me too," says Juliet. "But it was my idea, not his. Just so you know."

The waitress ignores her and quickly grabs our menus. "Great choices! That'll be out in a sec."

Juliet breathes in contentedly, and her eyelids dip slightly. "All right, question two. What's your favorite food? I know that seems like a random question, but we just ordered mine, and I'm curious about yours."

I think it over, then decide to be honest.

"Blueberries," I say.

She leans forward. "Like, just blueberries?"

I blush. "Yeah."

I'll never be able to explain this to her, but there's a reason blueberries are my favorite. They're the closest thing to candy that was allowed at the LIC, so I always ate as many of them as I could whenever they were available. Even now, they're my go-to whenever I feel like something sweet.

"I think they're delicious," I say. "And they're good for you, so I don't feel bad eating them. It's a win-win."

She narrows her eyes. "Huh. Well, now I know more about you, Caden, so this evening has already been a success. Now we should talk about the weather or something, right? I'm pretty sure that's what normal people do on dates."

"Why would I want to be normal? Normal is boring. I want to know about your inventions."

She shuffles forward in her seat. "Really? Most people's eyes glaze over when I start talking about anything even remotely related to science. I've learned to avoid it as a conversation topic."

"I'm genuinely interested, Juliet."

"Well, if you want to know, I'm guessing you want to hear

about stuff like the Bolt Gloves, right? Stuff that can blow things up or hurt people."

"You know me too well!"

"You're such a boy. So, well, I'm working on this suit that's inspired by Black Widow. You know, from the Avengers? She can do all these spinning kicks and stuff because she's got full range of movement, right? Well, I started thinking about how awesome it would be if it was real. Like, to have a suit that would let someone move as much as her, yet made sure they were fully protected from bullets. So I've been working on that a lot, and it's almost done. Natalie's been helping me with it, actually, as a body model. But she still won't let me shoot her when she's wearing it for some reason. I guess she doesn't trust me."

"That sounds so cool! But if you're going to make a suit based on one of the Avengers, you really should go with Iron Man."

She chuckles. "My family does okay, but we're not *billionaires*. Oh, and there's this other thing I'm working on that's pretty cool. I know you're going to judge me for this name, but I'm a scientist, not an advertiser. Anyway, I call them Black Hole Bombs. It works like a grenade, only the explosion can be perfectly timed and contained. I'm trying to make it nonlethal, but at the moment it's so strong it can vaporize pretty much anything instantly. The explosion they make looks sorta like a black hole, hence the name. I'll have to take you out into a paddock one day and show them off. They're pretty cool."

"That sounds awesome."

We chat about our favorite movies until the waitress returns holding two steaming plates. She places the first down in front of me. It's a sliced chicken breast with crispy golden skin over a pile of green sauce and a bed of fresh, glistening fettuccini. I grab my fork and stab it into the chicken. I cut off a small piece and then bite down. The chicken is tender and moist, and the sauce is creamy, salty, and slightly nutty.

"Oh God," I say. "This is the best thing I've ever had in my mouth."

Her mouth is also full. She swallows. "Right? You're welcome. You're *also* welcome that I didn't make a sexual joke just then. But that's the only time tonight I'm going to let you off that easy. Set me up like that again, Caden, and I'm going to have to go for a punch line. And trust me, it's going to be glorious."

We eat in silence, but it's not awkward; it's very clear it's because the meal is delicious. Once I'm halfway through my dish I look up at her. She's cutting into a piece of chicken.

"Hey, I've got a question for you."

She swallows and wipes her mouth, even though there was no food on it. "Shoot."

"Why do you like me?"

I recall how I felt when I asked Dyl the same question. That time, the whole world seemed to fade away as I waited for his response. Right now all I can think about is the fact that her answer will never mean as much to me as Dyl's did. He's already answered that question correctly, so she doesn't stand a chance.

Her right eyebrow arches. "That's a loaded question for a first date, isn't it?"

"Sorry. You don't have to answer it if you don't want to."

"No, it's cool. I guess it's a lot of things. I know this sounds superficial, but there's something about your face that I like. Maybe it's your eyes, because they remind me of the ocean, or maybe it's how you always look at everyone in such a friendly way, like you care about them even if you know nothing about them. I like how the way you look at me is different from the way you look at everyone else, because it makes me feel special. And I like your hair, especially how it's always kinda messy but looks good, and I'd be lying if I didn't mention your body, because it's freaking ridiculous. But the thing I like the most about you is how you make me feel. You make me happy every time I see you. Even when you're not around, I think of you and I smile. Is that enough for you?"

It would be, if Dyl didn't exist.

"It definitely is."

"Great. Now let's finish eating. It's not as good when it gets cold."

We finish our meals. Despite her objections, I pay, and then she drives me to my place. She parks in front of my house, then we walk to my porch. Once we're there, she stands facing me, swaying slightly, her hands clasped in front of her.

"That was so much fun," I say. "We have to do it again."

"Definitely."

I'm watching her body language. She leans forward and shifts her feet so they point at me, which is good, but her hands are still clasped together. At the LIC I was taught what both of these separate actions mean, but they never told me what both of them *together* is signaling.

It's too risky to go in for a full-on kiss, so I step forward and kiss her on the cheek.

"Really, Juliet," I say. "I want to do that with you for the rest of my life."

"Whoa, slow down. It was a first date. We aren't getting married or anything."

"You're right. Well, I'll see you tomorrow, I guess."

"That you will."

She turns and walks away.

"Oh, and Caden," she calls as I reach the front door. I turn and look over my shoulder. "Next time, give me a proper kiss."

She opens the door to her car and climbs in. Smiling, I step inside the house. It's dark, the only light coming from the TV. M is asleep in front of it. D's snores are soft down here, but the fact that I can hear them even this far away means they'll be booming upstairs. I close the door and lean against it, the events of the date replaying in my mind. The way she smiled. The taste of the food. Her weird yet still funny jokes. The softness of her cheek when I kissed her.

How'd I do, Kaylee?

She likes you a lot. It's almost over, Caden. You did really well.

Suddenly Dyl is all I can think about. His laugh. His eyes. Him, in his entirety.

Kaylee said I did well.

So why does it feel like I failed?

CHAPTER
TWENTY-ONE

AS SOON AS I STEP OFF THE BUS, I SEE NATALIE and Trevor waiting for me by the school gate. I wave and make my way over to them. It's a warm, windy day, and orange leaves are tumbling across the parking lot. I didn't sleep much the past two nights, so my head is fuzzy and my body feels lifeless. Unfortunately, my exhaustion doesn't mean anything to the LIC, so I need to think of a way to wake myself up before I answer a question incorrectly or do something out of character. Being Nice is always difficult, but it's almost impossible when everything is annoying and all I want to do is sleep.

As soon as I'm within earshot they lean forward.

"So," says Trevor. "We need details."

"We do!" chimes Natalie. "Start from the beginning. What were you wearing? I was expecting a Snapchat but Juliet never sent me one. Quick, Juliet will be here any minute and I need the details from you before she tells me what *really* happened."

"Okay, um, I was wearing a suit. White shirt, black pants. Leather shoes."

Natalie grins. "Very traditional. I like it."

"Is that specific enough for this postmortem?"

Trevor looks like I hit him. "*Mortem*? God, it wasn't *that* bad, was it?"

"No! It's an expression. The date was nice. We talked for a while and ate delicious food and then I paid and that was it. I think she likes me. My only worry is that I came on a little too strong."

Natalie closes her eyes and then slowly opens them. Her eyelashes are long and full, yet they don't have the obvious tar-like consistency of mascara. Her eyes also aren't brown—well, technically they are, but they're brighter than most, almost the color of almonds. She really is unnaturally pretty.

She clicks her fingers at me. "Why are you looking at me like that, Caden?"

"Sorry, I was lost in thought."

"Well, don't go falling for me. Not only because Trevor would murder you if you even thought about touching me, but because I think Juliet seriously likes you. Wait, here she comes now, I guess we're outta time." She points, and I see Juliet pulling up in her gold Mazda. "Oh, and don't forget, it's nationals tonight. Do you still want to come? Trevor would never admit it, but he thinks you're a good luck charm. It'd mean a lot to him if you came."

Trevor grins. "I'll happily admit that! You're my friend, Caden, and it would be awesome if you came. Also, if watching a stunningly handsome swimmer break a world record isn't a draw for you, Juliet will be there. So it could be your second date!"

"Sounds great!" I say.

Juliet closes her car door and starts jogging over to us.

And I see the truck. It's an orange pickup, sort of like mine, and it's cutting right through the lot, heading right toward her. And it's not slowing down. The driver is some kid who is screaming and he isn't even holding the steering wheel—he's slapping it like that'll do something. *Oh God, it's going so fast, it's going to hit her!*

I go to cry her name and someone hits my shoulder and I spin, then fall to my knees. On the ground, I look up just in time to see Dyl take a running dive at Juliet. He grabs her and tucks her against his body. The two fly out of the way just as the pickup speeds past. It bounces over the sidewalk, then hits the school fence hard enough to bend the metal.

Holy fucking shit, did that just happen?

Natalie's hands are clasped to her mouth, and Trevor is slack-jawed.

"What the fuck," says Trevor. "What the actual fuck."

The pickup driver clambers out to be greeted by a bunch of students who flocked over because of the noise. He's crying, and he has some blood on his face, but he's definitely up and moving, which is the important thing.

Dyl and Juliet are on the ground, with Juliet lying on his chest. They're looking into each other's eyes. He raises his hand and brushes a strand of hair out of her face.

Oh.

That's what just happened. It was a set piece.

I make my way over to them, but when I reach them they don't even react. Dyl brushes a tear off Juliet's cheek with his thumb and asks her, "Are you okay?"

She nods, then pushes herself up off his chest and stands on shaking legs. "Yep. Yeah. I'm super."

He rises quickly, then offers his hand to her. "Come with me. I've wanted to show you something for a while, and now's the perfect time. It'll help, trust me."

She nods slowly and takes his hand.

———————

JULIET AND I ARE LEANING AGAINST THE FENCE that surrounds the school, waiting for our lift to nationals. Trev's dad, who is also his coach, has organized a limo to take us all to the stadium.

I'm glad school is over, because after the crash, classes were canceled so that everyone at the scene could get counseling. My counselor kept trying to get me to calm down, telling me that accidents are a part of life, and that I should be *so* grateful no one was seriously hurt. She's clearly good at her job, but her attempts to help me process what happened didn't work at all because I know no one was ever in danger. Well, except maybe me, because Dyl's play was such a big success. I couldn't even think about explaining that to her, though.

On top of that, I can't stop thinking about Dyl and Juliet talking in private after the set piece. I've been trying to keep my mouth shut, but it's only a matter of time before I crack and ask Juliet about it. It's an itch I have to scratch.

I shouldn't ask.

But I *really* want to.

I crack. "Where did you go?"

Juliet turns to me. "Huh?"

I cross my arms. "With Dyl, after, you know. Where'd you go with him?"

Caden, calm down; that's none of your business and you're coming across like you're jealous.

Juliet sighs. "Nowhere, honestly. It was nothing, Caden. I was, well, I was so grateful to him for saving me, I went along with it. I mean, you saw him—he was like a freaking superhero. Once the adrenaline wore off I realized how weird it must've looked. And I'm sorry about that. But how do you turn down an offer from the person who just saved your life?"

But he didn't save you. All he did was lie.

"It's no problem, Juliet, it was a scary situation and you dealt with it really well. I have no idea how I'd deal if that happened to me."

"Caden, if it's all right with you, I'd like to stop talking about it now. Honestly, I'm weirdly fine about it. Sure, it was scary, but it's also not that big a deal, and I don't want to let it ruin tonight. Is that okay?"

Is it okay? Not really. I want to pick at this thread to expose Dyl for the liar that he is. It's way too risky, though, as by exposing him I could reveal myself. Then we'd both be killed, and all my stress would've been for nothing.

I mimic zipping my mouth shut as a white limo pulls up to the curb and parks right in front of us. The tires crunch the gravel. Natalie clambers out in sky-high silver heels and a tight sparkly dress. Her hair and makeup are perfectly done. Juliet and I are both still wearing our school uniforms.

"Oh crap, was this supposed to be formal?" asks Juliet.

"Hello!" says Natalie. "It's only the moment that could shape the rest of Trevor's life! But there's obviously no helping you two, and I'm too stressed to care about you being underdressed."

She closes her eyes and breathes in through her nostrils like she's meditating. "Okay. You're about to enter a no-negativity space, all right? I'm a mess, and Trev's pretty nervous as it is, so please be nice to him. Make him doubt himself and I'll throw you out of the limo."

The limo window slides down, revealing Trevor. His hair has been buzzed super short, so much so that I can see pale scalp beneath his dark hair. He leans forward and pokes his head out of the window. "Hey babe, you know I can hear you, right? And you don't need to threaten them, I'm fine. My headspace is golden."

Natalie sulks back to the limo with her shoulders sagging. Juliet and I follow her. Inside, it looks a lot like the limo that first took me away from the LIC. Leather seats, strips of blue light on the ceiling. Trevor sits wedged between Natalie and a man who looks exactly the way Trevor will in twenty years. They have the same friendly twinkle in their deep-set brown eyes and the same broad shoulders.

"Hey," says the man who looks like Trevor. "I'm Donnie, Trev's dad."

He offers his hand. I notice that his muscular body is covered in an obviously homemade green shirt with the words TEAM TREV written across the chest.

"Caden," I say as we shake.

He turns away, signaling the end of the conversation. I turn to Trevor, who is staring at me.

"Hey," I say.

He drums his hands on his calves and exhales. His hands are shaking. "Hi, Caden."

I have a strange realization: I want him to do well. We only met because I'm fake, but my friendship with him is real. I care about him and I genuinely want him to achieve his goal.

"Good luck today, man."

"Thanks."

"Okay," calls Natalie. "No more talking. I'm too worried someone will say something that'll make him nervous. So let's listen to music."

She presses a button on her iPhone and an upbeat electronic song starts to play. I recognize the tune, but can't for the life of me figure out who the artist is.

The stadium is just over two hours away, and the drive ticks by slowly. I spend it staring out the window, thinking about Dyl. No one is allowed to talk, so the only real distraction is Natalie's playlist, which, thankfully, is pretty great.

Once we reach the stadium, the five of us climb out. People bustle around us, moving in both directions up and down the street, ignoring us. The stadium is illuminated by massive columns of white light from spotlights anchored to the floor. We walk up to the front counter, where a short man is trapped inside a smudged box made of thick clear plastic. His expression, which looks alarmingly like the disappointed emoji personified, doesn't change when we reach him.

"Hi," says Trevor. "I'm competing. Like, today, I'm going to swim."

"Tickets and ID, please."

I pause, because I don't have a ticket. Suddenly I'm worried that I should have one and it's going to be really embarrassing to admit that I don't. Thankfully, Trev's dad steps forward and slides a piece of paper into the slot in the plastic.

After we produce our student IDs, the disappointed pool employee hands Trev's dad a bunch of tickets and we walk inside. The room smells like chlorine. People are rushing about everywhere, buying snacks, heading to their seats, taking photos. The whole place is buzzing.

"This is it," says Trevor. Behind him is a long hallway. A bunch of guys carrying duffel bags are walking down it toward a set of navy double doors. I assume it's the professional version of the sign-in area from the school swim meet.

"We'll scream super loud," says Juliet.

"Go crush them," I say.

"Thanks, you guys."

Natalie leaps into his arms, pressing her body hard against him, and places a kiss on his open lips. Donnie makes a show of looking away, but he's smiling.

"You can do this, babe."

"Thanks, babe."

Juliet and I glance at each other. She smirks but doesn't say anything. Nat and Trev separate, then he and his dad head toward the lockers.

The rest of us go in the opposite direction, up to the bleachers. Our assigned seats are in the very back row, giving us a freaking fantastic view of the entire pool. The tiles are sky blue and the water is clear. Above the pool are triangular red and yellow streamers. In the very corner of the room is a large screen that shows a bigger version of the events happening in front of me. It cuts to commentators, one male and one female, who are sitting in a booth. I had no idea this was televised, and for some reason that makes it seem so much bigger and therefore scarier. The stadium is already almost full, which really adds to the intensity level. I don't know what I was expecting, but this is obviously a huge frigging deal, and it feels kind of weird that someone I know is such a big part of it.

A horn blares, and a bunch of muscular girls in one-piece bathing suits step up to the starting blocks. A few of them swing their arms, others fiddle with their goggles or swimming caps.

"He's already got a good time," says Natalie, more to herself than to anyone else. "He doesn't need to win. He just needs a good time."

Juliet places her hand on Natalie's thigh. "He will win, though, right?"

"I hope so."

A horn blares and the girls dive into the pool. They slide into the water making only tiny ripples. I scratch my chest, remembering how red it was after I dived in during the school's swim meet.

"My boyfriend is out there," says Natalie. "He could be a star by the end of the night. He'll be on TV and everything. It feels like he's doing what he was made to do, you know? Living his destiny."

"Lucky him," I say.

"You'll get there one day, Caden. I can tell. You have a destiny."

I look out at all the faces in the crowd. How many of them have accepted that they can't have everything they want? Not many, I'd guess. "The problem is that everyone feels that way."

Natalie purses her lips.

Juliet is staring out at the pool. "It's so weird," she says. "This whole world exists and I wouldn't even know about it if I didn't know Trevor. It's like the world is full of all these little worlds that only matter to some people. It's kinda nice, but kinda exclusive in a bad way. I'm not sure how much I like it."

"You're getting a bit existential, aren't you?"

"Yeah, watching one of my oldest friends live his biggest, craziest dream is having that effect on me. People always forget but, of our group, Trev and I have known each other the longest. You and Natalie came later. Trev's been the most stable person in my whole life. And I'm so damn proud of him." She leans closer to me, her voice almost a shout so that I can hear it over the sound of the crowd. "Hey, I want to tell you about something."

"What is it?"

"So, Dyl is having a party at his place to celebrate the end of the semester. And he doesn't want you to come."

"I can't say I'm shocked."

"Well, screw him. I'm inviting you. I want you to come to the party with me."

The speed of my heartbeat doubles and my stomach clenches. "Really?"

The lights of the stadium make her dark hair shine. Her eyes don't leave mine. "Really. I want you there with me."

Is three dates enough for the LIC? Are they preparing the Stalker right now?

"Then I'll be there."

After about two hours, Natalie leaps to her feet and screams. "Oh my God!" she says, looking at Juliet. "He's there! He's there!"

She points down at the pool. A line of eerily similar-looking guys walk out to the pool. Trevor is third from the right, and he's wearing a silver warm-up suit. He unzips the jacket, then takes it off and puts it in his bag.

I count the competitors. There are eight of them. Trevor is jumping up and down, his arms slack against his body.

"This is it," whispers Natalie. "Everything has led to this."

A horn blares, and the boys step onto the blocks. Trev crouches.

3.

2.

1.

The horn blares again. Trevor dives forward, his arms out in front of him, his body stretched out.

"That was a good dive," says Juliet.

"Swim, you beautiful boy!" screams Natalie.

I scream with them. In the pool, it seems like everyone is level. The crowd screams and cheers. I cup my hands to my mouth and shout Trevor's name. The wall is coming up. *Go, Trev, go!* They all touch the wall. I turn to the screen to see Trevor lift his head up out of the water.

The camera is focusing on him.

"He won!" screams Natalie. "Oh my God, he broke twenty-three!"

I look at his time, which is being displayed in big white numbers on the screen: 22.89.

She tilts her head down and smiles. "My boy did it."

We clap and cheer along with everyone else as the competitors climb out of the pool. Trevor looks up at the crowd, his dark eyes flitting from left to right. We wave, but his eyes move right by us. He obviously can't make us out from all the faces in the crowd, but he keeps scanning, looking for us, which makes me grin.

A woman in a tight jacket and an even tighter skirt waddles up to Trevor. She waves a black microphone in front of her face as a cameraman crouches in front of them. "Congratulations," she says. "Do you realize what just happened?"

The pair of them are on the screen, with Trevor as the focal point. On screen, he somehow looks different. His eyes are clearer and his muscles are more pronounced. His massive chest is covered in droplets of water. He looks like a bona fide superstar.

He runs his fingers through his hair, shaking off the water. "No, not really."

The reporter clamps her hand down on his shoulder. Her fingernails dig into his muscle. Trev smiles a wide, slightly goofy smile.

"You, young man, just scored a time six-tenths of a second under the previous trials' cutoff. So I think it's safe to say that you, Trevor Flagg, are going to compete in the Olympic trials!"

Trev's smile grows wider, and his eyes light up. "Wow, I mean, I can't even . . . Wow. That's huge. I did it? Oh wow, I actually did it!"

The reporter turns away. "And that, viewers, is the face of an extraordinary young man's dreams coming true. Remember the name Trevor Flagg: he will be a champion soon!"

A dangerous feeling fills me. If Trev can achieve his biggest, craziest dream, what's stopping me from doing the same? Why can't I find a way to stay alive *and* make sure they don't kill Dyl?

I grit my teeth. These thoughts are pointless and make me hate myself for thinking them. I'm not Trevor. He's free, and I'm a Love Interest. We aren't the same. Only a moron would compare us.

"He's done it," says Natalie. "He's done it."

For some reason, her smile fades. Her teeth sink into her lips and she can't seem to stop staring at Trevor. I go to ask her what's wrong, but she catches me looking and shakes it off, the smile returning to her face.

CHAPTER
TWENTY-TWO

MY PHONE VIBRATES, MAKING A SOUND LIKE AN angry wasp. I reach out and grab it from under my pillow. It's a text from Juliet.

Panic stations. I repeat, panic stations. Come to the park in front of the library. We're here.

I go to type a response and my phone vibrates again.

Actually, no. Go to Trev's place. Try to talk some sense into him.

I swing my legs over the side of my bed and sit up. I call her. It rings twice, then she picks up. "Hello?"

"Hey, it's Caden. What's up?"

"Trev broke up with Natalie. She keeps saying she's going to kill herself, and I don't think she's being dramatic. Actually, I need to get back to her, to make sure she doesn't do something dumb. Talk to Trev. Fix this."

My mouth drops open. "Ummm, oh, okay. I'll do it. Text me his address."

I pull on the closest clothes, a pair of black jeans and a red hoodie, then run out of the house to my truck. The idea of driving makes my hands shake, but I don't have a choice. Using the GPS app on my phone for directions, I drive toward Trevor's place. As I drive, I think about my approach to this situation. How do I stay in character when Trevor is doing something that's so out of his? I can tell being a Nice in front of him is going to be almost impossible. I just don't have it in me to do anything other than be brutally honest with a friend who is making a dense, life-ruining decision.

Once I reach the house I park and run up to the front door. It's a small, squat building. The cream-colored walls are faded. I knock on the screen door.

Trev's dad answers it.

He eyes me warily. "Caden, right?"

"Yeah, is Trev here? Can I speak to him?"

"He's in the gym. I'll show you."

He walks me through the house to a set of glass double doors that open onto an orange-tiled patio with an old treadmill and a set of weights. Beyond the equipment is a lap pool. Trev is standing beside the weight machine holding a dumbbell. He's wearing a navy jersey and basketball shorts. The shirt is darkened from his neck to the middle of his chest.

He raises the weight, wincing as he moves. I dig my fingernails into my palms.

"Hey, Caden," he says. "Did Nat send you?"

"Juliet, actually."

"Figures. How's Nat holding up?"

"Do you want me to lie?"

He passes the weight to his other hand and lifts it. "Kinda."

"Well, I'm not going to. She's not doing that well, man. She might even be suicidal."

He raises the weight again.

My eyes narrow. "She was your world, man. Why did you do this? It doesn't make any sense."

He places the weight down on the shelf. The metal screeches.

"Love is complicated, Caden. More than anything, that's what it is."

"Not with you and Natalie. You're so perfect together, everyone is jealous. Fine, I'll say it. *I* was jealous of you. I want so badly to have what you had. And you just threw it away? Why?"

He finally meets my eyes. His eyes are bloodshot. "I cheated on her, man. And breaking up with her was easier than dealing. It's hell, but it's easier."

It hits me like a punch to the gut, and all the energy leaves my body. I lean against the wall to stay upright. "Whoa, um, okay. What happened?"

"Did you see that reporter from last night? The hot one? She came for me in the locker room. I was so excited about everything and she made these sultry eyes at me. And then she invited me to the bathroom and she kept making those eyes at me, like I was the man I want to be eventually, but it was like I was him in that moment. Like I was already successful and famous. I think she could tell what I wanted, so she grabbed me and led me into the bathroom and she got on her knees and pulled my pants down and I . . . I didn't stop her. Natalie had never done *that* for me; she thought it was gross. So I leaned back and closed my eyes and . . ."

His enormous chest heaves in a sob. He raises his hands and covers his face.

I place my hand on his shoulder. He doesn't shake me off so I leave it there. "She might understand, man."

He shrugs his shoulder and turns away. "I know she'll forgive me. But that's why it's not fair to her, man. She doesn't deserve to be with someone weak and scummy like me. Someone who has sex in a bathroom, where people piss on seats and take shits. I'm dirty and she's pristine. She's too good for me."

Kaylee, can you help?

This is sorta out of my area of expertise, Caden.

"Don't give up on what you have. Not yet. Talk to her."

"I don't know if I can bear the pain. It'll kill me."

I step toward him. "What you're doing now is killing her." There's anger in my voice, making it deep and making it tremble. His eyes widen and he takes a step back. "Right now you have a choice. You can take some of the pain from her or you can leave her on her own with it all. It's all up to you, Trevor. I advise you to make the correct choice, because if you don't, you'll have to deal with me."

I walk back through the house. I pass Donnie, who is sitting at his computer. His watery eyes follow me as I pass.

That wasn't very Nice, Caden.

Honestly, I don't really care about that right now.

She gasps. I'll pay for saying that later, I know I will, but I can't stress about that now. I pull out my phone and stare at the contact list. It reads:

Juliet.

And then, beneath hers:

Dyl.

I want to call Dyl, but Kaylee is listening, so I press Juliet's name. It rings twice and she picks up. "Did you talk some sense into him?"

"I tried my best."

"Was it good enough? Did he at least explain why he broke up with her? I think that's what's hurting her the most, she thinks she screwed up royally in some massive way that she can't remember."

"It's not something she did, it's something he's done. But he seemed to be in a daze. I think it's best that he tell you himself, if he wants you to know. It's pretty private, and I feel weird knowing it myself."

"Fair enough. Caden, hang on, Natalie wants to talk to you."

I hear the muffled sound of the phone being passed from one hand to another.

"Caden?" says Natalie.

"I'm here."

She lets out a tired sigh. "Juliet, I want to talk to Caden in private. Is that okay? Caden, are you alone?"

I hear a door shut through the speaker.

I turn around. I'm on the sidewalk, surrounded by silent houses. Two blocks down, an old woman is clipping a hedge with a massive pair of shears. Other than that, the entire street looks deserted. "Yeah, I am."

"Did you speak to Trevor?" Her voice is soft. "Did he tell you if he was going to get back together with me? Like, ever? Or are we officially done?"

"It's not my place to say, Natalie. I'm so sorry, I don't want to screw things up by telling you things he doesn't want you to know. I couldn't live with myself if I made things worse between you."

A harsh sob sounds. "There never used to be anything he didn't want me to know." She laughs a harsh laugh. "I'm dead. This is it, I'm dead."

"Natalie, don't hurt yourself over this. He's just a guy, and even though you love him you'll get better in time. You'll eat ice cream and watch movies that make you cry and then you'll get better. Don't you dare kill yourself over this."

"You're not listening to me," she says, her voice cold and clinical. "If he dumps me, I'm dead. Do you get what I'm saying, Caden? If Trevor breaks up with me I'm dead."

I picture her perfect eyes, her flawless skin, and impossibly white teeth. The extraordinary, almost unnatural length of her eyelashes. Her faultless model's body.

She's like me.

She's a Love Interest.

I force myself to say, "Meet me at the lookout."

————————

NATALIE IS SITTING UPRIGHT ON THE LOOKOUT bench, running her fingers through her hair. Her eyes are red but her cheeks are dry.

"You're . . ." I say as I step toward her.

"I'm a Love Interest," she says. "There. Now your coach can't get you in trouble for disclosing it. It's not like it matters anyway. They're probably already programming the Stalker to come for me as we speak. Hardwiring its circuits, planning the kill strike."

Does it work like that, Kaylee?

No response comes.

I sit down beside Natalie and put my arm over her shoulders. She nestles into my chest. Her breath is warm and it makes my shirt flutter. She smells sweet, like strawberries. "I suspected you were one as soon as Dyl appeared. You always act weird around him. When you both started courting Juliet I knew for sure. Plus, the fact that you're both ridiculously good-looking kind of clued me in to what you really are."

The label offends me. Does she know what I am? Does the term *Love Interest* define me? If she knows I'm a Love Interest, does she know everything she needs to about me?

Or am I something more?

I look down at the top of her head. "I suspected you as well, at first—when I saw your eyelashes, because they're way too long and perfect to be natural. But you're obviously a better actor than I am, because you fooled me. I was *so* sure you were in love with Trevor. It made me think I was just being paranoid."

She pushes her head away from my chest and meets my eyes.

"I *do* love him. With everything I have."

I roll my eyes. "Okay."

She blinks once. "I do, Caden. I love him so much that I can't even tell if what I'm feeling is fear because I'm probably going to die, or grief because I love him and he dumped me. Wait, you don't feel that way for Juliet? You must be a pretty good actor yourself—you seem pretty smitten with her."

I cross my arms. "Maybe I do. I'm an expert on making people fall in love, not on what love feels like."

"Here's a test. When you're bored, what do you think about?"

I bite my lip. "I don't know. Death, I guess. Either mine or Dyl's."

She leans back into my chest and sniffs. "I feel sorry for you, Caden. But not that much. Because I think this hurts more than the incinerator will. I guess I'll find out if that's true soon enough."

"Don't talk like that, it's not over. He could want you back. He's the one who screwed up, not you. Your coach must know that."

"Yeah, I called him, and he thinks it's not over yet. Apparently Kaylee told him about your conversation with Trev, and how upset he was over cheating on me. I don't know. The only thing I can think about it is that maybe Trev knows, deep down, that our relationship started under false pretenses. Because Trev's such a good guy, the best really, and it's so unlike him to do that. Unless he knows there's something wrong with me. Plus, Caden, a girl . . . a girl is dead because of me. I never talk about it, obviously, but I think about it constantly and I think it warped me. I know I won, but, like, when she got taken away I changed so much that I'm not even sure if I'm lovable anymore."

"You're extremely lovable, Nat. And there's nothing wrong with you. Nothing. You've done what you had to do to survive. It's admirable."

"That's so kind of you to say, Caden. Thanks. But it's something you should prepare yourself for if you can, because the LIC doesn't prepare us at all for how it feels to win. They make it seem like winning will be this big party, but it's really not."

I picture Dyl being taken away, and know that I could never prepare myself for that.

"And I'm sorry about this," she continues. "But I have more

bad news. You need to hear it, though, because it could save your life. Here it goes: Juliet is planning on making her choice at Dyl's party."

The whole world slows down.

"Are you sure?"

"Yeah, she's sick of toying with you both. She doesn't think it's fair to either of you. So she's decided she'll choose as soon as the party ends."

This is good, Caden.

I start to shake. I sit up straighter, trying to contain myself, because I can't let Natalie know how awful I feel about this. She's expecting me to be happy about it, so that's how I must act. Even though she's a Love Interest, I *still* have to lie to her.

"You're in the home stretch," says Natalie. "And I'd bet on you. Dyl will be dead by the end of the week."

I gulp. "Great."

She meets my eyes. "I take back what I said before—you're not that good an actor. At least you're not when you're hiding what truly matters to you."

CHAPTER
TWENTY-THREE

TO KILL TIME, I'M ON THE FLOOR BESIDE MY
bed doing push-ups. Up, down. Up, down. My muscles burn, all
the way from my wrists to my chest.

I need to be big, I need to be strong.

My "Nicki's Greatest Hits" playlist is playing through my laptop speakers, because I had hoped it would distract me. But now
even Nicki reminds me of Dyl, and my mind is trapped in an endless cycle of Juliet making her choice. I picture her choosing Dyl,
forcing me to accept that I'm going to die. Then I picture her
choosing me, and having to watch as Dyl is dragged to his death.

I'm not sure which is worse.

I drop down so my face hovers an inch off the carpet. I'm so
close I can see the wiry individual strands, and the little white
flecks of dust and dirt that are deeply entrenched in the fibers. My
entire body starts to tremble. A drop of sweat falls from my forehead to the floor.

Caden, you need to go to bed. Big day tomorrow.

Can't sleep. Last chance to make sure I'm perfect.

You'll get bags under your eyes and no one likes those. Go to bed. That's an order.

A knock sounds on my window. I rise to the top of the push-up and look forward. Dyl is there, crouching outside my window. He's wearing a black T-shirt, skinny jeans, and boots. I stand up and walk over to the window, rolling my aching left shoulder as I move.

I push the window up.

"Can't sleep?" I ask as I turn back and press the space bar, stopping the music.

"No way. I'm kind of stressed about tomorrow. Judy thinks if it goes well I'll make up some lost ground. Then, the day *after* the party, I've got this big thing planned. I can't tell you about it, obviously, but it's so cool. I'm already memorizing my lines."

He doesn't know that she's going to choose tomorrow. He doesn't know how close he is to death. I should play along, but I can't win this thing with an unfair advantage. I just can't.

"Dyl, there isn't going to be a day after the party for one of us. She's going to make her choice tomorrow."

His face drops. "Are you sure?"

"I'm certain."

"I . . . I haven't done enough. If she's making her choice tomorrow, she's going to pick you." His eyes go wide. "I'm going to die."

I can't lie. I can't do it.

"I think so," I say. "Dyl, I—"

"Nope, I'm not going to give up, and I don't think you're ready to give up on me. We're smart, so we can figure a way to get out of this. If we make sure we're both really important to her, then they'll have to keep me around, right? I don't know, maybe the LIC could repurpose me as a long-lost brother or something? Come on, man, start coming up with some ideas! The only way for us both to survive is to make sure we're both important to the plot, so how can we do that? There has to be a way. I mean, if Cho Chang can make it to the Battle of Hogwarts then we can get through this. Maybe we could copy her? If I somehow find a way to make myself important to the school, then they'll keep me around. Right?"

"I just don't think that's our story. Trust me, I wish I could tell you it'll work, but I promised I'd be honest. And it won't work. Our story is going to end with one clear victor, and as soon as he's crowned, the other needs to vanish. *That's* our story."

His pupils twitch, and I can almost see the cogs in his mind processing this. He gulps, then looks up at me. "So this is my last night alive. Fine. I've known this was coming for a while, so it doesn't change anything. But can we do something fun tonight? I don't want to spend it alone."

Don't be stupid, Caden. He could kill you. It's happened before. Don't go with him.

"Kaylee thinks you want to kill me."

Dyl's jaw is clenched tight and his cheek muscles are twitching. I notice something weird: he's shaved. It makes him look younger and makes his eyes seem kinder somehow. His bloody perfect eyebrows are slightly raised, and his skin is so clear it looks like it's glowing. He rubs his hairless chin and catches me looking at him.

"I'm not going to kill you, Caden. I'm not even trying to win anymore. What's the point? It's over, I know it is. You beat me.

And I'm okay with it, really. But I want to enjoy this wild world for one last night before they burn me. I don't think it's too much to ask, given the overwhelming shittiness of the hand I've been dealt."

He's right, it's not too much to ask. "I'm in," I say. "But I have to get changed."

"You know, Nice guy, I wouldn't object to a sympathy strip show. Just saying."

Huh. If I could trust him, I'd be flattered. But that line sounded heavily scripted. I imagine Judy sitting by herself in a dark room, writing down things for Dyl to say to me. Is he *still* playing me?

Then again, what if he's genuine? What if I'm so messed up I can't even recognize that he legitimately likes me? The prospect makes my heart do a happy dance. "Are you saying you like men, Dyl?"

"I'm saying I like sex, Caden. And I'll take what I can get."

Staring into his eyes, I pull my shirt over my head and drop it to the ground. I straighten my shoulders and tense my chest, trying to make myself as impressive as possible. He's staring at me and suddenly all I want is to know what he's thinking. *Why not ask?* My first instinct is that I can't, and that I'm stupid for even considering it, but why can't I? Kaylee will probably think it's weird, but Juliet isn't here and that's all she cares about, so there's no real reason to deny myself this.

"What do you think, Dyl?" I ask. Suddenly I don't know what to do with my arms. Then I remember that I'm a Nice, so I tuck them into my pockets and give him my best puppy-dog eyes. "Of me."

He steps close to me and the air between us fills with energy.

Is he going to touch me? Kiss me? God, I want him to touch me. Slowly, he looks down, his gaze moving from my face to my chest, studying me. His jaw clenches tight.

Finally, his stare meets mine. "I think you're perfect."

I gulp. He takes a step backward and leans against the windowsill. He's being odd, but I'm not sure if I think that because I really wanted him to kiss me and he's not, you know, doing that. I peer closer and notice that his eyes have filled with tears. He's blinking, trying to stop them, but it's too late, and he starts to sob.

"Dyl, I . . . Hang on, I'm going to get dressed."

He covers his face with his hands, and I spin around, grab a clean shirt, and tug it on. Then I pull a pair of jeans over my boxers and make my way back to him. His bottom lip is wobbling, and his eyes are focused on the window frame. He's dug a little hole in the paint, revealing the spiky white wood beneath.

"Sorry," he says. "It's just, you just made me think about everything I'm going to miss out on. Because I'm going to die, Caden. I'm going to fucking die. And I can't pretend I'm okay about it anymore, because I'm not."

Oh fuck.

My heart drops. "I'm so sorry, Dyl."

He pushes off the windowsill and moves toward me with small, hesitant steps. I don't know what he's doing, but then he lifts his hand and wipes his nose before looking at the floor. I think he wants me to hold him, but he's too nervous to ask. I step forward and press him against me, wrapping my arms around the entirety of him. He feels small, and cold, and I can feel his bones through his shirt. He places his chin on my shoulder and sobs, so

I move my hand up to the middle of his back and press him as close to me as possible. It feels like our ribs should slide between each other's cracks, filling the gaps.

But they don't.

I rub his back. "It's all right, Dyl. Think of all the people who've died in all of history. If they've done it, you can too, right?" I wince as soon as the words leave my lips. I'm such a freaking moron.

He sniffs. "I suppose."

After a few seconds, he steps away and wipes his eyes. "I have a question for you. Do you like me? Juliet didn't like me. But did you like me?"

Of course I like you. I like three things: Nicki Minaj, Star Wars, *and you.*

"Don't talk about yourself in the past tense. Just . . . don't. I do like you, Dyl. You're . . . you're my favorite person."

He smiles like a child, hopeful and full of wonder. "Really?"

"Really."

He wipes his eyes again. "Okay, that makes me feel a bit better. I've been thinking about the fact that she chose you over me a lot. Like, what does it mean? I gave the contest everything I had, and I still wasn't good enough. What does that mean about me as a person?"

"It means I'm a better actor than you. A better liar. That's it. I only won because I'm a bad person."

"I'm not sure that's it, Caden. There's something about you, something that's wormed its way into my brain and hooked itself in so deep. And I can see by the way Juliet looks at you that she thinks it too. You have this thing about you, an X factor if you will. Whatever it is, it's strong."

I raise an eyebrow. "I don't feel strong. I feel confused most of the time. But I thought you wanted to do something fun tonight. And this conversation is as far from fun as possible. So, do you have something planned?"

He nods. "It's a surprise." He steps outside. I follow after him, treading into the cool night air.

When we reach the car he pats the hood. "What do you think they'll do to this? Once, well, you know."

"I don't know."

But that's a lie, because I have an idea. It'll be given to the next Bad. That car has probably gone through a few hopefuls like him. And, after tomorrow, it'll be given to another.

"Let's ignore all that," he says. "From now on, okay? Let's ignore the fact that I'm about to die and enjoy ourselves."

"I'm here for you, Dyl. I'll do whatever you want."

"Be careful with your words, Caden." He's smirking. "There is a lot of stuff I haven't tried yet, and I'd rather not die a virgin."

I slam the door. "Please stop with the jokes. It feels like you're messing with me, and I can't handle that. So please, Dyl, listen to me and stop."

What I don't say is how much I want him, or how much I want to believe him. I wish I could grab his hand and take him back to my room. Once there, I'd take his clothes off and kiss him and we'd just keep going until we were under the sheets, sweaty and exhausted. But I can't. I don't have it in me to trust him that much.

"I'm saying what I feel, Caden. Believe me, it's not scripted. Judy pretty much gave up on me. She's already planning for the next Bad. So I have the luxury of being able to speak my mind. But I understand that you don't, so I'll stop."

I want to move past this, to forget how mistrustful I am, even if it's just for a second, so I pick his iPod up from the space between us and press Play.

I nestle against the seat.

He drives.

The stars blur above us.

After some time, he parks the car and I open my eyes. In front of us is a carnival, a stretch of glowing yellow and pink lights. A massive Ferris wheel spins in the background. The air smells like burning toffee, mud, and mowed grass.

I glare at him. "We're in *public*, Dyl."

"So?"

"Do you think I'm an idiot? What if Juliet is here and sees us together? What if anyone from school sees us? They'll think it's a date. If this is some sort of tactic to try to claw your way back I—"

He slaps his forehead. "I didn't think, man, honestly. It looked fun."

"Take me home, Dyl."

"What?"

"I . . . I can't do this. I want to go home."

I remember what I said to Trevor, about taking the pain from others, about how it's braver to take some pain from them, to bear it, than it is to leave them suffering alone. Dyl's shoulders are slightly hunched and he keeps blinking, like he hopes I won't notice what he's doing.

Preventing himself from crying.

Because I'm not the only one who feels things that need to be hidden. He's the person I'm the most like my real self with, but I still downplay some things, like my feelings for him, when we're together. Now I know that he's doing something similar: downplaying how he feels about tomorrow.

I open the car door and step outside. "Screw it." I slam the door shut. My shoes sink into the damp ground. "Let's go. I don't care if they see us."

"You sure?"

I nod, and he climbs out and locks the door behind him. We start walking through the carnival.

"Don't stand so close," I say as I approach a stall. I run my fingers through the fur of a teddy bear that's on display. "I don't care if they see us together, but I'm not actively suicidal."

He raises his hands in mock surrender. "As you command, Nice guy."

I hand over a fifty-dollar bill to a bubbly young woman and she hands me six juggling balls and two twenties.

"Get a ball into the container and you win a prize," she says. "Get more in and you get better prizes! Good luck!"

I hand three of the balls to Dyl, then take aim and throw. The ball hits the middle of the container and bounces out. *Damn it!*

"Rookie," says Dyl. He takes aim. His eyes narrow in the way they always do when he cares about something, and he holds the ball beside his head, his biceps flexed. Even through the jacket it looks fantastic. I notice I'm staring at his arm, and blood rushes to my cheeks. I kick the dirty ground as he throws. He gets the ball in.

I throw again. I miss.

He crosses his arms. "Are you pretending to be bad at this? You know, to make me feel good about myself?"

I give him the finger.

He throws and it bounces out. The crack in his perfectness makes me want to laugh, but I keep my lips pressed together.

Now it's my turn to throw again. *Come on, impress him. Show him you're good at something.* I throw the ball. This time I miss completely.

He gets his shot in. *Of course he does.* He pumps his fist when he makes it.

"Congratulations," says the girl. "You can take your pick from the back wall."

Dyl leans back and peers at the wall like a scholar. "Surprise me."

The girl hands Dyl a pink stuffed dinosaur. He squeezes it and it squeaks. "What I've always wanted. Thank you."

She laughs. "You're welcome."

We walk away.

"Do you like my dino?" he asks. "I'm thinking of calling him Mr. Huggles."

I frown. "Are you serious?"

He lifts an eyebrow, then walks up to a family that's waiting in line in front of the cotton candy stall, leaving me alone. He waves at them, getting their attention, and then he starts talking to the parents. A small girl, maybe four at the oldest, is hiding behind her father's legs. Dyl crouches, then offers her Mr. Huggles. She reaches out and snatches it from his grasp, then returns to her safe place. The parents laugh, and then Dyl makes his way back to me with his hands tucked into his pockets.

"That was the furthest thing from Bad I've ever seen," I say. "It was, dare I say it, adorable."

He shoots me a back-the-eff-off look. So I drop it.

"Let's go on the Ferris wheel," he says, pointing at the structure that towers above everything. It's large and white, and candy-colored lights have been attached to each carriage.

I tilt my head up. It's really high. What if one of the carriages snaps? We'd die. Is a silly ride worth it?

Dyl is staring at it with wide eyes.

I gulp, and wipe my sweaty palms on my thighs. "I don't like heights, but it's your call, man."

"Then let's go."

The line takes about twenty minutes; we stand slightly apart just in case someone from school sees us. I already have a lie planned if we run into someone: I'm here with a group, but none of them wanted to go on the Ferris wheel so I'm going alone. Being next to Dyl is a total coincidence, I didn't even recognize him. It's not my best lie, but it's unlikely I'll have to use it. I already texted Juliet to see where she is, and she's at home studying. I also checked with Nat and Trev, and they're both busy. Nat's at an author signing in DC, Trev is training. Dyl has no other friends, so there's no danger there, and I'm not sure anyone else knows us enough to know that this pairing is unusual. They might even think we're just on a date and not care at all. I like the thought of that.

I lean against the cold railing and watch Dyl as he watches the crowd. He looks at everyone, but his more intense focus seems to be drawn toward couples.

We reach the front of the line and he faces me. "You know, the only way you can know in public if someone is a couple is if they hold hands. Like, we're together, but no one thinks we're a couple. But if we held hands, they would."

"I guess. What's your point?"

"Well, maybe it's because I've never been close enough to someone to hold their hand, but it seems like people only do it to prove to others that they're in a relationship. They're like, *Screw you, strangers, I found someone and you're alone, and I want you to know that.* You know?"

"Maybe they like each other a lot? Maybe they just want to hold the hand of the person they love and they don't give a damn what anyone else thinks."

He tilts his head to the side. "You really are a Nice, aren't you?"

"No, I'm not."

"Someone who wasn't at least partially Nice wouldn't have said that, Caden. They just wouldn't have."

"Next!" calls a man in blue overalls. We pay at the booth, then walk toward the carriage. I climb in first and sit down on the wooden bench. Dyl sits down beside me, closer than he needs to. I guess it'd be pretty hard to explain this away as a coincidence, but oh well, it's too late now. The small booth rocks forward, then swings back. I grip the railing tight, and my sweaty palms cool against the metal.

Dyl laughs. "You look so scared, man. Have you ever been on one of these?"

I shake my head. "Nope."

Caden, what the hell are you doing? I left for a while and now I'm back and you're doing this? Why? Don't you know that this looks a hell of a lot like a date?

So what if it is, Kaylee?

Talk to me like that again and I'll . . .

He's dying, and he wants to do this with me. Once he's gone I

*promise I'll be a perfect Love Interest. But right now, I need to be
here for him.*

*He could be trying to get pictures of you together or . . . It's
wrong, Caden. On so many levels. You shouldn't be doing this with him.*

Well, I am, Kaylee. Sorry.

*I can't be here for this. Just know that I think you're being an
idiot. A massive idiot.*

Dyl is staring at me. Like always, it settles me, deluding me
into thinking everything is okay even though all the evidence
points to the contrary. "Kaylee?"

"Yep. She thinks I'm stupid for doing this with you."

"Do *you* feel stupid for doing it?"

Our feet lift up off the ground.

I shake my head.

We lift higher into the air and I grip the railing tighter. The
crowd shrinks, and then is replaced by the horizon. In the distance are the lights of the town, but there's also an awful lot of
navy sky.

"It's beautiful," he says.

The carriage steadies, and suddenly it isn't so scary. I move
one hand to rest on the seat between us. His eyes move down and
focus on it, and his Adam's apple bobs up and down. He seems
nervous, like he's unsure what to do now that we're so close. I instantly know he isn't going to make a move, but fuck that, we're
here, and I want this moment to be something more than it currently is. I guess that's the problem with Dyl: what we have now
isn't enough for me. I all caps WANT MORE.

"You know," I say. My voice is shaking. "You and I, we're
pretty close. Maybe we're not in love, but we're close, right?"

"Sure. What's your point?"

"If you want to hold hands with someone, I'll hold your hand."

"So you'll take that bullet?"

"Gladly. Seriously, Dyl, you've shown me so many cool things, so if there's anything I can do for you tonight, I'd like to do it. And I'd be lying if I said I didn't want to try it. So are you going to hold my hand or not?"

He moves his hand across.

And places it on top of mine.

I flip my hand so our palms are touching. His skin is rough, yet his grip is soft. Our eyes meet as our fingers intertwine, and he smiles like I told a joke. And that makes me smile as well.

I've kissed him.

But this feels closer.

The Ferris wheel keeps moving up and the moon gets bigger and bigger and the whole thing feels like it's never going to stop rising.

But I'm smarter than my feelings are.

And I know the descent is coming.

CHAPTER
TWENTY-FOUR

I'M STARING AT THE MIRROR IN MY BEDROOM. I'm wearing a white shirt, black slacks, and dress shoes. I fiddle with the top button.

How much man-cleavage should I show, Kaylee?

None, obviously. Button it all the way up. And wear a tie. You need to be the best-dressed boy in the room.

It was a joke.

Well, it was very funny, Caden. Now hurry up, I want you to be early. It's sweet, like you're excited about this party.

I do up the top button. *Hey, I have a question. What happens to our relationship if Juliet chooses me?*

Well, we won't talk as often, because they'll remove your implant. You'll still have my mobile number, though, and you're always welcome to call me if you have a question. So I become a free, always accessible relationship counselor. It's a pretty great service. Lots of people would benefit if they had someone like me in their life. They really would.

Good to know. And hey, thanks for helping me through all this.

It's my job, Caden. I had no choice. But that's sweet. Thank you.

Once I'm dressed I leave my room and head toward my truck. When I reach it I open the door. Sitting on the passenger seat is a bouquet of pink tulips.

For me? How sweet.

Kaylee doesn't respond, so I slam the door and turn on the engine. Then I drive to Juliet's house.

Juliet and Natalie are sitting on the front steps of Juliet's house. Juliet is wearing a frilly white dress. It's cute, and she looks great, but it's nothing compared to her space dress. Natalie looks characteristically stunning in a skintight green number. I park in front of them and they both stand and walk to the car. Their heels click against the driveway.

"You look beautiful," I say, handing her the tulips. Juliet presses them to her face and inhales deeply.

"Thank you, Caden. They're lovely."

They climb into the backseat and clip on their seat belts.

"Do you know the way?" asks Natalie.

"Sure do."

"Then let's go."

I turn the steering wheel and pull onto the road.

Juliet turns to me. Her face is covered with simple makeup, making her skin paler than usual, and her lips are glossy. "So you're comfortable with driving now? Before you weren't."

"Yeah, I am. Now that I'm doing it, it's not so scary."

She looks out the window. "Yeah, and it's freeing, right?"

"More than anything in the world."

She closes her mouth and I grip the steering wheel. My palms are slick with sweat, which makes the plastic slippery. This kind, lovely girl is going to kill someone today. She'll never know what she's done, but that won't stop it from being true. And, if I win, I'll have to spend the rest of our life together knowing that her choice killed Dyl.

"How are you doing, Natalie?" I ask, in a lame attempt to stop thinking about how much everything is going to change tonight.

I flick my eyes up and look at her through the rearview mirror. Her arms are crossed and her shoulders are slouched. She moves her eyes up and meets my stare. "I'm doing about as well as you'd expect, Caden. But it doesn't matter. Tonight, I'm going to win him back."

"She's pretty certain," chimes Juliet.

"I'm certain because I know Trevor, and as much as he doesn't think so right now, I know how he thinks. I know exactly why he's doing what he's doing."

"But aren't you mad? That he did what he did?"

"Honestly, I don't care that he cheated. I know I'm supposed to, because it's been bombarded into me by every single TV show ever, but I don't want to listen to them. Like, I'm not going to dump him because a bunch of TV writers told me it's the right thing to do. All that matters is that I still love him."

The GPS barks a command, and I pull into Dyl's street. "I get where you're coming from. If I loved someone I'd forgive them anything. That's where the unconditional thing comes from, right? It's not, like, unconditional unless they do something bad. It's just unconditional."

"Right."

Juliet smiles. "Right. Plus, Nat, if he rejects you we can still get super drunk."

"Jules, I'm right with you. If my talk with Trev doesn't go my way, I'm going to become a hot mess of supernova proportions."

I park the car, and take a deep breath in through my nostrils. Juliet rubs my arm. "Ready?"

No freaking way, I want to say.

I nod. "Yep."

Dyl's house is a massive one-story building with white walls and lots of glass. Dark-green shrubs line the stone pathway that leads to the front door. Rows of cars are parked around the block, filling the street. Up ahead, a bunch of guys in suits are leaning against a silver convertible. They stare at us as we pass. Or, more accurately, they stare at Juliet and Natalie. One of them wolf-whistles, and both Natalie and Juliet shoot him scathing looks.

Natalie's arms are crossed. "Who knew Dyl had this many friends? He doesn't seem to talk to anyone aside from you, Juliet."

She shrugs her shoulders. "There's a lot about that boy I don't get."

We walk up the steps to the front door. A black man in a suit is standing there, his huge frame blocking the entire doorway.

"Names," he says. His eyes are focused on a clipboard.

Juliet steps forward. "Juliet Stringer."

His eyes move down the list, then he moves his hand up and scrapes his pen across the paper. Of course she's on the list. He turns his body and Juliet slides past him.

"Caden Walker," I say.

He scans the list. I'm not going to be on it. Why would I be? Why would Dyl make this easy for me?

The guard raises his hand and swipes the pen across the paper again. "Move," he growls.

I rush past him and Juliet grabs my hand. She's beaming. The hallway is long and white, illuminated by circular lights embedded in the ceiling. The floors are rich, varnished timber. An overloaded coat rack stands beside the door. So I'm in. But why would Dyl do that? Maybe he truly has given up on the contest.

Or maybe he just wants to spend time with me.

Juliet lets go of my hand. "Caden, we're in! And this party . . . I thought it was going to be a kegger or something, but oh my God, this is ridiculous. I mean, he has a freaking bouncer. How can he afford this?"

"Who knows? Let's just have a good time!"

"Good call."

Natalie joins us, and we walk through the hall toward the thumping music. We pass through a glass sliding door into a large lounge room. A dining table that's full to the brim with trays of small, immaculately presented pieces of food sits in the middle of the room. There are tiny quiches, slices of smoked salmon, and bite-sized berry pies. People in formal clothes, neat black suits for the men, evening gowns for the women, are standing in small circles around the table, either chatting or nibbling at the hors d'oeuvres. My mouth waters.

A middle-aged woman with hair the color of gold, like the metal, approaches us. She's wearing a tight black dress that dips low, revealing her collarbone and her clearly surgically improved cleavage. A silver necklace hangs around her neck. Her posture is rigidly, almost uncomfortably upright, and her smile is wide but seems genuine.

"Hello," she says. "I'm Dylan's aunt. He's been living with me ever since, well, you know. And who are you?"

She's looking only at Juliet, who fidgets, her fingers bunching up her dress. "I'm Juliet."

"Oh my gosh, I knew it! From the look of you I knew it. Dyl talks about you all the time, you with your precious little science experiments. He's so smitten, it's honey sweet."

Juliet leans her head back. "He's what?"

"I've never seen him like anyone as much as he likes you." She raises her hands to her mouth. "Oh my, he's going to be so mad if he finds out I said that to you. I know he's got his big tortured-soul persona going, but believe me, deep down he's a big softie. Now, excuse me, I need to go before I say anything else that will embarrass him."

She strides away, heading straight toward another small group of kids. They gape at her as she reaches them. Juliet is staring at the floor, her expression alarmingly unreadable. *Wait, was that scripted? Maybe Dyl is still fighting?*

Natalie is scanning the crowd. "Any signs of Trev?"

"I can't see him." I turn to Juliet. "Do you want a drink?"

Juliet nods, and I step forward and approach a waiter who is holding a silver tray filled with flutes of champagne. I grab two glasses and pass one to Natalie, then give the other to Juliet. I spin back around and grab another, mouthing thanks to the waiter as I lift the glass off the tray.

"But there's Dyl."

I lower my glass. He's standing in the doorway, staring at us. He's wearing a black blazer over a white dress shirt and a skinny black tie. His hair has been pushed up and over his forehead, so it stands as a wave. The partygoers around him all stop what they're doing and gape at him, but he ignores them all, keeping his attention fixed on us. His mouth curves into a lopsided grin. I grin back at him, even though it's out of character. I can't help it.

"You made it," he calls. He approaches us, and now it's my turn to look at the floor. *Here we go, he's going to ignore me again,* I think. I notice his shiny shoes are pointing in my direction. I look up and see that he's staring at me. His lips curl up into a small smile, like we have a secret, and he offers me his hand.

"It's Caden, right?"

"Right."

We shake hands.

"I'm glad you made it." He lets go of me and kisses Natalie on the cheek. Then he faces Juliet.

"Juliet, you look lovely."

"Hi, Dyl."

"Can we talk?"

"Listen, Dyl—"

"It's fine," I interrupt. Juliet raises an eyebrow at me as her tone rings in my ears. That was the voice she used with me when she told me she couldn't do the art project with me. So it's the voice she uses when she's about to let someone down. And if she lets Dyl down, it's game over. He needs time to recover some ground. I don't want him to overtake me, but I also don't want this to be the end. Maybe if they talk, Juliet will reconsider her decision to decide tonight. "Hear him out."

Juliet uncrosses her arms. "Okay, fine. See you later."

They walk away, leaving Natalie and me alone. As soon as they mix into the crowd, Natalie slaps my chest. "Caden! What are you thinking? You just let that happen!"

"Yeah but, like, it'll show her I'm not threatened by him, which is good for me. Trust me, I know what I'm doing."

Her narrowed eyelids tell me she's skeptical. "Okay, but be careful, all right? You haven't won yet."

"Noted. Thanks, Nat."

I take a sip of my champagne, which tastes sweet and crisp, like a slightly underripe green apple. It's okay, but it's obviously not real champagne. Rather, it's a nonalcoholic rip-off. It's probably unfair to compare them, but it's nowhere near as nice as beer is.

Natalie and I walk onto the wooden deck. A DJ with blond-and-green dreadlocks has set herself up in the corner. Loud electronic music is pumping from the large black speakers beneath her table. A group of guys is standing beside her, trying to get her attention.

The deck declines into a small stretch of sandstone before it drops off into an infinity pool. Two guys and two girls are already swimming. The girls are wearing frilly bras and underwear. They're sitting on the shoulders of the guys, laughing like this is the best moment of their entire lives. The guys move toward each other, and then the girls grab each other and start wrestling.

"Looks fun," I say, pointing toward them.

Natalie scowls. "Why don't you join them?"

I sip my drink. "I didn't bring my trunks."

"What's that about trunks? Are you talking about how good I look in mine?"

A hand slaps down on my shoulder. I turn and see Trevor. His cheeks are covered in a couple of days' worth of stubble, and his eyes are bloodshot. Somehow, his massive chest looks smaller, like he's deflated.

"Hey, man," I say. Natalie crosses her arms. "I'll leave you be."

"You don't have to do that," she says, but I ignore her and walk toward the pool. I sit down on the edge and stare at the skyline. I pull my shoes and socks off and dip my bare feet into the water.

Behind me, clusters of people dance under the lights. In the pool, a girl in a red bra swims up to her friend, and they sit on the step. I stare at their practically naked bodies. *Do they turn you on? They're everything a man should be attracted to in a woman.*

I turn away from them. The boys are now on their own. The tall, lanky one with red hair grabs the other and shoves him under the water. They sink under, then both kick up, spluttering for air. The redhead laughs, then leaps at the other boy, tackling him down. He's not muscular, and his skin is pale, yet I find I can't look away from him.

I recall the attraction I felt toward other guys at the LIC. Toby excluded, I never felt anything particularly strong for anyone. But in general, I felt it every time a cute guy would smile at me, or when I was fortunate enough to be around someone shirtless. So I felt it, sure, but I didn't understand it, and I figured it'd stop when I met my Chosen. We'd meet, and the weird feelings I had would go away. Then we'd get married and have babies and I'd do all the stuff I'm supposed to do. I guess I thought I was straight just because everyone treated me like I was, and no one ever gave me a chance to think otherwise.

Speaking of guys I'm attracted to, Dyl appears in the living room. A second later, Juliet steps down off the staircase and faces him. He touches her hand, which makes my heart race, and then they separate. The sight fills me with a weird, deflated feeling. Like, I'm so glad she shook him off, but I'm also a bit crushed that he's trying so hard and failing. Can't she see what I see in him?

Juliet heads toward the bathroom, and Dyl just stands there, his posture floppier than usual. He takes in a breath, which perks him up a bit, and then turns around and walks up the stairs, presumably back to his bedroom.

I put my shoes and socks back on and stand up. Dyl, my Dyl, is currently upstairs, alone. If this truly is the end, I need to see him one last time. There aren't many things in life that I truly need, but spending time with the real him one last time is definitely one of them. Doing this probably isn't the *best* idea, but Juliet's in the bathroom, so I have a bit of time. As long as I move fast, it'll be fine. It's reckless, sure, but if I'm careful it won't ruin my chances with her.

With that in mind, I walk back through the party. When I reach the staircase, I do a quick check to make sure no one is watching, then I duck under the little black chain that's blocking the entrance. Once I'm through, I check again and realize that no one has noticed I've committed a party foul. They're all too obsessed with themselves. Grinning, I jog up the stairs.

At the top of the stairs it's still and so quiet. The staircase leads into a big open area with two white leather lounge chairs in front of a fireplace. A foosball table is in the corner. At the far end of the room is a single door. It's ajar, the light is on, and faint punk music is playing. My shoes click against the polished timber as I cross the room. When I reach it I knock once, which makes the door swing inward slightly.

"Juliet?" he calls.

"Try again," I say.

"Caden? What are you doing here?"

"I wanted to see you."

"Oh. Um, okay. Give me a sec, I'm getting dressed."

I tuck my hands into my pockets. There's no questioning it, this is weird. It's a big, important night, the biggest ever, really, and I should be with Juliet. Instead, I'm here, and I couldn't be happier. I'm actually surprised Kaylee hasn't told me to stop. Usually things that make me happy piss her off.

I'm still here, Caden. Just so you know.

Oh. You know what I'm going to do, right? Does your silence mean it's okay with you?

She sighs. *I still think you're being a massive idiot, but I can't stop you, so I'm going to make you a deal. I'll let you do this, but this has to be your last hurrah with him. Do you hear me? This is the end of the two of you. Even if the contest doesn't end tonight, this is it. No more drives, no more anything. You've done everything I've asked, so I'm going to give you some time to end it, but as soon as you go back downstairs it's over, all right?*

Agreed.

Great. Now, I'm going to give you two a bit of privacy. You have ten minutes, Caden. Do what you have to do, and then I want you downstairs with Juliet.

You're the best, Kaylee. Truly.

I know, Caden. Don't make me regret it.

The door swings open, revealing Dyl. He's now wearing white pants and a white shirt. The shirt is unbuttoned, showing his chest. He narrows his eyes, and it takes every bit of self-control within me to keep my feet planted. All my brain wants me to do is charge forward, grab him by his shirt, and kiss him. He'd stumble back until his legs hit the bed and we'd fall down together and . . .

His perfect eyebrows furrow and he starts buttoning up his shirt, silencing my urge to kiss him. "What are you doing here, Caden?"

For some reason, he's mad, and trying to kiss him now might result in him breaking my nose. I've decided to trust him, but that doesn't mean he's suddenly incapable of hurting me.

"Juliet is looking for you," he says. "You shouldn't be here. You should be with her."

"I told you, I wanted to see you."

The crease between his eyebrows gets deeper. Wait, his expression isn't anger; his eyes are too soft for that. What he's feeling is concern. For some reason, he's worried about me.

"Dyl, I know what I'm doing. She's in the bathroom, so we've got a bit of time. We don't have much, but it's better than nothing. Do you want me to go?"

He looks past me, checking the foyer.

"No, I don't want you to go. Come in."

He moves aside and I enter his bedroom. He closes the door behind him and locks it. As the lock clicks into place, I wonder why he did it: is it because we're Love Interests and we can't be seen together, or is it because he knows what I'm about to do and wants privacy? I really hope it's option two.

"Sorry if I seemed weird before," he says. "I'm just confused. This is so unlike you."

I pause. "What do you mean?"

He runs his hand through his hair. His shirt is now fully

buttoned up, but it still pulls up a bit, giving me a glimpse of his stomach. Now I get why Love Interests are taught to do it; it's a pretty big turn-on. "It's just, well, you normally do everything by the book. Whenever Juliet is around, you're always the perfect Nice. But the perfect Nice wouldn't be here. He'd be downstairs, with Juliet. And yet . . . you're here."

I nod. "That I am. Again, if you'd like me to leave, I'll go."

He smiles. "I'm not complaining, not at all. It's just worth noting, I think. So, what do you think of my room? Do you now know why the LIC spent so much time designing it? Is it, I don't know, making you fall in love with me?"

I glance around his room. It's a lot bigger than mine, and it's really freaking adult. That's my first thought: *this is a man's bedroom, not a boy's.* I mean, there's art on the wall! Not a movie poster or something, but actual art! His bed is a double, and the blanket is light gray, buried beneath dark-gray throw pillows. An e-reader sits on the wooden bedside table, beside a shiny chrome lamp.

The best part of the room, though, has to be the window. It takes up most of the far wall, and it's framed by soft-looking navy curtains. Through the window I can see trees and the night sky.

"Actually, yeah, it does kind of work. I mean, it doesn't make me fall in love with you, but I do know more about you now. For example, now I know that you prefer e-books to print books, you monster."

He laughs. "That's actually true. Print books are so heavy, and I always wreck them, which makes me feel bad. What else?"

I point to his record player. "You still listen to records, for some reason."

"It's all about the sound, man. There's nothing like it. Anything else?"

I nod toward his bed. "Your bed is a double."

"And what does that mean, exactly?"

"It means you want a partner. Or maybe I'm thinking about it too much. You could just like extra space. I don't know."

If I want to make a move, this is my one chance. How much time has passed since Kaylee left? Maybe five minutes. That leaves me with only five more minutes to spend with him. And chatting is nice, but we're alone in his bedroom. I repeat: *we're alone in his bedroom*, and he's told me twice now that he doesn't want me to go. This is the best chance I'm ever going to get.

"Hey, Dyl?"

He looks at me. "Yeah?"

"I'm going to do something, and if you want me to stop at any time, you can tell me, okay?"

All he does is nod, so I reach out and grab his wrist. I hang there for a second, my thumb drawing circles on his skin, waiting to see if my touch is acceptable. He doesn't move away or say anything. Instead, a cute smile lights up his face. I pull him forward a step, so he's directly in front of me, and then I grab his shoulders. He's gone soft, pliable, and it's so fucking hot. I squeeze him maybe a little bit harder than I have to, just to feel how firm he is, and he seems to like it, because he bucks slightly, his knees relaxing. I guide him back a few steps to the spot where I want him, with his back pressed firmly against the window.

"Is this good?" he asks.

"It's perfect."

I place one hand flat on the cold glass beside his head and then lean forward so that we're almost touching. "Are you okay with this, Dyl?"

He nods. "I am."

I lean forward and kiss him. He kisses me back, slower than he did at the shed. Unlike last time, I don't feel like ripping his clothes off, but this . . . this is better. Softer. Kinder. More like I've finally found a way to express how frigging much I like him.

He closes his lips and pulls back a little bit. His hands are on my hips, his fingers playing with the edge of my shirt. I breathe in, taking in some much-needed air.

"We're out of time," he says.

I want to say he's wrong, but I know he's right. Seconds are all I have, so I kiss him again. He kisses me back, but it's different—lighter, hesitant. He closes his lips and rubs my arms.

"Caden?"

"Yeah?"

"We need to go."

I clench my hand into a fist and tap it against the window. "Yep."

I press my forehead against his.

"I'll give you some time," he says. "I'll give you a couple minutes to find her, and then it's game on. And hey, Caden?"

"Yeah?"

"I'm rooting for you."

I close my eyes and press my forehead against his just a little bit harder. "I'm rooting for you too."

I tap the glass one last time, then I take a step back. The air away from him feels cold, and I know why: I will never be that close to him again. That kiss was it for us. I want to say something to him, to tell him how much I wish I weren't competing against him, or how much I want him to be my boyfriend. But I've already spent more time than I should've here, and he's right. I can't stay.

Somehow, I leave his room without looking back.

And the grand finale begins.

CHAPTER
TWENTY-FIVE

I STEP DOWN OFF THE STAIRCASE AND SCAN the crowd for Juliet. I peer around a tall guy in a bad suit and spot her. She's standing in front of the pool with her arms crossed. I stride over to her.

"Juliet!" I call as I open the pool gate. "There you are!"

She turns, faces me, and smiles the biggest smile I've ever seen on her.

"Caden!" she says. "I was looking for you! Where'd you go?"

"I was looking for you! I guess we just missed each other."

"Huh. Anyway, I'm so glad I found you, because I have news. Dyl invited a bunch of scientists to this party. Or, his aunt did. Apparently she has a bunch of connections in the industry. This is, like, seriously life-changing stuff. If I can get one of them to even think about giving me an internship, this could affect the rest of my life. Seriously, Caden, this could be the start of my career. See, look, there!" She points to an Indian man standing beside the punch bowl. "That's James Batra. He's the son of Jairam Batra, and they both work at Harvard. Look at that, James freaking Batra at the same party as me." She runs her fingers through her hair.

This is . . . unexpected. The scientists obviously mean that Dyl is still playing the game. Or maybe he isn't? Maybe he just wanted to do one last nice thing for Juliet? That's totally something he'd do. But why didn't he tell me? No, he'd have told me if he were just being kind, so he's still competing. I can't be mad, I told him to keep fighting after all, but I guess I just didn't expect him to try this hard.

"Should I talk to him?" asks Juliet. I blink, then realize she's talking about the scientist. "I don't want to seem overeager or anything, even though I am. What should I do, Caden?"

"Be yourself. It's enough."

Her gaze softens. "You're amazing, you know that, right? This incredible thing is happening to me and the first thing I wanted to do was tell you about it. I know we haven't defined our relationship, but I like you a lot, and . . ."

Kiss her now! She wants you to!

I . . .

Kiss her right now! I'm not asking, Caden.

I step closer so that our bodies are almost touching. Her eyes go wide but she doesn't pull away.

"Caden, what are you . . ."

I lean forward, tilting my head to the side. My lips are right beside hers. I pause, because I . . .

Keep going, Caden. If you stop now I'll . . .

I know what you'll do, Kaylee.

I close my eyes and kiss her. Her lips are even softer than

Dyl's, and sweeter. It feels nice, tender and soft. Yet it doesn't claw at my chest like kissing Dyl did, and a part of me knows it never will. She tilts her head to the side and kisses me again, her hand curling inward against my chest. I pull back and meet her eyes.

This is it: the grand finale. Am I doing this? Can I do this? Tears form in my eyes and I blink rapidly to get rid of them before Juliet notices. My heart aches, the pain so strong it almost knocks me to my knees. I have to do this. I have no choice. He must know I have no choice, just like he had no choice but to keep fighting for Juliet. I can already tell that I'll hate myself for the rest of my life if I open my mouth. But the worst part of it is that I know, and I think I've always known, that when it came to this moment I would go through with it.

"I love you, Juliet," I say. My voice comes out clear and strong, just how I practiced it. "I think I always have, ever since I first met you all those years ago. And now I'm telling you all the things I wish I had had the courage to say back then. If you want me to be your boyfriend, all you have to do is ask."

There. It's done.

She closes her eyes. "Caden, I like you too, and I want to be your girlfriend, and you have no idea how happy I feel right now that you said that. But like I said, there are a lot of people here who could start my career and that matters a lot to me. So I know this is going to suck to hear, but would it be okay if I pause this conversation and talk to them?"

"Juliet, I'd be upset if you didn't. Go crush it. I know you will. I'll be waiting."

She grins, takes in a deep breath, and makes her way across

the room. James Batra looks up from his cup of punch and smiles at her. She shakes his hand, and they start to talk.

I need to sit down. I feel light-headed and dizzy, like I could faint at any second. That was *so* close. The night isn't over yet, and she didn't give me a concrete yes, which means the contest isn't over. For now, Dyl is safe, which is the only thing that matters. Still, the queasy feeling lingers, and I know if I don't sit down soon I'll throw up. I almost killed Dyl. How could I do that? What's wrong with me? I scan the crowd. Yes! There! Across the deck is a spare seat. I take a step toward it.

The lights snap off and a piano starts to play. Everyone goes totally still. A spotlight illuminates, revealing Dyl. He's standing at the end of the deck in an all-white suit. A single red rose is in his hand. He steps forward to stand in the center of the light.

Oh no.

"Juliet," says Dyl. He's wearing a microphone, so his deep voice booms around the entire room. "Where are you?"

Juliet places her cup down on the table and walks out onto the deck. Everyone has stopped what they were doing to watch them.

"Dyl, what are you doing?"

He steps forward to stand right in front of her. The spotlight moves, illuminating them both. It looks like the two of them are the only people on the deck.

"There are some things I want to say to you, Juliet, but it's hard, because you're wearing that glossy stuff on your lips you wear sometimes depending on how fancy you want to be. I'm just a guy standing before you, and you're so beautiful I never get tired of looking at you." He licks his lips and smiles. "I'd steal a blue French horn for you if you wanted one, because I don't know how to quit you. If I was marrying someone else I'd say your name at the altar. Our story is epic, Juliet. And I know that every single possible way to say I love you has already been said, which is why I didn't try to be original. But I love you, Juliet. And I hope you love me too."

He extends the rose.

The crowd leans forward.

"I—I—" stammers Juliet. "I'm sorry, Dyl, I really am. But—" Her eyebrows furrow. Dyl's mouth drops open and his eyes fill with tears. He knows it's done. He knows *he's* done. "This whole thing, it's not for me. It was all for you! And I don't want to be a bit player in the spectacle of *your* life. I'm my own person, Dyl. And on top of all that, I'm sorry, but I love someone else, and I want to be with him. I don't want to be with you. Not now, not ever."

Juliet spins and walks away. In the bright glow of the spotlight, Dyl's face falls and his shoulders slump.

Game over.

CHAPTER
TWENTY-SIX

I DROP MY GLASS. IT HITS THE GROUND, AND I do nothing but watch as the liquid sloshes onto the wooden slats of the deck. Around me, snorts of laughter break out.

Congratulations, Caden! That's enough for them. It's done. You won! And I'm sorry about threatening you before, I just thought you might need an extra push to seal the deal. Now, I have a date, so I have to go. Drink something! Celebrate! You did really well.

That's enough. They're going to kill Dyl.

The boy who stood outside my window, the boy who drove me through the night, the boy who is obsessed with rock music and who is so much nicer than me, the kind of guy who should've been a Nice. I picture him waiting outside my room, framed by my chipped wooden window frame.

He's about to die.

I need to process this. I won. Dyl will be executed. Everything is going too fast. The world is too loud, bright, and cruel and I can't focus on anything because Dyl, my Dyl, is about to be murdered. It's so horrific it's almost abstract, like it can't really happen. But it will. A Stalker will claim him, and if he runs, it'll decapitate him.

I bend down and pick up the dropped glass. Dyl breaks out of the spotlight and forces his way through the jeering crowd toward the exit. He ducks through the doorway and moves out of sight.

I walk over to the table and place the cup down. As it touches the tabletop I realize how violently my hand is shaking. Why do I feel like this? This is what I wanted. All along, ever since I arrived at the LIC, this was the thing I wanted. To win. To survive.

But now that I have it I don't want it. In fact, I hate it.

I want the boy who came to my window at night. I want him whole, and I want him with me.

Juliet appears out of the crowd. "Caden, what's wrong? You look like you've seen a ghost."

"Where did Dyl go?"

"His aunt said he went to the lookout. She looked so mad at me and I—"

"He's going to kill himself. I need to go. Right now."

Her eyes widen. "Oh God. I'll come too."

Together, we run through the party back into the house. At the kitchen, I pause. I walk up to the wooden block filled with knives with silver handles. I grab the smallest one, then spin and chase after Juliet.

We step outside the front door. Juliet grabs my arm. "Why'd you grab that knife?"

I shrug her off me. "We can't talk now. Come on."

Kaylee, are you there?

Thankfully, there's no response.

I reach the truck and swing the door open. Juliet stands beside it with her arms crossed. Her heels are digging into the soft ground. "Caden, what the hell are you doing? How do you know what Dyl's going to do? He wasn't even sure he knew your name at the start of the party, and now you're upset because I rejected him?"

"I can't explain, Juliet. I don't have time."

"That's not for you to decide. I told you this was a big night for me and then Dyl ruined it and now you're making it worse. Caden, you're scaring me."

"I'm a liar, Juliet. So is Dyl. I *should* be scaring you. It's the rational emotion to feel when you're around me."

Tears fill her eyes. "What do you mean? I told you I want to be with you and now you're freaking out because obviously you've changed your mind and don't want to be with me anymore."

"That's not it. Trust me." I take a deep breath. *Am I doing this?*

I picture Dyl, naked, a tear running down his cheek. Orange fire hurtling toward him. Him closing his eyes like he's accepting it, but his bottom lip is shaking. The image makes the decision for me. I don't want to live a life where Dyl is dead and I'm a liar.

I can't be a Love Interest anymore, so I'm going to do it: I'm going to sacrifice everything I've worked for to give him a chance to survive. I'm going to put my head next to his on the chopping block.

I don't have a choice.

It's who I am.

"I'm a Love Interest, Juliet. And so is Dyl. For most of our lives we've been owned by a company that monitors important people like you. They want you to fall in love with one of us so that we can spy on you for the rest of your life. We tell them your secrets, and then they sell them. In order to make sure we comply, they kill whoever doesn't get chosen. They burn him like garbage."

She nods, her stare intense. Her eyes are watery.

"Do you hear what I'm saying, Juliet?" I shout. "I've been spying on you! I've been lying to you this whole time! I'm the worst fucking person you've ever met."

The confession overwhelms me, and suddenly my eyes fill with tears. I lean forward, my chest heaving, and press my forehead against the steering wheel. I'm stupid, so stupid. What does crying achieve? Nothing. I can't fall apart, even if I want to. I need to save him. I take a deep breath. The air smells like plastic.

A hand touches the middle of my back. I flinch and look up, expecting to see a dark, eyeless face staring at me. It's not a Stalker, though. It's Juliet. Her lips are pressed together and her cheeks are shiny.

"Caden," she says. She's shaking, but her tone is even. "If what you said is true, that means, because I chose you, they're going to kill Dyl. Is that right?"

I nod, my strength coming back to me. I roughly wipe my cheeks.

"They want to," I say. "But I think he's going to kill himself before they can. I . . . I know him, and he's too proud to let them kill him. That's why I need to go. I need to save him."

She walks around to the other side of the truck and climbs in.

"What are you waiting for?" she asks. "Drive!"

I plant my foot on the accelerator and speed away from the party.

CHAPTER
TWENTY-SEVEN

WE'RE DRIVING THROUGH THE QUIET STREETS toward the lookout. Juliet has turned in her seat so that her back faces me. Her shoulders are hunched, making her look small. Occasionally her shoulders move and she lets out a tiny sob, and each time I hear the sound, so soft and weak, a flare of pain hits me. I'd say anything to make her feel better, but I can't think of anything to say that can fix this. So I just drive, and try not to think about the fact that I'm responsible for turning a sweet, wonderful girl into the suffering thing beside me.

She turns back to me. Her cheeks are glistening. "By telling me what you just did, did you . . ."

"Put you in danger? I did, and I'm so sorry. But they probably won't kill you. They think you're important enough for Love Interests. It's not a thing everyone gets, only superimportant people. Or, at least, people who they predict are going to become important someday. I doubt they're not going to give you that chance, so you're the safest of anyone. I am sorry, though. For that, and for everything else."

"So this is the real Caden, huh?"

I nod slowly. "The one and only."

She looks out the window, turning her back to me again.

We reach the parking lot. The only other car in the large stretch of concrete is Dyl's black convertible. It's parked haphazardly, across two different parking spaces. An ice-cold shiver chills my blood.

Juliet sits up straight. "Do you want me to come with you?"

I shake my head. "You can't. I don't know how Dyl is going to act. Rejected Love Interests are famous for violence—they like to leave the world with a bang. Dyl's not going to do that, though, at least I don't think he is. Just . . . I'll go."

I know what I have to ask, but every part of me is saying it's too much to ask of her. It's awful, but I have no other option.

"And I need you to do something for me, well, for us. I know you hate me, and that's understandable, but Dyl and I are going to have to run. So can you go back to your place and get as much food and water as possible? Fill the back of the truck with anything you can think of that'll help us survive. Dyl and I are going to go seriously off grid, so we'll need supplies. Please, Juliet. I know it's not fair to ask this of you, but believe me, it's my only option. I can't let them kill him."

Juliet nods. "I'll do it." She smiles wryly. "You know, I wondered if everything happening to me was too good to be true. I kept denying it, but deep down, I knew something weird was happening. No one had ever shown any romantic interest in me before, so I should've known it was fake. I should've known."

Ouch. I want to tell her she deserves only good things, but I don't have time. Dyl needs me more than she does right now.

"So you'll do it?" I ask.

"I will. I'll meet you back here in twenty minutes."

"Make it ten."

I clamber out of the truck and kick the door closed behind me. Then I tuck my hands into my pockets and jog up the path to the lookout.

Kaylee?

Nothing.

My fingers grip the hilt of the knife. I need to get the implants out, and fast. Now that I've decided I won't let Dyl die, the thought will be racing through my mind constantly. Trying to force the thought away just brings it back stronger. If Kaylee decides to listen to me it'll take only a second for her to realize what I'm doing.

And then it's all over.

If I can get the implants out, I'll buy us some time. Not a lot, but it's better than nothing. Plus, Kaylee told me they're not bombs, but since when has the LIC cared about telling us the truth? I'm not an idiot and I don't trust them. The implants need to come out.

I break out of the forest and reach the top of the clearing.

Dyl is standing on the railing, his back to me, the pointed ends of his shoes hanging over the edge. His arms are stretched wide, and his eyes are fixed on the stars.

"Dyl!" I call.

"Caden?" He looks over his shoulder at me. The wind buffets his hair. "What the hell are you doing here?"

"I could ask the same of you."

"I'm ending it, Caden. That should be obvious."

I step onto the platform. "Don't."

He turns back to face the town. "Why not? There's no nobility in letting my owners put me down like a bloody animal. This way I get to rob Craike of his murder boner."

I step forward. "I said don't. I told Juliet what I am. What *we* are. I can't let them kill you, Dyl. So let's run. Let's get in the car and escape from everything. I'm as dead as you are if we don't run, so get down off that railing and come with me. Please."

He jumps down onto the platform and walks over to me. He grabs my shoulders. "You rebelled?"

"I did."

He grins. "You freaking idiot." The grin fades and he lets go of my arms. "Wait, it's not because of the, um, gay thing, is it?"

It feels like a punch to the face. I know instantly that what I feared, what I desperately hoped wasn't true, is in fact reality: he was playing me. Every moment we shared was part of his strategy to take me down. I've always known it was a possibility, but here it is, my nightmare confirmed. He doesn't like me. His late-night visits. The drives in his car. The kiss in the shed. They were *all* scripted.

I barely suppress a whimper. "What do you mean, *the gay thing*?"

"The, you know . . . thing. Judy suspected that you, well, are what you are. And she suggested I play it up in hopes of derailing your efforts to make Juliet fall for you. And it was working, we both sensed you backing away, but Juliet had obviously already made up her mind. I'm not telling you this because I want to hurt you, because I don't. I just need to make sure you don't throw your life away because of something that wasn't real.

You're a great guy, and you're my friend, but I'm not in love with you. And I . . . I'm not gay. I like girls."

A sharp burst of laughter escapes my lips. It's totally fake, but I'm a good actor and he buys it. "Do you even hear yourself, Dyl? What in the world would make you think that after everything I've been through I'd want to be in love?"

He scratches the back of his neck. "I don't know."

"I'm rebelling because I'm not, nor do I ever want to be, the type of person who lets a friend die. That's it. Yeah, sure, I'm attracted to you. I guess that makes me gay. I'm not ashamed of that. Don't confuse *that* with this, because I'm not in love with you, Dyl. This is not a romantic gesture. I just don't want you to die, because you don't deserve it. Clear?"

Just like that, I'm back to being a liar.

"It doesn't matter why you're doing it, Caden. All that matters is that you're doing it. I . . . I have no idea how you can be so brave. You're risking everything to help me. It's more than I deserve."

"That's probably true. Now, shut up and sit down. I need to cut your tracker out."

He sits down on the bench and I pull the knife from my pocket. He stares at the blade and his lips part. "You've thought this through, huh?"

"Not really. But I'm glad it seems like I have a plan."

I touch the side of his stupidly beautiful face and push his head so it tilts to one side, with his cheek hovering above his shoulder. My fingers press against the skin at the very edge of his forehead until I feel a lump. He winces.

I move the knife up and position it above the bump. "This is going to hurt."

Dyl grits his teeth and closes his eyes. I raise the knife. It's going to hurt like hell, yet I don't feel bad about it. Maybe it's because I know it needs to be done. Or maybe a sick part of me wants to make him suffer. It feels like vengeance. I—

A harsh sob rings through my mind. It's a voice. A girl's, to be precise.

Kaylee.

Oh no.

I . . . I . . . I'm so sorry, Caden. I was checking in and I heard everything. I know what you're doing.

I take a step away from Dyl. My entire body goes slack. *No no no.* The knife feels cold in my hands. Dyl's eyes are searching my face.

Kaylee, please . . .

The Stalker is on its way. I'm so sorry, Caden. Goodbye.

PART
THREE

PROTAGONIST

TWENTY-EIGHT

"WHAT IS IT?" ASKS DYL. HE'S LEANING against the railing, holding his hair away from the lump where his tracker was inserted. "Why'd you stop?"

My heart is racing and my head feels fuzzy, like everything around me is crashing down. A sound like cymbals being smashed rings in my ears. I press my hands to my temples, trying to make everything shut up for a second so that I can figure out what to do.

I lower my hands. "It's Kaylee. She knows."

He turns around and kicks the railing. He moves his foot back and kicks it again.

"That means Judy knows as well; Kaylee would've told her."

"It doesn't change anything, Dyl."

But that's not true. This changes everything. This means there's no going back for me. This means I'm risking my life for the guy who tricked me into falling in love with him.

Even though I know this, it doesn't feel so bad, because looking at him now, knowing what he's done, I'll still do anything to save him. I'm probably the biggest idiot on the planet, but I can't turn off my affection for him, even though he has no affection for me.

Oh wow, he has no affection for me.

Still, I'm not going to let the LIC kill him.

But just: *ow.*

He moves back into position and tilts his head to the side. "You're right. Just do it."

I reposition the blade, right beside the bump. I push the blade in, and Dyl screams and shoves me with both hands. I take a few steps backward. Blood is spurting from the wound, running down his face onto his jacket.

He takes in a deep breath that fills his chest, then he gets back into position. "So the Stalker is coming?"

"Yep."

He scrunches up the material of his pants. "Then we need to hurry. Just do it. Come on, man, do it!"

A jagged red slash sits above his forehead. I step forward and peer closer. Peeking out through the slash are a few tiny red wires. I move my fingers up and go to grab the wires, pulling gently. Dyl roars, baring all his teeth.

"Stop!" he cries, shoving me in the chest again. I step away, raising my hands. He's shaking. "I felt it, Caden, I felt it in my brain. It's connected or something. You can't take it out. You can't. If you pull you'll scramble me." His eyes fill with tears. "I'll die."

Half of his face is covered in blood. It needs to be done, but I don't want to hurt him any more, so I step backward.

I start unbuttoning my shirt. "Then we're going to have to trust the LIC."

"What are you doing?"

"I need to stop the bleeding. It's something Kaylee taught me."

I pull the shirt off my shoulders and drop it. Then I take off my undershirt, ball it up, and hand it to him. "Press that to the wound. Can you walk?"

He nods, and raises the shirt to the wound and presses it in. He winces as the white material turns red.

I pick my shirt up off the ground and jog down the path to the street. Dyl follows me. My phone buzzes. As I run I pull it out of my pocket and look at the screen. It's a text from Juliet: *We're here. Hurry.*

What does she mean, *we're*?

"Come on!" I scream, and I pick up my pace. We reach the bottom of the hill, where Juliet is sitting in the driver's seat of my truck. The headlights are on, and they cast two white beams of light across the gloomy parking lot. I sprint toward the truck and swing the door open.

Trevor is sitting in the backseat. "Hey," he says with a wide grin. His hair is spiked up and he's wearing a brown leather jacket. "I heard you're a fugitive now."

"What are you doing here?" I ask him.

Natalie peeks her head out from the backseat. She's wearing a black shirt and jeans, but her hair is still perfectly styled and her makeup is immaculate; her eyes are smoky and her lips are covered in pale-pink lipstick. "I'm here too. We all decided that we can't let you die. Oh and, just so you know, Trev knows about me. I kind of had to tell him."

Trevor shrugs. "I'm a cheater, she's a liar. But we're happy and in love, and that's what matters."

"Aw, babe," says Natalie, and she plants a quick kiss on his cheek.

I stifle a scream of frustration. "Don't you see what you've done? Now we're all going to die!"

Natalie's eyes widen. "Yeah, we will, if you don't stop whining. Now hurry up."

I want to argue more but I quickly realize it's stupid, so I jump into the front seat. Dyl climbs in after me, wedging himself between Natalie and Trevor. They both stare at him like he's a confusing piece of art. He looks down at his calves.

"Go!"

Juliet plants her foot on the accelerator and the truck surges forward.

Natalie crosses her arms. "Does your coach know you've rebelled?" Dyl and I both nod. "Shit, that means we're already running out of time. Juliet, you need to drive as fast as you can and get us as far out of town as possible."

Juliet gives it some more gas and the truck picks up speed.

"I know this might be an unpopular opinion at the moment," says Trevor. "But shouldn't we go somewhere public, like a mall or something, and then call the police?"

I'm staring out the window at the flat, barren earth. "The LIC has enough money to bribe anyone. The police can't help us."

"We could make a video explaining what happened to you and post it online, and . . ."

"People have tried," says Dyl. "They all died, and the whole thing is covered up so fast it was like it was never posted. They were tortured for days before they were sent to the incinerator. And they say they lowered the heat settings for those people, so their deaths took longer. I'd call bullshit, but I heard the screams. It took hours. My point is that the LIC doesn't want anyone to know they exist, and they'll never let the word get out. Ever. And *every* conceivable way of spreading the word has been tried, and they all failed. Our best chance is to hide and hope they give up or forget about us."

Trevor leans back in his seat and sighs. "I guess you've thought about this more than I have. It's still so huge, I can't even fathom it."

"Then why are you here?" I meant to sound curious, but it comes out sounding mean. I press my lips together, then realize it doesn't matter that I did something that wasn't Nice. The LIC wants to kill me anyway, so there's no reason to be Nice ever again. I turn and look out the window as that sinks in.

I don't have to pretend I'm someone I'm not ever again.

Trev winces. "Well, you're my friend, Caden, and I'm not going to let some shady group of people treat you like a slave or kill you. And Natalie, well, she's the most important person to me on the planet. I'll do anything to protect her." He looks over his shoulder. "And Dyl's all right too, I guess."

"So is there somewhere we can go?" asks Juliet. "Like, some-place where people have made it away from them?"

I shake my head. "As far as we know, no one has ever survived running from the LIC. A Stalker always catches them. Always."

"What's a Stalker?" asks Juliet.

"It's a killing machine," says Dyl. "It's designed for one purpose: to keep Love Interests in line."

"Specifics, please."

"It's a robot," I say. "A big robot strong enough to pull people apart. They're also expert trackers, and they're scary fast. So far, they've got a perfect track record of catching fleeing Love Interests. No one gets away from a Stalker."

"But they're not us," says Natalie.

"Everyone thinks that," says Dyl. "Everyone thinks they're the exception."

"No, she's right," I say. "They've never had to face us. We have a shot."

Silence falls over the truck. Juliet reaches a stop sign and the truck slows to a crawl. We're already at the outskirts of town, and after this corner there's a long stretch of road surrounded by paddocks. I stare at the rearview mirror.

Out of the darkness, an eyeless face emerges. The swath of shadow unfurls, revealing the rest of the Stalker in all its horrific glory. The little rivers of light on its chest glow like fireflies in the darkness. Its toeless foot steps forward.

"Go!" I scream, my hand slapping the steering wheel. *"Go!"*

Juliet's eyes dart to mine, then she follows my stare to the mirror and her mouth drops open. She plants her foot on the accelerator and the truck skids around the corner, sending up smoke. We skid across into the opposite lane, which, thankfully, is empty, and then she corrects course and pulls into the other lane. She absolutely guns it. The entire cab vibrates as we shoot forward.

CHAPTER
TWENTY-NINE

"IS IT STILL CHASING US?"

We've been driving now for almost five hours. My eyes feel dry and heavy, as if they're being pushed out of my head. My hands are numb, and the hair on my arms is standing up. I peer over my shoulder. Behind me all I can see is a massive wall of darkness. I turn to the left and notice that the earth around us is flat and barren, broken apart only by the occasional tree.

Trevor leans forward. He's smiling. I grind my teeth together. He shouldn't be here. He should be safe, in his bed, asleep. So should Juliet and Natalie.

"Want a sour worm?" asks Trevor, offering me a bag filled with neon-colored candy. He's chewing with his mouth open. "They're good. And you need to keep your sugar up. It's almost time to switch dri—"

"I'm fine," interrupts Juliet. Her eyes are red and puffy. "Really."

"No, he's right," I say. "We need to switch." I pull a sour

worm out from the bag and pop it into my mouth. I bite down hard, cutting off the head. I feel the sugary energy creep through my blood, rushing to my heart and settling the shakiness of my arms. "Let's do it now. Park, and we'll both run around then get back in. It'll take two seconds."

"It's going to be out there, Caden," says Dyl. "It could've caught us if it wanted to. It's doing what they always said it would. It's tormenting us."

I shudder. "I know. But it'll end it for sure if we crash. At least this way we've got a shot."

Juliet puts her foot on the brake and the truck slows. "Now!" she calls.

I jump out and land on the road. I take a few quick steps to regain my balance, then I turn and run toward the front of the truck. Juliet passes me. I reach the front door, which is open.

Natalie screams, high and loud.

I look up.

The Stalker steps out of the darkness.

"Caden!" screams Juliet. "Get in!"

I leap into the truck and slam my foot down on the accelerator. *Please please please.* The truck charges forward. I grip the wheel and turn it, and the truck skids back onto the road. Wind whips in through the open door. In the rearview mirror the wall of blackness moves forward, covering the Stalker. It raises its mannequin head and meets my stare as the darkness covers its face.

With one hand, I reach out and slam the door shut. The sound vibrates around the cab, then silence falls.

"It's messing with us," says Natalie. "But that's a good

thing, right? It buys us time. We just need a plan, and Juliet, you're the only one who can think us out of this. So you need to sleep, because we need you at full brain power to get us out of this."

"I'm fine," says Juliet. "I can think and keep watch."

"Nat's right, we need you to sleep," I say. "You've been out-voted, so do it."

She stares at me for a second, then opens her mouth. Her eye-brows furrow and she pouts before turning and leaning her head against the headrest. Why is she acting so strange? It hits me: that was the first time I've ever bossed her around. The power in our relationship has shifted, and now she has no idea what to expect from me. I want to explain myself to her, to tell her that I'm not an awful person, I'm just not the meek boy she thought I was. I want to tell her I understand this change must be a shock to her, but that I'm still pretty much the same guy, only better, because now I can finally say what I truly think and feel.

I want her to know the real me.

I open my mouth, but she closes her eyes and pretends to be asleep. If she doesn't want to talk, I need to respect that. It's the only way I'll ever rebuild any form of relationship with her.

"So after Caden, I'll drive," says Natalie. "Then Trev, then Dyl. And then the cycle repeats. And I know what you're thinking, Trev, but I've driven in a car with you so I know you're actually a pretty decent driver. Much better than you think you are, anyway. So you can drive on your own for a few hours. You'll be fine."

Trevor scratches his forearm. "Yeah, because *fine* is exactly how I'd describe our current situation."

IT'S BEEN EIGHT HOURS SINCE WE WENT ON THE run, and the red gas gauge has started flashing. I've watched it flash so many times now it's burned into my retinas, and the image lingers even when I close my eyes.

Dyl's driving, and I'm in the middle of the backseat, wedged between Natalie and Juliet. No matter how I try to position myself, my thighs are always touching one of them. Juliet hasn't said a word to me since I moved to the backseat, and when I look at her she always turns her head and looks out the window.

"We need to stop," says Dyl. His voice is deeper and more gravelly than usual. "Are you sure there's a station up ahead?"

Juliet chews her bottom lip. "It doesn't matter, because that thing's not going to let us refuel. But we can do something about it. Come on, you guys, I know we're all thinking it."

"I'm not thinking anything," I say. "What are *you* thinking? You're the genius."

I meant it as a compliment, but like most things I've said recently, it comes out sounding harsh.

Juliet fiddles with a long strand of her hair. Her long, slightly pink fingers are shaking. "I think we need to fight it."

"I was *not* thinking that," says Dyl. "It's a killing machine. There's no way we can face it. No way. It'll butcher us all. There was this video they showed us, back in the LIC, of it ripping a Nice's head off with its bare hands. It's unstoppable."

"I have weapons," she says. "They're in the back of the truck. While Nat and Trev were loading the truck I went to my lab and grabbed some of the things I'd been working on. I brought your suit, Natalie, and the Black Hole Bombs and the Bolt Gloves and a few other things. We can fight it if we plan our attack. If we run out of fuel and it catches us we're all screwed. If we plan ahead, we can at least try to take it out."

"So what's the plan?" I ask.

Juliet grins. "I say we blow it up." She rubs her palms together. "The bombs, they're strong enough to do it. If I can get to the detonator and we plant it in its path, I can destroy the Stalker. I know I can. All we'll need is some sort of building to hide in while we plant the bomb."

Dyl sighs. "How do we even know a bomb will work?"

I roll my eyes. "What else are we going to try, Dyl? Should we just give up and die? If that's what you want to do go right ahead, but I want to at least try something, and this is the best plan we have."

"No, you're right," he says. "Sorry. Wait, you were saying we needed a building? Because look." He points out his window. The sun is slowly rising, and against the pink sky is the outline of a barn. "Will that do?"

Juliet nods. "It's perfect. Okay, we need to do this now. Is everyone ready to run? Dyl and Caden, I'm going to need you to be bait. Nat and Trev, run in the opposite direction in case anything goes wrong. Okay?"

"Wait, what?" says Natalie. "What are we doing?"

"When the truck stops, get away from us. Caden, run to the back and find the black backpack. That's the one with the bombs. Grab it and then run toward the barn."

The barn is rapidly approaching.

"Stop, Dyl! Make it look like the gas ran out."

Dyl puts his foot on the brake and the truck rolls to a halt. Trev grabs the door handle, swings the door open, and jumps out; Juliet follows him. I leap out after them. I turn for a second and look down the road. In the distance is a lone figure. It lowers its head and moves into a sprint position.

I wrench the tarp off the back of the truck and start searching for the backpack. Natalie and Trev leap off the road and sprint toward the forest. I scramble through a pile of clothes, then a pile of cans, then my fingers touch scratchy canvas. I grab one of the straps and pull, revealing a black backpack. I turn. The Stalker is about five hundred yards away and closing fast. Juliet and Dyl are in front of the barn, where Dyl is pushing up a plank of wood, trying to open the door.

I sling the bag over my shoulder and run. The bag jostles as my feet pound against the damp grass. Dyl drops the plank of wood and the barn door swings open, creaking as it moves. I reach them and pass the bag to Juliet.

"Is this it?" I ask, my voice harsh from breathlessness.

"It is." Her eyes go wide. "Now move!"

I look where she's looking. The Stalker is standing beside the truck. It's bent over, its black fingers gripping the bottom. It straightens up, lifting the truck clean off the road like it weighs nothing. The Stalker pauses there for a moment, holding the truck above its head.

Then it turns and faces us.

I grab Dyl by the shirt and pull him a few steps forward. This yanks him out of his stupor and he starts running. Juliet follows us just as the Stalker throws the truck. It soars through the air toward us.

I dive forward as an orange blur rockets through the side of the barn, sending up a spray of wood chips. The truck hits the other side of the wall and crumbles, spraying glass and unleashing a pungent smell of gasoline. Orange fire spreads from the hood, spewing black smoke.

Juliet crouches beside the wreckage and unzips the backpack.

"Get away!" I call as I stand up. "It could blow!"

She ignores me and keeps ferreting around the bag. "Yes!" she says as she pulls out a black boxlike item. She places it on the ground and presses a button. A light on the side turns from red to green. Then she pulls a small black thing that's shaped like a pen from the middle of the device. Smiling, she grabs a handful of straw and covers the object with it.

Through the smoke, the Stalker appears. Juliet scrambles away, joining us. We're pressed against the back of the barn. I offer my hand to Dyl. He grabs it. His palm is cold and sweaty.

The detached door of the truck is embedded deep in the ground. The Stalker swipes at it. The door lifts up, spins once, then falls and digs itself deep into the ground, sending up little clods of brown earth.

Dyl lets go of my hand and steps forward. The Stalker's head pivots to the side, staring at him.

"Take me," says Dyl. His voice is hoarse. He pounds his fist on his chest. "Leave them, take me." The sound of his fist hitting his flesh is the only noise in the entire barn. Or at least it seems that way.

I notice his feet are crossing, and he's moving slowly to the left. Toward the bomb.

The Stalker moves into a sprint position.

"Now!"

The Stalker transforms into a blur of darkness, its hand stretching out to grab Dyl. Juliet presses her thumb down on the end of the pen. The hand grabs Dyl's shirt and yanks down, slamming him into the ground.

A maelstrom of intense black and purple erupts out of the ground, swirling viciously. The air turns freezing cold, like all the warmth has been sucked out of the room. A vortex of color has enveloped the Stalker, save for its hand.

With a snap, the ball of color folds in on itself. The Stalker's detached hand is all that remains. It drops, then lies still on the blackened, smoldering earth.

"Oh my God!" says Juliet. She jumps up and down and pulls me into a hug. "It worked! Do you know the ramifications of this, Caden? I've discovered a way to create a truly contained explosive. All of the destructive power, none of the risk. The potential for this . . ."

Dyl is still lying facedown on the ground. *Oh no.* The straw surrounding him is red with blood. His blood. There's a lot of it.

I go to say something, but my throat clamps shut and I freeze. *Please, please let him be okay.* Juliet releases me.

She sees Dyl. "No way. Not now."

I crouch beside him.

"Dyl?" I say softly. I touch his shoulder and roll him onto his back.

His nose is leaking blood, and his face is pale and sweaty. He opens his mouth, and his Adam's apple bobs up and down.

"Caden?" he says.

His eyes close.

CHAPTER
THIRTY

DYL IS LEANING AGAINST A TREE USING A ROLLED-UP jacket as a pillow. His head lolls to the left and his eyes are closed, but he's breathing. We're in the middle of a grayish-blue forest, surrounded by smooth-barked white trees. I'm sitting beside him with my legs out in front of me, waiting for him to wake up. A sane person would be sitting with the others in front of the fire, where it's warm and dry, but I wanted to be there when he woke. He stirs and I straighten up.

"Hey," I say softly as I shift closer to him.

He looks down at his chest. He's shirtless, but most of his chest is covered by a white pad. When the Stalker slammed him into the ground, the force was so strong it took a lot of the skin off. His face glows white, and his hair is damp and pressed down over his forehead. Damn it, the LIC was right. Wounded guys *are* hot.

Thankfully, the cuts are quite shallow, little more than grazes, and Natalie thinks he passed out from shock. While I was carrying Dyl away from the barn, Juliet raided the wreckage of the truck for food and other supplies. She managed to salvage a few cans of food, some singed clothes, and a kit filled with medicine and matches.

I raise a white pill, a Tylenol, to Dyl's chapped lips.

"Here," I say. "It'll get rid of the pain."

He waves my hand away. "It's fine. I can handle the pain." He scratches his arm. "The cold is slightly harder to handle. Can you get me a shirt?"

I stand up and brush the leaves from my pants. Then I walk through the forest to the others. Trevor and Natalie are curled up together on the ground, with Trevor's massive arm covering most of Natalie's torso. Juliet is sitting on a large moss-covered rock, her legs dangling over the edge. Her hair is straggly and she's fiddling with some wires: the Bolt Gloves. Her eyebrows are furrowed and her lips are pursed.

She places the wires down and picks up an open can of beans. She offers it to me.

"Baked beans?" she asks. "They're cold and terrible, but they made me feel a little bit better. So maybe they'll work on you."

I grab the can and raise it to my lips. I fill my mouth with the metallic-tasting beans. I swallow, then place the can back down on the rock.

"Caden," says Juliet, "I've decided to forgive you."

I wipe my chin with my sleeve. How can she forgive me so fast? How can she be over it when I haven't even begun to forgive myself for what I've done to her?

"You don't have to do that, Juliet."

"I know. But I've decided I want to. So I forgive you. We're okay."

"You have no idea how much that means to me," I say.

I'm being totally honest.

"I think I do," she says. "It's why I'm forgiving you. But enough about that. How's Dyl?"

"He's awake. And he's all right, I guess, considering what happened to him. He can move, at least. How are you?"

"I'm okay. Not good. Just okay. I'm trying to come up with a way to get out of this alive. To do that, I need to know more about the LIC. Nat's told me a bit, but your memory is fresher, so I'd also like to ask you some questions. How much do you know about it? They spy on people they think are important, right? Why? What does that achieve?"

I cross my arms. "Juliet, they don't tell Love Interests everything. We're on a strictly need-to-know basis."

"I understand that, but someone as smart as you must know some things about their operations. Please, Caden, this is important. If we're going to escape them, I need to know more about them."

I sit down. "Fine. All I know for sure is that they sell the information they collect. That's what Mr. Craike, who is the leader of the place, told me. He asked me how much I thought someone would pay for information that could destroy a president."

"No," she says. "They can't be . . ."

"But they are! This goes *really* deep. If you think of anyone who has ever been anyone, chances are they had, or have, a Love Interest beside them. That's the thing, Juliet. This has been going on for centuries. He showed me this hologram of all the Love Interests throughout history, and there were hundreds of them. These people have been lurking in the backgrounds of history for generations, collecting secrets for the LIC to sell. We live in a world where a piece of information can kill careers or start wars. The people who run the LIC have been taking advantage of this for years."

She nods, taking it all in. "It's actually kind of genius. Of course people are going to share secrets with their loved ones. That's kind of the whole point of having them in the first place. What the LIC is doing is disgusting, but it's genius. That said, I think I've found their weakness."

"I'm all ears."

"Secrets are their business, but their existence itself is a secret. I imagine their clients are small in number, or maybe they don't even know how the LIC gets its information. My point is that people who know about the existence of Love Interests are dangerous to the LIC. It's why they want to kill us so bad. If word got out that they're using loved ones to spy on people, they'd lose all their power. If we could find a way to tell the world about Love Interests, then . . ."

"A Stalker will—"

Her eyes light up as she interrupts me. "That's the thing, Caden. It *always* comes down to the threat of Stalkers. Without them, the LIC would just be . . . people. And that's the thing about technology—as much as I love it, it becomes a crutch. I'm sure they had ways to keep Love Interests in line before they invented Stalkers, but now I'd bet they'd be lost without them. If we could find a way to destroy the Stalkers, we would buy enough time for Love Interests to come forward. We'd need a lot of them to do it, but that would destroy the LIC for good."

I breathe in the clear, crisp air. It's too nice, too easy, to be true. If this plan were feasible surely someone must've tried it. "Well, maybe that's true. But right now all I know is that we need to move."

But I can already feel her idea worming its way through my brain, finding a spot to nestle and take root. *We can fight back.* I pick up a black shirt from the pile beside Trevor's head and walk back to Dyl.

He's standing with his hands in his pockets. I grip the shirt tight. This boy tricked me, and tried his absolute hardest to kill me. I should want to beat the crap out of him. Yet the sight of him standing there only reminds me of our nights together. *It was fake*, I think. *It was all fake.* I can't long for those moments because they weren't real, and I can't keep treating Dyl like he's the guy I thought he was.

I pass him the shirt and he grabs it with one hand.

"It's Trevor's," I say. "So it'll probably be a bit big. But it's black, so I thought you'd like it." I wince. I guess it's not as easy as just deciding to stop being nice to him. "We need to move," I say, my tone harsh. "Is that a problem for you?"

He shakes his head. "No, it's not. I'm fine."

"Are you lying to me?"

"Don't you trust me anymore?"

"Just . . . put your clothes on. We're moving."

Keeping eye contact with me, he pulls the shirt over his head, flinching as the material touches his chest. Once it's on, he smoothes down his hair.

"So what's the plan, Caden?"

We rejoin the others. Natalie and Trevor are now standing. She is stretching, and he is yawning a massive yawn that shows all his teeth.

"We need a new car," I say. "So we need to get out of the woods and buy one."

Trevor clears this throat. "We should be pretty close to Brookman Bay. It's a pretty quiet town but it has a great pool. Dad used to take me there for meets sometimes. I'm pretty sure it has a lot of used-car dealerships—it's that type of town, one that reeks of desperation."

"They'll be able to trace my card if I use it," says Juliet. "I've got two thousand in cash, but dealerships probably aren't going to accept that much seeing as it's so freaking sketchy and it puts them at risk. So we might have to use the card and then run as fast as possible."

"But where are we running to?" asks Dyl.

Juliet turns and faces me, her eyes wide and questioning. I nod slowly.

"We aren't running anymore," she says. "We're going to fight them."

THIRTY-ONE

JULIET AND TREVOR WERE CHOSEN TO BUY THE car. I advised them to buy the second-cheapest one, because that wouldn't look desperate, just budget conscious. Everyone volunteered to go, but that pairing was selected because a white heterosexual couple is the least remarkable and therefore least memorable pairing, should someone decide to interrogate the salesperson. Trevor was chosen over Dyl and me as we figured they would be looking for people with our descriptions, not his. Also, of all of us he looks the oldest, which might be an advantage. Juliet told us that, legally, one of us would need to be eighteen in order to register a car. So all we can do is hope that either the salesperson skips that step, or we find someone who is a little bit sketchy. It's not ideal, but we don't have a choice.

While we wait, Natalie insists we remove our implants.

So I'm standing in the woods, in my underwear so as not to get blood on the only clothes I have, with Dyl's rolled-up belt in my mouth. Natalie advances, holding the knife. My teeth clamp down on the leather. It tastes dry and earthy.

"This isn't going to work," she says, with a flourish of the knife. "You're too tall. You're going to have to lie down."

Dyl is pacing back and forth. He's worn a little trail into the mulch. "How do you know this is going to work? How do you know this isn't going to scramble him?"

I take the belt out of my mouth. Why does he care so much? He wanted me to die before, and now he's worried about my safety? It doesn't make sense. Yes, I tried to kill him as well, but at least I was backing away toward the end. He never hesitated in his plan to take me down, so he doesn't care about me. But that doesn't explain why he looks so worried right now, or why he took my hand when I offered it to him when we faced the Stalker. "I'll be fine, Dyl."

Natalie lifts her hair up, revealing her scalp. A large, dotted scar is visible above her ear. It curves, following the shape of her skull. "After Trevor chose me, I was brought back to the LIC one last time and they removed it. Apparently they reuse them, which is too gross to think about. The point is I know this will work. His scar won't be as pretty as mine, but he won't die, Dyl, I promise. Caden, please lie down."

I pop the belt back in and lie down on the rocky outcrop. I lie on the very edge, so my right arm hangs limply in the air. I tilt my head to the side and Natalie rests the point of the knife against my skin. I close my eyes.

"Ready?"

I nod.

The side of my head explodes. The knife digs in over and over and over, parting my skin and scooping out the gelatinous red flesh beneath. Every part of me is cold save for the side of my head, which is a burning inferno. The belt feels like it's climbing down my throat, choking me, so I try to spit it out but it's caught and I can't and I start choking. Two weights clamp down on my arms, the sensation stronger than the pain. I open my eyes, and through the tears I see a blurry face. The face moves away, then returns. My vision clears, and a pair of green eyes meet mine.

Dyl.

He pats my shoulder. "It's done, man."

I blink and sit up. Sharp pain burrows into my brain. "Is it out?"

He nods and starts unbuttoning his shirt. His shaking fingers fumble and he finally just rips the shirt off. I gaze at his chest for a second, then look down at my hands.

"It's done," he says. "Now move; I need to get mine out."

I roll to my trembling feet, then fall forward. My chest slams into a tree and I cling to it as the entire world vibrates. The forest jumps up and down and left and right. I grip the rough, cold wood and breathe in. The shaking at the edges of my vision gradually returns to normal. I breathe in deep, then push away from the tree. Dyl screams, and the sound hurts me more than the knife did.

I stumble toward him. When I reach him I place my hands on his bare shoulders and hold him down, just how he held me. Natalie's mouth is a firm line, and she's holding the knife steady. She flicks the tip of the knife, and a small silver ball falls out of the cut. It lands on the stone with a clink.

I grab Dyl's hand and pull him up to a sitting position. He sways, but remains upright.

"We're back!" calls Juliet. She and Trevor are making their

way through the forest toward us. They're both smiling. "And we were excellent! Well, Trev was. He got us a great deal on the car, plus he had the genius idea to get you two some more comfortable clothes and some tents to sleep in. We . . ." She reaches us and falls silent.

Trevor raises his hands, revealing three large black canvas bags that are full to the brim. "It's just a bit of blood, Jules, they'll be fine. Don't let them take our story from us, because it's a cracker. So the girl at the store, she was—"

Natalie interrupts with a grim smile. "Babe, I love your stories, but now is definitely not the time."

He sighs. "Fine. The car was four grand, so we had to use the credit card. We figured we may as well spend as much as we can, seeing as they'll know we're here anyway. So Jules and I went on a spree and bought you guys a bunch of crap."

Juliet hands me a plastic bag. "These are yours, Caden. I hope they fit."

I open it and peer inside. It's a plaid duffel coat, a gray shirt, a pair of dark jeans, and black dress boots, the kind that hipsters love. She's staring at me expectantly, her eyes wide.

"Thanks, Juliet," I say. "These look great. Truly."

She presses her lips together, then turns and walks back to the others.

I walk into the woods and get changed. The boots are a little too tight, maybe one size too small, and they pinch my toes, but the material is soft and the ache that's been building at the bottom of my calves starts to lift. Everything else fits perfectly. I walk back into the clearing. Dyl is now wearing a navy button-down, and he's holding a black leather jacket. The side of his face is covered in blood, matting down thin strands of dark hair to his scalp.

Juliet picks up her bag of gadgets. "You two need to get washed up before we go back into town. We passed a creek on our way here." She points to her left. "Wash the blood off, then we'll go."

Dyl and I trudge through the forest. I lead the way.

He climbs over a rotting log. "Does it still hurt? The cut, I mean."

"What else could you be referring to?"

"A lot of things, I guess."

We reach the creek Juliet was talking about. The water is only about an inch deep, a thin stream of clear water running over dark pebbles. *Dyl lied to me*. I should ignore him, or do something, to tell him our friendship is done. We're alone right now in this quiet forest, so it's easy to pretend that he isn't the person he is. Like this is just another moment, like our kiss or the drives. But it's not another moment, so I need to start treating him like the person he really is.

He pushes up his shirt sleeves and crouches beside the water. I do the same, scooping up a palmful of icy water and splashing it onto my face. The water comes away pinkish. The contact doubles the pain, and I grit my teeth. Dyl dips his hand into the water and then rubs his bloody skin. He's cringing and his eyes are full of tears. I start to say something to comfort him, then I remember everything he's done. Instead, I scoop up a handful of water and hurl it at the wound on the side of my head. The water slaps my flesh and feels like a million bee stings. All energy leaves my body and I fall to my knees.

Breathe in.

Breathe out.

I reopen my eyes.

Dyl is looking at me. "Are you all right?"

I nod.

He shuffles forward, raising his hand. "You missed a spot."

My head jerks back.

His right eyebrow rises. "That move was platonic, I swear. I'm a bro helping out another bro who has blood on his face."

I roll my eyes. "You're so full of crap. Stop pretending to like me at all, Dyl. Just be yourself. It's why we did all of this, so you may as well be honest."

I stand up, using my left hand to find the last remaining spot of crusted-on blood. I dig my fingernails into it, scraping it off. It feels gooey, and clings to the edges of my nails.

I walk away from the creek back to the clearing, where the others are standing in a small circle. They've all changed into more casual clothes, jeans, T-shirts, and jackets. Juliet is wearing a pale-pink hoodie under a gray winter coat that reaches her thighs. Her hands are covered in fingerless gloves.

A branch behind me snaps. I turn and see Dyl standing there, a tiny speck of blood on his forehead.

"You missed a spot," I say before I step into the clearing. "Bro."

Sitting on the rock beside a puddle of blood are our trackers. I step toward them. "Which one was mine?"

Natalie points to the one on the right.

I crouch down and pick up a rock that's about double the size of my fist. It's covered in dirt and mulch. I stop beside my tracker, then bring the rock up and slam it down. The orb breaks with a satisfying crunch. I raise the rock again. The orb is now a jumble of eggshell-thin pieces of metal, tiny red wires, and silver powder.

"Stop!" calls Juliet. She grabs my hand and holds it tight. "Don't break them!"

"Why not?" asks Dyl. "That looked fun."

"Yeah," I say. "Plus, they're using them to track us, remember? They need to go, right?"

She rolls her eyes. "Yep, they're tracking us, but they're also our only shot at finding the LIC, and I can't do that if you smash them."

"I don't follow."

"Think about it, Caden. They're sending a signal to the LIC. That means that, if I had the right tech, I could use the trackers to track *them*. For my plan to work, we're going to need to attack the LIC directly, and we can't do that if we don't know where it is."

Dyl pouts. "Oh, you're still on this dream. Good to know."

Natalie steps forward, grabs the orb, and tucks it into the front pocket of her jacket. "We have to go. As my mom says, we can fight in the car. But, for the record, I'm with Juliet."

The girls bump knuckles, then we walk out through the clearing to the road. Parked on the side is a small red car. The paint has faded, and the passenger-seat window is cracked.

Juliet opens the front door. "Caden, could you sit in the front? I'd like to talk to you. I need to pick your brain for more info about the LIC."

"Sure."

I walk around the front of the car to the passenger door. In the window is my reflection. My skin is überpale, and there are

Godzilla-sized bags under my eyes. My hair hangs limply over my forehead, and the patchy beginnings of a beard are growing on my cheeks. I raise a hand and rub my prickly skin, my fingertips running along my jawbone.

Trevor catches me staring at myself and smirks. "You're not so hot anymore, huh? Don't worry, we all look like shit."

"It's not that," I say, peering closer. For the first time I can recall, the boy staring back at me matches my image of myself. "I look human. It's weird, but I like it."

"Sure is. Now get in."

I open the door and step inside as the trunk slams. Hot air is blowing from the dashboard. I clip on my seat belt.

Juliet turns on the engine.

"Is everyone ready?"

Silence answers her.

"I'll take that as a yes." She flicks on the turn signal and pulls onto the empty road. "Let's get as far away from here as possible. And then we can come up with a plan."

———

WE STOP AT NIGHTFALL AND PARK ON THE SIDE of the road, then find a small clearing and go to set up the tents Juliet and Trevor bought.

Right now, we're all crowded around the trunk, looking at the three bags. "This is awkward," says Trev. "We should've bought four. Nat and I are going to share, obviously, but . . ."

"I can sleep outside," says Dyl. "That's fine."

"Don't be silly," says Juliet. "You'll freeze. Caden and I have been friends for . . ." She slowly closes her eyes, then reopens them. "Actually, yeah, I want to go alone. I'm sorry, I won't sleep otherwise. And I'm so tired that's all I want to do. I can't go another night without it."

"Let's set up," I say. "And then we can decide later. I'm freezing."

We carry the tents to a small circular clearing, where we drop them. It's a wide stretch of short grass, broken apart by large gray boulders. The shade from the stones sends long stretches of black across the damp ground.

Trev looks up at the pink sky. "It's going to get dark soon. We need to set up. Like, right now."

I grab a two-man tent and then walk to the edge of the clearing. Once I finish assembling the base tent I notice the others are done too, and are now sitting in front of a fire. Dyl isn't with them.

"How's it going, Caden?"

Dyl is leaning against a boulder with his hands in his pockets. He detaches from the stone and strides over to me. I start to flatten out the tarp.

"I don't need help," I say.

"It's not that, I know you don't need help. I just realized I'd be dead right now if it weren't for you."

I drop the tarp and meet his stare. "Oh."

"And I realized I don't want to be a dick to the person who saved my life."

"Don't be dramatic, Dyl."

"I'm not being dramatic, Caden. Or we're in a dramatic situation and I'm acting accordingly. So I wanted to say I'm sorry for manipulating you when we were competing. You're a nice guy, no, a *good* guy, and it was mean. You didn't deserve it."

Using my foot, I push the last peg into the soft ground. It sinks in easily. This is an apology, which I guess is a good thing, but it hurts because it's confirmation that everything we had was scripted.

"We agreed early on," I say, "that we were going to give it our all. Giving it your all meant manipulating me, and I get that, Dyl."

"I want to ask you something."

His eyes flick toward the others, huddled around the campfire about fifty yards away. I'd say we're just out of earshot.

I scratch my forearm. "Shoot."

"Would you have still saved me if you knew what I was doing? Or did you only save me because you thought we were in love?"

"I never thought we were in love."

"Tell me the truth, Caden. I know the real you well enough to tell when you bring out the Nice guy."

I clench my fists, and I feel the blood rush to my cheeks. I wipe the end of my nose with my jacket sleeve. "I don't know what you want me to say. Yes, Dyl, I was beginning to like you in a way I've never liked anyone else, and yes, I thought you maybe liked me back and that was scary and exciting. So I don't know what I would've done if I didn't like you in the way that I do or if you weren't particularly special to me. And if that's the case I'm glad I started to feel that way toward you, because I don't want to be the type of person who is okay with someone innocent dying. I just don't. And if feelings for you are what made me wake up and see what's right and what's wrong, then I'll always be thankful for them, no matter how this all ends."

He's staring at me.

In the distance, the fire crackles, an orange spark in all the hazy blue.

He breaks eye contact and walks past me toward the fire. I step aside to let him pass. Then he stops and looks back at me. He digs his hands into the pockets of his jacket.

"Just so you know," he says. His voice is trembling. "You're a cute guy, Caden. I'm sure you're going to make some lucky boy really happy one day."

"Um, thanks?"

"I know you will, because I . . . I liked our time together. It may have started as a lie, but I did enjoy spending time with you. In fact, it was maybe the most fun I've ever had. I thought you should know that." He turns and heads toward the campfire.

I feel the smile coming and am powerless to stop it.

So, in the middle of a freezing forest:

My stomach fills with butterflies.

CHAPTER
THIRTY-TWO

"CAN YOU PASS THE SPAGHETTI, CADEN?"

We're all sitting around the campfire. I'm holding an ash-covered, fire-warmed can of spaghetti. I use a plastic fork to scoop up one last mouthful. The spaghetti is basically mush, but weirdly I like the taste. I swallow, then pass the can to Juliet.

She takes it silently and starts to eat, taking quick, big mouthfuls.

I turn my attention back to the flickering orange flames and move my hands out in front of me so my palms heat up. The biggest log, the one in the center of the fire, is gray and ashy, yet the end that's out of the fire looks untouched.

"Juliet's right," I say. "We can fight them."

Dyl murmurs something under his breath.

"Speak up, Dyl."

"I said we can also die trying."

"Maybe we will. I'm all in, but that's my choice, and I don't want to drag any of you into this unwillingly. So, Dyl, if you or anyone else doesn't want to fight, you can leave. I won't hold it against you."

Dyl places an empty can of beans on the grass, then wipes his hands on his jeans. "If I leave and they catch you, they'll torture you to find out as much as they can about my whereabouts. I . . . I wouldn't be able to handle that, knowing they're torturing you just to find me. But that's not the only reason I'm staying. I want to fight them as well."

"So do I," says Natalie. "More than I've ever wanted anything."

"I'm here for Natalie," says Trev. "So I'll do whatever she wants. So it looks like I'm fighting too."

Juliet clambers to her feet. "This feels like too serious a decision to make over breakfast food." She pulls her phone from her pocket and places the battery back inside. "But whatever. I'm going to try to see if I can figure out where the signal from the trackers is being sent. And then we can make our way there. I was trying most of last night, and I think I'm pretty close to getting it down. Give me a couple more hours and I'll have it."

After six agonizing hours in which all we do is wait, Juliet returns. She's grinning, holding the phone up beside her face. I rise slowly. *No way.*

"I found it," she says. "I did it."

I rush toward her, grabbing her hands to look at the screen. It's Google Maps, and a red light is flashing on it. The LIC. I stare at the blinking red light, my hands clenching so tight my nails dig into my skin. Mirrored hallways. Glass.

Hell on earth.

I remember who I used to be. Then I met Dyl and everything changed. I'm only just starting to discover who I am, and it's all because I got out of there.

And I'm about to go back?

The others get up and crowd around us, each one of them trying to get a good look at the screen. Juliet slides her phone back into her pocket. "It's about two days' drive to the east of here." She pulls out the tracker, then offers it to Dyl. "Here, you can smash this. I've got the signal locked, so it's useless now."

Dyl takes it from her and places it on the ground. One quick stomp and it's done.

Natalie sighs. "Juliet, I'm so impressed you found the LIC, but what are we going to do when we get there? There are only five of us. And they have killer robots, an entire army of trigger-happy guards, and maybe even military support. How are we possibly going to break into that? We'll get shot outside the walls and then they'll burn us. *All* of us."

"No, we won't," I say. "Because not all of us are going to go in. Not at first, at least. They want to take me inside to incinerate me, right?" Natalie and Dyl nod. "I say we let them. That way, I'll be let in, and I can find a way to break free and then I can find a way to let you guys in. Then, together, we can use Juliet's weapons to take them down."

"It's risky," says Dyl. "I don't like it. Maybe we should keep thinking—"

"We don't have time!" I say. "Sitting here now is risky, because at any moment a Stalker could find us and rip us apart. At least this way we have a shot, even if it's a bad one. If you can think of something better, we'll do that. But if you can't, this is happening. All right?"

He sighs. "Fine."

"It's settled," says Juliet. "We leave in half an hour."

———————

TEN MINUTES LATER, I'M STANDING ON THE stony shore of a small creek. I pull my shirt off, then drop my trousers and wade into the water. My whole body goes tense. It's fucking freezing. Still, I have to get rid of the lethargy that's gripping me in order to survive the rapidly approaching battle. *I can do this. Three. Two. One.*

I lower myself into the creek. The so-cold-it-hurts water just reaches my chest. Still, there's a satisfying clarity to the pain. This hurt, at least, is easy to understand. I lower myself until I'm fully horizontal. The water surrounds my face. Through a gap in the trees, I can see the gray sky.

"Hello?" calls a voice.

I sit up and press my knees to my chest as Juliet walks into the clearing. Her hair is loose and knotty, and a pink towel is wrapped around her waist. Her legs are bare.

She stops when she sees me. "Oh, Caden, I didn't know you were here." She smiles. "I was just going to wash my face. And you're in the water? Why?"

I fan my fingers through my damp hair. "It seemed like a good idea. Now that I'm doing it, I know it is in fact the worst idea I've ever had."

She laughs, making her way over to a smooth rock on the

shore. She sits down on it so her feet touch the water. "Can I ask you something? I've been thinking about it a lot and I don't think I'll be able to focus until I know for sure."

"You can ask me anything, Juliet."

"Do you love Dyl?"

My cheeks go red and I look down at the water. It's crystal clear. "I don't know what love is."

"Come on, I already know it's true. You can barely keep your eyes off him. You love him, don't you?"

I can't keep lying to her. Not after everything she's done for me.

"I think I do," I say. "It doesn't matter, though. He tricked me into developing feelings for him as part of the contest. He wanted me to fall for him so I'd back away from you. The scary thing is that it was working. I was already doubting whether I could do anything that would kill him. If you hadn't made your choice when you did, I would've lost and you'd be with Dyl."

"That's part of the reason I'm helping you," says Juliet. "As much as it sucks to be a Love Interest and everything, being tricked into falling in love with someone is pretty awful too. So I'm doing this for all the people out there who deserve to be in love with someone who genuinely loves them back. No one deserves to be lied to for their entire lives."

My chest starts to ache. "All I can say is I'm sorry. I'll never be able to fix it all."

"Thanks for the apology, Caden, really. Anyway, isn't it pretty normal for a straight girl to fall for a gay guy? All the sitcoms treat it like a rite of passage, something that all girls must go through.

You're pretty and kind and way too good to be true. At least I've ticked that box now."

"I . . ." I don't exist to teach her a lesson, and it irks me that she thinks labeling me is okay now. Like, by liking guys, I automatically take on *that* role in her life. That I'm suddenly a supporting character in her story rather than the hero of my own.

She leans forward. "But Caden, you need to know something. Your feelings *do* matter, because Dyl likes you back. Everyone can see it."

I shake my head. "He doesn't. It was all fake."

She laughs. "God, guys can be *so* thick sometimes. That boy is in love with you, Caden. It's obvious to everyone but the two of you. He—"

"He said he likes girls, Juliet. He straight up told me he isn't gay and that he likes girls."

She narrows her eyes. "Caden, stop and think about it for a second. There are three very plausible explanations for him saying that. Maybe he's lying; he's done it before, so he could be doing it again. Or, you know, he might be bi. He totally could like girls *and* you, so don't dismiss that as a possibility. He might also be in denial. The world is getting a lot kinder, but coming out is still a big thing, and the process is different for everyone. Maybe he's just not ready to admit how he feels yet."

I sink lower into the water. Everything she's saying is too nice to be true. If Dyl liked me, why wouldn't he just tell me?

I scratch the back of my neck. "It feels weird to be talking about this."

"Good, that means it's weird for both of us. But, Caden, I want you to know, in case you're as blinded by love as I used to be, to the point where you can't see the obvious: *he likes you.*"

"How can you tell?"

"You know how I said you can't keep your eyes off him? Well, as soon as you look away from him, the first thing he does is look at you. It only lasts a second, but I'm a scientist. I notice minute changes. It's what I do." She slides off the rock and brushes her hands clean. "Well, I need to get ready, so I'm going to find my own spot. Big day tomorrow, huh?"

"The biggest."

"See you later, Caden. Think about what I said."

Like I could ever think about anything else.

CHAPTER
THIRTY-THREE

"EAT UP, CADEN," SAYS DYL. "YOU NEED TO BE strong." Everyone is still asleep, or at least pretending to be, so it's just us, sitting in front of a dying campfire. The sun hovers above the horizon.

We're two hours' drive away from the LIC, which means that, as soon as the sun starts to set, we're going to start the final leg of this journey. First, we're going to drive until we're within walking distance of the LIC, then I'm going to walk to the doors and scream until they capture me.

Dyl is offering a can of tuna. I grab it and crack open the lid, then scoop up a large chunk and put it in my mouth. The fish tastes too salty but feels weightier than the other food I've eaten recently, and it settles nicely in my gut, restoring a precious amount of energy. I take another mouthful, then pass the can back to him.

He shakes his head. "No way, man. You'll be in the most danger, so you're the one who needs to be strong."

"You'll be in danger too—"

"Stop being stubborn, Caden, and eat the damn fish."

I pout but scoop up the last few flakes anyway. I swallow then look up at the sky. "How long until the sun goes down? It feels like it's taking forever."

"That it is." He stretches his arms out in front of him. "Do you want to practice with the Bolt Gloves again? I could wear some sort of chest armor and then you could actually attack me."

I look down at my right hand. Wrapped around it is a glove made of wires. The pads are electric blue. I bring my hand up to my face and turn my wrist slowly, marveling at Juliet's creation.

"It's probably too late now. I've learned as much as I can, and there's no point tiring myself out for peace of mind."

"Let's hope you're right." He leans forward and picks up a long stick. He pokes the ashy remnants of last night's fire. A log tips over, sending up a spray of tiny orange sparks. "I miss what we used to have."

I tilt my head to the side and narrow my eyes. "What do you mean?"

He shrugs. "It was nice, you know, when we were friends, or whatever our relationship was. When I could come to your window late at night and hang out. I liked those times, well, a lot more than I like these. Don't you feel the same?"

I shake my head. "Not really. Dyl, I've spent my whole life pretending to be someone I'm not. It's only now that I can actually say what I think and what I feel. Do you not know how important that is to me? Those nights with you were the best nights of my life, but they weren't real. So I prefer now."

He meets my eyes. His stare is almost desperate. "Please don't die tonight, Caden. Please."

"I won't."

I turn my attention back to the fire. "You know," I say, "if this all goes well, you could become a paramedic after all. If you still want to, that is."

He drops the stick he was holding and looks at me. "I didn't think you would remember that."

"Well, I do."

"I . . ."

We hear the sound of a tent being unzipped. Dyl shuts his mouth and I straighten my posture. It's Juliet. Her hair is puffy and frizzy, and her nose is pink. She climbs out of the tent.

"So here are my boys," she says as she stands. "My two boys. You have no idea how proud I am of both of you."

I can't think of anything to say, so I stare down at the fire. She walks past us and heads toward the forest.

"She deserves better," says Dyl. "Than us."

I watch her as she walks away in her awkward, lopsided gait. "She sure does."

"Morning," calls Trevor. His face is poking out of the tent, and he is smiling a dopey smile. I can see his bare, muscular shoulders. Natalie's long, thin arm wraps around his neck. She places a soft kiss on his cheek.

He turns and kisses her back, then climbs out of the tent.

"Is Juliet pissing?" he asks as he pushes down his spiky hair. "'Cause I need to go."

As he says it, Juliet reemerges from the tree line. Trev grins and walks toward her, his massive hands undoing his belt. Natalie moves forward and crouches beside me.

"You know you don't have to be with Trev anymore," I say. "If you don't want to."

She sits down. "I can't go through this without him. Once this is all over, we'll see where things stand, but for now, we need to be together. I can't do this alone."

She notices the Bolt Glove and raises an eyebrow. "You're wearing it already?"

I nod. "I'm trying to get as familiar with it as possible. If Craike or a Stalker or anyone notices it before I take my wool glove off, then they'll win and I'll be incinerated. Everything depends on me getting inside wearing the glove without them noticing. I—"

"The sun's going down," interrupts Dyl. "And just so you know, that rule was dumb. We don't actually have to do this right now if you don't feel up for it, Caden."

I love the way he says my name. CaYYYden. He says it in a way only he can.

I shake my head and stand. "No, the reason we set it is that we'd always postpone if we could. We'll never feel one hundred percent ready. So let's do it. Juliet, are you ready to go?"

She shakes her head. "I need to get changed. And so do you, unless you want to stick it to the man in the shirt you slept in. Everyone, get ready and then we'll leave in five."

Dyl and I head toward our tent. It used to be mine, and Dyl spent half a night sleeping outside. Then I caved and let him share, so now it's ours. We both pause in front of the doorway.

"You first," he says. "I'll keep watch."

"Fine."

I step inside and reach my pile of clothes. The tent flap rustles.

Dyl is standing there.

I gulp down a breath. "What are you doing?"

He steps forward. "Just this."

He grabs my wrists and lowers them so they hang beside my hips. Then he steps close, so his chest is almost touching mine, and he turns his head and closes his eyes. His lips press against mine. They linger there for one, two, three seconds. He closes his lips, then he pulls away. I open my eyes. *When did I close them?* His forehead is pressing against my forehead, and his hands are holding mine.

We stand there for a moment, just breathing.

He pulls back an inch. This close, his eyes truly are spectacular. They're green, sure, but they're also speckled with all these different shades: some light, like grass, others almost black.

I bite my lip. "What was that?"

He bends down and picks up a shirt and a jacket. "No incentive," he says as he shrugs off his old shirt. He pulls the fresh T-shirt over his head. Then he wraps the jacket, a dark one that seems to be made primarily of pockets, around his lithe body. It's a size too big and hangs off him, yet he somehow makes it look cool. "I had no incentive, Caden. None at all."

He lifts the flap of the tent and walks outside.

That's why I'm doing this. Is it worth it?

Hell yes.

I take off my old shirt, then pull on a clean gray T-shirt and put on my plaid jacket. I'm grinning. *He likes me he likes me he likes me.* It's real. I'm not a foolish child chasing something I can never have. What I felt was real.

Now I need to save it. All I have to do is take down a centuries-old organization that's armed with the most sophisticated killing machines on the planet. I run my fingers through my hair, spiking it up, then step out of the tent.

They don't stand a chance.

Outside, everyone else is ready. Trevor's wearing a brown leather jacket and designer jeans. Natalie's wearing skintight black pants and an oversized pink sweater. Juliet's wearing skinny jeans and a royal-blue coat fastened all the way up to her neck. They don't look like rebels; they look like an average group of kids.

Juliet heads toward the car and gets in the driver's seat. I let Natalie, Trevor, and Dyl clamber into the back, and then I climb in.

I pull on my seat belt. "It's funny, I'm about to go into a scenario where death is highly likely, and I still have to buckle in."

Juliet turns on the engine. "That's a good thing. It means you're not an idiot. Have you ever seen the stats? There are so many deaths every year that could've been prevented if they'd been wearing a seat belt." She plants her foot on the accelerator and the car moves forward.

"Juliet," I say. "Do you know that you're incredible?"

She turns to me. The wind coming in from her open window is blowing her hair. "What?"

"I said you're amazing. I want you to know I think that about you."

"Thank you, Caden."

"I think you're amazing too, Jules," says Trevor. "I hope you know I think that."

"I do. Thanks, Trev."

Silence falls over the car, becoming so thick it would take

something really worth saying to break it. Juliet is staring forward, her eyes slightly narrowed, her shoulders hunched, her hands gripping the wheel at nine and three o'clock.

She looks like Dyl. They're more alike than they realize, both super intense and confident. I'd bet most of the people at school don't know Juliet is a science prodigy, even though she is literally the best at it in the entire school. It doesn't matter to her that no one knows she's so talented. She's also incredibly brave and already saved my life once by destroying the Stalker. If I didn't know before, now I totally know why the LIC wanted to monitor her.

I nestle into my seat and stare out the window. The forest blurs past.

After about an hour and a half, the trees start thinning, leaving gaps of foggy gray air between the smooth white trunks. Up ahead is a long stretch of flat earth. Fog fills the air, and the grass glimmers with frost.

Juliet pulls onto the side of the road and parks.

"This is where we leave you," she says. "We can't risk driving out in the open. Well, until you get the door open, that is."

I step outside. I push my arms out in front of me, and feel the satisfying cracking of my vertebrae as they click back into place.

Juliet walks around the front of the car and stops in front of me. "Give me your hand, Caden. The one with the glove."

I raise my gloved hand. She picks it up and starts fiddling with the wires. Then she presses the button above my wrist. Blue light streams from the base mechanism. With a buzzing sound, the wires start to glow neon blue.

"There," she says with a proud grin. "It's working perfectly."

She passes me a pair of gray wool gloves.

I put the left one on my free hand, then hesitate. "Won't the contact activate it?"

She shakes her head. "Nope, you need to press pretty hard in order to make it work. Like, really push into what you want to electrocute. It'll be fine."

Slowly, I pull the wool glove over the wires, then flex my fingers.

Juliet pats my shoulder. "Are you nervous?"

Of course.

"Yeah, I am."

"You shouldn't be. You've got this, Caden."

She grips my shoulder one last time, and then she walks back to the car and steps inside.

Dyl walks up to me and offers his hand. I grab it with my free hand and we shake. There are too many words and not enough time to say what I want to say, so silence feels right. Once he moves away Natalie gives me a tight hug, then lets me go and joins Juliet in the car.

"What's with the silence?" says Trevor. "Caden's about to risk his life, for pete's sake!" He grabs me in a rough hug. "Go smash it, Caden. I know you will. And Dyl, so help me God, if you don't hug this glorious boy right now I'm going to have to punch you."

"If I have to," says Dyl with a sheepish smile. *He looks like a Nice.* He walks across to me and extends his arms. I step forward, and he grabs me and pulls me to his chest. He smells like the campfire and coconut shampoo. A few long strands of his silky hair press against my face. In my ear, he whispers: "Do it for us."

Us.

Not him. Not me.

Us.

I want to ask if he means a capital *u* Us, like a capital *w* We, but he lets me go and moves back to the car. Dyl, the real freaking Dyl, referred to the pairing of the real me and the real him as an *us*. If that doesn't give me strength, then nothing will.

Or is he talking about us as in Love Interests? Maybe that's what he meant—like, I should make all the bastards at the LIC suffer on behalf of every single child who was forced into that hellish existence. I want to ask him, to know for sure what he meant, but he's already climbing back into the car.

I walk to the side of the road and stand on the marshy ground. The car's engine turns on. The twin beams of the headlights illuminate the path I must follow: the path that will lead me directly to the LIC. I don't look back as I hear the sound of tires spinning against the road. Then it grows quieter and quieter.

And I'm totally alone.

CHAPTER
THIRTY-FOUR

STOPPING ISN'T AN OPTION. I KNOW IT ISN'T. Yet my gut is practically begging me to turn around and sprint toward the forest. Still, I keep going, marching with my head held high toward a place where my death is a very real possibility.

The air is so cold I can see my breath. It's thick and white, like smoke. I can't believe I'm returning willingly. I used to think the only way I'd ever go back would be in a body bag or as the prisoner of a Stalker.

But here I am, walking back to the LIC. I can already see it. It's smaller than I expected, just one square building, not much higher than a house. There's nothing else around for miles, save for the occasional lonely tree, so I know this is the right spot. Plus, it's probably nerves, but there's a strange heaviness in the air, a constant weight pressing me down. As if I didn't already know there's something seriously wrong with this place.

My feet make grating sounds as they thump down on the road. I lighten my tread and the sound softens. How many steps have I taken since I left the others? I spin and look behind me.

The tree line is about three hundred yards away, although it's hard to tell due to the murky darkness. I turn back around and check the LIC. It's about half a mile away.

Now that I'm closer, I can see the square building leads to a runway, one that's protected by a wire fence. *I've been here before.* This is the bunker. This is where I was taken when I was first assigned to Juliet.

I scratch the bare bump of bone that connects my hand with my forearm. The wires are poking out from above the wool glove. I tug the sleeve of my jacket down, covering them.

Dyl's smiling face appears in my mind. His real smile, the genuine one, not the one he learned at the LIC. The one that reaches his eyes, lighting them up. The smile he made when he was outside my window. My life has had so much darkness but it's the sparks of joy, like his smile, I think of now. Kisses. Laughter. Friendship. Those are the things I want to remember, and the things I look forward to.

I guess that makes me an optimist.

I guess that makes me Nice.

A chain-link fence appears. Atop it is a massive curl of razor wire. I reach the gate and loop my fingers through the cold metal.

Time to out-act Craike.

"Help me!" I scream, taking all the frustration I feel and funneling it into a different cause. My eyes fill with tears. "Please! I need help!"

At the top of the fence is a black security camera. It pivots, and the reflective end faces me. A spotlight turns on, covering me with a circle of white light.

I jump and point at the camera. "There! I know you see me!"

A few tense minutes later, the door of the building swings open and Craike steps out, wearing a black suit and a canary-yellow tie. In his slender hands he's holding a silver handgun. He strides across to the gate and aims it.

Right at me.

A blur of darkness streaks out of the door and stops directly in front of the gate. I stare into the Stalker's chest. A little galaxy of silver light glimmers where its heart should be.

That's where I'll aim.

Craike stops beside the Stalker. He's holding the gun steady, aiming it right between my eyes. A gust of wind opens his jacket, revealing a second gun strapped to his hip.

"Caden," he says. "Welcome back. We missed you."

"Before you do anything, please hear me out," I say. "I was dragged into rebelling. I didn't want to run but Dyl tricked me into doing it. I came here to hand him over in exchange for my freedom."

"You expect me, of all people, to believe you've fallen out of love that fast?"

My face falls. "I was delusional, and he was playing me. You know love can drive people to act irrationally. But I'm smarter than my feelings and now I know it was all a fantasy. I want to get back to reality. So please, let's put this behind us. That's all I want. I'm good at being a Love Interest, you must've seen that, so I'm valuable to you. Let me tell you where Dylan is and then we can . . ."

He types a password into the square screen beside the gate. It flashes, then the door swings open.

I step forward. "So we have a deal?"

He grins. "Throw him."

What?

The Stalker's hand shoots out and grabs me by the neck. It jerks to the side, sending me spinning through the air. The earth rushes toward me. My face grinds into the grass, filling my mouth with dirt clods and warm blood. I place my hands on the ground and push myself up. My mouth is full of warm and salty liquid. I spit, spraying the grass with red.

"Again."

Hands grab the back of my shirt and yank me up off the ground. The collar of my shirt digs into my throat. A button pops off my jacket and falls, spinning, to the earth. I'm high off the ground, and my body is straining against the material of my clothes. The hands holding me release, and I follow the button down. I barely have time to raise my right hand to protect my head before I land. My nose and my balls take most of the force, and my nose gushes twin jets of blood. As for my balls, well, they feel like mini supernovas of pain, sending an ache right into my core, to the part of me that sits behind my stomach. I curl up, whimpering like a kicked dog.

I failed. I . . .

Fingers wrap through my hair and pull. I scream and am wrenched to my feet. *Craike. I'll kill him.* I want to shock him now; I want it more than I've ever wanted anything. Yet I leave the wool glove on, and scramble forward with tears streaming down my face.

The back of my head is pushed, and I land hard on my hands and knees.

Craike is sneering at me. He's standing about a yard away,

aiming the gun at my forehead. Instinctively, I raise my hands, like surrendering will save me.

"Back when you were first released," says Craike, "I told you what we do to rebels. And you're a smart boy, Caden, so I think you know that you're about to die, no matter what your intentions in coming here. But, in case you're confused, I'll explain what is about to happen. I'm going to take you to the incinerator." He turns away and taps on the screen that's embedded in the wall. It's a touch-screen keypad. I watch his fingers: the code he enters is 2484972. Easy. "And you're going to burn."

I realize the only reason he didn't try to disguise his password is that he doesn't think I'm going to survive long enough to ever use it. I swallow, and find my mouth is parched.

The door rolls upward, and Craike grabs me by the shirt and pulls me to my feet. He moves around and places his hand on my back. With a push, I stumble inside. A white jet sits in the middle of the bunker. He presses the barrel of the gun into my spine, and the metal digs into my vertebrae.

I have only one trick left up my sleeve: to be myself. Maybe if I stop acting like the meek, sensitive boy he expects me to be, he'll be entertained enough that he keeps me alive a little longer. It might buy me enough time to finish my mission.

We reach the silver elevator, and Craike presses his plastic key card against the wall beside the door. The machines start to whir. The doors open, and he turns to me. He's so close I get a whiff of his icy cologne. "Get inside."

I walk into the elevator, then spin and face the open doors. Outside, the massive metal door is slowly descending. Past that, the moon is rising. The Stalker struts inside, its cold forearm pressing against my shoulder. I roll my wrists, which makes a cracking sound. The door closes.

The elevator descends, as signified by the streams of white light that pass outside and the general sinking feeling. Craike scratches the tip of his nose.

"Well, this is awkward," I say.

They both ignore me.

The door slides open, and the Stalker grabs me by the biceps, its grip tight enough to bruise, and pushes me forward into a serene mirrored hallway. Instinct makes me try to step backward, away from this hellish place, but the Stalker is holding me too tight and I can't move. *Relax. Deep breaths. It's okay.* After this, I'll never come back here. One way or another, this is it for me and the LIC.

A guard dressed in red steps toward us. He's holding a long black baton. I turn away from him and come face to face with my reflection. Staring back at me is a thin young man with messy hair and hunched shoulders. It takes a second to register that the scruffy kid is actually me. I look more Bad than I ever have, and there's this intense, fiery look in my eyes. I look nothing like the boy I was when I lived here.

I freaking love it.

"Is everything under control, boss?" asks the guard.

"Don't talk to me," barks Craike. We proceed down the hallway. The guard steps into the elevator and then the doors close.

Save for the elevators, there's only one door on this level, and it's at the very end of the hallway. It's made of black glass.

We reach it, and Craike swipes his card. The two panes of glass separate, up and down, to reveal a massive room. The walls, the roof, and the floor are all seamless brown glass. A massive polar bear rug lies on the floor in front of a solid glass desk that's adorned by a laptop. The polar bear's mouth is open in a sneer, showing its red tongue and its pointy teeth. One wall is devoted entirely to a glass bookshelf filled with ancient leather-bound books. On the far right wall is a fireplace that houses a ball of blue fire, yet the room is freezing.

Craike walks around his desk and sits down on a leather arm-chair. He gestures toward the much smaller chair at the other side of the desk. "Please sit, Caden. And don't worry about getting blood on my furniture. I've already arranged for it to be cleaned once you leave. My visits with rebellious Love Interests tend to be messy."

"No offense, but I don't want to know about your sex life."

His eyes light up and his mouth curves into a grin. The Stalker releases me. I rub my bruised arm and make my way across to the seat. My shoes click against the smooth, shiny glass. He watches me.

I sit down. The chair is firm and high-backed, forcing me to sit rigidly upright. "Who'd have guessed you worked in a Lady Gaga music video."

"I hear you're quite the fan of hers."

I chuckle and cross my arms. "So why are we here, Craike? What do you want from me?"

"You're in a rush to get to your execution? Don't worry, Caden, within the hour you will no longer be with us. What I want is to talk to you for a few seconds. I try to understand people, Caden; that's what I do. That is why I would like to speak with you, man to boy, before you die."

I shrug. "Well, I'm here. Ask your questions."

He fiddles with his tie. "How do you think I got this job?"

I'd never thought about it. Ever. In my mind, he had always had the position and that was it. He'd always had it and he always would.

"Did you graduate with honors from Hitler's School of Evil?"

He tuts. "I got this job because I wanted it, Caden. It was, and still is, my dream job. And that's not because I'm sick in the head and enjoy killing teenagers. Disciplining Love Interests is the worst part of my job. I enjoy managing, and selling, the information you acquire for us. *That's* my passion. I love discovering a nugget of information, giving it to the perfect client, and then leaning back and watching as empires fall. You have no idea how much I've shaped the world. In many ways I'm the most influential person alive, even though no one knows my name."

"What's your point?"

He sighs and rubs his temples. "My point, Caden, is that you are so determined to make me your antagonist, to make me the person who is stopping you from getting what you want, but that's not who I am. I'm just a man doing my job, a job countless people have done before me and countless more will do after. You aren't special to me; I don't hold a grudge against you, nor do I particularly care about your little love story. I don't know you enough to care. I even had to look your name up on the system when I saw you screaming outside the fence. And then you stride in here like you're this important hero, and that's not who you are to me. At best, you're an employee who isn't smart enough to know his place. At worst you're a little shit who is getting in the way of me being able to do my job. In the story of my life, *you're* the antagonist. Can't you see that?"

I nod. "I can see that, but it doesn't change anything. I like Dylan, I maybe even love him, and you're stopping me from being with him." I imagine Dyl laughing. *They want to kill him.* "So I'm going to bulldoze you."

Craike's eyes light up. "You know, I think I like the real you. He's feisty. It's attractive. Anyway, your actions have a price, and you seem willing to pay it. I respect that. But I have one last question. You do know that gay people need Love Interests, right? It doesn't make any sense to me why you didn't tell us your orientation so we could've assigned you to someone more applicable."

I blink. It's not something I've ever thought about, and it certainly wasn't . . . Wait. It's a trick. He's trying to mess with me, throw me off my game. Or is he?

"If you think *that's* why I've done what I've done," I say, "then you weren't paying attention. I want to be free."

Craike leans forward and lays his handgun on the desk. The metal skitters against the glass. "The only true freedom in life is death, as you are about to discover. It's time to go. Walk to your death like a man, Caden. I'll give you that. Come on now, stand up, and let's end this little tantrum."

NOW!

I yank my glove off and leap for the gun.

CHAPTER
THIRTY-FIVE

THE STALKER MOVES AS A BLUR, STREAKING across the room in a heartbeat. Pain flares in my shoulder blades. It's behind me, wrenching my left arm behind my back. I have one shot before it pulls my arm out of its socket. Just one. I spin and push my outstretched palm, the one covered by the Bolt Glove, into the pulsing orb of light where the Stalker's heart should be. I grit my teeth and grunt, putting all my strength into the push.

Its mannequin head tilts slowly down to look at the hand that's groping its chest.

The glove hums, glows electric blue, and sends a shit ton of electricity right into the Stalker's "heart." The robot spasms. Its arm flings out and smashes into the chair, which shatters. I pull my hand away. The wires are steaming.

The constellation of lights on the Stalker's chest dim, then fade completely, and its body goes rigid. The head lolls and its chin touches its chest. Its knees collapse, and the behemoth body falls and crashes into the floor. *Crack!* A lightning-shaped fissure appears in the glass.

I turn back. Craike is reaching forward, going for the gun. I grab his wrist just as he touches the handle.

The Bolt Glove activates again. Craike spasms and falls limply to the desk, right onto the gun. *Thank you, Juliet.* I push him up and grab the gun with my free hand. I aim it at him. My finger twitches on the trigger. If I pull it now his head will explode.

He groans and looks up at me, his eyes opening groggily.

I press the gun to the side of his temple. "Open the front door." I jab it in harder. "Now!"

"As you wish."

Craike stands up and opens his computer. I walk around the desk, keeping the gun aimed at his heart.

"You know you're on camera," he says. "I'd say you have about a minute before guards flood in and riddle you with bullets."

"What's that thing you told me once about actors? I don't believe you. There's no way you'd have cameras in your private office. Now open the door or I'll shoot."

He taps on the keys. A box in the corner of the screen shows security camera footage of the front door opening, revealing the bunker. I step forward and zap Craike again. He falls face-first to the desk and lies still. I place the gun down, then retrieve my phone from my pocket and start texting.

Juliet. It's open. Password 2484972. Hurry.

On our way.

I put the phone back in my pocket and aim the gun at Craike. Even though he looks passed out, I know better than anyone that appearances can be deceiving.

I check the gun and see that it's loaded, but it contains only one bullet. Carefully, I try to open his drawers to look for more ammunition, but they're all locked. A quick scan of his bookshelf doesn't reveal anything that could house bullets. So I have one shot. I'd better make it count.

I glance at the computer. On the camera feed, I see my four friends sprinting past the jet. They reach the elevator. Juliet punches the code into the keypad. Come on . . . Yes! The doors open.

Craike is stirring. His face is pale and one side is smeared with blood, yet he's grinning a massive grin.

"You brought them to me." He laughs. "Thank you for that."

I jab the gun into his temple. "Tell me where the Stalkers are kept."

He continues laughing, high-pitched and maniacal. Slowly, he pushes himself off the desk and stands up.

"Sit down," I growl.

He squares his shoulders, and his eyes meet mine. "You aren't going to shoot me. You're just a Love Interest."

"No, I'm not." I lower the gun and aim it at his right kneecap.

Even though I've been through hell, even though I've been told I'm worthless my whole life, even though I'm gay, even though the world wants me to bow down and accept that who I am makes me insignificant, the following is true:

"I'm the protagonist, fucker!"

I pull the trigger.

A burst of red blood darkens his slacks, and he drops. It was the perfect protagonist move. It was violent, sure, but Craike will survive, so I don't have a death attributed to me. I'm the hero because I only hurt him when he would've killed me. He will re-cover from this wound, which means I will as well.

I run my fingers through his shiny hair then make a fist. I yank his head upward. "Tell me where they're kept or I'll kill you. I'll do it. You always thought you could see through me, Craike. Well, am I acting now? Am I?"

He grinds his teeth together. "Fine," he spits. "They're kept on level ten. Good luck getting there in one piece."

I slide my hand into his pocket and pull out two crumpled tissues and his wallet. I pull the key card from the wallet, then drop it and the tissues. They land beside his head.

I lift up my shirt and scrub my face with it, mopping up blood until my skin feels raw and clean. I hang on to the gun, even though I'm out of bullets. If I'm convincing enough, anyone I come up against will automatically assume it's loaded. I head out into the hallway. Thankfully, it's still empty. I sprint toward the elevator. The plastic card sticks to my damp palm.

The elevator beeps and the door opens. Inside are Natalie, Trev, Dyl, and Juliet. They all look pale and sweaty.

Trevor blurts out, "This place is so trippy!"

Everyone ignores him. Natalie is wearing a skintight black suit, the same one that hung in Juliet's garage. Her hair is tied back in a high ponytail. I walk into the elevator and press the button marked 10.

The door closes.

I move to the back of the elevator to stand beside Dyl. "Hey," I say.

"Hey."

Juliet clears her throat. "So the Stalkers are on level ten?"

I nod.

The elevator stops and the doors open. Outside is a long

hallway. The path to the right leads to a gray glass door that's guarded by two men. One of the guards looks up. He looks young, I'd guess early twenties, and has a friendly face, with wide brown eyes and pale lips. The other is ridiculously buff.

I turn my head and look down the hallway. It stretches on for about five hundred yards, then banks to the left. We can't run. They'll shoot us all before we reach the corner. The harsh neon lighting makes my eyes water.

The guards shout something, then dash forward, their hands reaching for their weapons.

Natalie charges past me. She sprints, pumping her arms and taking giant leaps toward the two guards. She reaches them before they can draw their guns. Fluidly, she drops down to the floor and sends a sweeping kick. Her shinbone hits the calves of the guard on the right. He flings his arms into the air and collapses. Natalie turns her attention to the other guard, her eyes narrowing as she moves. She ducks under his punch and sends a quick jab right into his throat. His face goes crimson, then he falls to his knees, his hands clawing at his throat. Natalie bends down and pulls their guns from their holsters.

She stands. "Thanks, boys."

She spins, flashing a smile, then strides down the hallway back toward us. She hands one of the guns to Juliet.

"Babe," calls Trevor. "That was seriously the most badass thing I've ever seen. I love you so freaking much."

He grabs her by the shoulders and kisses her on the cheek.

Natalie tugs at the sleeve of her suit. "It's easier because of this, knowing I'm bulletproof, so you have to thank Juliet as well."

"No way," says Juliet. "That was *all* you, Nat. But enough back-patting, we've got work to do."

"Agreed," says Natalie.

I pull Mr. Craike's card from my pocket and step toward the screen. "Let's hope this is a master key."

Trevor's face drops and he leaps in front of Natalie.

Bang.

Bang.

My ears ring. Trevor collapses. The guard at the end of the hall does as well, his blood smearing the mirrored wall behind him. His eyes roll back into his head. His mouth is hanging open, his tongue sticking out against his puffy lips. Natalie's gun is smoking.

"No," says Natalie. Her arms are trembling.

A vast chunk is missing from the middle of Trevor. It's like someone gouged a giant shovel into his chest. His body is convulsing and blood is flowing from his mouth, covering his lips and jaw. It's . . . it's not good. No one could survive that. Trevor might not be dead yet, but he's not going to survive this.

"No," says Natalie. She's staring at him, pulling at her hair. He goes still. Natalie hasn't even noticed yet. Oh God, Natalie hasn't noticed yet. "No. I'm bulletproof. The armor . . . It . . . it . . . Trevor, you idiot! Trevor!"

She looks down and sees the corpse. Her mouth opens but no sound comes out.

"We need to go," says Juliet. If she's struggling with what happened to Trevor, it doesn't show on her face. How can she be so practical? Trevor is dead. It happened so fast and it's so bizarre I can't believe it, even though it just happened right in front of me. Trevor, the boy who made a stupid joke mere seconds ago, is now dead.

"Right now," says Juliet. "Or we're all dead."

Juliet grabs Natalie by the arm and pulls her forward. I watch them leave. Trevor's guts are showing. His blood is splattered on the walls. He's—

Dyl grabs my wrist and pulls me from my thoughts.

"Caden. We need to go. Come on!"

I let him pull me forward and then we run down the hallway.

CHAPTER
THIRTY-SIX

I PRESS THE CARD AGAINST THE SCREEN. IT shows Craike's face, and the sheet of glass descends, sinking right into the floor. Juliet goes first, holding the gun in front of her. We all step through after her.

"Oh my—" says Juliet.

At the far end of the room is a small army of Stalkers. Rows and rows of them, all standing perfectly still. They're all dormant. At the very back of the room, in a glass cabinet, is a Stalker made of white plastic. It's bigger and chunkier than the others. My first guess is that it's a prototype.

The rest of the room is taken up by a lab eerily similar to Juliet's, albeit one that's much cleaner. It's filled with silver benches covered with neatly organized scientific equipment: test tubes, circuit boards, microscopes.

Sitting at one of the desks, peering through a microscope, is a man in a long white lab coat. He has thinning brown hair and a gaunt, bony face. Square glasses sit at the end of his nose, making his brown eyes look much bigger than they really are.

I step in front of the others, shielding them with one arm.

He looks up from the microscope. "There's no need for that nonsense, Caden. I'm not going to hurt anyone."

"How do you know my name?"

He stands up and makes his way toward us, walking around a peculiar device. It's a circular pad, about a yard in diameter, that sends up a pillar of soft blue light. The base of the pad is attached to a thick gray cable that leads to a computer.

"Of course I know your name," he says. "You have destroyed two of the most important advances in human history. Two of my creations. My children. You butchered them. So when you're marched to the incinerator, and trust me, it will happen, I'm going to watch with a smile on my face."

"What happened to not hurting anyone?"

"I won't kill you myself, you idiot." He turns to Juliet and bows. "Hello, my dear Juliet. My name is Dr. Scheinman, and I'm incredibly excited to meet you. A mind like yours, well, it's like mine, rarer than one in a million. In the future, you will create as I have created." His eyes focus on the Bolt Glove on my right hand. "And you already have. It would take an extraordinary weapon to destroy my extraordinary weapons. And you made this with minimal training in a shed in your backyard. You have so much potential, Juliet, and if you align yourself with an organization that can provide you with the right resources, you'll conquer the world." His eyes light up. "Speaking of, if you continue to create like you do, my employer will become interested in employing you. In fact, I believe they already are. The others must die, but you can live if you join us."

Juliet crosses her arms. "Thanks, but no thanks. I have no intention of inventing things that assist slavery."

He barks a harsh laugh. "But you're willing to kill people? Come on, Juliet, you're a creator, like me. You are as close as possible to the beings all those feebleminded religious people pray to. You are a goddess, Juliet, an inventor. It doesn't matter what lesser people do with what you make, all that matters is that you made it."

"You're wrong, that's *all* that matters. Also, you're a murderer, so no offense, but there's no way I'm going to take career advice from you."

"How many people have you killed?" growls Dyl. "You created the Stalkers, right? They captured Love Interests and brought them back here to die. No, not Love Interests, they captured *kids*. Kids who are now dead because of you. You're disgusting."

The scientist rolls his eyes. "And you're a gullible fool. But it doesn't matter. What matters is that . . ."

I realize what he's doing. He takes another slow step to the left. Toward the blue light.

"Stop him!" I cry.

It's too late.

He leaps into the light. Pinpoints of blue neon illuminate each of his joints.

At the back of the room, one of the Stalkers lights up. The man steps forward, and the Stalker mimics his movements. It sprints toward us.

Dyl dives forward with his arms outstretched. He flies through the blue light, his arms wrapping around the man's frail torso. The light flashes red as they both sail out of the column. They hit the ground and roll once.

"Get off me!" cries Dr. Scheinman. Dyl pushes him away and stands up. The scientist remains on the floor.

The Stalker is standing in the middle of the room, rigidly upright, but motionless. It's now totally black.

I tilt my head to the side and step toward Dr. Scheinman. "You were controlling them?"

Tears fill his eyes. "They are not lesser for having to be controlled by me! They are the future."

"They're puppets," I say. He winces like I hit him. "Just big, scary puppets."

I recall the Nice's head being cut off. I imagine this man's hand squeezing, doing the deed.

"*No!*" he screams. "They are genius brought into this world! They are perfection! They are mine!"

"Shut up," says Juliet. She walks to his computer. "And tell me your password."

He glances at me, then says, "It's Layla. It's my—"

"No one cares," snaps Juliet, putting her gun down on the bench. She types the password and the screen lights up. The sound of her fingertips hitting the keys is the only sound in the room.

Juliet leans backward and puts her hands over her mouth.

"What is it, Juliet?" I say.

She looks up. "I can't access the files. It scanned my fingerprints and came up with an error message. It says the control program can only be operated by Dr. Scheinman. He's the only one with a clearance level high enough."

What does that mean? Why does she look so sad?

"I don't get it," says Dyl.

Juliet is shaking. "It means that that man"—she looks down at the doctor—"is the only person on earth who can control a Stalker."

"Of course I'm the only one," says Dr. Scheinman. "Do you think someone as smart as I am would trust the world's most secretive spy organization? I did this to keep myself safe. If they could get rid of me, they'd do it in a heartbeat. I made sure that . . ."

His voice trails off as he realizes what's about to happen.

I turn to Juliet. "Hand me the gun, Juliet."

His face falls.

Juliet shakes her head. "Caden—"

"Just . . . just give me the gun, all right?"

She picks up the gun and passes me the handle.

I grab it and she meets my eyes. "Your thought is right," she says. "It has to be done. It's the only way to stop them. Getting rid of him will save so many people, Caden. It needs to be done. If you can't do it, I will."

The scientist is on his hands and knees, whimpering. *Don't think about it.* He runs his fingers through his thin hair. He looks so small and weak, groveling on the floor. He reaches into his wallet and pulls out a photograph. It's beaten and tattered, and the corners have yellowed. It's of a woman holding a baby girl.

I aim the gun at him. *Can I do this?* I don't know if I can, but I know that I must. I failed Trevor, and I need to keep the others safe. This will destroy me, but I must do it to protect them. If someone is going to be ruined it must be me.

It has to be me.

It has to be.

"Please," he whimpers. "I have a—"

A gun goes off. I look down and see blood welling above the

doctor's heart. He gasps, then falls face-first to the floor. A red circle of blood appears on his back.

But I didn't pull the trigger. *How?* I look up and see Natalie aiming her smoking gun at him.

"He took more from me," she says. "And I can survive this. You probably couldn't. You've done so much, Caden, but you're not the only hero in this story. So let's play to our strengths, huh? You tell us what to do and I'll deal with anyone in our way. Okay?"

"You're right," I say. My brain is all over the place, but I need to focus. "Okay, Juliet, you have to blow up the Stalkers. Just in case we were wrong."

Juliet runs toward the Stalkers at the back of the room. When she reaches them she slides her hand into her backpack and pulls out a bomb. She places it on the floor, then starts tinkering with the wires.

Dyl is standing to my left, looking at me. "He deserved it, Caden."

I look down at the broken body at my feet. "I know. It's just, you know. He was still a person."

He places his hand on my shoulder. "I know, man. I know."

"Guys," says Juliet as she walks toward me. "The bomb is ready to go. Should I detonate?"

We all nod, and Juliet presses her thumb down. With a roar, a huge whirl of purple and black appears, devouring the army of Stalkers. The whirling color snaps them out of existence, leaving only a few mangled, smoking parts.

"Now what?" asks Natalie.

Everyone is looking at me.

I have one idea, and it's risky. But it *is* what a protagonist would do.

I clear my throat. "There's one last thing. But you guys, don't do this if you don't want to." I look at my friends and know that they're going to follow me, so I smile. "We're going to end this once and for all."

THIRTY-SEVEN

TREVOR'S BODY IS STILL IN THE HALLWAY.

Natalie's eyes fill with tears at the sight of him, but she keeps moving.

The guard is also in the spot where he died, slumped against the wall with his head leaning forward. There's so much death here, and I'm leading them back through it. I didn't keep Trevor safe and I didn't kill the scientist. I *can't* make any more mistakes.

We jog forward.

Once we're all inside the elevator, Juliet presses the button marked 1. The elevator zooms upward.

"We'll have a funeral for him," says Dyl. "When we're free."

"For both of them," I say, thinking of the scientist. I remember the guard. "No, for all of them."

The elevator stops and the doors open. A guard is standing in the middle of the hallway. He gasps and reaches for his baton.

"*No!*" cries Juliet. "You moron! Why are you here?"

He steps forward. Natalie raises her gun.

"You," I say with a jab of my pointer finger. "It's four against one. And we *will* kill you. If you want to live, I suggest you play dead or get the hell out of our way."

He drops his baton. It clatters against the concrete. "Fine. Please don't hurt me."

As we approach, I reach out and grab his wrist. The lights on my glove flash, and his body stiffens. He falls against me. I lower him to the ground, then advance toward Craike's office. I press the card against the screen and the panes of glass separate.

Craike is slumped against the glass bookshelf beside his desk. His eyes are closed and his legs are stretched out in front of him.

"His computer's there," I say, pointing. "Juliet, can you figure it out?"

She nods and walks across the room to the laptop. She steps over the fallen Stalker's massive body and then leans forward to stare at the monitor. Her fingers tap against the keys, filling the room with a clicking sound.

Natalie is eyeing Craike warily.

I make my way over to her. "I just wanted to say thanks. You know, for what happened in the lab."

"You're a lot of things, but you're not a killer, Caden. Killing him would've destroyed you. Me, well, I just wish I'd made him suffer a bit more. So you don't need to thank me. To be honest I'm glad I'm the one who got to make him pay for everything he's done. I—"

"Hey, guys!" interrupts Juliet. "I've found it! I—"

A static hum fills the air, and a grid of red light appears just in front of the desk. Juliet looks up and realizes she's trapped. I turn to Mr. Craike. His eyes are now open, and he's holding a silver pen. Or at least it looks like a pen. His thumb is pressing down on one end.

Using his free hand, Craike reaches into his jacket and produces a gun. He aims it at Juliet. My mind flashes back to when he greeted me at the gates. He had two guns. One in his hand and one strapped to his hip. I took the first, but I forgot about the second.

I raise my gun. I'm out of bullets and he probably knows that, but I need to do something.

"Drop it," growls Craike.

"Okay," I say. I bend my knees and place the gun on the floor. Craike's arm is shaking and his grip on the gun is going slack, like he's struggling to keep it upright. From that, and the way his eyelids are drooping, I guess he's only a few minutes from passing out. I just need to stall him. I rise and lift my hands above my head. "It's over. Just put the gun down and—"

Craike barks a harsh laugh. "It's not over yet, Caden. There's something you need to know before you can call it a day."

A gun goes off. The grid of light sends out sparks, then returns to normal. Natalie is holding her gun, aiming it right at Mr. Craike. She shot at him. It was a good plan, but with the barrier up, he's untouchable.

"As I was saying," says Craike, "you can either listen to me or I can kill Juliet. It's up to you."

"You wouldn't do that," I say. "She's too important."

"She's nothing now! She knows about us, so she'll never trust anyone again. And if she doesn't tell anyone her secrets, I'll never get paid. Because of you, she's disposable. But that's not what I wanted to tell you. I have something to tell you about Dylan."

I turn and look at Dyl. He's standing with his arms crossed. What could Craike possibly know about him that could damage me? What else could he be hiding?

"You've got nothing," says Dyl. "You don't know me."

"Look at me, Caden," says Craike. "I want to watch as the horror sinks in. Look away and I'll shoot her."

I suck in a breath, then turn and look at him.

"We were never going to kill Dyl. Do you think we would waste resources unnecessarily? We just transport the unchosen Love Interests to another country, wipe their memories, and have them try again until they're picked. Your whole crusade has been for nothing."

He's lying. He must be. He *always* lies. I study his face, taking note of the twinkle in his eyes and the width of his smile, and realize he's telling the truth. He's doing what he always does, destroying an empire with a perfectly aimed piece of information. Everything that brought me here, everything I've done, was to save Dyl, and he wasn't even in danger. People have died because I'm a gullible fool.

"That was beautiful," says Craike. "Remember how stupid you've been while you grieve."

He turns the gun on Juliet and pulls the trigger. His hand goes limp and his head lolls. He's unconscious. He held on just long enough to do the unthinkable.

Juliet smacks the floor, her body alarmingly limp. I rush forward and crouch down in front of her. I can't touch her because of the barrier, but I get as close as I can.

"Juliet?" Did he hit her? It'll be close, but . . .

A circle of blood appears between her chest and shoulder.

NO NO NO NO NO.

It's my fault it's my fault it's my—

Her eyes open and she takes in a deep breath. *She's okay.* Using her right hand, she props herself up and inspects her wound.

"Juliet," I say, "you need to get to the pen and bring the barrier down. Then we can get you out of here."

"Oh my God, you think I don't know that?"

I shut my mouth. With a grimace, she drags herself forward, moving toward the pen. She pulls herself forward another inch, then collapses. *Come on, Juliet, get back up. You're almost there.* Her arms are shaking, but she manages to pull herself a bit closer. With a desperate lunge, she grabs the pen. She presses the clicker at the top and the barrier fades away.

Natalie and I rush forward. I reach Juliet and bend down beside her. Natalie goes straight to Craike. He's unconscious, but she takes the gun from his slack hand anyway. Then she grabs him by the hair and smashes his head into the bookshelf. She pulls it back, then smashes it in again.

I wrap my arms around Juliet and stand up. She's surprisingly light. Her cold fingers scramble against my shirt, but her grip is weak. A clean hole is ripped right through her shoulder, and her shirt is wet with blood. Maybe I thought too soon; maybe she's not okay.

She looks into my eyes and her eyelids flutter.

"Juliet!" I say. "Hey, stay with me, okay? Listen, I love you. All right? I love you. It's okay. I love you."

Her eyes close.

"Juliet!" I can feel her breath on my neck. She's not dead. Not yet, at least.

"We need to move!" I cry.

CHAPTER
THIRTY-EIGHT

THE CAMERA FEED SHOWS THE LOVE INTERESTS flooding into the hallways. The guards that are on duty are quickly outnumbered. She did it. Juliet freaking did it.

"Caden," says Dyl. "What do you want to do now? Don't lie to me."

I never will.

"It's awful," I say. "But I want to leave right now. Juliet doesn't have much time. We can find a way to save the others later." I look down at Juliet. "I can't let her die, Dyl."

"She won't," he says. "The wound is bad, but she won't die from it. The fact that she's still breathing means the bullet missed all her essential organs, which is good, obviously. We have enough time to save the others. Caden, she won't die. You trust me, don't you?"

"I do," I say. "So we'll do it."

"Is that really what you want?"

I nod.

He smiles. "I believe you."

"Good. The key is in my pocket. I'm not putting her down, so you're going to have to do it."

He moves to my side and slides his hand into my pocket. He pulls out the card, then places his hand on my shoulder and squeezes. "Thanks, Caden. Let's move!"

He releases me, then we run through the doorway. Natalie joins us.

We reach the elevator; Dyl presses the button marked 2 and the doors close. The elevator descends. Juliet is shivering. Finally, the doors reopen.

Standing outside is a group of about thirty guys. They're all crowded around the door, each one pressing forward. They're wearing the same clingy sky-blue shirts that are burned into my brain. The memory of the cold, silky, constrictive feel of them makes me shiver.

"You saved us!" cries one, a big guy. The sleeves of his shirt have been cut off to reveal his huge biceps. I look up. Oh wow, it's Robert, the Bad with the massive back. His eyes are watering. "We're free. Come on, guys, clap for them!"

They begin to clap and cheer. Their faces contort into smiles, an expression that feels like a punch to my gut. *Trevor. Juliet.* Was it worth it to let them get shot so these people could smile? Was it really?

"Come on!" I say.

They rush forward and fill the elevator. I'm pressed to the back. Dyl places his hand on my shoulder again. His palm thumps with every heartbeat. Boy, he has a strong heart. The strongest I've ever felt. I focus on the sound. Each individual beat. His heart is still beating, so it's going to be okay.

We reach the top level and the door opens. Two guards descend, their batons raised. One boy's face cracks under the black metal, but another takes his place. He shoves the guard to the floor and everyone pounces on him, kicking and clawing. The other guard screams, high and loud, as he's dragged to the floor. The crowd settles, leaving the guards a bloody mess.

I turn to Dyl. His bottom lip is trembling and his hands are balled into fists. His eyes are brimming with tears. He can't die. Not Dyl.

"You need to go," I say. "So does Juliet, and Natalie. Dyl, if you take her, I can go back and . . ." My eyes flick down to the boy's body. His forehead is crushed inward like a dropped boiled egg, revealing fragments of skull and brain. That could've been Dyl. Or Juliet or Natalie. "I need to free the others. It's what Juliet would want."

He raises an eyebrow. "There's no way you're going back in there alone."

"You've done enough," says a deep voice. It's Robert. His hands are in his pockets. "Give me the key, I can take it from here. The four of you can go and I'll free the others."

"Great plan," I say. "But I can't trust you—you seem too keen." I pick the boy standing beside Robert, a boy with curly red hair and the beginnings of a beard. He's clearly a Nice. "Will you go with him, just to make sure he doesn't try anything?"

He nods. Dyl hands him the key card.

"Then go!"

They spin and run to the elevator. The rest of the Love Interests are sprinting toward the massive open door. Juliet is in my arms, Natalie is to my left, and Dyl is to my right.

"Ready?" I ask.

We run.

We pass through the open door into the cool night air. The sky is navy and the air feels charged. We reach our car. Natalie climbs in first, then, gently, I lay Juliet down on the backseat so that her head rests on Natalie's lap. Dyl gets into the driver's seat. Once I'm sure Juliet is safe, I climb in and sit on the passenger seat.

As I buckle my seat belt Dyl turns to me. "Caden, do you want to go for a drive?"

I picture him back on the roof, sitting beside me, looking into my eyes, asking me the same question. Back then, the prospect of driving with him was exciting. A tiny taste of freedom, of rebellion. I look through the windshield and the world is so large and so vast. I can go anywhere. Now we're really driving, now we're actually free.

It's not exciting.

It's exhilarating.

"Don't make this a big thing, Dyl. Just drive."

He plants his foot on the accelerator and the world blurs away.

EPILOGUE

I ROLL OVER, TILTING MY HEAD TO FOCUS ON the soft sunlight that's streaming in through my bedroom window. I can see my garden. It's small, and admittedly not much to look at, but it's really important to me. The simple and repetitive task of maintaining it clears my head when things get bad, which used to be quite often. Those episodes feel distant now, though. How long's it been since I last had to use it? I don't know exactly, but my garden is practically all weeds now. I take that as a good sign, and I smile.

I could spend my day trying to fix it, because I'm not going to my lectures, and I gave a bullshit excuse to get out of my library shift tonight. This year's excuse was the funeral of my grandma, which is officially the last time I can use that one. But that's a problem for future Caden, not me.

I look over my shoulder. Dyl is on his back, shirtless, his arm stretching out beneath my pillow. He's got the day off too; he got out of his internship at the hospital. He's wearing black boxers,

I know he is, but his lower half is covered by a white sheet, so it's easy to imagine him completely naked. If I wanted to, that is.

His chest rises, filling with air, then falls. His biceps are slimmer than before and his stomach is soft, extending out from his pecs a little bit. Like I did, he lost his abs pretty quickly after we freed everyone from the LIC. It doesn't matter; he's still the most beautiful thing I've ever seen. I think about the moment on the plane, when I saw him looking so different, and how him not being *him* hurt me.

Now I wouldn't change anything about him. I lean forward and place a soft kiss on his damp forehead, my lips pressing down the dark strands of soft hair. Then I spin around and grab the jeans that lie in a pile on the floor beside the bed. I shuffle my butt forward and pull them over my calves. The bed rustles. Lips press gently against the middle of my bare back, along with the bristle of Dyl's early-morning stubble. It tickles, so I grin.

He kisses me again, this time at the base of my neck. The soft, slightly wet touches move along my shoulder.

"Are you aware of the time?" he asks quietly. He nibbles my shoulder.

"Acutely."

"Then you're lucky you're cute."

I stand up and jump into my jeans. Once the belt is buckled, I spin around.

He's rubbing his eyes. "I can't believe it's been a year. One freaking incredible year. Come back to bed, Caden. I want you . . ." He taps his chest. "Right here."

I fight the urge to lie down beside him and rest my head on

his chest. He'd be warm and he'd stroke my hair and . . . *Focus, man!* I've been thinking about this morning for weeks and I don't want to ruin it now. "Actually, I was thinking we could watch the sunrise? If you do I promise we can do whatever you'd like for the rest of the day."

He laughs. "*Whatever* I'd like? Wow, someone's feeling brave this morning! What if I told you I want to spend all morning listing all the reasons Nicki is actually the worst rapper ever?"

I pick up a pillow and hit him over the head with it. "Take that back!"

"Never!"

I pull back the pillow to hit him again, but then he grabs my wrist and pulls me, laughing, onto the bed. I'm on top of him now, looking down at him, and he's so frigging cute I just have to kiss him once.

Okay, maybe twice.

After the third kiss I roll sideways so that I'm lying next to him. "I wasn't joking, Dyl. I really want to watch the sunrise. You in?"

He nods. "Of course."

I get up as he pulls on a pair of black jeans.

"Hey," he says. "Speaking of plans, I was thinking we should invite Nat and Jules over tonight. We could make a nice meal, see what they're up to." He bounces out of bed. "Sound good?"

I take a red shirt from the drawer beside the bed. From the same drawer I retrieve a black one and toss it to him. He catches it with one hand and puts it on, then he makes his way over to me.

"That sounds great," I say. "Is Jules still with that singer? You know, the one with the dreadlocks?"

He shakes his head. "Nope, she's with a marine biologist now. As soon as she said it I thought for sure he was a Love Interest, but then I remembered how badass we are."

Together, we walk out of the bedroom and through the kitchen. It's simple, with wooden counters and an old-fashioned gas stove, but I love it. The white oven dish Dyl used last night to make lasagna is still on the counter, between a stack of library books and a wooden bowl filled with fruit. I open the glass door and step out onto our porch. The sky is clear, and shiny drops of dew have collected on the wooden railing.

The view is of the hills that surround our property. I reach the balustrade and place both hands on the cold, wet wood. He mimics me.

Two small trees are growing beside the house, just in front of a gray concrete water tank. One for Trevor, one for all the others. Trev's is a red maple. The other is an elm.

Dyl sniffs and rubs his nose. I'll never leave him, and I think he knows this. The cost for us to be together was just too high for me to ever give up on us. But that's a problem for another, darker day; right now he makes me happier than I've ever been.

I look up. The sky is really freaking blue today. It's cloudless and immense.

"Hey," says Dyl. He isn't looking at the sky. He's looking at me, smiling that Bad boy smirk of his. "I love you."

I smile so big it's probably lopsided.

I don't even care.

ACKNOWLEDGMENTS

I honestly can't believe I'm writing this! *The Love Interest* has been such an amazing, life-changing whirlwind for me ever since I started writing it, and there's no way I'd be writing this without the input, support, and general awesomeness of all the people listed here.

First up: my mum, Helen Dietrich. You've never doubted that I could get a book out there—even when so many other people did—and I appreciate that so much. We did it! You're amazing.

The rest of my family is also the freaking best: Shaye, for being enthusiastic and wonderful and for all your ideas in this book that I shamelessly stole. And for reading it in one day, when I finally let you read it. Also for freaking out about the Arkham games, *Game of Thrones*, and Pokémon with me—you liking that stuff makes it way better. THANK YOU! To Selam, who is the most amazing future world conqueror: I love you so much and hanging out with you is my favorite thing. Dad: for being yourself, and for being so nice and so supportive when I decided to follow a pretty out-there life path. Lastly, Kia: I dedicated this book to you because you're a badass. Enough said.

Zeima, Sarah, Asha, Lauren, Maddy, Becky, Andrew, Jacob, Jack: I <3 you all. To my two favorite teachers: Ms. G and Mrs. T, for being so incredible, plus Anthony Eaton, who taught me so much about YA.

Now the writing side of things: the reason I'm writing this is because Leon Husock, my agent and good friend, took a chance on me. I knew you were my dream agent the second we started talking about female Thor in our first Skype call, and you've totally lived up to that label. *The Love Interest* wouldn't be a thing without all the work you have put into it, so thank you so much.

To Liz Szabla: working with you has been so freaking great. Your notes and insight constantly amaze me, and you've shaped *The Love Interest* into something way better than I could've done on my own. Thank you so, so much. An equally huge thanks to the entire team at Feiwel and Friends. Publishing a book has always been my wildest dream, and this team has made it more fun, rewarding, and thrilling than I ever even imagined. You're my faves.

My writer friends: I LOVE ALL OF YOU! Seriously, all of you. If I've ever interacted with you on Twitter, you deserve a place here. Some people that have been particularly important to *The Love Interest* are: Holly Jennings, for all the chats/advice; Max Wirestone, for your enthusiasm; Becky Albertalli, for being so amazing and for making me feel welcome in the YA community when I was brand new (Tim Tam Slams FTW); Kimberly Ito, for being a great friend and for the notes that made *TLI* what it is (seriously); Everly Frost; all of Leon's clients; Clay Wirestone; Mia Francis; Phillip White; Kaitlyn S. Patterson; Kevin Savoie; Shelly Z; Adam Sass; Jay Coles; Sage Collins; and Caleb Roehrig.

To the Swanky Seventeens: I feel like I hit the biggest jackpot with this debut group. You're all so talented, friendly, and funny, and have made this whole debut thing an absolute blast. Jilly, Tricia, Andrew, Anna, Stephanie, Angie, Nic, Tristina, Breeana, Emily, Carlie, Sonia, Kayla, and everyone else: thank you so much.

Lastly, I want to give a shout-out to the LGBTQIA+ people out there. If you're LGBTQIA+ and reading this, know that you are perfect, and valid, and you deserve only the best. I hope *The Love Interest* managed to get my feelings about you across, but just in case, I'll make it crystal clear here:

I love you.